The Pulse Effex Series:
Book One

PULSE

L.R. Burkard

Lilliput Press

Cover by Design Xpressions, Dayton, OH
Contact TheDesignXpressions@gmail.com

PULSE
Copyright © 2015 by Linore Rose Burkard
Published by Lilliput Press, Ohio

Library of Congress Cataloging-in-Publication Data
Burkard, L.R.
Pulse/ L.R. Burkard
ISBN 978-0-9792154-8-3 (print)
ISBN 978-0-9792154-7-6 (ebook)
1.Apocalyptic—Fiction   2. Post-Apocalyptic—Fiction   3.YA Suspense—Fiction   4. Christian—Fiction

Printed in the United States of America

COMPELLING

"A must read for people of all ages!...I look forward to reading the sequel."

DOUG ERLANDSON, Top 50 Amazon Reviewer

REALLY ENJOYED IT

"I really enjoyed *PULSE*! L. R. Burkard does a fantastic job depicting what life might be like for those that are prepared--and those that are anything but. (If you wonder why some people bother "prepping" read this book!) I also enjoyed the strong emphasis on faith and how focused on Christ some of the characters were."

CHRIS RAY, PreparedChristian.net

A PAGE TURNER

"*PULSE* is a page turner from the very beginning!

JOY BICE, Pastor's Wife, Author

RIVETING

"L.R. Burkard's *PULSE* is a riveting story of the effects of an EMP that takes place in the United States. Blended with loss and hope, *PULSE* is full of surprises making it a great read. Considering the times we are in, I find it a must read for the church."

REGINA GROEGER, Ordained Minister

REALISTIC AND FRIGHTENING

"I loved this book! The story of each teen gradually unfolds and includes carefully researched details that make you really feel what it would be like to go through this!"

CAROL RIFFLE, High School Science Teacher

HEART POUNDING

"Loved it! Loved it! Loved it! I cried...my heart pounded...! Holy Cow, guess I better invest in a rifle!"

C. KLEPEIS, Reader, Virginia

EXCITING

"*PULSE* is exciting, thought provoking, and hard to put down! I enjoyed every page!"

D. SUMMERS, Reader

FASCINATING

"*PULSE* is carefully researched and fascinating, with gripping subject matter and compelling characters. Highly recommended!"

DONNA J. SHEPHERD, Pastor's wife, Author

EXCELLENT BOOK!

Found myself burning the midnight oil to find out what happened next!

"THE Qs," Amazon Reviewers

THIS BOOK BRINGS IT HOME

Get it, read it, get young adults to read it—and prepare!

C. REINEMANN, Disaster Preparedness Consulting, LLC

HAD MY WIFE READ IT

Just finished the book and had my wife read it as well. Definitely a page turner to pick up as soon as you can!

BRIAN B., The SouthernPreppers.com

CHILLING DYSTOPIAN NOVEL

Stories like this one get me very excited for today's young adult reader.

DEENA PETERSON, Blogger, Reviewer

FILLED WITH INTRIGUE AND SUSPENSE
Emotions run high at times and fairly leap off the page!

ANNE PAYNE, Amazon Reviewer

A MUST READ NOVEL
Wow, what a book!

JUDITH BLEVINS, Amazon Reviewer

GRABBED MY HEART AND NEVER LET GO!
Had me spellbound! You won't want to miss this gritty and powerful series.

NORA ST. LAURENT, BookfunMagazine.com

AN ALL-AROUND GREAT READ
Exciting, informative and entertaining!

CYNTHIA L. BALDWIN, Amazon Reviewer

SUCH AN EXCITING READ
I absolutely loved this book! I kept reading it and reading and reading. I just couldn't put it down!

LYNDA, Amazon Reviewer

To see more reader praise for PULSE, see its Amazon Listing!

Acknowledgments

Special and heartfelt thanks to my beta readers, all of whom helped strengthen the manuscript in the final stages of writing. Gina Groeger, Carol Riffle, Joy Bice, and my own smart and beautiful daughter Bethany, for careful reading and comments; Dana Summers for her enthusiastic feedback; my husband Mike, and Brad Sanders for their knowledge of firearms; and Jessica Orme for her equine expertise.

Thanks also to the numerous and growing body of preparedness bloggers from whom I have learned so much about the world of prepping (which, by the way, is often light-years away from Hollywood's version seen in such shows as, "Extreme Preppers.").

Above all, I thank my Lord and Savior, Jesus Christ, without whom I can do nothing!

"Son of man, speak to your people and say to them, If I bring the sword upon a land, and the people of the land take a man from among them, and make him their watchman,

And if he sees the sword coming upon the land and blows the trumpet and warns the people, then if anyone who hears the sound of the trumpet does not take warning, and the sword comes and takes him away, his blood shall be upon his own head."

Ezekiel 33:2-4, ESV

PART ONE

ANDREA

AGE 16, JANUARY 11
DAY ONE

So my dad got all upset because when he went to leave for work the car went halfway down the driveway and died.

His *precious* Mercedes.

I was just walking out to wait for the school bus and he hurried towards me in a huff, yelling something about how the starter wouldn't even turn over.

"What'd you do to the car, Andrea?" he demanded. I stared at him. I couldn't believe he was trying to pin it on me.

"Nothing."

"What'd you do to it?" he asked again. I turned and stalked blindly down the driveway to wait by the mailbox. My heart was pounding. Normally I'd enjoy the crunch of snow beneath my boots and the way the pines lining our driveway are blanketed in white; but I barely noticed either.

Leave it to Dad to ruin my day before it starts.

Yesterday Mom let me practice driving for about thirty-five minutes and the Mercedes drove just fine. So I'm supposed to know what happened? I'm guessing it's frozen because we're having a mean cold spell. The bottom line is Dad loves his car more than me (he loves lots of things more than me). I blinked away tears that felt cold on my skin the moment they appeared. Where was that bus? I wanted to see my friends and forget about home.

I waited, beginning to freeze. Designer boots aren't made for warmth. I waited a long time; I knew the bus should have come already but I didn't want to go back—Dad would say I overslept and missed it on purpose or something like that.

Finally, I had to go in. Sure enough there was Dad, hands on hips, glaring at me.

"Why are you back?"

"The bus didn't come."

He stared at me as if he didn't believe me.

"So walk to school," he said. I gaped at him. Was he kidding? We live, like, five miles from my high school. My mother called him from the kitchen. I turned and stared out the window. Our secluded circular drive was a winter wonderland. In nice weather it's a beautiful manicured front, maintained meticulously by landscapers. Today it was a world of white, so cold the snow glittered. No way was I going to walk to school. Anyway, my father says things he doesn't mean when he's mad so I took off my coat and boots in the mud room. (There's rarely an ounce of mud in it but that's what we call it.)

I went to heat water for hot chocolate but Mom said, "NOTHING'S working, Andrea. NOTHING. We're having a black out." Our house is like, all electric—the stove, our heat and even the pump for the well. So when we lose electricity we're pretty much without everything. Mom's sort of freaking out about it. I'll bet her and Dad had one of their fights. We've lost electricity before and the world didn't end. But when my parents actually have a fight as opposed to just being mad at each other silently, everything and anything makes them crazy.

———◆———

Dad's been outside tinkering with his car for the longest time but it still won't start. I hope he can fix it. I can't stand the thought of being home all day with him here. My little brothers are home (their bus didn't come, either) and so I'm stuck with the whole family but no one to talk to.

I'd call Lexie except I can't get my idiot cell phone to work. Of all times for this to happen! I charged that phone all last night and we had power then because when I woke up my alarm clock showed the

2

time—5:05AM. I asked Mom if I could borrow her cell and she said, "All the phones are dead. Something's going on."

"What do you mean?"

"Nothing's working!" She tossed her head at me, looking exasperated and creeped out.

"The house phone doesn't work?"

"No. Nothing." She took off with baby Lily to put her down for a nap.

So I can't even text anyone. I can't check online to see if my friends have posted anything. I can't watch YouTube, and just now I turned on my iPod, only it didn't turn on. It should have, but it didn't. There's nothing to do. I may as well have gone to school.

———————◆———————

Okay, so Dad said power lines might have been knocked down by the weight of the snow. That doesn't explain why we have no cell phones but, whatever. I really don't care why this is happening. I just want it to be over.

Mom is still freaked out, nervously going around the kitchen like she doesn't know what to do with herself. She taped the refrigerator shut so we can't let out the cold air, and she unplugged all the appliances.

I heard my father come in the side door to the garage, muttering to himself.

"Why didn't he take the Lexus to work?" I asked, keeping my voice low so he wouldn't hear me. I knew he preferred the Mercedes, but I couldn't see why he'd be picky at a time like this.

My mom turned and went to the counter and leaned against it, her arms folded across her chest. My mother is a pretty woman, slim, and a dark brunette like me, but she often looks strained and unhappy. I figure if I were married to my dad I'd look that way too.

"That's not working either," she said.

"BOTH cars are dead? At the same time? How did that happen?"

"I have no idea." She looked disgusted. She went to the sink and started rinsing dishes with water from a plastic jug.

"Great, I hope that doesn't last," I said. One day with my father was more than enough for me. I thought of his motorcycle. The motorcycle was Dad's nod to freedom, to his old self, the man he was before the corporate monster mentality owned him. He hardly used it, even in good weather, but he'd never gotten rid of it.

"Too bad it's snow cover or he could use the motorcycle."

My mom didn't turn around but said, in a monotone voice, "That isn't working either."

This was shocking. "He actually TRIED the motorcycle? In this weather?"

"Just to see if it would start," she said, still not turning around.

So dad was definitely home for the day. I decided to keep a low profile by disappearing to my room. Upstairs I got in bed and picked up my iPad. When it wouldn't power on, I flung it down on the mattress and stared at it. Why wasn't anything working? Even with a power outage, my cell phone and iPad should work.

I felt depressed. I wished I could talk to Lexie. We'd laugh about having the day off from school because Mr. Sherman, our World Geography teacher would be totally frazzled that class was off schedule. Mr. Sherman follows his schedule like a Nazi. At least that was something to look forward to at school tomorrow—hearing Mr. Sherman bemoan our day off.

I tried to sleep but got bored, so I headed back downstairs. The boys were sliding down the wide mahogany banisters of our marble staircase. They're not supposed to do that, but I stood watching, enjoying their glee. The real estate agent who sold us the house called the staircase a "showstopper." I think it's why my dad bought this stupidly big house. Just to show off. Anyway, as I waited to see them crash at the bottom, I suddenly heard a strange, muffled sound. In a few seconds I realized it was baby Lily—wailing from her room!

I rushed down the hall to her room and opened the door. She was on her back in the crib really going at it, screaming like a little banshee, arms and legs flailing. I leaned over to pick her up. Her wide-eyed terror made me hold her to my chest, saying softly, "Poor baby! Poor Lily! It's okay. We didn't hear you! Andrea's here."

I looked at the baby monitor and realized we'd forgotten it wasn't working! Lily's first stirrings are usually heard by one of us so she never has to work up to full-fledged crying before we get her. She was unused to being ignored this long. Even in my arms, her little lower lip still trembled and her whole tiny body shuddered now and then. I held

4

her close, rocking back and forth before changing her diaper, but she continued to fuss so I knew she wanted my mother.

Lily has the biggest, most beautiful blue eyes. I don't know where she got them because all the rest of us have green or brown, but I'm glad she does. She doesn't have a lot of hair yet, but I think it's going to be blonde and that's different from the rest of us too.

Downstairs I found Mom searching for batteries in a closet. I shook my head. "Mom, Lily was screaming her head off. This idiotic house is so big we couldn't hear her!"

"Oh, my goodness!" Mom held out her arms and took the baby, who let out a gurgle of satisfaction. She snuggled Lily to her chest, covering her little head with kisses and headed for the kitchen.

"How did you hear her?"

"I was in the hall."

"Did you change her?"

"Yup."

"Thank you."

My mother looked upset, so I added, "She's fine, mom. Babies cry."

She reached for the fridge and then stopped. "Oh. I can't heat the bottle." She looked at me.

"I'll make her a new one."

"She likes them warm. How will we warm it?"

"Don't we have anything?" I asked. "Doesn't dad have a space heater?"

She nodded. "Yeah. It's electric."

I sighed, turning to get a clean bottle from the cupboard. "Well, she's going to have to drink it at room temperature today." Mom stood nearby as I measured the powdered formula into a bottle, then added water from a jug. She took one of Lily's hands to kiss it, but gasped.

"Her little hand is cold!" she cried. "I put her down for her nap not even thinking how she'd get cold up there." She tore off a sock to feel her foot, then put a hand behind her neck and sighed. "Her neck is warm. That's a good sign."

"She's fine, Mom." But I had begun to notice the temperature in the house dropping too. Who would have thought one day without power would do that?

I took over hunting down batteries and heard my dad come in. He said he'd gone to speak to the neighbors to see if they knew anything. Our plat has about five roads and maybe two dozen houses. Turns out none of our closest neighbors were home, but he found a family home at the far end of the street. They're in the same boat we are. Everything's dead—cars, computers, phones, cell phones. Like us, they're hoping only this area was affected and that outside our neighborhood everything is okay.

If nothing changes by tomorrow, Dad's gonna walk a few miles down the main road with one of the neighbors to find out. He says we're blind as bats with no TV or radio or phones. It's depressing. I hate being stuck at home with this useless family and nothing to do.

EVENING

I never knew a house could get cold this quickly. We really felt it when the sun went down. Whenever we've had a power outage before, Dad just took us to a hotel. Now we're stuck here. We have this gigantic fireplace—at least, I've always thought it's gigantic, but now that we need it for heat it seems hardly big enough. It's really the stone-flagged mantle and dark mahogany bookcases flanking it that make it seem huge. Anyway, Dad spent a long time getting a fire going, even with a fire-starter, but we still have to stay close to feel its warmth. We moved all the furniture into a small circle around it.

Mom got a camp stove from the garage (which I forgot we had. We haven't gone camping since before the twins were born) and by putting it over the logs, we could actually heat the tea kettle. Now we can warm the baby's bottles and I finally got to drink that hot chocolate I've been wanting all day!

So we sat around the room together, which is hugely odd. My family never sits and hangs together. Well, not with my dad, anyway. The boys had dragged in their bucket of building blocks and the baby was asleep in a portable crib near the fireplace.

I looked at my father. "When do you think power will be back?" When he didn't answer right away—he seemed to be thinking about it—my mom said, "I hope it's soon. But I don't get it—how come everything is out, even our cell phones and cars?" She was looking at my dad as though she expected him to explain it all. He shook his head.

"I don't know. Those cars should start if it's zero degrees and it only got down to twelve today." He stared into the fireplace. "If it was

6

only one of the cars, I could understand that. A fluke. But none of them work. I don't have an answer to that."

With nothing else to do, I tried reading with a flashlight but I guess the batteries are dying because it's too dim. We have a few candles on the dining room table but it's pretty dark in here, even with the fireplace. My little brothers are giggling and being silly like it's a family camp-out, but my mom and dad aren't even playing along. The baby is blissfully unaware that anything's changed; I envy her. Dad is worried because all we have are a few logs left from the holidays to burn besides some fire starters and cardboard boxes in the basement—but that's it. And the temperature is now below zero outside.

I'm not too worried—we've never had a long outage before so why would we now?

I tried to sleep in my room but woke in the middle of the night—*freezing*. Carrying blankets and my pillow, I groped my way in the dark and went downstairs. Everyone else was in the family room. Mom and the baby had the best spot, asleep on a sofa that had been moved in front of the big stone fireplace. The boys were on the floor in front of that. Dad was asleep on another couch, moved so that it was adjacent to the one with Mom. I put down a few blankets and my pillow and slept on the rug like the boys. I'm only warm on the side facing the fireplace, though.

I managed to fall asleep earlier without my music but right now I'm wishing I had it. I'd give anything for one working iPod! If I at least had that I might be able to forget about everything else.

I hope the power is back by tomorrow.

This house is lonely and quiet and boring without electricity.

JANUARY 12
DAY TWO

Wretched morning. I had to get ready for school with no hot water or shower or anything—and then Dad walked out with me when I went for the bus. He wanted to talk to the driver and see what he could find out about the outage. The bus never came. I was so disappointed. I'd prefer a normal day at school (even without a shower) to this grind. Home with nothing working. The whole time we stood out there waiting he said, like, two words to me. Sometimes he creeps me out.

So the living room looks like a campsite with our extra blankets and pillows around. We have to dress in layers to keep anywhere near warm. If I need to use the restroom, I wear my coat! Speaking of which, the toilets stopped working last night. My father wasn't too concerned because he figured we can keep them flushing by bringing in water from the well. Even though it's powered by electricity, we have a manual hand pump. But after he went out to bring in the first bucket of water he returned shortly, cursing up a storm. The pump handle was frozen. And when he tried to force it to operate, it came apart right in front of his eyes.

Seems he should have slowly defrosted it with heat instead of trying to force it to work. Now it's useless!

So I was given the lovely task of hauling in snow—bucket after bucket of it. I am SICK of snow. We have four bathrooms in this ridiculous house and I was supposed to fill *all* the tubs. After filling just one my arms and legs were aching and my hands were starting to freeze. I begged Mom to let me rest. The layer of ice on everything makes it real work to get that stuff in a bucket and then into the house and then into the bathroom.

Mom said I could do more tomorrow. I thought, *Perfect! We'll probably have power by then!* I got warmed up by the fireplace and then went up to my room to hide. I didn't want Dad to see me and make me do more hauling. While I was out there he did help a little because he was making a depression in a wall of snow to put a cooler with the rest of the food that was in our freezer. (Even though the house feels so cold, it's still colder outside and he thinks it will keep better out there.) But his mood was still foul because of the broken pump and I had to ignore a good deal of "colorful" language while he dug.

I asked my mother why he's so angry. She says it's because he can't get to work or even call in and it makes him feel crazy. He's a workaholic, so this is sort of killing him. He's also worried he'll get fired for not going in. And she thinks he's worried that other people are still going in and getting their jobs done while he's helpless out here in the plat, which is kind of isolated by surrounding farmland.

"Why would they fire him?" I asked. "He can't be expected to get to work when there's no power and no vehicles."

"They won't fire him," she answered, taking the single big black pot we've been using for heating food. She opened a few cans of stew, emptying them into the pot and I followed her as she brought it to the fireplace and positioned it on the camp stove. "He's just worried because he's like that."

It figures that my father is more upset about work going on without him than he is about what's happening here. This is the gist of what's really getting to Dad. HE CAN'T DISAPPEAR TO WORK AND BURY HIMSELF IN HIS JOB. What if his co-workers have power? What if things are going on without him as usual? He can't handle the thought. He's worse than I am about having to live without my stuff working.

A strange thought hit me, though: Maybe he's just afraid. He's used to being in control of things and feeling like he's good at what he does, like in his office. Here, I don't think he knows how to take care of us with this outage. He's in upper management and calls the shots at work. Now he's only got us to boss around. Otherwise he's as powerless as our gadgets.

When I returned to the living room the boys were doing a puzzle on the floor and mom was sitting with the baby, just staring ahead. It was like she was watching TV, only of course it wasn't working. Our useless big-screen sits in the corner like an altar. At first it looked like mom was staring at it. But she wasn't. She was staring at nothing, lost in thought. I want to throw a sheet over that huge, silent TV. It's just a reminder of what we can't do.

JANUARY 13
DAY THREE

I woke up to find Dad's been burning my books for heat! I can't believe it. Of all the stuff he could have picked, of course it had to be books that were mine. And he had the nerve to complain they weren't burning well! He says today we all have to scour the property for branches and anything that will burn or else he'll start using furniture!

"Can't we wait and see if the power comes back?" I asked.

"It's ten degrees out there, Andrea," he said. "We can't wait."

It's not like we have a forest out there, either. Our property is one acre, most of which is carefully landscaped lawn and flowers when it's not covered in snow. So we have a small stand of trees and bushes before you reach someone else's property. Mom calls it a natural privacy fence. Dad said it's the best place we've got for finding anything to feed the fire.

PULSE

We've never had long outages before. We were always lucky, even after a bad storm that took out electric for thousands of people, 'cos we live near a substation. Since they always get that up and running quickly we've always had power restored really fast. After last year's hurricane we only lost our electric for a day and a half. And my cell phone still worked. And our cars started. *What is going on?*

So Dad walked all the way to that power station today. Normally you can't walk on our main road, at least not safely. If you leave the plat you take your life in your hands because everybody speeds on the main road. But today it was eerie quiet, Dad said, and he passed four cars that were dead and abandoned in the middle of the road. He wanted to ask questions but the substation was empty. Dad's not sure if it was empty because there's nothing they can do or if it's because no one could get to it. Another thing—usually if you get close to the station, you can hear wires crackling. Today Dad said he heard only one thing: a whole lotta nothing.

I so want to wash my hair. And I really want to talk to Lexie. I wish I was at school! Just so I could do something normal instead of having to haul in snow and now look for wood! And with all that snow and ice? How will it even burn if it's frozen?

I trudged out to the stand of bushes and trees hoping someone was going to lose their job over this. Somebody somewhere must have done something wrong to cause this power failure. If you ask me, heads should roll!

When I got there I was glad to be alone for a change. Even the silence didn't bother me. Snow cover always brings a muffled quality with it but today it felt different. It took awhile for me to realize it was because there wasn't a single sound of civilization; no one warming a car engine before leaving for work or to go shopping; no one using a power blower to clear their sidewalk or drive of snow; no one's radio or television turned up too loud and wafting out from their house. There wasn't a single sound except my own feet crunching in the snow.

I didn't find much to burn. Sure, there were bushes, but I had nothing to cut them with. I gathered the few sticks and branches that were sticking up out of the snow but everything else is covered. It didn't amount to a lot. When I went in complaining my feet felt like ice, Dad said, "Just be glad we have a fireplace." I wanted to give him a sarcastic answer because he's said about a hundred times, 'It's a good

10

thing we have a fireplace.' A hundred times. And if you ask me, a fireplace is not good enough, because unless I'm right up next to it, *I'm still cold.*

EVENING

Jim is back! Jim is our neighbor on the right. Dad stepped outside and saw a faint flickering light coming from his house. He went to speak to him right away. Turns out Jim was at Wal-Mart when the power went out. Wal-Mart is about thirteen miles from here. Jim spent the first night at the store with other people who were stranded but he's been walking home ever since. Jim's not a young man, or he might have made it sooner. He managed to bring one bag of stuff from the store. He said he bought a lot more but had to leave it in his car.

"So there's no power there either," my mom said, flatly.

Dad shook his head. "Nope. Same as here. You should have seen Jim. He looked awful, like he barely made it home. He stopped by a few roadside fires people had going but he thinks he may have frostbite on both his feet."

"My goodness," said Mom. "Poor man." Then, "Does anyone know why?"

"Why what?"

"Why this happened to the electric? Was it the snow? And what about cars and cell phones?"

"No one knows for sure. It's anyone's guess."

My mother sighed. "Did you ask him about water?"

Jim's well has a manual pump like ours which hopefully isn't broken. We've been going through the bottled water my mom buys to mix up baby formula for Lily, but we're almost out of it. Hauling in snow and having to boil it is like sheer misery. I hope his pump works.

"I'll ask him tomorrow. He didn't want to talk right now." He paused. "He also said that if I had a gun, I should make sure it's ready to use." You could hear surprise in my father's voice.

"What does that mean?" I asked. I thought I must have heard him wrong. My dad looked at me. My mother was waiting to hear his answer too.

"He said we might need to protect our homes. Looting could start soon if help doesn't come. If the power doesn't return. He reminded me of what happened after Katrina."

"But we're out here in the country. Who's going to loot us?" Mom asked.

Dad shrugged. "I think Jim's a little paranoid."

"Did he see any looting going on?" Mom persisted.

Dad nodded. "Yup. He said people were starting to panic at Wal-Mart because they wouldn't accept anything but cash. And some people actually started walking out with their arms full of stuff they hadn't paid for." He shrugged. "I mean, who carries cash today? Nobody."

"But if you did have cash," I said, "you could buy food and water. At least people in cities can buy that stuff. Unlike us out here in the middle of nowhere."

Dad gave me a dark look. "Yeah. For a few days. And then it all runs out. And then they come looking for more."

"Well, they won't find it here," I quipped. I'd been noticing our pantry wasn't all too stocked. I didn't usually pay much attention to that stuff since it was mom's job to shop and cook. But already we were eating the less desirable items from the pantry like peanut butter and jelly. The boys actually like this so for them that's just dandy. I would be fine if I never ate peanut butter again in my life.

Anyway, we're going to run out of food, and then what? Nobody knows how long this is going to last. And no one knows why it's happening. I wish I could get on Facebook and ask my friends. I wish we could watch the News and find out. I feel so alone.

Another thing; the quiet inside the house is driving me crazy. Outside it seemed okay, even restful. But in here? I never realized how appliances make noise, but with nothing working in the house there's a strange silence that is grating on me. It's like a lull before the storm. It's quiet but not *peaceful.*

And I think the storm has already hit.

JANUARY 14
DAY FOUR

Today is the FOURTH day without power in this freezing house.
I hate it.

I can hardly believe it's been four full days. I never thought this would happen to *us*. I know other people have experienced long outages after a bad storm or tornado, but we didn't have a bad storm! We had snow, and it froze overnight, but that's happened before without causing a power failure. I'm really sick to death at how nothing is working. I WANT TO TEXT MY FRIENDS. I WANT TO TALK TO SOMEONE. I WANT TO USE MY COMPUTER.

It would help if we knew what was going on and how long we'll have to wait for power to come back. But there's no way to know anything—I feel crazy.

Dad went to the main road hoping to get information from someone—anyone—but when he got back his mood was darker than ever. I heard him talking to Mom.

"Yeah, I saw people. Pulling sleds loaded with stuff."

"Why?" asked Mom.

"They were heading to town to look for an emergency shelter."

"Maybe we should go there," I said.

"You really want to walk to town in this cold?" Mom said. "That's five miles. I won't take Lily out in this weather." She looked at my father. "Maybe if the car is working...?" He shook his head.

"Nope. I've tried it every day. I've tried them all."

"Do you think there is a shelter in town?" she asked.

"I have no idea." He shrugged. "Maybe in the Civic Center; or the school gym. Other than those places, I don't know where they'd be able to accommodate a lot of people."

I thought of trying to squeeze into the gymnasium with people I knew from town and thought better of wanting to go. Who would want to be stuck inside with all those people? Even the thought of seeing friends didn't appeal to me. I hadn't showered in three days and my hair felt like dry spaghetti. Then I wondered if they might have running water. If they did, I'd go, no matter how I looked. Hot, running water—the very idea filled me with longing.

"If there was a shelter would there be running water?" I asked.

"Not unless they've got power," said Dad. He looked at my mom. "If nothing changes by tomorrow, I'll make the walk into town and see what's what."

"What about those big water towers?" my mom asked. "They would still work, wouldn't they? Because of gravity?"

"For a couple days, maybe longer," Dad replied. "But once the pressure falls, they'll fail, just like everything else."

I thought of the three jugs of water mom had left for baby Lily's bottles. I got up and put on my gloves and a pullover hat.

"Where you going, Andi?" asked Aiden, scampering over to me with bright eyes. He looked utterly normal. The twins, seven years old, weren't feeling nearly as deprived as I was. They missed video games and television but didn't seem to mind that nothing else worked. They layered t-shirts under their clothes as if it were second nature, and couldn't care less that hot running water was a thing of the past. They liked the whole family being in one room every day.

I tousled Aiden's hair. "I'm gonna collect more snow. I think we might need it."

Mom looked appreciatively at me, though she said nothing. Dad was elsewhere, lost in thought. He was often like that; present, but not really there. I wondered what he was so busy thinking about.

"Can I help?" Aiden asked, looking up at me eagerly.

"You certainly can!" I replied.

"I can too!" yelled Quentin, not to be outdone by his brother.

I found two mop buckets this time and mom gave the boys empty Chinese food plastic tubs. She stood at the door and received our snow-laden containers to take them to the nearest bathtub, emptied them into it, and then returned the containers to us to fill again. With the boys and mom helping, we were able to fill up all the tubs. I was exhausted when we finally scrambled back inside and settled in front of the fireplace.

As I sat there cross-legged with Aiden and Quentin leaning up against me, their little faces red from the cold, I realized I was enjoying the fire. Both its warmth and mesmerizing depths. I liked the way different colors would appear within the flames here and there, and the crackle of a spark now and then would pop out like mini fireworks. I was even enjoying my little brothers being near me. It felt like we were a cozy family.

Then to my delight mom filled the kettle with snow and announced she was making hot chocolate. She brought in granola bars and crackers on a tray. The boys got a burst of energy and started dancing around the room.

Then Lily woke up and started fussing. I was ready to get her but mom asked my father to. It was the weirdest thing: When he picked up the baby I saw no emotion on his face. He sat back down holding her. I couldn't help staring, startled by the sight. It occurred to me that I never saw him holding her; Mom always had her. It looked truly strange. I wondered why he never held her, but I didn't say anything. He still seemed to be elsewhere anyway, even while he held her. He wasn't looking down or enjoying her the way most people enjoy a baby. He was staring at the fire, lost in thought. I felt sorry for Lily. Then I felt angry. My father is a loser! I don't care how much money he makes. I will never marry a man just because he earns a good income. I want a guy who looks into my eyes and sees who I am. I don't understand how my mother fell in love with my father. It seems impossible.

EVENING

It's dark and I'm restless. There's nothing to do except read. Dad found a couple more flashlights in the garage so I'm using one, but it's a pain. A flashlight doesn't seem heavy until you have to keep it at the right angle for reading. A candle isn't bright enough unless I hold my book right up next to it and that's not comfortable. So I only read a chapter and then I'm tired from the effort.

We had the last of the burgers tonight. I can't wait for this to end so we can get more food.

I miss hearing from my friends more than anything. I picked up my cell phone for the thousandth time just to see if it might work. (I knew it wouldn't but I couldn't resist trying.) When it just stayed black and didn't start up, I felt like throwing it in the fireplace. I would have too, except my father was in the room. I didn't feel like getting yelled at.

JANUARY 15
DAY FIVE

We are in much worse shape than I thought. I mean, regarding the power being out. I thought it was just temporary like in the past but my dad doesn't think so.

I was helping Mom get ready for lunch, taking out paper plates, napkins and plastic forks, while Dad was outside grilling hotdogs. Suddenly she said, "Your father thinks he knows what's going on."

I stopped and stared at her. "What? What's going on?"

She gave me a look. "He won't say. You know your father."

"Oh, wonderful, " I said. I was tempted to get on my mother's case and tell her she ought to force it out of him. We had a right to know, didn't we? But I thought about how moody and angry my dad is, and how if you push him, he just flies into a rage.

Mom added, "He says he doesn't want to believe it yet."

15

"Believe what?" I asked.

"What might be happening."

"I don't get it, "I said. "What might be happening?"

Mom turned and folded her arms across her chest. "I'm wondering if we might be at war or something." I felt a chill creep down my spine which had nothing to do with the cold. Such a thought had never occurred to me. My idea was that a major storm had taken down power lines but I never would have thought of war.

"Who would we be at war with?"

She shook her head. "I don't know. North Korea? Russia? Maybe radical Muslims? They've hated us forever."

I thought about that a moment. "My world history teacher said Islam is a peaceful religion."

"Ha!" said my mother. "Tell that to the Christians who have been beheaded over there this year!" She paused, and said more quietly, "He's obviously never read the Koran. That doesn't say much for his grasp of world history, either. More Christians were killed for their faith by Muslims in the past one hundred years than the number of Jews killed in the Holocaust."

I stared at her. The Holocaust was another thing my teacher had been fuzzy about. I wasn't actually sure how many had died in the Holocaust but I didn't want to say so.

"How would war stop our cars from starting?" I asked.

My mom sighed and shrugged. "I don't know."

Later while we ate hotdogs sitting around the fireplace, my father mentioned that some of the people he'd seen on the road yesterday were still trying to get home. They were stranded when the grid went down, he said.

"What do you mean, 'the grid went down?'" I asked.

"The electric grid," he said. "It's down, ruined, kaput."

"How could that happen?" asked my mother, putting down her hot dog. I felt my own stomach flip. Surely what he was saying was not possible.

"I was talking to Walt, you know, the guy down the road who owns the convenience store in town?" She nodded. "He said a solar pulse could do this. It affects all electronic circuitry, everything that has electronic parts."

"At least it's not war," Mom said. "And I guess that explains the

16

cars."

He nodded. "And our phones, and computers....you name it."

"But we didn't feel anything," I said. "How could that happen without our knowing it?"

Dad spread out his hands. "Okay, a giant sun flare sends out this huge pulse, a magnetic wave, but people don't feel it. It doesn't affect us. But anything electronic gets fried."

"So how long does it last?" I said.

"How long does what last?" he asked.

"The solar pulse. How long until it's over?"

"Oh, it's over," he explained. "It's over and done with."

"Okay," I said, trying to understand the implications, "so now we can fix everything?"

Dad looked as though my question had annoyed him. "Well, that's the million dollar question, isn't it?" He sounded angry. "How to fix everything. How do you get a new car motor? Or how do you know what got fried and needs to be replaced? And even if we have the parts (parts that did NOT get fried) how do you get them where they need to be if nothing's working?"

Mom had a disturbed look on her face, mirroring what I was feeling. I said, "You're making it sound like we're going to be like this for a long time."

He nodded, and a dark look came over his face. "That's exactly right."

Mom stared off sadly into the fireplace. Dad stood up. "I'm going to look for more wood to burn." We knew he meant he was going to scrounge around the basement and attic for old furniture.

Mom said, "Please don't use anything valuable."

He put his hands on his hips. "What's valuable if we freeze to death protecting it?" I felt bad for my mother, because she cares about furniture and antiques and things like that, but I also hoped my dad would find something to burn. I was frightened by what he'd told us. And angry, but I didn't know who to be angry at.

If it was really the sun that had caused this mess, there was no one to blame. No one but God, I guess. Was God punishing us? We certainly could have gone to church more. Now it was too late. We couldn't go anywhere.

Thoughts kept coming at me as I took in the enormity of what he'd said. If I'd been at school when it happened, I would have had to walk miles—in this weather—to get home. The idea scared me. I thought of the people Dad mentioned who were still trying to reach home. That could have been any one of us! I wondered if that was the reason we hadn't seen our two closest neighbors. I thought of Chase Jones, this guy at school. He lives the furthest of any of us—thirty-five minutes by bus. His house was right on the border of school districts so he was allowed to choose which one to go to and his mother chose ours. Imagine if he'd been at school when everything shut down! The thought made me shudder.

I felt as though gloom was deepening all around me, like I was being engulfed. Suddenly I couldn't stand it. I was suffocating. I shot to my feet.

"Where are you going?" my mother asked.

"I don't know," I said. I was appalled to find that I was crying. She had a look of pain on her face; I knew she felt badly for me but she just nodded, so I started walking aimlessly around the house, moving, I had to keep moving. I was tired of sitting in one stupid room all day to stay warm; tired of wearing heavy garments or my coat in the house; tired of not being able to take a shower, listen to music, or call a friend. I ended up in my bedroom, fell onto my bed and buried my face in my pillow and sobbed. I didn't want to believe what my dad had said. If I believed that this situation wasn't going to change for months and months, it would be unbearable. How was I supposed to survive alone with my family for months? How could I live without any friends or music or the internet? I felt as though I'd just received a death sentence. Goodbye, life. Hello, wretchedness.

After crying my eyes out, I suddenly had a new thought. My father didn't know for SURE that we'd had a solar pulse. Even Walt, that store owner, didn't know for sure. They were guessing. *Guessing!* That meant they could be wrong. I sat up, grabbed a tissue from my night stand and blew my nose. Maybe I was upset for nothing. Maybe I'd wake up tomorrow and everything would be back to normal.

I got up and went back downstairs, my stomach grumbling with hunger. I raided the pantry for cheese crackers and opened a can of ravioli. I felt better after I'd eaten. But I don't think it was the food that helped me as much as my decision not to believe what my dad had said about a solar pulse.

Right now I feel sure things will turn around soon. They have to.

JANUARY 16
DAY SIX

It snowed last night on top of the snow that's already there. I stood looking out my window at the street, all white, because no plow has come through. The snow didn't look pretty anymore. It looked threatening.

Latest calamity? When Dad went outside to get bacon from the cooler, we found out we're not the only hungry creatures around. Something managed to open the cooler—probably raccoons. Mom was mad as all get-out that my dad put the food outside to begin with. He thought it would stay colder that way, but boy is he sorry now. I refuse to cry about it but it's very aggravating. Our pantry supplies suddenly look paltry to me because there's no way to go shopping to replenish anything. I think I can safely say my father is clueless about what to do. And he always acts like I'm the clueless one.

So Dad and I and the boys pushed and dragged our refrigerator into the garage and put what was left inside it. We lined it with snow and ice first. It's plain to see that we are going to need more food—and water, for that matter. I'm still the one bringing in snow every day for mom to boil the heck out of in the kettle. I've been making the tea or coffee and washing Lily's bottles and bringing in wood, besides snow for water. But what happens when the snow melts? Not to mention I hate going out in the cold every morning—but at least we have something to boil and drink. Which reminds me that we've run out of milk. The cream ran out two days ago, so even though milk is a lousy substitute, coffee was still drinkable. Now with no milk I have to resort to using that horrible powdered stuff. I can't drink black coffee. I hate the thought that I'll never have another good cup. We've also used up our eggs. And pancakes taste lousy without milk or eggs. Today mom made us oatmeal—I hate oatmeal. She says it's all we've got for breakfast food. Ugh! I never in my life dreamed I'd go hungry! My dad has a big bank account! Who would have thought we'd ever go hungry?

Dad looks grim. He took Aiden and Quentin to gather sticks again. I'm glad he didn't make me go along. I have enough to do in here, heating water over the fire and other terrifically stupid things that only pioneer people should have to do. I'm sweating hot when I work near the fire and then I get numb with cold when I'm away from it.

Today I was waiting for some water to heat up in the kettle because I wanted hot chocolate; I could feel Mom looking at me. Suddenly she said, "You're going to have to change who you are, Andrea. At least until things get back to normal."

"What?" That's all I could say, because I had no idea what she meant.

"Life is going to be full of work until we get some power back..." She looked away and I could see she was holding back tears.

"Mom, what's wrong?" I hate to see her cry. No matter how mad she makes me, I still hate that. "It'll come back soon," I said. "We'll be okay."

She looked at me, her eyes teary and hopeless. "No, no," she said. "It won't."

My heart skipped a beat, but I decided instantly not to believe her. "How do you know it won't?"

"That's what your father said. He said if it's really a solar pulse that did this, it could take months or a year or more to see power restored." She sniffled and reached into her coat pocket for a tissue. (We're all wearing our coats—it's the only way to stay warm enough in this stupidly big house. The living-room ceiling is like nine and a half feet high—I've heard my dad brag about it. Right now I'd like to be in a little room that one fireplace could heat up entirely.) Anyway, I didn't like what I was hearing, so I said, "Well, how does he know? He could be wrong."

She shook her head again. She didn't look at me but stared at the fireplace. "He's right. If the cars were working, I'd think he was wrong, but nothing is working. He's right."

Baby Lily was starting to fuss on her lap so she got up. "We have to change her," she said. I automatically went for the baby supplies, all piled on a plush corner chair. There was no longer any use for the baby's room because it was too cold, so we'd moved all her changing stuff into the living room. I grabbed a diaper and saw that we only had about a dozen left. I didn't mention it to Mom.

As I did my best with a blanket to keep the baby warm while Mom changed her diaper, I asked—while trying to fortify myself to a possibly stinging reply—"What did you mean about me having to change, Mom?"

She shrugged and was silent a moment. "You'll have to get used to doing a lot more work than you're used to. So will I."

"Like I haven't been?" I was annoyed. "I've been doing my own laundry since Lily was born. But you said I'd have to change WHO I am. What does that mean?"

She had finished, and after we got Lily's clothes in order and buttoned up her little one-piece winter suit, Mom took her and returned to the couch.

In a raised voice, she said, "I mean, you'll have to stop thinking about wanting hot chocolate and using our little bit of boiled water for yourself only! We have to think about the baby first!"

I just stared at her. I'd gone out and gathered the snow for that tea kettle myself. And I'd been doing it for the baby's bottles, or for tea for her and dad and the boys, too. I felt tears forming in my eyes so I just left the room. I'm used to my father being insulting, but now my mother is too? I hate this. I walked around the house a little bit, looking at all the appliances that are dead and useless. I went into my bathroom, glad that it still smelled clean—thanks to all the snow we'd hauled in to fill the tub. With a sinking heart I realized I'd need to get more snow already—the tub was less than half full. As I stood staring at the snow level, knowing that the only way to get water for now on was by hand, I felt a terrible foreboding. What will we do if Dad's right? If there really was a solar pulse? How will we live?

JANUARY 17
DAY SEVEN

Today dad noticed how low our food supplies are. Like I said, he's always in a fog so it figures he wasn't taking stock until now. He'd gone looking through the pantry and then came at my mom, really angry.

"Why can't I find anything good to eat?" he demanded.

"How can I possibly buy food when I can't get to a store?" Mom said.

"You know what I mean, Tiffany," he sneered. "There's hardly anything on the shelves like in a normal home. What happened to stuff like bagels and chips? Where's the mac and cheese?"

"You know I've been trying to lose my baby weight," she said, her voice getting tight. "I stopped buying junk food weeks ago—if you were home more, you'd have noticed. I didn't want them in the house while I'm trying to lose weight. You knew that."

"Great," he said, with deep sarcasm. "Nice time to let the food run out." His tone of voice made me want to crawl under a rock. I hate it when they fight.

"How was I supposed to know this would happen?" Mom cried.

"How about the rest of us?" he asked. "The rest of us aren't on a diet. All you ever think about is yourself."

My mother just stared at him but I saw her eyes tearing up. I hated my dad right then. She went back by the fireplace and snuggled up with the baby. She was crying. Even the boys felt badly and went over to her for a hug. They'd been playing with toy cars on the floor but had stopped and stared during the argument. Sometimes they come to me when they're scared by my parents, but this time they just froze where they were until it was over. Mom kissed them and stroked their hair.

"It's okay. We'll get by."

I wonder if she meant it. I think she was just trying to make them feel better. I certainly don't feel better. I don't see how we can survive for long. My hair feels itchy and cruddy, and I didn't even THINK of putting on makeup or earrings or anything, today. It's like life has stopped. Maybe mom's wish is coming true: I am changing. I have no choice.

When dad stepped outside for something, I did some scrounging around in the pantry. I found a bag of chocolate chip cookies beneath a box of powdered milk. I'm not telling anyone. I'm hiding it. I grabbed the powdered milk for our coffee. I knew it would taste lousy but it was something.

When Dad got back, I heard him telling my mother he'd spoken to a neighbor who'd been out on the road towards town and passed a stranded car. He could see someone was in it. When he got closer it looked like a little old lady so he knocked on the window. She didn't move. He opened the door and there she was, just sitting in her car— dead! There was no purse or anything to identify her so he figures someone stole it. He asked my father if he'd help bury her as soon as the weather allows. I felt like I was in a movie. Things like that just don't happen in real life.

I guess they do now.

I was deeply disturbed after hearing that. I kept picturing this sweet little old lady dead in her car, right near our plat.

"Why did she die?" I asked.

Dad looked at me as though he'd forgotten I was in the room. He shrugged. "I don't know; could be from the cold, exposure. Or maybe she had a heart attack."

I am haunted by the image of that lady. Why didn't she leave the car and look for help somewhere?

My stomach is starting to bother me. I think I might be sick. I know I'd like to cry. I don't know if it was the story of that lady or because I'm starting to believe we really did have a solar pulse and we won't get power back for months, maybe not for a year. I didn't want to believe it. But the image of that dead woman tells me it must be true.

This whole situation seems unreal. I WISH I could talk to Lexie or Sarah! I want to forget about all this and go back in time to how things used to be. I thought my life sucked because I have a rotten father. Now it looks like I had it great.

I just didn't know it.

———◆———

Our little neighborhood started gathering outside today to exchange ideas. Normally we rarely see each other. Everybody minds their own business—we only know the neighbors on either side of us. But today probably everybody who lives here (and wasn't stranded elsewhere when the grid failed) was outside. Except for one guy at the end of our street who hasn't come out and doesn't answer his door. His name is Mr. Herman, which I know because I sold him chocolate bars for a school fundraiser once. I didn't like him then, and now I really don't like him. Why won't he come out? We know he's home because there's smoke coming from his chimney. It's like he's trying to hide or something.

Anyway, all we found out is that everyone else is pretty much as miserable as we are except for a few people who had a generator and some extra fuel. They've rationed their usage of it, but even they are going to run out of fuel soon. And having that generator didn't put any extra food in their pantries.

Mitchell Hughes was out there—he goes to my high school. I saw him just before we went back to our house. We nodded hello but that's it. We've never been what I consider friends. He's quiet or shy or something. He acts like a dork. Even though he rides the same bus as I do, we've never gotten to know each other. I like a guy to be friendly first—before I am. He failed to do that. But I was glad to see him today. It reminded me that I'm not the only teenager having to survive at home in a world that's stopped. I wonder if we'll become friends now that there's no way to see anyone else our age, at least not until this snow clears and we can get around.

No one knows any more about the cause of the power failure than we do. We'd love to know whether or not all of Ohio is like us, or the whole country, or the whole planet! One person has been trying to get a radio station all week with no luck—they have a battery-operated radio, imagine that. If they find a working station we may be able to find out if help is on the way. Dad says if the whole country isn't affected, either the government or charities will send help soon.

I hope so. I mean, we're not the only ones in trouble. There's got to be loads of people like us, people who will need help and food and who might not have a good heat source.

I'm also re-thinking that emergency shelter—if there is one. I think now that we should go to it.

More people were out on the main road today despite this awful cold. Dad said they probably don't have a fireplace like we do and have no choice but to seek shelter elsewhere.

"Maybe we should do what they're doing," said Mom. "If there's food and shelter somewhere, we'd be better off."

"Farmingham said there's no emergency shelter in town," said my dad. Mr. Farmingham lives in our plat. "So they'll have to go to Dayton. And if Dayton is powerless like us, it will be dangerous, worse than staying home. Every city without power will have looting and rioting. Remember Katrina."

I don't know why, but I wanted to see the road for myself—maybe just to see other people. I saw a whole family walking along together. Two little kids were bundled up on a sled and there was a baby in a backpack. I don't want to think about them being out there when it gets dark. Dayton is thirty minutes from here by car. So I told them what my dad said about cities. At first they looked startled. They asked what we were doing to stay warm and I told them our situation.

"You see? We can make it with the fireplace," the woman said to her husband.

"I guess," he said, grudgingly. I turned around to go home. I think they went home too because I saw them heading back the way they'd come. I was glad!

I passed one other young couple. The woman was pushing a stroller full of stuff but there was no child with them. The man had a big backpack on. They said they never used their fireplace and now it wasn't safe. Raccoons were living in the chimney or something so they had to seek shelter. I watched them go on with a heavy heart, but if it hadn't been for the cold, I would've wanted to go with them—just to get away from home.

I guess we are lucky to have the fireplace. I'm getting used to not having central heat. It's been a week and I feel okay if I'm layered up. (Now I see why they used to wear so much clothing in the old days. Like, in Shakespeare's time; did you ever see Queen Elizabeth's dresses? They look so heavy! But weight is warmth, I'm finding out. This is so not me—I don't even care what I look like, just so I'm warm.)

EVENING

Dad used a staple gun to put sheets over the doorways and now the living room is livable. It's bliss to sit around without feeling chilled. But I can't be alone in here, so even though the house is dark and cold I wander up to my room at least for a few minutes every day. For my sanity. It's driving me crazy, all this staying in one room all the time. Up there I can pretend nothing's changed. None of my stuff works, but I bundle up and hang out, visiting my old life. It doesn't work for long because my nose and fingers get cold. So I come back and sit near the fire, and then I'm hot. This is life now, hot or cold, never comfortable.

I keep hoping the whole downstairs will warm up from the fire, but Dad says most of our heat is lost through the chimney. I'm confused, because isn't that how they used to heat houses? With fireplaces? I don't get why it doesn't work anymore.

I wish I could fall asleep and then wake up to everything the way it used to be.

I miss my friends, and being online, and my music.

Even my brothers are bored. We all miss video games.

We're stranded like a bunch of helpless sitting ducks.

Nighttime is the worst. I can hardly sleep without my iPod. Sometimes I cry myself to sleep. But I have to be careful because I don't want the boys to hear me.

Last night was hard. I guess my mother heard me sniffling because she came and hugged me and I cried on her shoulder. I can't remember the last time she did that. She said things like we can get used to living without power. "Think of the Amish," she said, "they always live this way."

"Even the Amish have stoves and refrigeration," I said.

My mom was silent a moment. "Not anymore."

It makes no difference. I'll never get used to this.

JANUARY 18
DAY EIGHT

I can't believe I'm writing again today. I've never been this faithful about it before. I have time now and nothing else to do, I guess.

So this morning I was feeling sorry for myself and then I remembered the chocolate chip cookies. I went to where I hid them—in the drawer of a hallway table that no one ever uses. It's there just to hold an enormous vase with dried flowers—another stupid showpiece. Anyway, I took out the cookies and went up to my room. I got snuggled under a bunch of blankets and tried to pretend away my misery. I ate a cookie. I was only going to have a few cookies and share the rest. But one after another, they just kept going down.

I ate the whole box. Then I cried and hated myself for being a pig. It's all because of this power-outage! I would never have done that before.

I'm a selfish, gluttonous, pig.

———————◆———————

To my joy I found an old wind-up watch that seems to be telling the time! I told my dad and he tried to take it, but I fought for it. I can't explain it, but having a working watch feels like an unbelievable luxury. It's like SOMETHING is still okay in this world. I started crying because he was making me give it up, and that's what actually saved the day. He turned away in disgust because I was crying over it, but I don't care because now I have it.

Dad is changing. At first I couldn't put my finger on it but then I realized what it was. He's growing a beard. I can't remember ever seeing him with a beard before so it's sort of spooky, like he's someone else and not my father. Up to now he looked unshaven and sloppy, but now I can see he's been growing out a beard. I guess he's doing it because he can't go to work anymore. At his office none of the men wear beards. Or maybe he's just getting into this Davy Crockett thing with the rifle and hunting. (Did I mention he keeps a rifle out now? It's on the mantel, looking ominous. He says we may have to defend ourselves. I think he's nuts. He also says he may go hunting. I'll believe it when I see it.)

Yesterday he started building a small shed outside. He had wood in the garage for a project he never started. I thought, when he discovered this wood, that he would use it in the fireplace but no, he's building something. (Why? When we could use it for heat!) Every day we still go looking for wood and sticks but everything is frozen. It's a waste of time.

I didn't ask about it because he snaps at anyone who talks to him. But when I got too cold in my room and came down, Aiden and Quentin were arguing over something stupid and the baby started crying and I couldn't stand it. So I ran outside to get away from everyone and almost ran smack into my dad. He didn't look mad—just tired. I didn't know what to say, so I asked, "What're you building?" I looked at the shed. It was high enough to stand in, but not much bigger than what would hold one person.

"An out-house," he said, wiping his face with one sleeve.

I guess I looked shocked because he said, "Get used to it, Andrea. This is life—unless things ever get back to normal."

"Will they?" I asked.

He shook his head, looking around. He was silent for a very long minute. "I don't know."

He didn't say we are in serious trouble, but I'm wondering more and more what we'll eat when our food runs out. We can't drive to a store (we can't even walk to one; they're too far) and Mom says the shelves would be empty by now even if we could.

I asked again when help will arrive from the government and Dad says he just hopes the whole country didn't have an "EMP."

27

"What's that?"

"It's an electromagnetic pulse; a catastrophic high voltage power hit—like I told you. Could have been from the sun, or maybe terrorists."

He gave me a look that sent a shudder down my spine. I wish I'd paid more attention when Lexie talked about the ways her family practices homesteading. It seemed so unnecessary. Even stupid. So much work. But I bet they're warm and well fed and not so worried like my mom and dad.

Lexie is someone I wouldn't even be friends with except we both have twins in our family. Mom had dragged me along to a Twins' Club Meeting, and Lexie's mom had dragged her along. We got to talking for the first time—we'd never talked at school—and that's when I discovered how nice she is. And funny.

I don't think about it a lot, but I'm glad we're friends because knowing Lexie has been good. She's not into clothes or boys like I am, but she's smart and very religious—she talks about "The Lord" (like she knows him) and she says things like, "I'm praying for you," whenever I tell her something I'm struggling with.

I hope she's praying for me now because I sure could use some divine intervention.

I REALLY dread using that disgusting out-house. It's bad enough having to use snow every night to make the toilets flush, but an outhouse is like, primitive! Dad says if we had a constant water source we could continue to use the bathrooms when the snow is gone, but we don't have more water. Jim's manual pump handle is working but it will be a long haul just to get drinking water from there every day.

EVENING

All of a sudden my mother stood up tonight and said, "What is wrong with us? The Hendersons still aren't home, right?" The Hendersons are our neighbors on the left. We haven't seen them since the grid went down.

My dad nodded.

"THEY have a wood stove—on the first floor!" My mother shook her head like she couldn't believe it. "Why haven't we thought of this?" She started picking up blankets and wrapping baby Lily up more than ever.

"What are you doing?" asked my dad. "They aren't home."

"I know. We're going there. We're going to stay there until they come and chase us out. IF they come and chase us out. We can cook on the woodstove and maybe they even have food."

"Um. Aren't you forgetting something?"

My mother gave my dad a look.

"The house is locked." She straightened up and put her hands on her hips.

"Yes, Peter, the house is locked," she said. "You'll need to break in." She said the words like he was an idiot not to realize it himself. I sighed. It would have been nice if they were trying to get along right now, seeing as how everything else in life is so much harder. But no such luck.

My dad stared at my mom for a moment and soon I heard the garage door open. I figured he was getting some tools or something. Mom said, "C'mon, Andrea, don't just sit there. Grab some of our stuff. Take whatever food is left."

When dad returned about forty-five minutes later we were sitting with our arms full, ready to go. The boys were yawning but ready. Mom said, "What took so long?"

"They had some wood near the stove," he said. "I started a fire to warm up the place. C'mon."

So now we're in the Henderson's house with a real wood stove. The Hendersons are just a working couple with no children so there are no toys or anything like that. I can tell with just our candlelight and Dad's one flashlight that it's pretty here. I think they might even have more money than us. And the pantry is full! I know I shouldn't be excited about that, but I am. A week ago we would have been horrified at the idea of breaking into anyone's house, and here we are, gloating.

I wonder if the Hendersons were stranded somewhere and couldn't get home. I'm sorry they couldn't, but I'm also glad. I just hope they're okay. We don't know them well but I think they might have welcomed us here during this cold spell for the baby's sake. (Maybe not, but I want to think so.)

If they don't come back, Mom thinks we can manage on the food they've got—a least for a couple more weeks to a month, maybe more. I just can't think about what will happen after that.

PART TWO

LEXIE

AGE 16, JANUARY 11
DAY ONE

We would have used the truck to get me to school because it had all-wheel drive and Dad hadn't plowed the driveway yet. Only it wouldn't start.

"Must be the cold," my mother said, frowning. "Maybe the starter's frozen. C'mon," in her soft southern drawl, "you get the girls their breakfast while I get dad."

Inside the house, twins Lainie and Laura, six years old, were at the table waiting for their food. Justin, our toddler, was asleep upstairs.

"Is Lexie staying home from school?" asked Laura. Before Mom could answer they broke out in a cheer. "Yay, Lexie has no school! It's a snow day! Can we have a snow day, too, Mommy?" The girls are homeschooled. They often speak at the same time or at least it seems that way. And they say the same thing. They delight and exasperate me.

"Slow down, girls. No one said anything about a snow day," said Mom. "Where's your father?"

Lainie answered. "He's downstairs checking....um, checking something." She and Laura looked at each other. "*What* is he checking?" Lainie asked her sister.

Laura shrugged. "The broken? The toaster's broken!" She looked at Mom. "The toaster's not working, mama."

"Broken?" My mother went to look at it, at the same time saying,

"Why isn't the light on? Lex, hit that switch, please."

I did. When nothing happened, we realized there was no power. I opened the fridge. It was dark.

"Don't open it!" Mom warned. "Keep the cold air inside!" Her shoulders slumped a little. "Oh, well. There goes my baking day."

"Maybe it won't be out long," I said. Dad walked in.

"Power's out?" Mom asked, even though it clearly was. He nodded. "It's not a popped breaker."

"And I can't get the truck started," she said. "Can you give it a try?"

"Sure. C'mon, Lex. I'll take you in." Fifteen minutes later we were still home, and Dad had tried all the vehicles. None of them would start. He scratched his head.

"Could be they're just being ornery on account of this weather."

"How'm I gonna get to school?" I asked. Then, in a carefully even tone I added, "Maybe Blake can pick me up." Blake Buchanan is eighteen, two years older than me. I guess you could say we're pretty good friends. He's not your average guy. He's a science geek and very intelligent. He's also quieter than most people, but when you get him talking on a topic he likes, he can talk as fast as anyone. Blake drives by the farm every day on his way to school but my mother prefers taking me herself. Blake and his family go to our church and my folks are good friends with his, so I'm holding out hope they'll let him start driving me in before he graduates. I've had a small crush on him since forever.

Inside, Dad got his laptop while I hit Blake's number on my cell phone. "Um. My phone is dead."

My father grinned at me, while he dug in his pocket for his cell phone. "Here. How many times do I have to tell you to charge your phone every night?"

I took his phone but protested, "I did charge it last night! I know I did." I sat down with the girls who were eating granola with milk. Waffles were off the menu.

"Hmm," he said, teasingly. "I don't know. A charged phone wouldn't be dead."

I took his phone. It wasn't working either.

"You're both hopeless," my mother said good-naturedly. "Use the house phone, Lex, and HURRY." Meanwhile dad took his phone back and was trying it himself. "I just used this about an hour ago," he said, puzzled.

I tried the house phone and then turned to my parents. "Um, guys. This phone doesn't work, either."

My mother and father looked at each other.

"That's odd," said my dad. His laptop was sitting open on the counter and he went to the keyboard. "Laptop's dead, too." There was a deep silence for a minute while they pieced together what was happening. My mother gasped.

"Oh, my."

My father said, "Wow."

"What is it?" I asked. They had both realized something. "What is it?" My dad was silent for a minute while I waited.

"We've talked about this," my dad said. "You remember— something happening that could take down the grid?" My mother had sat down, looking grim.

I suddenly realized what he meant. See, we're "preppers." We'd long ago taken seriously the idea that something catastrophic could render the country helpless in a matter of minutes by shutting down the entire electric grid. Heck, we almost expected it. My parents even had enough emergency supplies in storage to last through such a disaster. *But had it really happened?*

"You don't think...it's really happened, do you?" I felt suddenly drained of energy. Fear rolled over me, making my legs weak. I wasn't ready for this, whatever had happened. I guess I never thought it really would because if it had, I wasn't taking it very well. I sat down at the table, tears popping into my eyes. *Why am I not prepared for this?* I wondered. My family had been storing supplies for a long time just in case of a disaster, natural, economic, or political. For anything that could disrupt the electric grid.

But who can really prepare for life to change in a moment to something new and unknown?

Dad said, "Let's not jump to any conclusions. But I'll get the generator going." We have a whole-house generator that is kerosene fueled, and we'd always wondered if it would work after something like an EMP. Now we were going to find out.

I was still sitting with a despondent heart. My mother saw the look on my face and came over and rubbed my back.

"It's okay," she said, soothingly. "We'll be okay."

"I know we've talked about this," I said, shaking my head. "But I can't believe it. Think of all we've just lost, Mom!"

She shook her head back at me. "No. Think of all we still have."

I stared at her a moment. I expected her to say, "At least we're all in this together, that sort of thing. But she said even more than that. "We have each other, and we have God, and because we have God, we have everything we need."

I stood up, still crying, and went into her arms, glad no one was around to see it. "How will I ever see my friends again?"

"Oh," she said, in that same soothing tone, "Listen to what your father said. Don't jump to any conclusions. We don't know what's happened. And no matter what, even if it really is an EMP, once the weather warms up we'll be able to travel some. You'll see your friends again, I'm sure of it." Her voice sounded soft and reassuring in my ears, but the possible magnitude of the situation was still coming at me, like a long, slow train that you're waiting and waiting to let pass.

I lifted my head to study her face. "Mom, it's January! If we have to wait for warm weather to see anyone, that will be months!"

"Shhhh," she said. "We don't know anything for sure, yet. Let's wait until we know what's going on before we worry over it."

Dad hadn't returned yet so Mom and I began breakfast clean up. I went to the nearest storage area which was a front closet and pulled out some water jugs. It was strange to do that, because in the past we'd only used stored water when we were replacing it with newer, fresher water. We did that with all the supplies, rotating usage to ensure that nothing in storage got too old. This time I had no replacements to put back.

When dad returned, he announced the generator did work. Nevertheless, I abandoned the dishes in the sink and sat there morosely while he and my mother discussed the situation. I was still obsessing over the fact that we had no working vehicles. This was probably less important than the loss of power, internet, and so on, but for some reason I could only think about my world narrowing down like the way clogged arteries do, which we'd studied in Health class. I felt sorry for myself, truth be told. I mostly saw my friends only at school. Our homes were too far apart to walk the distance, even in good weather.

Dad disappeared downstairs again while we finished cleaning up.

Afterwards I got out the school books for the twins and called them to the table. Dad walked in.

"Okay, I got on the broad-band and heard some talk. We've had some kind of a catastrophic hit. Either there's been an EMP from the sun, or an enemy of our country set off a bomb which caused it. Either way, there's definitely been a catastrophic pulse, at least to Ohio."

"Can I listen to the talk?" I asked.

He shook his head. "Not right now. I put it back. Just in case there are more blasts, or pulses. We'll use it sparingly until we know better what's happening."

Dad had put a few essential items, like his ham radio and a regular radio, into a homemade "Faraday cage," a shielded, reinforced container designed to protect sensitive circuitry from damaging surges of currents like those caused by an EMP. Lots of preppers do this. I knew Blake's family had. At least I wouldn't lose touch with Blake.

"No one knows what caused it?" Mom asked.

"Not yet. But the good news is, no one's reporting seeing or hearing a blast or a detonation, so it was more likely a solar flare than a bomb."

"If it detonated over Kentucky or Kansas we wouldn't have heard or seen it. I wouldn't be too quick to assume anything," Mom said.

"You can see or hear a blast for hundreds of miles," Dad responded. "I don't think there's been one or someone on the radio would have reported it by now." He paused. "Anyway, there are a few things we need to do." He looked at the twins. "You two go on upstairs and play for now; your mother will call you when it's time for school."

"I think we'll pass on that for today," said Mom. "I'll have enough to do getting out supplies for when the generator runs out."

"Yay, it's a snow day!" shouted Lainie. The two scampered happily off.

"Dad, are you absolutely certain we've had an EMP?"

"Absolutely certain?" He paused, thinking. "No." He looked at me. "If it was just the electric that was out, I wouldn't think so at all." Then he pointed out that the phones are dead, and took his cell phone and plopped it on a stack of school papers that were on the table.

"This is all it's good for now," he said. "A paperweight." He looked seriously at me and added, "When the cars won't start, phones are out, computers are dead, it all adds up to an EMP. I can't think of any other explanation. But it is hard to believe...." He paused. "I think we ought to treat this like any other black out until we know definitely."

"So," Mom said, folding her hands calmly in front of her. "What do we do, now?"

My father looked thoughtful for a moment. He reached his hands out, clasping one of ours in one of his. "We pray."

———————◆———————

Afterwards I wanted to run outside, expend energy, do something to use up the surge of unrest that was filling me at the thought of what was happening. I'd done my chores in the barn before it was time to leave for school so I asked, "Can I put the doe with the buck?"

"The rabbits?" Dad chuckled. "So much for treating this like a routine blackout; that wasn't my first line of action, but sure, why not? May as well get a start on it. The more we breed them, the more meat we can offer our neighbors and friends—or trade—if it comes to that."

"I want to do it! I want to do it!" yelled Laura, coming out from behind the doorway into the kitchen. Lainie, her partner in crime, was right behind her.

"You little stinkers," my mother said, in her southern drawl voice, "You were supposed to be upstairs."

"We want to help," said Lainie, who wasn't usually so altruistic. "Can I put the rabbits together, daddy?" asked Laura.

"No, I'm gonna do it!" Lainie protested, giving her sister a shove for emphasis.

"You apologize to your sister this instant," said Mom. "And neither one of you are going to do it, because Lexie will."

"Sorry," Lainie said, not looking at Laura.

"Look at your sister when you apologize," my mother instructed. "An apology doesn't mean a thing if you can't look someone in the eyes when you give it."

The girls had heard this a hundred times of course, but always managed to forget. Lainie looked hesitantly at Laura. "Sorry."

"It's okay."

"Now, git!" Dad said and the two ran off, this time going upstairs to their bedroom.

"Sweetheart," he said to my mom, "Maybe you can dig out the emergency candles and a bunch of those oil lamps you and Lex made that time. We'll use the generator just for refrigeration and hot water. I'll check the wood and fill the bin in the mud room." We all spun into motion. You'd think we'd been practicing for this sort of thing, the way we scattered and got busy. As I went out to the rabbits I realized that in a way, we had. My mother and father had anyway, mentally, a hundred times. It stood us in good stead at the moment.

The rabbits had portable housing so we could move them around the property. Right now they were in the barn on account of the cold. I opened the female's cage, moving aside the oilcloth cover.

"C'mon, sweetie. Time to put you to work." The doe moved away from me, her whiskers twitching. I spoke softly to her. In a minute she turned in my direction. That was my cue, and I took her by the scruff of the neck and then cradled her in my arm.

I opened the door to the buck's cage. "You're gonna like this, big guy," I said, placing the female in the far corner from where he was. We never pushed the rabbits close to one another. They had to decide on their own when to get friendly. But once they do, they breed quickly and we would be counting on them for meat.

I liked to watch and see how long it takes for the animals to approach one another, not to mention we needed to know if they'd mated. But I was too restless and returned to the house, making a mental note to check on the rabbits again in an hour. I'd just removed my coat and gloves when I heard knocking at the front door. We live far off the road and get few callers, but my heart lifted at the thought that Blake had arrived. Who else would come all the way down our quarter-mile drive this early in the morning? Maybe dad was wrong about an EMP! If Blake's truck worked, he had to be wrong! Mom came rushing out before I could get to the door, and opened it.

"Hello!" she said, surprised.

I joined her. There was a man in the doorway holding a little girl in his arms. It wasn't Blake.

"Hey," he said. "I'm a school bus driver. I need to use your phone. My bus broke down on the road." He nodded sideways, indicating where it happened. "And I guess you don't get good cell reception out here 'cos my phone's dead."

"Our phones are out," Mom said, "but come on in from the cold."

"Your phones are out, too?" he asked, stepping forward. Behind him we now saw there were about eleven more kids trailing towards the

36

house. He saw our gaze. "Oh, I didn't want to leave anyone in the bus in this cold."

"Of course not," said Mom, looking worriedly out at the line of youngsters. "You all had quite a walk to get here!" she said, marveling. The kids looked weary. But she smiled for them as they filed in, looking curiously up at her and then me. Despite the huge realization dawning on us of how life had instantly changed, we had to help these kids without scaring them.

"Bless your little hearts!" my mother drawled in her most southern sounding accent as they marched in. She grew up in the South. It only came out strongly now and then, her drawl, but when it did, it was straight from the heart o' Dixie.

I welcomed them, noting how cute they were, all bundled up in their winter clothes. Some were shivering despite that.

I led them into the living room and around the wood stove as Dad came and spoke with the bus driver. I pulled off gloves and mittens, showing them how to safely warm up their fingers. Then I helped them remove all their gear while Mom got out the big cast iron kettle and filled it from the water jugs. She put it on the wood-stove to heat up for hot cocoa, and then went to talk with Dad and the driver.

Kasha, our golden retriever, was delighted with the extra company. I supervised her eager explorations of the kids, while they shrieked with excitement. Hearing all the noise, the twins rushed downstairs. They stood open mouthed, taking in the scene.

"Wow!" Lanie breathed.

"Wow!" echoed Laura.

"Let's get our dolls!" In minutes the floor was strewn with what I call the world's largest collection of Barbie dolls, as well as children, pillows, and Kasha running wildly about in the midst. I joined the adults in the kitchen.

The bus driver, who said his name is Roy, did not believe my father's assessment that a probable EMP had occurred. He had to try our phone for himself and our cell phones. Then, surveying us and the warm atmosphere he said, "You all don't seem very upset about this."

"Oh, we're not happy about it," my mom interjected quickly. "We're just not that surprised."

"Really? You expected this?"

I figured this was going to launch a conversation about politics and terrorists, or divine judgment and I got up to find disposable hot cups for the hot chocolate. From the pantry, I could hear the conversation.

"We didn't expect it," my dad said. "We knew it was possible, because NASA's been warning the public for years that a solar flare could take down the grid."

"Solar? You mean the sun did this?" The man sounded dumbfounded.

"It could have, yeah," dad said. "But whatever caused it, our first order of business is getting these kids home."

"Oh, man," Roy said, as I came out. He shook his head. "My first pick up was ten miles from here! How we gonna get them back if our vehicles don't work?" He looked at my dad. "How long do you think this will last? More than a day or two?" My father's eyes met my mother's. I hastily went to check on the kids. The bus driver clearly had no idea how the rules of the game had changed and I certainly didn't want to be the one to tell him. The children of course, had no inkling. I looked at their beautiful young faces and wondered if their parents had done any food storage. I hoped that when we got them home, they would be okay.

Without asking my mother or father I took a moment to run downstairs and grabbed some packages from the storage room. Back upstairs, I announced, "Time for hot chocolate." A chorus of happy cries ensued. In the kitchen I got a big tray and loaded it with what I needed.

"I still don't get how come I never heard about this, about a solar flare," Roy was saying.

Dad shrugged. "The media never really picked up on it." He tipped his cup to get the last bit of his coffee. "I saw an article here or there, but I guess no one wanted to take the threat seriously."

Roy shook his head. "Sounds like our government, doesn't it?"

I got busy making the hot chocolate and handing around cups. I made the kids sit in a row, with strict orders to be still while they drank. I gave out raisins and cookies, too. Back in the kitchen, talk continued.

"We need to get these kids home," Dad said. "Look, it's snowing again." He nodded towards the window. "It's only gonna get harder to move around, not easier." He looked at Roy. "Can you ride a horse?"

The man's face blanched. "Unh uh. I haven't been on a horse since I was a teenager."

Dad frowned. "It'll take more trips, then. I was hoping to have three riders."

"I can ride," my mom put in.

Dad shook his head. "You'll need to stay with the girls and Justin."

"I can do that," said Roy. He looked embarrassed. "I mean, since I can't ride, I may as well help out somehow."

My father looked at him thoughtfully, but he slowly shook his head. I knew that was coming. No way would my father trust a stranger with the care of his children.

"No, my wife will stay with the baby," he said. "We have a toddler." The three little ones shared a room which even had its own insulated wood stove, a round modern marvel that Dad had specially fitted. We often used it in winter, so I knew the baby was snug and warm.

"I've watched babies before," the man said, "so I know I could handle a toddler." There was eagerness in his voice—or something—that set me on edge and I guess my folks felt the same way. My mom said, "No need. I'm staying." He looked ready to protest but I spoke up.

"Um, you HAVE to come with us." Everyone looked at me, so I explained. "These kids are too little to show us how to get to their houses. You're the only one who knows where they live."

The driver scratched his head. "She's right. But how will I go? I don't ride."

"Dad, we ought to try the cart," I said. My father gave me a warning look but I'd already said it, so I added, "Otherwise, we'll have to go back and forth who-knows-how-many-times and all the while these kids' parents are worrying their minds out."

"They're not worrying," Dad said. "They think the kids are safe at school."

"Still," I reasoned, "Do you want to be doing this all day? The cart will be quicker."

My mother stood up to collect cups. "I think you're right, Lex," she said, with an apologetic nod at my dad.

"The cart's never been tested with a lot of weight," my dad said, thinking it out. "You think it'll hold them all?" He looked at the roomful of children, most of whom were all over the floor again playing.

"It'll have to," my mom said, softly.

He nodded, accepting that his hand-built cart was going to get that weight test, ready or not. "Lex, go and harness Spirit and Promised Land to the cart. You'll ride Rhema and take one or two of these little ones with you on the saddle—think you can handle that?"

I nodded, certain I could. I often took the girls with me for rides around the property or on our horse trail.

It was the harnessing I wasn't so sure about. Dad had demonstrated how to do it but it was a long time ago and I never actually used the cart with the horses. He'd built it, showed me how to harness it up and then used it a few times himself. That was it. Now its day had come. I prayed as I walked out there that I wouldn't make a mistake getting it ready for such a precious load of passengers.

I did the best I could, and then covered the bottom with handfuls and handfuls of hay. Hay is a great insulator from the cold. Back in the house, I helped Mom get the kids ready. It took some doing to match everyone up to the right boots, coats and hats and gloves. Then there were the inevitable last-minute bathroom breaks, which meant some kids had to get OUT of their coats and gloves all over again.

In a few minutes one little boy came and gazed at me solemnly with big, brown eyes. He was uber-cute.

"Yes?"

"Your baf-room is broken," he said. "It didn' work." I stared at him for a moment, uncomprehending. Then it dawned on me. The plumbing would be affected by the electric failure. A toilet will flush once or twice before it runs out of water from the holding tank, but that's it. It had evidently run out, since lots of the kids were visiting the restroom.

I nodded. "I know. I'm sorry."

He shrugged. "It's o-tay."

"What's your name?" I asked.

He smiled, revealing a missing front tooth. "Max."

I smiled back. "I'm Lex."

He held my eyes for a moment with that inquisitive look kids have and then unexpectedly drove his head into my stomach, making me gasp. I tousled his head, realizing I'd been given a sure sign of approval from a kindergartener.

"C'mon, y'all," I heard my mother call. I grabbed Max's hand and helped him into his coat and hat and gloves.

"You're nice," he said, this time, our faces close while I zipped him up.

"So are you." I tweaked his nose. One day Justin would be his age. It was a cute age. I tied a scarf around his head to cover as much of Max's head as possible, but he pushed it back down towards his neck.

"No," I said, gently bringing it up again. "You'll be glad to have it over your face once we're out there." I nodded towards the front door.

He let me fix it.

Outside, we piled the kids in the cart. They were thrilled, as if it were a joyride. I took out the box of treats I'd grabbed from our storage room, giving one granola bar to each child. Roy looked at me expectantly, so I handed him one, too. Somehow, even though a single granola bar isn't much, I couldn't let those kids go home empty handed. My dad looked on and nodded at me approvingly.

"You sure I can't try to get the bus going?" Roy asked.

My dad shook his head. "There's no point. It won't work."

Under his breath to me he said, "I hope this cart holds up to the load." He was looking at Roy, and I saw that the driver was dad's biggest worry. He was a large guy, maybe two hundred fifty pounds. Coupled with the weight of a dozen youngsters, it did seem like a lot.

The children were practically on top of one another but I liked the fact they'd keep each other warm. I encouraged them to dig into the hay. When they were settled, I said in a loud voice, "Okay, who would rather ride with me on horseback?"

I realized my mistake instantly when every single hand but Roy's went up and the cart started creaking as they all jumped to their feet, crying, "Me! I want to!"

"Whoa!" shouted my dad. "Sit down, all of you!"

They did. My father is a big teddy bear at heart but his voice can sound tough if you don't know him. He surveyed the children and picked out the two biggest kids. "Think you can fit them, Lex?"

I looked at the kids. They may have been big for kindergarteners, but they were still just kids. "Yup," I said.

Once my dad got them in front of me, where I circled them with one arm and showed them how to hang on, we started out, moving slowly. My father rode Spirit, a good-natured thoroughbred, so he wouldn't add more weight to the cart. The bus driver sat against the front rail, telling him which way to go.

Snow was falling and I felt the light flakes settling on my face and eyelashes. A few of the kids were sticking out their tongues to catch the flakes. I smiled. But my dad looked at the cart worriedly every time it creaked or groaned over the uneven driveway.

With Roy directing us, we managed to drop off the first child in about twenty minutes. The home had a circular drive, allowing us to take the cart right up to the front. The boy's mom opened the door before Dad even had a chance to knock. She stared at our cart like it was an incredible sight, but seeing the bus driver in it seemed to settle any doubts she had.

Dad explained quickly about the bus breaking down. Whether or not she knew yet that nothing was working I couldn't tell, but we had to hurry on to get the other kids home before we all froze. Or, we would have hurried except that when my father went to help the child climb out of the cart, Dad saw that I hadn't harnessed the horses to it properly. He gave me a reproving look while he fixed the hitch.

I hate getting that look from my dad. I'm glad that he caught my error before the horses became unhitched, perhaps while we were moving. I doubt it would have caused an injury to anyone but I would have felt a lot worse.

At the next house the mother greeted us with anxious, excited tones. I couldn't make out her words since I remained at the street but my dad spoke to her and I saw him gesturing and then her gesturing, and finally he turned to go.

"She don't like it," said Roy, watching. "Neither do I. But we're all in the same boat."

I nodded.

"Except for you guys. You're ready."

He sounded resentful. I didn't know what to say, so I said nothing. As my father neared us, we heard the woman call to him. "What should I do?"

Dad turned his horse. He called, "Do you own a woodstove?"

She nodded, yes.

"Build a fire! Stay warm," he said.

I could tell he didn't enjoy leaving a woman with so little help or information, but what choice did he have? As we left, I turned to look back. The sight of that woman holding her child, staring at us forlornly as we left, seemed sad. Was there a husband and father who had gone to work and could be stranded somewhere? Would he make it home to help his family? I didn't know.

Two hours later we were down to the last child, my passenger, whose teeth chattered despite the blanket and my arm wrapped around him. The cart waited at the street while I rode him up the driveway to the door. Both parents were home. Like all the others they were eager to ask questions. I was surprised they expected me, a teenage girl, to have answers; or else they were just desperate to talk like most people with no means of communication with the outside world.

Anyway, the cold was starting to numb my fingers right through my gloves. Roy, who probably did not have wool socks like Dad and I, had laboriously climbed out of the cart at each stop; and then lumbered his big bulk over the rail and into it again. He used the time to stamp his feet, trying to hold off the numbness and threat of frostbite.

"Okay, which way to your place?" Dad asked.

"I need to get back to the bus before I go home," Roy said. "I left my stuff there." Dad shook his head.

"Didn't you say you lived north-west of here? The bus is south. Can't do it."

"I need my stuff," he returned. "I left my wallet there."

"Look," said my father. "I'll get your things and get them to you at a later time when it's not this cold. But I'm not heading in the wrong direction. We want to get home so we need to take you to where you belong right now."

Roy hesitated. "Why don't I go home with you and I'll get my stuff tomorrow?"

I felt decidedly creeped out. Roy wanted to come home with us, no doubt about it. I looked at my dad, silently pleading with him not to agree. I gave him what I hoped was an intense stare. His cheeks and nose were red from the cold and I realized mine were likely the same.

To my relief Dad said, "I'd rather not have to make this trip tomorrow. We'll take you home now."

"Look, my house keys are on the bus. I won't be able to get in without them and I don't have a woodstove like you all. I'll freeze, even if I could get in."

Dad took a breath. "How do you heat your home?" he asked.

Rhema stamped one foot impatiently. I felt exactly the same way.

"Propane," said Roy.

"Then you've got the means to start a fire," said Dad, as if that

43

settled everything.

"What—what—I don't know how to do that! I'll blow the house up!"

"I'll help you," my father said.

"But the keys," he persisted.

"We'll get in." I loved my Dad's firmness at that moment. There's nothing like a good man standing strong to make a girl feel secure. Rhema snorted and Dad looked at me. "Hey, Lex, I want you to go on home. I'll get Roy to his house. No sense in both of us staying out in this cold any longer than we have to."

I gave him a worried look. I wanted to go home alright, but not until I knew for sure that Roy wasn't coming too. I shook my head.

"That's okay. I'll wait for you." Dad almost grinned. He understood me so well.

"No, sweetie. But you know what? Let's switch what we're doing here. You take the cart back and I'll take Roy on Rhema."

"What? I got to get up on that horse?" Roy exclaimed.

"I'd rather wait for you, Dad," I said. He motioned me over to him and reached for something from behind his back. Keeping it out of sight from Roy, he pulled out his Glock 26 and handed it to me. Surprised, I searched his face.

"Why do I need this?"

"Because I've read too many disaster scenarios where people get violent. You've got horses. People on foot may want a horse. That's why."

"I don't want it, Dad." There was no way I would ever shoot a person, I was sure.

"It's loaded but not chambered," he said, in a low voice. "Keep it in your front coat pocket. It's safe unless you pull the trigger." He paused. "You know what you're doing."

I did. Mom, dad and I were all well-versed in gun safety and how to use a firearm. And I wasn't surprised Dad had it with him; he was licensed to carry. But I was reluctant to take it. This wasn't target practice. He was giving it to me so I could use it in self-defense. This was different. This was a real life situation.

"I'll never use it, Dad!" I whispered, fiercely.

"You shouldn't need to use it," he returned, calmly. "Just be ready to show it. Nine times out of ten that'll be enough."

44

His eyes looked deeply into mine. My Dad has a way of really being with you, of meeting you where you are by looking into your eyes.

"You won't need to use it," he repeated, reassuringly. "It's only day one. Most people aren't even aware yet of what's ahead. But I need to know you have it with you. And in case any trouble should start, all you need to do is show it."

When I still hesitated, he added in that same gentle tone, "I need to know you have it."

I took the gun, my hands instantly remembering how to handle it. I tucked it in my pocket, making sure it was in as deep as it could go. I didn't want to lose dad's favorite firearm. I felt an eerie sensation at the thought that I might need to defend myself. But I also felt skeptical: Wasn't this the sort of thing that people made fun of preppers for? Being paranoid? Thinking that every disaster meant the coming of the apocalypse? Was my dad becoming one of those paranoid extremists, like they showed on National Geographic's "Doomsday Preppers"? We'd actually rolled our eyes at what some of those people felt they needed to do to "prepare," like building deadly traps around their properties for the zombie hordes they expected to come after them, or buying a grenade launcher. We were nothing like them, just an ordinary family hoping to get by if times got tough.

The gun in my pocket didn't feel ordinary.

"Don't stop for anyone, no matter what. I'll be along shortly on my way back and if there's someone who needs help, I'll get to them. But don't you stop." He gazed at me. He knew I'd normally stop for anyone or for an animal in distress.

"Got it?"

"Got it."

"I think she's right and we should all stick together," called Roy. I'd almost forgotten he was there. I wanted to stick together—but only with my dad. Hearing Roy say it filled me with fresh distrust.

"Go on, Lex. I love you, honey," Dad said.

"I love you, Dad," I said. Under my breath I added, "Be careful!" He nodded.

"You, too."

LEXIE
JANUARY 12
DAY TWO

When night fell the dark was heavy, even with snow on the ground. From my upstairs window I couldn't see a single light outside other than the "canopy of the heavens" (that's from a poem I read). I'm thankful we have oil-lamps inside. They glow softly and cast shadows, making things feel cozy. Except Dad still isn't back.

It's hard to focus on anything else. I had no trouble getting the cart home. And I saw no one on the road at all, just the same few empty cars we'd passed earlier when we were taking the kids home. Roy obviously wasn't the only one who got stuck out there but I have no idea where the other motorists went.

Anyways, I'm worried; I keep praying that the bus driver didn't turn out to be a psychopath—you never know. Mom and I agree he gave us a bad feeling.

Laura and Lainie are watching us for clues on whether they should be worried or not, so we pretend everything's fine and Dad will be home shortly. But Mom and I got off alone and agreed in prayer for Dad's safety. Actually we prayed for a lot more than that. With this EMP, there'll be a lot of people without adequate shelter or food. Mom and I prayed for everyone we could think of and for our country. We prayed for our friends from church, and I prayed for friends at school and their families. You'd think that would be a downer but I usually feel better after prayer, and yesterday was no different. I still wish he'd walk in the door but I feel deep inside that he is okay. *Thank you, Lord!*

But we're short on distractions. Once the girls are put to bed, I'm usually on my PC, or I watch a movie with my folks if I'm done with homework. I can't quite believe that movies and news and documentaries are now a thing of the past—for now, anyways. I wonder how Andrea and Sarah are taking this. Besides Meredith at church, Andrea and Sarah are my best friends. I can't get on Facebook or send a text and it gives me a strange powerless feeling. I hope Andrea is okay. She isn't always happy at home.

I stayed up late last night hoping Dad would walk in the door. It started snowing again when I was out there star gazing and it seemed beautiful and poignant—but also sad. Anyways, I camped out on the sofa so I would hear when he got in. Only he didn't. Mom slept on the other couch for the same reason.

"Mom?" I had trouble sleeping. I wasn't sure if she was still awake but she answered me, sleepily.

"Mmmm?"

"Do you think we should have let Roy come to the house? Like he wanted to? Dad would be here, then." She was silent for a moment.

"I don't know, honey. We had that bad feeling about him. I think he's a polecat. (That's southern for 'a bad person.') I do wish your dad would get back, though."

"What do you think's held him up?"

She sighed. "Could be Roy wanted company, I don't know."

That sounded weak and in a moment we both chuckled.

"Well, it could be horse trouble," she said, in a tone with more conviction. I felt a pang of concern for Rhema. We've been together for five years and I love my horse dearly. But I hoped mom was right, surprising even myself. I'd much rather think horse trouble was keeping dad than human trouble. Because if it was people trouble, it would be serious. But he would give a horse time to rest if it needed it.

LATE MORNING

I'm going to the Buchanans' to see if they'll help me look for Dad. Blake and his family are good friends as well as being part of our church body. They live on the other side of town, which sounds close but our town is larger than some counties. It's certainly not walking distance. I should be able to get there on Rhema in maybe an hour. Wait, Dad has Rhema! I'll use Promised Land. I'm going to be cautious and stay off road where I can, sticking to the edge of fields like deer do. I know my dad would want that.

I think my parents are extreme in their caution, but it's such a part of the prepper worldview that I guess they couldn't altogether avoid it—and maybe it's passed on to me, too. Anyways, the Buchanans are preppers like us. They won't be in a panic over this. They'll help me search for Dad, I know it.

I told Mom my plan. She frowned but then slowly nodded. "I guess one of us will have to go but I think it ought to be me."

"Mom, you have to stay with the little ones," I said. "What if something happened to you? We'd be orphans."

"Don't say that," she scolded. "I believe your father is perfectly safe. He's just been held up." She stared at me like she couldn't comprehend why I'd uttered such a negative statement.

"I didn't mean it that way," I said. "I just meant it would seem like we were if both you and Dad are gone." I felt my face get red. I hate it when my face gets red. Whenever that happened at school, I always wished I could climb beneath a rock. At least it was just my mom seeing my red face.

"If he's not home soon I guess I'll have to let you go." She looked at me worriedly. "You'll have to take the firearm."

Like I said, I guess my parents are a little extreme in their caution. Maybe all preppers are.

———————◆———————

Time is going by and tension is mounting here. We can't keep our minds off Dad. Mom and I dragged in wood, heated water, washed dishes by hand and checked our lamps for nighttime, but I'm itching to be off.

Two days ago we could have reached Dad by cell phone. Now, it's like we're living in another century.

———————◆———————

I've had enough. I'm going to saddle up and go talk to the Buchanans.

———————◆———————

I've gone and returned home and Dad still isn't here. I was so hoping he'd be back! All I got from the Buchanans was bad news. Here's what happened: When I got to their house at first no one came to the door. I saw their vehicles in the driveway, so I knew they hadn't got stranded elsewhere—they had to be home. I led Promised Land around the house and knocked on the back door. I banged on it. Then the basement door. When there was still no answer, I banged on a window. Hard. I was getting angry. Why didn't they answer? Then I started calling for Blake.

I searched the windows for movement, hoping he would answer. I was just ready to give up (and ready to cry, too) when I saw the drapes move, and there was Blake! He looked surprised, but I couldn't help noticing that he was not happy to see me.

A minute later the back door opened and I hurried over. Mr. Buchanan came out—at least I thought it was him—because he was covered with a tarp-like poncho and wore a gas mask! I felt a little frightened, honestly, by his appearance. But when he lifted the mask and started to speak, I felt better. It was Mr. Buchanan alright. The same Mr. Buchanan who supplied our church every Sunday with coffee and tea and donuts or other goodies. He was not a super smiley man, but he was nevertheless jocular if you spoke to him, and always helpful. My parents were good friends with him and his wife. I trusted him implicitly.

"What are you doing here, Lexie? Is everything okay?"

"Dad's missing."

He frowned. "You'd better come in." He was looking me over in a strange way though, like looking for a wound or something.

"I'm fine," I said.

"Uh, no," he said, bending down and picking up a yellow plastic thing. He handed it to me. "You'd better put this on over your clothes. Just in case."

I stared at the yellow plastic in his hand.

"It's a haz-mat suit," he said. "I can't bring you to our safe room unless you put it over your clothing."

I thought it was a strange request, but I took the suit. He waited while I tied up Promised Land and positioned a feed bag beneath her head; then opened the door and allowed me to move inside ahead of him. I put the one-size-fits most suit over my clothing while he shook off his tarp and stomped his boots. He gave me light blue thingies, and said, "Put these over your shoes." I felt like I was a leper or something—I had no clue why he was making me do this, but like I said; We trust the Buchanans. I did what he asked. Only later did I find out the reason—which was to avoid possible fallout in case the EMP had been caused by a nuclear warhead. I'll get to that in a minute.

"Where is everyone?" I asked. I wanted to say, "Why are you

wearing that mask?" but I was afraid it would embarrass him. A gas mask isn't exactly macho looking.

"They're in our safe room," he said. "I'm wondering why you're not in yours."

I stared, surprised by the question. "There hasn't been a storm or anything." He gave me an inscrutable look.

"Something took down the grid and until we know for sure it wasn't a terrorist's bomb, you should stay safe. Radiation levels are worst right after a blast."

I felt myself gaping. "Radiation levels? How do you know there's radiation?"

"Well, we don't know for sure; we actually have a radiation detector but we can't find it. How's that for being prepared, huh?" When I didn't smile, he added, "Do you guys have a detector?"

"I don't know."

"Well, here's the thing," he said, "If we've had a solar flare, then it's safe to be outside; that sort of radiation doesn't pose much more of a threat than normal sun. But if it was a bomb there will be nuclear fallout, and until we know for sure where it hit and which direction the plume went, we need to play it safe. At least for the first few days." He paused. "Unless there are more bombs, in which case I don't know how long we'll need to stay sheltered." He studied me. "You rode here all by yourself?"

"I didn't want Mom to leave when Dad's already missing."

"Okay," he said. "Tell me what happened. How is he missing?" I told him quickly about Roy and the school kids, adding that I didn't trust that bus driver from the start. His frown deepened.

"We'll need to pray about this," he said. Where does he live?"

"Who?"

"The bus driver, Roy." I felt like a dimwit and I blushed. My mind seemed to have latched onto the words "nuclear fallout" and I couldn't think straight.

"Well, I'm not sure, exactly. I know it was north-west of us, I heard my dad say so."

Mr. Buchanan's expression changed as soon as I said I wasn't sure.

"If you don't know where he lives, I don't see what we can do. It'll mean spending many more hours out there, not knowing if we're exposing ourselves. Do you see what you're asking, Lexie?"

I nodded miserably.

"But I'll tell you what, we will pray for your dad's safety."

I thanked him and turned to go.

"Hey, how long did you guys spend outside yesterday taking those kids home?"

I thought for a moment.

"Three or more hours, easy," I said. He nodded, but his face went blank. I could see he wasn't going to say if that length of exposure to fallout might be really bad.

"Come and get warmed up before you go," he said. I peeked out at Promised Land. She's such a good girl. She was munching, patiently hanging in there, despite the long ride and now being left standing in the cold. I followed Mr. Buchanan to the basement safe room. Mrs. Buchanan greeted me really warmly, and the whole family seemed especially happy to see me. I felt so ridiculous because as they surrounded me with hugs, I started crying. The Buchanans are good friends but they aren't usually THAT affectionate. I think they were happy to see someone else after being isolated in their safe room for a day and a night.

"Lexie's just gonna warm up before she has to ride back home," Mr. Buchanan said. He proceeded to talk with his wife, telling her my tale. I wiped my eyes and got a hold of myself as the younger ones bulleted me with questions.

"How did you get here, Lexie? On Rhema?"

"What are the girls doing?"

"Is your family staying in your safe room like we are?"

"Weren't you afraid to leave the house?"

"Give Lexie some room," Mr. Buchanan ordered. The little Buchanans instantly obeyed and I busied myself warming up by the kerosene heater, admiring the fact that they'd thought to install a heat source into their safe room complete with an outside, tiny air vent. Blake came over and stood next to me, saying nothing. He shoved both hands in his pockets and rocked a little, as though he was trying to think of something to say. Somehow I felt he was being supportive, and I turned to gaze up at him gratefully. Blake's tall and sandy haired, "one tall drink o' water," my mother would say. You can see at a glance that he's the mild-mannered type. I guess some people would call him a geek.

"You okay?" he asked.

"No," I said, and then in the next minute I'd told him the story of Roy and the kids. The whole family fell silent as I spoke. Talking about it filled me with fresh worries about my dad. Mrs. Buchanan came and put an arm around me.

"Let's pray over her," she said to her husband. The family surrounded me. Each one touched me, the little ones hanging onto my jeans or putting a small hand tenderly on my arm. The adults had a hand on my shoulders; Blake put one of his around my elbow. Mr. Buchanan prayed, and then Mrs. Buchanan. It was deeply comforting. I suddenly felt…well, protected. I don't know how else to describe the cocoon I seemed to feel around me during those prayers.

I thanked everyone and got ready to leave. Mrs. Buchanan pushed a cup of hot soup into my hands saying, "Here, don't go on an empty stomach." The soup was wonderful. Finally I went to leave but Blake came over to me, his eyes pensive.

"Hey, I'll be praying your dad gets home soon."

I nodded, but stared at the floor. "Thanks." It wasn't the help I'd hoped for. But I liked the way I had his full attention. Blake was the sort of guy who seemed chronically busy thinking so that when you spoke to him you could never be certain whether he had heard you or not, or, if he had, if it would penetrate the fog of his swirling thoughts enough to register. But I was definitely on his radar at the moment, and I liked it. It occurred to me that if anybody had a good handle on what might have happened if we'd indeed experienced an EMP, it would be Blake. I peeked up at him.

"Do you think there's dangerous radiation out there?"

He frowned. Then he shrugged. "Hard to say. We don't know what caused the pulse…You know how parents are," he added with a little smile.

"I know. My mom and dad are making me carry a firearm." He said nothing and just nodded, making me think he agreed with that caution.

"What if it was just a solar flare?" I asked hopefully. The visit had definitely given me new things to worry about. "A solar flare wouldn't cause dangerous radiation, would it?"

He looked uncomfortable, shifting on his feet. "Well, the thing is, whatever caused such a widespread outage is likely to set off a chain reaction leading to nuclear fallout; even if it wasn't terrorists." He looked almost apologetic. "But you'll be okay for now if it was a flare. See, the radiation from a flare is stronger than usual but not deadly. The real danger is what happens afterwards because of the grid going down. Like at Fukushima. Nuclear power plants depend on electricity to function properly, so we could see multiple leaks throughout the country…that's a danger regardless of how the grid went down."

My heart lifted and then sank at his words. We may have escaped contamination so far; but it might be coming anyway. He touched my arm as if he was going to say more but his dad said, "I'll walk you back upstairs."

As we left Blake added, in a louder tone so I'd hear him. "If the reactors blow, it'll be in two weeks or so." When I looked back at him with a worried frown he said, "With two weeks to shut things down, even manually, they may never blow." I realized that was supposed to be good news, so I gave him a weak smile.

"We gotta pray they don't," he added.

"Yeah. Thanks."

Mrs. Buchanan hurried over to give me a last hug. "Give your mom our love and tell her we'll continue to pray for your dad's safe return." I nodded my thanks to her.

"I'm sorry we can't search," Mr. Buchanan said as he led me back up the stairs.

I couldn't bring myself to say anything expected like, "That's okay," or, "I understand."

I did understand—if the Buchanans were right about there being radioactivity about, I couldn't blame them for staying in their shelter. But I was too raw to be kind. As I mounted the horse, Mr. Buchanan watched with the door opened a crack. It opened more.

"Hey, just in case. Change your clothes and put 'em outside when you get home and get your mom and the kids into the safe room and live in there for the next 48 hours, okay?"

"What about my dad?"

"If he gets home and can't find you, he'll check your safe room."

I turned to leave. Tears filled my eyes. I'd really thought the Buchanans would jump into action, joining me on horseback to search for Dad. The prayers had felt great and I really appreciated them but now, back in the cold white silence, I was immediately in worry mode.

The idea struck me to ask some of the kindergartener's parents where the driver lived. I remembered where some of the houses were where we'd dropped off kids. One of the parents was bound to know where Roy lived. But then I realized it didn't matter. I couldn't go there alone and expect to be any help if my dad hadn't been able to handle that guy. And maybe we were all dead anyways, from nuclear fallout we hadn't known was around.

I thought of those kids sticking their tongues out to catch snowflakes. Was it clean snow or deadly contaminated snow? Suddenly the magnitude of being totally in the dark about the outside world and what had happened to cause the EMP felt overwhelming. I wished I had taken the time to practice using dad's amateur radio. We needed it desperately.

I rode Promised Land hard, trying to keep down a sense of panic. I even gave up the fields, taking the roads I knew well because they were faster. I saw people walking and headed to the opposite side of the road. One man motioned at me and waited as though he wanted to talk, but I remembered my dad's words and I let Promised Land gallop past.

"Hey!" he called, in an angry voice. I didn't care. I just wanted to get home. If there had been fallout, then he was dead anyway, just like me and dad, and Roy and the kids.

At home I planned to drag out an encyclopedia and read about radiation poisoning. (Yeah; we have encyclopedias. When they were selling for a song because all the information was available online, my parents picked up a set. I have to hand it to them for being far-sighted.) Anyway, if we were poisoned, I wanted to recognize the signs. I thought of how we'd prayed for Dad and the feeling of assurance I'd gotten from the Lord. Had I been mistaken? Was I imagining that feeling? And just now, at the Buchanans' house—hadn't I felt safe? As in a cocoon?

But maybe it was all an illusion, just wishful thinking. Maybe all those years of prepping for a disaster were pointless, too. All that effort, the years of storing food little by little, putting aside what we could, the wood-stoves and solar panels, the cost of the safe room. I reflected bitterly how we'd given up Disney one summer to fix up that room. On and on it went, my mind raising images of all we'd done to prepare— the gravity-powered water filter, so effective we could take water from a pond and it would become drinkable after going through it.

What good was it now? What good, any of it? I pictured our

storeroom lined with shelves of products, all for seeing us through an emergency. And now I pictured all of us dying from radiation poisoning despite it all. The tears kept trickling as I rode, making painful rivulets as they hit the icy air on my exposed cheeks and face. I urged Promised Land faster, anxious to get home.

If I was going to die, I wanted to die at home.

How could You let this happen, God?

At home, I took care of the horse, crying harder when I saw Rhema's empty stall. When I got back in the house I sat down at the kitchen table and cried some more. It was colder in the kitchen than in the main living area but I didn't care.

"Mama, Lexie's crying!" I looked up. Lainie was staring at me with big eyes.

"Are you crying 'cos daddy's not home yet?"

I nodded. That was partially why. And then it hit me that Lainie and Laura and Justin hadn't been outside yesterday. It was only dad and I who had taken the kids home. And mom had been outdoors only briefly. This meant they may not have been exposed! I suddenly felt a little better but not a whole lot, because I might still be dying. But it was a great relief that we weren't all dying. Mom came out, holding Justin on one hip.

"What's the matter?" She hurried over to my side and stroked my hair. "What did the Buchanans say?"

I looked up at her. Mom's still really pretty in her forties. Even when she's worried. We're both blondes but I look more like my dad than her.

"Mom, do we have a radiation detector?" She looked at me for a moment and then comprehension dawned and her eyes widened.

"Oh, no!" she said. "What did they tell you?"

"Do we have a detector?"

"What is it, mommy? What is it, mommy?" Lainie cried, tugging on my mother's shirt.

"Did they find radiation? Are we in a fallout zone?" Mom asked.

"What's radiation, mommy?"

We both ignored Lainie.

"They don't know," I said. "They can't find their detector. But they're staying in their safe room just in case."

She stopped. "You mean they won't help us find Dad?"

I shook my head. "Nope."

"Hmph!" she said. "Here," and she handed me Justin. "I think I know where ours is. Hold on."

"Is Daddy LOST?" Lainie asked me, her little face frozen with fear.

"No, he's not lost!" Mom cried, hearing her as she left the room.

Lainie turned to me. "IS daddy lost, Lexie? Is that why you're crying?"

My heart was pounding but I tried to focus on my little sister. Thing was, instead of tears, now that I'd shared the news with my mother, I just felt restless energy. I forced myself to smile. "Daddy will be okay," I said. "Jesus is taking care of him." I said it by faith, not feeling it in my heart. Lainie nodded at me dubiously but she turned to go back to playing with Laura in the family room.

It felt like a long time until my mother returned. I had to keep settling Justin, who wriggled every few minutes to get down. Lainie returned.

"What is mom getting, Lexie? What's a 'tector?"

"Nothing. Go and play," I told her.

"No!" She crossed her arms and glowered at me. "I want to know!" I might have smiled at her puckered up little face except I was in no mood for smiling.

"I'm staying right here 'til you tell me!"

"Well, I'm not telling you, so just stay there if you want."

Lainie continued to nag until I was ready to shout at her. I was so tense that if I hadn't been holding Justin I might have really lashed out. But suddenly it occurred to me that her standoff wasn't about knowing, really. She just wanted an answer, any answer. Lainie hated to think we weren't telling her something; it didn't matter what it was.

"Fine! She's getting a radiation detector." I watched Lainie's face and could tell (as I suspected) that she had no clue what that was.

"Okay," she said, and just like that, turned and walked away. I sighed. And then mom was back, holding the detector.

"I'm not sure how to use this thing," she said, "but I'll give it a try."

"Wait, Mom," I said, after watching her get her coat on. "I've been outside a lot already; let me try." She hesitated, and I could see she didn't want to let me.

"Mom, if I'm sick already there's no sense in letting you get sick too."

Reluctantly, she handed it over. It was two pieces, attached by a cord. One looked an awful lot like a magnifying glass except that wasn't its purpose at all.

"Here's the information it came with," she added, pulling some folded papers out of her back pocket. "I guess we'd better read up on how to do this." She sat down, taking Justin from my arms. "We practiced using most of our stuff, but I never honestly thought I'd have to use this thing. I think your dad knows how to use it."

"Give it to me," I said. I spent the next ten minutes poring over those instructions, wishing my dad was there to be doing it instead of me.

"It measures alpha, beta, gamma and x-ray radiation," I said.

"I'm pretty sure we only have to worry about gamma rays," said Mom.

"I'm trying to figure out how to tell which it's measuring," I replied. I looked up at her after a few more minutes. She was feeding Justin from a baby food jar. The baby seemed impervious to the fact that the house, overall, was cooler than in the past. He was happily accepting each proffered spoonful, his messy mouth evidence of his enjoyment.

"Mom, I don't know what I'm doing," I admitted. She looked over at me.

"Okay. Can you finish feeding him? I'll see if I can make heads or tails of that." I took over feeding the baby. After a few minutes she said, "I think I got it. I'm going outside. I'll be right back."

I met her eyes. "Sorry, Mom."

"What for?"

"I should be the one doing that."

"Actually no, you shouldn't be," she said. "I almost forgot. Radiation is cumulative. If you've been exposed already, the last thing you need is more of it."

About ten minutes later mom came back in. She was flushed.

"I can't seem to get anywhere with this. I'm not even sure it's working," she said unhappily. "Maybe I'm missing something very simple, but I don't know what." She paused. "I guess we'd better grab some stuff and move into the safe room. It's probably too late to avoid the worst exposure but just in case it might help, we have the room, we may as well do it."

57

We both started collecting things to take with us but then I remembered something.

"Mom, don't we have those pills? To counteract radiation?"

"You mean potassium iodide," she said. "That wouldn't help much if we've been exposed to gamma rays—they might protect the thyroid but that's about it. Gamma rays are the worst kind; too powerful to be diffused by taking something." She gave me a sad "chin up" sort of smile and turned and started locking up the house. I began carting stuff down the steps to the basement.

After the first trip I said, "We're going to be cold down there."

"I'll load the stove in the basement," she said, "which ought to help. If it's really too cold we'll just have to come out, is all."

The safe room had just about everything we could need for at least two weeks—except a means of independent heat. Guess we never thought it would be freezing weather when we might need the room.

I tried to brush away worries about Dad as I gathered up things for the girls and the baby. Inside I felt a sinking hopelessness; it was likely too late. Definitely too late for me but maybe even for all of them. Before we shut ourselves in I grabbed the correct volume of the encyclopedia--P-Q-R—and brought it with me.

I'd like to say that what I read was reassuring, only it wasn't. The first few hours following a blast are the deadliest for gamma rays. But one thing stood out to me: It talked about avoiding fallout and brushing it off your clothing if you saw it. It said wash up, change clothes, leave contaminated objects outside of your shelter. In other words, it seemed to imply you could SEE it. Other than snow, I didn't see any unusual dust cover or anything else out of the ordinary. Neither did we feel any sudden strong winds, or heat; and we didn't hear anything exploding. I guess I'm saying I feel pretty certain we were not near the detonation site—IF there was a detonation—and so I'm less worried. I showed Mom what I read and she feels better too.

The girls are whining to get out of this room and go to their bedroom but Mom says the prudent thing to do is at least stay the night.

LATE NIGHT

When the girls and Justin were asleep Mom told me that if Dad isn't back by tomorrow morning, she's going after him. She knows how to handle a firearm and a horse. Mom and I often practiced shooting or riding together.

I just never dreamed we were practicing survival skills when we did it.

LEXIE
JANUARY 13
DAY THREE

Dad is back! He woke us up this morning, knocking on the door to the safe room. Mom and I seemed to wake up at the same instant. She scrambled up to let him in but when she opened the door and saw him, she froze.

"Oh, my goodness!"

When I looked at him, tears sprang to my eyes. Dad looked like he'd been through hell. My mother sort of lost it.

"Do you have radiation sickness?" she cried, pulling him into the room to sit him down. She was instantly in a panic.

"What? What? No, I'm okay," he said, and he pulled her into a hug. Mom started crying.

"What happened to you?" she asked.

I'd gotten up and so I went and hugged Dad. I was also crying. He put one arm around each of us. "I'm sorry," he said, softly. "I'm okay, really."

The little ones had kept on sleeping. And then we were all trying to talk at once. Mom was asking what happened to him and he wanted to know why we were in the room and I tried to tell him about radiation exposure and then the twins woke up and shouted, "Daddy's home! Daddy's home!" as if no one knew it yet.

"QUIET, EVERYONE!"

My dad would make a good movie director. He knows how to call the shots.

In the sudden silence, Laura asked, "Where WERE you, daddy?" She stumbled towards him, still wiping sleep from her eyes. Her question was exactly what we all wanted to know.

"Mommy was worried about you," added Lainie from her sleeping bag on the floor. But then she got up and scampered to Dad, hugging one of his legs.

"I know; and I'm sorry, girls." He released me and mom to bend down and give the twins a kiss atop their heads. Suddenly Justin made a sound. He'd not only woken up but had pulled himself to a standing position in his portable crib. He was rocking back and forth holding onto the side, gurgling happily at dad. It seemed to break the tension as we all chuckled and mom went to pick him up.

"I want a better kiss, daddy," Laura said, and so Lainie had to get a better kiss, too. But Laura had noticed that her daddy's face was very red and rough, and his hair was a mess.

"Did you fall off your horse, daddy?" she asked.

He smiled, "No, honey, I didn't fall. I had a very long walk, though."

Mom gasped. "Did you have to walk in this weather?"

He nodded.

"That's enough, girls," Mom said, "I want your father now. I want to hear every bit of what happened to him."

"What happened to Rhema, Dad?" I asked. My voice was tense. If dad had been walking, then something had happened to Rhema or he'd have been riding.

Mom turned to me. "We'll talk about your horse later. Right now I want to hear what happened to your father." I didn't like that, but there was no arguing. Not when mom talks in that tone of voice.

"What about the radiation?" I asked.

"What's all this about radiation?"

I told him what Mr. Buchanan had said about fallout and he cocked an eyebrow but said, "If we were in the worst of the fallout it would be evident by now. Lexie and I would be sick already, if not dead."

"You don't exactly look wonderful," Mom said.

He gave a wry grin. "I'm not sick. Just weather-beaten." He looked around. "Is that why you came down?"

"Yes; Gerard told Lexie to get us down here. I tried the radiation detector but I don't know how to use it," she told him. "I thought we may as well be safe."

"Sure," he said, nodding. "Where's the detector? Just to be sure, I'll go check."

"Wait a minute," Mom said, wide-eyed. "You haven't told us what happened to you!"

He paused and a look of distaste passed over his face. "I'll tell you everything when I get back." He looked weary.

I was glad to have him back in one piece.

"Oh, no, you don't," said Mom. "I'm going with you."

"Can I come?" I asked.

"Stay with the little ones," said Dad. "We'll be right back." Mom handed me the baby who started to fuss until I shoved a bottle of ready-to-feed formula into his mouth. Mom had breast-fed Justin for the first six months of his life and then tried to switch him to a cup. He didn't want any part of a cup, so we still gave him bottles. I was glad we'd stocked the room.

As my parents left, dad turned back to say, "Lock the door behind us."

"Really, Dad?" This seemed silly and unnecessary to me.

"Really."

They left hand in hand. I locked the door, looked at the twins and shrugged. Dad was acting like an extremist prepper but so what? At least we had him back!

When they returned Dad was shaking his head. "That was an expensive mistake," he said to my mom.

He looked in at us. "C'mon, we're going upstairs. We'll take our chances. I don't see any evidence of fallout."

"What did the detector show?" I asked, as I hefted Justin more securely on my hip.

"Nothing. It's useless. It works with an electronic pulse, ironically enough."

"It uses a *pulse*?" I asked, incredulously.

"Yeah. According to the instructions it has this Geiger tube which generates a pulse, an electric current, if radiation passes through the tube. The pulse (or current) is 'electronically detected.' Sheesh! You'd have thought they'd make a radiation detector to withstand an EMP."

"Maybe some do," my mom said.

Well, either I'm using it wrong or this one doesn't," Dad stated.

As we got settled upstairs and Mom stoked the fire in the woodstove, Dad went to get cleaned up.

"Did you find out what happened to Dad, yet?"

Mom straightened up and removed her leather heat-resistant gloves. She pushed back a strand of hair. "Not yet. He'll be ready to talk after he washes up."

"It looked like he was limping," I said.

She nodded. "He's sore from so much walking."

When Dad returned, Mom placed a plate of flapjacks in front of him. She'd been making flapjacks whenever we went camping since I was a kid so it was no stretch for her to whip them up with a pan and the wood stove. I served the little ones, keeping my ears open. I was dying to know what had happened to Rhema. My theory was that he'd lent her to someone more in need than himself. I was hoping that was the case rather than something bad happening to my horse.

"Okay," he said. "This is what happened." Everyone's eyes were glued to Dad. Even Justin seemed to know that he could not vie for attention right now. I tried to ignore the redness and blistering on his face, a result, he said, of frostbite.

"Roy is as helpless as a baby. I don't know how that man made it to be a bus driver," he said, shaking his head. "He insisted I help him get in the house—which took far too long because he didn't want me to break a lock. Finally I was exasperated and ready to break a small window but he cried out not to and produced—what do you think? The keys."

Mom and I gasped. "What a creep!" I said. "He lied about not having his keys!"

Dad continued, "So we had to freeze for that extra hour just because he was hoping I'd give up and bring him back home with me." Again he shook his head. "Then he wanted me to walk him through accessing propane for a fire. After spending some time doing that I happened to see he had a kerosene heater! And kerosene. I made him use that. But he just kept peppering me with questions as if he'd never had to get by without electricity in his life. I tried to reassure him that as long as he could ration his food and keep warm he'd make it until spring.

"Man, I don't have enough food to last me three months," Dad mimicked Roy's voice, and Mom and I both cracked smiles.

"I said, 'Hey, you've wanted to lose some weight, right? Here's your chance. You're going to. But you'll survive."

I recalled Roy's wide middle and had to grin. But what dad said next wiped the smile from my face.

"So then he says, 'Okay, just help me get my flashlights ready for the night.' He sent me to the basement to bring them up. I should have known no one would keep all their flashlights in a basement but I just wanted to get home and I went—and he locked me in."

Mom and I gasped. "He *locked you in?*"

"Dad, why didn't you make him get the flashlights?" I asked. "It was his house; he should have known where they were, not you."

"He said he'd climb up to the attic to get his extra batteries while I got the flashlights."

Mom sighed.

Dad nodded, remembering. "So he locked me in and said he wouldn't let me out until he was sure his heater could keep him warm and that he'd be able to survive."

"What did you do?" I asked.

"Well, the basement was pretty dark and it was getting really dark as the sun went down, so I looked around for a way to get out. It wasn't a walk-out basement. If I was going to get out, it would have to be through this little window by the washer and dryer. The dryer hose was in it so I had to pull that out and unscrew a few screws for the screen holding it in place. I didn't have a screwdriver, so I used my pocketknife, but that took a while."

"At first I thought he wouldn't possibly be serious about keeping me down there. I yelled out to him that it was mighty cold in that basement. He said, 'I'll let you out. Soon.' Every time I called he said, 'Soon.'"

"Well, my hands were getting numb with cold, making it harder to use my knife to undo those screws but I finally did. Then, I had to remove snow from around the window so I could crawl out; and then I found out there was no way I was gonna fit through that little window. After all that work."

"So how'd you get out?" Mom asked.

"There was a wooden frame around the window. I pried it off, top and bottom. That was enough for me to squeeze out, but it hurt like the blazes." He rubbed his ribs, showing us where it hurt.

"Anyway," and he looked right at me. "I went to get Rhema and she wasn't there! I figure Roy got rid of her to make sure I wouldn't go anywhere. I think that man was just terrified of being alone. All because the lights went out."

"You don't think he hurt her, do you?" My heart had flown into my throat.

"No, I think he ran her off."

"How stupid of him to get rid of a horse now!" I cried.

"So you walked *all* the way?" My mother asked, as though the idea was impossible.

Dad nodded. "Had to. I kept hoping to find that animal along the route but I didn't see her. I didn't see anyone. I DID stop at Mrs. Preston's."

"My gosh, I haven't even thought of her!" Mom moaned.

I felt a stab of concern for Mrs. Preston. I'd known her all my life. She lives about two miles from us and used to go to our church. When she started needing oxygen she didn't want to drag the canister with her to church, so she stopped going and began listening to the messages via the internet. The church records our pastor each week and posts the link on a Facebook page. So Mrs. Preston had Blake set her up with a laptop and speakers and everything. Gotta respect an old lady who does that.

Anyways, we usually bring her a meal on Saturday or Sunday since her meal service for the elderly doesn't deliver on weekends. Sometimes we bring her here to have dinner with us. She always has chocolate for me and the girls.

"It's a good thing I stopped there," Dad was saying. "She was asleep in a chair covered with a blanket, but her house wasn't much warmer than outdoors. I got a fire going in her little stove. It looked as though she'd tried to start one herself but couldn't do it. I'm thinking she would have just frozen in her sleep if I hadn't come by."

"So she's okay?" Mom said.

"She is for now. So are the cats. But we have to bring her here. She'll never be able to keep up that wood stove on her own."

"Wow," I breathed. "Thank God Mrs. Preston's house was on the way!"

Dad nodded. "You're not kidding. I was getting worried about frostbite, but I got all warmed up there and I changed my socks and found a different pair of gloves, dry ones. It made all the difference."

"Not for your face," I said, feeling sad. Dad's nose was so red he looked like a caricature of a drunk. Mom must have thought the same thing. She reached over and touched the tip of his nose. "You've got a little frostbite there on your nose."

Dad rubbed it. "Nah. I can feel it."

"I'll bet she was happy to see you," Mom said, and we all smiled. Mrs. Preston loves company.

But Dad was yawning. "I've been up all night. I need to take a nap."

"Would Roy try to come back here?" I asked, as he rose from the table. Dad thought for a moment but almost smiled, like it was an absurd idea.

"He's not in shape to make that walk, let me tell you. And there are plenty of closer folks he'd probably pester before us. So the answer is, no, I don't think so. Not while the weather's cold like this." He gave me a sideways look. "You still have my Glock, don't you?"

I'd actually forgotten about it. It was still in my coat pocket so I went and got it and handed it over. He examined it briefly. Looking at me he said, "So you rode all the way to the Buchanans and back?" He looked tired but I could see a glint of something in his eyes. Was it anger? I braced myself for having to defend my actions.

"Yes, I did."

He nodded. "That's my girl," he said. Then, "Maybe you'd best rest up too before we go get Mrs. Preston."

———————◆———————

Later I found out Rhema slid on a patch of ice when she was carrying Dad and Roy. It was a small miracle she hadn't broken anything or that neither man took a fall. And the irony of the situation is that Dad had just about decided to spend the night and let the horse rest. He'd taken a few handfuls of hay from the cart, stuffing them into his coat and saddle bag, so he even had food for Rhema. But Roy blew it. By trying to force my father to stay with him, he lost an ally. We might have felt badly for him and tried to check on him now and then—but not now!

I'm still wondering if there's radiation out there and we just don't know it. There's no way to find out unless we start getting sick. Dad says he'll go talk to Gerard (that's Mr. Buchanan) as soon as he can, but today we need to get Mrs. Preston. He's afraid to wait until tomorrow because of this freezing weather. Our outdoor thermometer reads 12 degrees right now.

I wish I could talk to Andrea. We should have devised some way to keep in touch if electricity ever failed—but how? It feels like so many things have happened since the power went out. I wonder if she feels the same way.

AFTERNOON

I'm ready to go but Dad's still sleeping. I meandered out to the barn—probably to mourn over Rhema's empty stall—and suddenly remembered. The rabbits! I'd left them together in one cage! A nasty doe could castrate a buck if she got tired of his pestering. With a terrible feeling of foreboding I rushed to the cages. If I'd let that happen, it would mean a whole lot less meat for the family as well as other people who might have traded with us.

When I got there the animals were in two separate corners and my heart sank. I saw the buck move. I took the doe out and looked her over—no blood anywhere. I could breathe again. I hurried her back to her own cage and then went to check out the buck. He growled at me a little as my hand approached, but I sweet-talked him for a minute and then suddenly I had him. I turned him over with my heart in my throat. He was okay! Whew! Dad would have been so disappointed with me if anything happened to him.

We'll put aside a buck from the first litter and maybe a doe from the next one to have more breeders. We've butchered rabbits before, so I know better than to get attached to them despite how pretty they are, but I was feeling awfully fond of that buck right then.

I'm so grateful we still have him.

LATE AFTERNOON

"You let me sleep the day away!" Dad scolded, coming into the kitchen where I was sitting with a hot cup of tea.

"Mom said to." My mother walked in, holding a crying Justin.

"I had to, honey," she said. "You looked so tired and worn out." He went and peered outside. "It's getting dark already and there's no moon to speak of. It won't be easy but we have to go."

"Can it wait 'til morning?" Mom asked. "Justin's got a fever."

Dad paused, looking at his son. "What do you think it is?"

Mom shrugged. "Don't know, yet. He hasn't been pulling on his ears, so I don't think it's an ear infection. Could be the beginning of a cold or flu."

"We shouldn't bring Mrs. Preston here until we know what he's got," I said. "She's so old, what if we got her sick?"

"You may be right," Dad said, nodding at me. "I'll just ride over quick and make sure her fire is built up."

"Oh, here we go," said Mom, in a defeated tone. She looked at him pleadingly. "Please be careful!"

My mom and dad are acting like we've had a zombie apocalypse. I had to roll my eyes.

"I will," he said. He walked over and gave her a kiss. Then he gave one to Justin who had quieted some but was still sniffling. "You feel better, young man. Daddy'll be right back."

Justin merely eyed him tiredly, keeping his head against my mother.

"We have medicine for him, right?"

My mother nodded. "Oh, yes."

"Lex, you coming?" he said.

"Sure."

Mom said, "I'll need her to be my arms. I can't put down a sick baby unless he's sleeping."

I was relieved, actually. My bottom was still sore from my trek to the Buchanans', not to mention taking the kids home the day before. This was way more riding than I usually do. But I walked Dad out to the barn because I hadn't done the milking yet. We were still yards away when Dad said, "Lex, the door is open!" He started sprinting forward, as much as the snow would allow. "You forgot to lock it!" he scolded.

The morning the power went out he'd told me in no uncertain terms to be sure and lock the door to the barn for now on.

"I thought I locked it," I said weakly when I caught up. But I knew in my heart I must have forgotten. I was so happy about the rabbits being safe that it flew my mind. I'm not in the habit of doing it, yet.

Dad sighed. "Let's find out if anyone's gone." He was referring to our stock. My heart had crept up into my throat. What if our cow was gone? As our only source of milk, without her we'd need more water for drinking, we'd have no cream and no butter, and Mom wouldn't be able to make any more cheese.

Inside I held up my lantern—and there was Rhema, munching on some hay outside her stall! This was proof I'd left the door unlocked; it must have swung open a little but I didn't care. My horse was back! I ran to her and put my arms around her large head, stroking her nose and telling her how happy I was to see her. None of the animals were missing.

Dad was happy too. He not only failed to chew me out for my forgetfulness but as I brushed down the horse I noticed he stopped and gave her an affectionate scratch behind the ears and spoke nicely to her. He's as glad as I am that we haven't lost her or that no one stole her.

I finished brushing and threw a blanket over her. I moved on to Milcah, suddenly feeling that her milk was coming much too slowly. Usually I enjoyed the minutes I spent by her side. It was a favorite time for me to think. Finally, she was emptied out; then I finished distributing hay to the other animals. Now I had to water them. This is the chore I dread most in winter as it takes twice as much work. I have to use an ice pick because their water freezes solid.

LATE EVENING

Dad says tomorrow we'll need to get Mrs. Preston whether Justin's still sick or not. The girls are delighted because we'll be getting her cats too, Moppet and Butler. Kasha may not like our new animal houseguests, and Mom's not happy about Mrs. Preston's cats, either; ("more mouths to feed," she says). But Mrs. Preston would be very upset if we didn't take her beloved pets.

I was going upstairs for the night when I heard my dad and mom talking. "You can stop worrying about radiation sickness," he said. "If Lex and I were exposed to anything major we'd be truly sick by now, if not dead. We'd have known it sooner, in fact." I watched them hugging in the doorway and felt a sudden contentment.

When I had to use rationed water to brush my teeth I lost that feeling. But at least I can brush my teeth.

LEXIE
JANUARY 14
DAY FOUR

"C'mon, girl, the sky looks threatening," Dad urged me. We'd finished breakfast and he wanted to fetch Mrs. Preston as soon as possible.

Justin is still feverish. I hope it won't endanger our elderly friend, but Dad says we can't keep riding to her house to keep up a fire and she can't keep it up by herself, so we have no choice.

When I saw my father putting a saddle on Spirit, I asked, "Aren't we going to use the cart?"

"We can't take the road," he said. "I saw a lot of people on foot yesterday. I was only out there because I had to be; I don't know why folks don't just stay home until it warms up some. Anyway, if we take the cart, everyone we pass on the road'll want a ride."

"I saw hardly anyone when I was out there," I said.

Dad nodded. "People are figuring out they may not have electric for awhile, and they're on the move. They seem to think there's help out there." He shook his head.

"But how will we get Mrs. Preston back?"

"She'll fit on my saddle." He sounded sure of it, but I had to chuckle.

"I can't see Mrs. Preston on a horse, Dad!"

"She may not like it," he acknowledged. "But she'll come. She has to." He stopped and smiled at me. "You couldn't imagine her using a laptop either, but she does it."

He was right. She was a typical old lady in many ways, but a surprising one in others. She seemed frail and often needed oxygen. But she still grew a vegetable garden, and even did a little canning each year.

We set off. The air was bracingly cold. Last week on the news—which feels like a lifetime ago, now—they said this cold spell was a record-breaker for Ohio. So much for global warming!

As we rode, I admired the frozen landscape, beautiful in its white silence. I hadn't been able to do so on my ride to the Buchanans'. I was too consumed by worries, then. Today the silence was deep, punctured only by the sound of the horses breaking ground in the snow.

Silence, I realized, was going to be a constant companion for now on. We can't watch the news or get on the internet or listen to music. We can't make a single phone call! Life is really different. I have yet to fully comprehend how much that's true. Even though here we are on horseback to pick up an old lady in the middle of winter!

I felt sad. We would have no more movie and popcorn nights; no more surfing Netflix for new releases; no more listening to my favorite music while I did chores in the barn or at home. And no more drives with music just for enjoyment. No more drives anywhere! No more weather reports. We could be in for a blizzard and never know it in advance.

I thought of Andrea and other kids I knew from school and felt a deep ache in my heart. Would I ever see them again? What about Grandma and Grandpa in Maryland? What about my aunts and uncles and cousins, some of whom were clear out in Colorado?

A lump was forming in my throat. But then we turned into some low brush and I had to coax Rhema on. We came out right smack behind Mrs. Preston's old white house. I pushed my musings aside.

After tying the horses and fixing feed bags for them, Dad unlocked the back door. We have a key for when we bring meals. Inside, I hurried to her parlor, where she was asleep in a chair.

When Dad caught up he stopped and surveyed Mrs. Preston. "I don't believe she's moved since I was here yesterday," he said. He got on one knee and opened the door of the wood stove to take a peek inside.

"Still going, but it's dying down. Good thing we got here."

I took one of Mrs. Preston's hands as I gently called her name but I stopped, startled.

"Her hands are cool!" I nestled one against my cheek but realized I wasn't feeling it all that much. My cheeks were numb with cold. But my dad shook her shoulder and when I looked up Mrs. Preston's eyes popped open.

"Oh!" she cried, and smiled. "Lexie. Oh." But she closed her eyes again. "I'm sorry," she said, feebly. "I'm so tired today." She gave my hand a weak squeeze.

"Lexie, go and get some of her clothing. Fill a bag or whatever you can find."

"Am I going somewhere?" Mrs. Preston asked faintly.

"You're coming home with us," Dad said. He must have told her the night before, but she'd already forgotten.

"Oh, how nice," she said and smiled again, still keeping her eyes closed. I felt as though she was only half with us But then she said, "Don't forget about the bowl in the hallway." I had to smile. She never lets me leave without taking a few pieces from her ever-full candy bowl.

When I returned to the room I went up to my dad. "Do you think she can make the ride?" I kept my voice low.

He looked at our neighbor. She was wrapped in a quilt, her feet encased in fluffy slippers. Her gray-white hair was being held in with an old-style hair net. She used the net when her hair lost its set. Normally a hair dresser came to the house once a week to set her hair. She was obviously due for a new set.

"We'll get her nice and warm, and then bundled up tight."

"Okay." I went to pack up more of her things.

Dad moved Mrs. Preston's chair with her in it right up to the stove. I searched for her coat and hat and a thick scarf—she didn't have a thick scarf, just a whole bunch of colorful polyester ones, the kind my grandmother always covered her head with. I grabbed a pair of black boots. I took all the sweaters I saw, a throw blanket and a nice, thick one that I hoped was woolen. As I took the blanket from the closet, a black form darted past me.

"Butler!" I knew at once I had to catch that cat. Mrs. Preston would fret and fret about it if we didn't take her latest animal rescue friend. She also had a calico named Moppet, but I wasn't worried about catching her. Moppet loved company and would come to me to be petted if I took a seat. As I was leaving the bedroom I saw a bunch of prescription medicines on the dresser and I swiped them all into the bag. In the downstairs hallway I was about to pass the candy bowl and then stopped and emptied it into the bag, too.

"Have you eaten anything today?" I heard my dad asking, as I came back with a few bagfuls of stuff. I saw the cat's bed and took it, stuffing it into another bag. I started seeing other things to bring, not to mention checking for any food we could use. In the kitchen, I found that Mrs. Preston had more plastic bags than any one person could probably use in a lifetime. It seemed she devoted a great deal of cupboard space, in fact, to saving that one item. So I filled as many as I thought we could cart back.

I surveyed rows of canned goods, including peaches. Not as much as she sometimes had, which I figured was on account of her getting older and slowed down. I suddenly thought I ought to ask permission before taking any. Back in the parlor with her eyes closed, Mrs. Preston still knew I'd returned. "You'll find the cat food in the cupboard, and Butler's favorite toy should be here on the rug somewhere."

"Should I take the canned goods?" I asked. I looked at my father as I asked, too. But Mrs. Preston said, "Oh, take anything you like!" as though I wanted it just for myself.

Embarrassed, I wanted to explain myself. I wanted to clarify that she was moving in with us; that what we took would be for her as well as the rest of us, but Dad caught my eye and just nodded at me to get packing.

"Did you eat anything today?" he repeated to her, as I turned to leave.

The old lady was silent a moment. "I gave Butler a can of his food," she said, in a wavering tone. "I think."

"What about you?"

"I don't think so," she said at last. I could hear them from the kitchen.

"Lexie," Dad called. "There's a gas stove and probably a reserve of gas still available; go and heat up a cup of tea and put plenty of sugar in it."

Dad was right and I was able to use the stove. Only a few days ago this would have been boringly routine, but already I had a feeling of slight awe as it clicked a few times and then burst into a bluish circle of low flame. Our stove was electric so it had died on day one of the outage. I'd always taken stoves for granted, but right now I couldn't help myself and made a second cup of tea. It felt like a luxury—doing it with a working stove.

When I brought the tea I had to spoon feed a few sips to Mrs. Preston, who smiled after each one. "Oh, that's good," she said, as if I'd just given her lobster bisque. "Thank you for coming," she said. "Is the power back yet?"

"Not yet," dad said. Our eyes met.

"Dad, if gas stoves still work, why didn't we get a gas stove?"

"It won't work for long," he said. "Once the pipe is empty or loses pressure, it'll be out of gas and useless, just like our stove."

"But can't you add gas to it? Like we do to a car?"

"It's not the same kind of gas, hon," he said. "And you can't store gas; it degrades over time."

Soon afterwards he said, "It's time to go, Loretta."

"Oh?" She said. "Okay." Her eyes were open, now. Watery blue eyes that were kind and docile.

"Butler won't come to me," I told her.

"Oh, he'll come," she said. "Give me a can of his food, and a fork or spoon."

When I did, she took the can and hit the spoon against the side of it a few times. In seconds the sleek black form was there, and jumped lightly onto his mistress's lap.

"Is Moppet here?" she asked.

"Right here," I said, bending over to grasp the cat. She'd been rubbing her fur against my legs, circling around, and waiting for me to pick her up.

We had to unhook Mrs. Preston's oxygen tube. And then get her positioned in front of her walker. She didn't absolutely need the walker, but she liked to know it was there just in case.

"Can we bring my walker?" she asked, as we went through the hallway towards the back door.

"Don't need to," said Dad. "We have a walker at the house."

"You have a walker?" she asked, surprised. "Why is that?"

"That time I broke my ankle," Dad said, "I needed it for a few weeks after the surgery."

"I'm glad you saved it," she murmured. But then, "Do you have my oxygen tanks? I need my oxygen, you know. I'm sorry."

"We have your oxygen," Dad said, loud enough to reassure her. To me he added, "'I put all the tanks together yesterday. See how many you can fit into your pack. I'll need to make another trip for some of them, I'm sure. Possibly a few trips to get all she'll need from here."

"I have two sizes of tanks," Mrs. Preston warned. "The smaller ones for traveling are in a corner of the parlor, in a box."

They were just the size to fit in the saddle bags, so I took as many as I thought we could carry. I'd have to leave some of the other things I'd packed, but Dad could get those when he returned. I grabbed packages of plastic tubing for the tanks and the other accessories, like nose clips. The tanks themselves were surprisingly heavy. When we got outside, both horses were stamping their feet, unhappy being tied up in the cold.

Mrs. Preston watched my dad mount Spirit in silence; I was waiting for her reaction, but she only looked puzzled. Suddenly it dawned on her that we were going to take her home on horseback, and she froze, her eyes wide. From his saddle, Dad told me to lift her up. She was on the back steps so she was already higher than if she'd been on the ground.

Mrs. Preston looked at me and she looked at dad. I was sure she was going to refuse to come. But suddenly she smiled.

"I haven't been on a horse since I was a girl!" She let me lift her up—but I had to put her down after my first try, since she was heavier than she looked. Taking a deep breath, I hoisted her again—never underestimate the weight of a little old lady, I thought—and then dad's strong arms pulled her the rest of the way while she giggled like a child. I handed Butler to her, and then Moppet. Dad settled her with the cats in her arms in front of him, keeping one of his arms around her, while the other held the reins. Mrs. Preston was so bundled up you couldn't see the animals at all, and only the older woman's eyes shone out from a mound of blanket. She looked cute, like a little child.

"Oh, oh, oh!" she cried, looking at me. "I forgot. Butler's on medication for an infection. It's in the refrigerator." I glanced at dad and he nodded, so I went for it. In this cold, I was sure everything in the refrigerator was probably still good. I hoped so for Butler's sake. While there, I grabbed two more plastic bags and stuffed in anything else from the fridge that I thought we could use. I'd put the bags in front of me like a passenger. Later mom said that was good thinking.

On the way home I found myself picturing us doing for Andrea what we had just done for Mrs. Preston. But it couldn't be just Andrea, could it? We'd have to take the whole family if we went for her. We couldn't very well leave the others to fend for themselves.

She and Sarah always teased me—affectionately—about being a farm girl. Now I felt sorry for them because they're not.

When we got back, I went to take care of the horses as soon as we unloaded. When I got back inside, Mrs. Preston was happily settled in the corner chair she likes best in the family room, the rocker with a quilted pillow.

Mom was still carrying the baby. She told us she'd had to give him acetaminophen because the fever was nearing 103.

"Oh, my," said Mrs. Preston, gravely. "Poor baby. Have you prayed?"

"Not today," said Dad. She was already holding out open arms and my mother automatically handed over Justin. Mrs. Preston always rocks him on her lap when she visits. Justin went to her now, even being sick, when a child usually only wants their mother.

We held hands and prayed over the baby right then.

I'm going to like having Mrs. Preston with us.

Over dinner—which Dad grilled outside—we talked about how people are hopefully managing to get by. Mrs. Preston's hearing isn't good so she just sat and drank her milk, smiling at us as though we were discussing something happy. Dad said people living near stores could buy supplies if they had cash—until the stock sold out. There would be no more deliveries though, to replenish the shelves. "That's when the real trouble will start," he said. "When the stores are emptied out. People are going to have to ration their supplies, and concentrate on keeping warm."

"How long will that take?" I asked. "For the stores to run out of stuff?"

He shook his head. "Could happen in a day, if people panic. You know how before a storm everyone runs out and gets water and food and suddenly the shelves are empty? Well, for those who can get to the store and back, they'll be buying everything they can cart with them. We're going to be without electronics for a long time. Credit cards and bank accounts will be virtually worthless. The banks won't open, because they can't give everyone their money—they don't have it. People will have to make do with what they've got—"

"Or what they can steal," added Mom, in a low tone. She was staring at the tablecloth, deep in thought, Justin half-awake, half-asleep on her lap. "Remember what happened after Hurricane Katrina in Louisiana? This is so much worse. There'll be riots."

"Lots of violence too, I expect," added Dad.

"And no one can call the police or an ambulance!" The realization sickened me.

Lainie was suddenly by my side. "Play checkers with me?" she asked. "Laura won't play and I'm bored!" I was ready to refuse but out of the corner of my eye I saw my mom nodding at me to do it. "Okay," I said, getting up. "Let's play checkers." I think I was a little relieved; it would take my mind off the awful prospect of what was in store for those who didn't have anything stored.

Mom said, "Hey, don't forget. You can still use that bin of toys in the safe room. It's not just for when we're in the room. I put it together for any power outage."

I looked at Lainie. "Want to do that?"

She nodded. "Yeah!"

As we went through the bin, I felt grateful my mom is such a whiz at planning ahead. I pulled out a book of Crosswords; Lainie grabbed a flat dress-up doll with Velcro accessories. Laura joined us, pulling out a jump rope and promptly putting it to use. There were also board games, cards, little easy-sew kits, and lots of other stuff, all of it non-tech. I recognized some things from the Amish General Store we'd visited last spring while on a family outing. I'd always wondered what life must be like for the Amish—now we were actually finding out.

Ready or not.

LEXIE
JANUARY 15
DAY FIVE

Chores take up more of my day than they used to. The barn chores don't bother me so much because I'm used to doing them. Gathering eggs, milking Milcah (yeah, her name is a pun), cleaning the horse stalls, giving out feed, and so on. The animals are why we're doing so well now without power. It makes me worry about my friends, though. The very stuff they teased me about is what's making life bearable with the grid down.

As I poured the day's water into the top of the filter, Mrs. Preston shuffled into the kitchen using Dad's old walker. She seemed tired but offered me her usual cheery smile. "Morning, Lexie."

"Good morning," I smiled, heading to the coffee percolator on the woodstove. She liked her coffee black, so I poured her a steaming cup while she got herself seated in the blue corner overstuffed rocker. When I handed her the cup she took a sniff, closing her eyes. "Ah," she said, contentedly, "The nectar of the gods!" It was a saying she favored although she was a devout Christian and didn't believe in "the gods."

I watched as she fiddled with her oxygen tubes, getting them settled comfortably in her nostrils. I was glad we had all the tanks now. They stood in rows in the hall closet because we couldn't risk their being near the heat of the stove. I tried not to think about what would happen when they ran out. Maybe by some miracle we'd have power back by then. Maybe we'd find a way to get more tanks from the nearest hospital or medical center.

Mom called for breakfast, so I helped Mrs. Preston get out of the comfortable chair. Sitting next to me at the table, she watched as Butler jumped onto my lap.

"He likes you," she said.

"He likes me too," Laura volunteered, and Lainie immediately echoed the statement. "Of course he does," purred Mrs. Preston to the twins. "Butler is a cat of good taste."

I stroked Butler's sleek black fur, expecting my mom to make me push him away at any moment. She has this thing about animals being near the table. But she said nothing, so I kept petting him. I think she was distracted because Justin's fever still hasn't broken, and I know she was up with him a lot last night.

"Is there any way we can help Andrea and her family"? I asked. My dad's fork stopped in midair as he took in my question.

He finished the bite of scrambled eggs and then asked, "What did you have in mind? What kind of help do you think they need?"

"I think they need everything," I said, nodding my head as I spoke.

"Everything?" He gave a glance at my mom. "That's a lot of stuff. That's also vague. What kind of 'everything' are you talking about?"

"I mean everything, Dad," I said. "Food, water, shelter—"

"Isn't Andrea's family the one with all the money?" asked Mom. "I'm sure they're all right."

"I think so, too," Dad said. "They've got that big house—"

"Yeah, with a fireplace for heat," I said, rudely cutting him off.

"Is that all they have?" asked Mom. "Maybe they've got a back-up generator."

"I doubt it," I said, and I meant it.

"Well, I'm sure they've got something—charcoal for a fire outdoors; a grill; maybe a camp stove."

"Would we be getting by without our indoor woodstoves?" I asked.

He chewed his food for a moment. "Well, not comfortably, I give you that."

"We need to help them," I persisted.

"And what about everyone else? You want to help the whole population who may be suffering right now? Where do you draw the line, Lex?"

"Andrea is my closest friend! I know we can't help everyone. But I also know we need to help the Pattersons."

"We can pray for them," Dad said.

"Dad, I mean REALLY help them."

He frowned. "Lex—prayer is the best thing we can do sometimes and that is real help. If you don't think prayer is real help, you're about wiping out God's favorite method of helping his people."

"I don't mean that prayer isn't real help, it's just that we can't JUST pray for them."

He took another bite of eggs and then looked across the table at me. "Unless they show up at our door, there's no way to do anything else. They're what—fifteen minutes from here by car? Twenty? That's gotta be fifteen miles, maybe more."

I happened to know it was eighteen minutes by car since I'd timed it in the past, but I didn't volunteer that information. I said, "They won't just show up. They don't have horses like we do or a wagon."

"It's possible they could make it here."

"Andrea has a baby sister," I said. "Could mom take Justin that far? How could they make it here in this weather?"

His shook his head. "I don't know, Lex."

"Why can't we take the cart and go get them? That way, they could live here with us—at least until the cold breaks."

He reached his hand across the table and covered one of mine.

"Lexie, honey," he said, softly. "Andrea's got a father who will take care of his family."

"Dad, you know yourself that Andrea's father is not a nice guy."

He shrugged. "What has that got to do with it? He's still a father. Fathers take care of their families."

"Just because you do, you're a good father, doesn't mean all men do, you know."

He looked at me quizzically. "Do you have any reason to believe that Andrea's father would not do everything in his power to see to the needs of his family?"

I fell silent, thinking for a moment. "Well, I guess he'd try, but he's never been home a lot, and maybe he's not even with them. What if he got stranded somewhere? What are they gonna do without a woodstove?"

"Use their gas generator or propane heater," said Mom. "I think you're jumping to conclusions, assuming they NEED help. It's not been a week without power, yet. Most people are managing to get by somehow or other. Even if they don't have a good heat source they may have friends in the neighborhood who do. Stop worrying about other people right now and concentrate on keeping our house running. I have Justin to worry about, and I notice you haven't been jumping to wash dishes for me."

I looked down. It was true. There was so much to do on top of my usual chores, and I hated having to heat up water just for washing stuff. Dad was using the generator to keep our refrigerator working but had stopped powering the water heater.

So I returned to the subject I wanted to talk about. Because parents just don't get it. How was I supposed to be okay having our basic needs met while I knew Andrea and her family are in trouble? Sarah lives in the city so I figured she had social services there. (Later Dad told me cities most likely did not have social services; that all services would have been crippled with the grid down, but I didn't know that then. I'm glad I didn't know or I'd have been just as worried about Sarah as I was about Andrea.)

I said, "I'm surprised at you two. I thought one of the reasons we were preparing was so we could help other people."

"Look beside you," Dad said, motioning towards Mrs. Preston. "We have a new family member. Plus two cats more than what we had before. We can't take in whole families, Lex. Yes, we've prepared a little extra, hoping to bring an occasional meal to someone in need, but if you bring another family here, there's no way our supplies will last. Then we'll all starve. How does that help anyone?"

"We won't starve; you can hunt," I persisted. "We have enough land."

"Hunting is something I plan on doing," he agreed. "But not every day. And think about how many times I've gone hunting and come back empty-handed. It's a heck of way to have to eat by, and the more mouths to feed the harder it will be." He paused. "And how long do you think there'll be anything to hunt? When everyone out there's doing the same thing? This is Ohio, not Africa. We have a limited supply of game out there."

I knew deep in my heart that Dad was right but I felt miserable about it, so I said, "I think you just don't want to be bothered!" I stood up.

"We feel just as badly as you do for anyone in trouble," he began, "but you must realize it isn't a matter of not wanting to help—it's a matter of resources. We don't have the resources to help a lot of people."

I still resisted his logic. "How do you know we aren't meant to help everyone we possibly can, for as long as we can, until we all run out?"

Dad looked thoughtful a moment. "Honey, when Jesus taught in the synagogue in his own hometown, he pointed out there were many widows in Israel in the days of Elijah and even though a great famine came over the land, Elijah was only sent to *one* of those widows. And though there were many lepers in the time of the prophet Elisha, only one of them, Naaman the Syrian, was healed. Think about that. God has reasons for allowing suffering. C.S. Lewis says without suffering there's no free will, because so much of human suffering is caused by our own devices. Whatever caused this power outage, it is still within the sovereignty of God. And in any case, my responsibility before God is to take care of my family, and that's what I'm doing."

"Just think about it, Dad," I pleaded. "I'm not asking you to help the whole town. Just Andrea and her family." Mrs. Preston, surprisingly, laid her hand upon my arm and patted it. I didn't think she could follow a conversation unless we were speaking really loudly but I suppose she heard our tones, which was enough. Her concern was sweet—but it didn't help me feel better.

In a last ditch effort I spilled my guts, so to speak. "I just keep seeing Andrea pleading for help," I cried. "Like Paul saw the man from Macedonia, remember? I can't help it! I wish I wasn't! But I keep seeing this image of Andrea and her baby sister and brothers, all cold and alone in their big expensive house! What would *you* do if you kept seeing that?" My voice cracked, which embarrassed me. But at the same time I was glad they could see how upset I was.

My parents looked at each other.

"Maybe we should pray about it," my mom said. I loved her so much at that moment.

"Okay," Dad said. "We'll pray about it." I loved them both. My folks are really good people at heart even if they can be a little thick now and then.

Later as I did my afternoon chores, I heard wind howling outside the barn and it made me shudder. That feeling of the Pattersons needing us came back, stronger than ever. Then I thought of Sarah in her apartment building, knowing I couldn't dare ask my dad to rescue them too. Besides, I wasn't getting the same urgent sense of needing to help them as I did when I thought or prayed about Andrea.

I did have to wonder how on earth Sarah's family was managing to stay warm, though. Could they have found a community shelter? Maybe they had a kerosene or propane heater. And maybe Andrea's family did too. Mom was right; Andrea's family was rich, it would make sense for them to have a back-up generator. We, who were not rich, had one. It made sense they would too, right?

It did. But I couldn't shake the conviction that we needed to go and get them. Something about their situation was not good and God was letting me know it. The question was if my parents could trust my perception of God's leading. Was I even sure of that, myself? How can you be sure of something like hearing God's voice, when even the Bible says it is a "still, small voice?"

All I knew is that every time I got to my knees at night when I prayed for the Pattersons, I got the same urgent feeling that we ought to help them. Soon. When something keeps coming back to you every time you pray, there's a good indication that God is trying to tell you something. If it lines up with Scripture, (and helping people surely lined up) then why should I think it wasn't God's voice?

LEXIE
JANUARY 16
DAY SIX

Last night Mom came up to "the bedroom." There's only one bedroom we use now because it's got the wood stove. I miss sleeping alone in my own room but the little ones fall asleep earlier than I do, so it isn't too bad. I can read by oil lamp. It's just strong enough for reading but not too strong to wake anyone else. It seems kids sleep like rocks anyways.

So my mother came up and we had a talk while the little ones slept. She asked me more about the Pattersons and we discussed my concerns.

"Have you considered waiting a week or two at least?" she asked, regarding getting them.

"Why? It's so cold right now. What if they aren't warm enough?"

"Lex, they surely have coats and blankets and can find a way to stay warm. I'm not saying they'll feel like they're at the Hilton—heck, we don't even feel that way. But they CAN stay warm; and I'm sure they're not starving. Nearly everyone keeps some extra food in the house and Andrea's family is well-off, so why would they be an exception?"

"Mom," I said, looking earnestly into her pretty blue eyes. "How could they stay warm, really? With sub-zero temperatures at night like we've been having?"

"Honey," she said, shaking her head for emphasis, "People find ways. Besides fireplaces, there's kerosene heaters, propane heaters, gas generators, gas lamps, oil lamps, even candles, and, if they've got ventilation, charcoal grills or barrel fires. Also, they can raise the temperature of a room just by sealing it off and staying in one room."

"That is no way to live," I answered, annoyed. "They can't stay warm with candles! And how do you seal off a room to stay warm? You can't LIVE in that room until spring!" I shook my head and pretended to read my book, hoping my mom would leave. She was trying to get away from her promise to pray about helping them, it seemed. It made me angry.

"Well, I just wanted you to know that your father and I will pray about this. But we both think the situation is not desperate yet for most people, and that we likely still have plenty of time before we try to get to their house. I have to see Justin get well first, too, before I take on any more of a challenge. This hasn't been easy for me, any more than you," she said.

I looked at her. "You seem fine. You act like you've been ready to live this way. You've had dinner every night for us and breakfast every morning." Lunch was usually just pre-packaged food, processed stuff we didn't often get as mom believes it's unhealthy. I was actually enjoying the change.

"I was somewhat ready for it," she acceded. "But I'm *tired* of it, Lex." She'd drawn out the word, 'tired,' sounding like weariness itself. I'd been so caught up in my own worries that I hadn't really stopped to consider how my mom was busy from morning to night. She was keeping our house running despite having less and less help from the generator. Dad was rationing the use of it more every day. My mom sighed. "I'd love to sit back and watch a good movie and just relax right now." She took a deep breath and exhaled, lost in thought. "I'd love a good hot shower, too." Normally I would have smiled at that or told her I wanted a hot shower also; but I was still annoyed, so I said nothing. She looked at me.

"SO—give us some time, okay?"

I stared at her for a moment. "Every time I think about Andrea I just want to cry." I paused, thinking. "Dad said once that a person can live for three weeks without food but only three hours without shelter in poor weather. And that's all we've had—really poor weather."

"They're not without shelter," my mom insisted. "Even a big house with only a fireplace still has a fireplace. Stop catastrophizing." She got up and left.

I felt badly after she left. Was I doing that? Catastrophizing? If so, I couldn't help it. I sighed and closed my book. I was using a roll-out bed, and I got up and then fell to my knees beside it. I really needed to know. Was I imagining this feeling of urgency regarding Andrea? Was I imagining it was a message from God? Maybe it was giving me a sense of importance, as though God could only speak to ME.

"Holy Spirit, help me. Dear Lord, please give my parents an assurance about doing this if helping the Pattersons is really Your will." I continued praying for a long time. At least twenty minutes or more. I'd like to say I prayed until I felt God answering me. I didn't. I didn't hear an answer. But as dramatic as it sounds, I feel no less sure that we need to save the Pattersons. You don't have to catastrophize, as my mom said, when the world does it for you—we were *living* a social catastrophe.

LEXIE
JANUARY 17
DAY SEVEN

Justin is still feverish and lethargic. Mom says fevers are more dangerous for babies than adults or older kids because they dehydrate quickly. And Justin refuses to eat or drink, so dehydration is a real threat.

It's the first time in my life I realize how important a doctor is. I mean I really get it, now. It's a thing I took blissfully for granted in the past. If you got hurt, you went to the doctor or urgent care, or even the emergency room of a hospital. Now there is no quick way to get to any of those places, and even if we did get there, who's to say whether there would be a doctor? Hospitals had medical personnel on site when the pulse hit but who knows whether they'd stay on the job with no power? They'd want to try to get home themselves. It's like every day a new aspect of the danger of this situation—living without power—is dawning on me.

Justin's eyes look sunken. I pleaded with him to take a few sips of apple juice when Mom was trying to get some down his throat, but to no avail. He just clamped that little mouth shut. When he even refused his next dose of medicine, Mom said, "That's it! I've had enough." She put a fresh kettle of water on the wood stove; then she took a dropper from a drawer and cleaned it with the water once it came to a boil.

(Meanwhile, Lainie came along and touched the kettle while it was hot and burned her hand. Mom had to stop and grab butter, which she rubbed over the burn. She's been studying home remedies for a long time. I guess they work because Lainie stopped crying right away. She's happily playing Boggle, Jr. with my dad right now just as if nothing happened.)

Anyways, Mom took the dropper and extracted the right amount of baby medicine into it. After strapping Justin into his high chair, she forced his mouth open with one hand while pointing the dropper inside his jaw, to the side. She explained that he'd have no choice but to swallow. He fidgeted and wailed and tried to stop her something awful, so I had to hold his little hands and arms. It worked, though! He swallowed the stuff. I felt sorry for him, like we were being mean. When she did the same thing with a few droppers of juice, I told her it seemed a little brutal.

"Would you rather have your baby brother die of dehydration?" she asked, casually.

I kept quiet after that.

A half hour later I noticed that Justin already looked better! I guess moms do know a thing or two.

I'm lucky to have my parents. Even my dad seems to have been born for a time of crisis. He says no one prepares better for a disaster than God, and by following biblical principles, he feels ready for this. King Solomon had twelve men in charge of providing food for his household, one man for each month of the year. So a long time ago my dad put mom in charge of storing food for one month at a time until she stored enough for two years.

But our family always prayed that God would raise up a 'Joseph' to store food for our whole country just like Joseph did for Egypt way back when. If people in ancient days could store enough grain to get through a famine, why shouldn't we, with all our knowledge, be able to do that today? But we never saw a Joseph rise up. When we talked about this once Mom said there's no Joseph because the world has Jesus. Jesus's offer of eternal life beats having grain in a famine, she said. Grain will perish, this life will pass away, but eternal life? That lasts forever! She thinks that if God allows our country to experience a catastrophic event that causes famine (and it seems that He has) it is because there are more important things than just eating and living mindlessly. She sees it as a national call to repentance. A call to come to the true Bread of Life.

I still wish we had a Joseph. Maybe I'm not valuing my salvation enough, but I still wish there was a way for everyone to be taken care of like we are.

I don't mean we'll be living like kings—Mom stored beans and rice and grains in huge quantities—but it will keep us alive. And because Mom loves good food, she stored all kinds of things to liven up the staples. Solomon's household needed tons of food each day—you can read about it in the book of 1 Kings, and I mean, literally, *tons*. For a single day his provision was "thirty bushels of fine flour, and sixty bushels of meal, ten fat oxen, and twenty pasture-fed cattle, a hundred sheep, besides deer, gazelles, roebucks and fattened fowl." This was for ONE day! There was "barley also and straw for the horses." My parents figured if Solomon's needs could be met, then so could our family's.

But life is harder now. Everything has to be done by hand. Tomorrow we have to do laundry. Up to now I've been spot-cleaning our clothing. If we have to immerse it in water, it's going to be a big job and a big mess and will take a lot of space to hang dry. I can understand why they only did laundry once a week in the old days. Even once a week will be too often for my liking now.

LATE AFTERNOON

Mrs. Preston wasn't feeling well. We found out her oxygen tank was empty! We didn't realize they would just run out with no sort of alarm or warning or anything. So now I know how to read the gauge on top of the canister and I've hooked her up to a new one and she's back to rocking in her favorite chair. And Justin seems to be improving! He got interested in Butler, rousing from his usual stupor to grab the cat's tail. When he did, Butler turned and whipped his claws out, raking the baby's hand. When Justin didn't cry, I checked his hands and found nothing, not the slightest scratch.

Mrs. Preston scolded the cat something awful. When she finally turned to see the damage, her eyes got *so* big. She couldn't believe it. It was like a miracle. We talked about it for minutes—how we'd both seen the cat scratch him. How could he have missed? How often does a cat miss? I think that was the Lord watching out for my baby brother. And if he can keep him from getting scratched by a cat, he can heal this fever.

But I still worry about Mrs. Preston because of the tanks. The larger ones only last a couple of days and that's if we ration her use of it. She doesn't need it much if she just rocks the baby, but she often insists upon helping us with chores. Her favorite activities—besides holding Justin—are peeling potatoes or carrots (which we have in bulk in the root cellar) or sifting through clothes to spray with stain remover.

Her needing oxygen made me think about other people I know who are dependent on medicines like my friend Craig Densen. He's in two of my classes and we've become friends over the past year. He's a Christian like me so we've had lots of talks about the Bible and theology. But he has Type I diabetes. And so does Mrs. Wasserman, my History and Geography teacher. She lives alone with her two dogs—what will happen to them when they run out of insulin?

Dad told me once that Type I diabetics used to die young before they had insulin shots. I'm starting to cry as I write, thinking about Craig.

I asked God why this is happening, but I didn't really expect an answer.

Here's a secret: If I get deep in prayer—falling on my knees and maybe even on my face—I've felt the presence of God. It's awesome. It's almost scary, except that I know God is love, and loves me. How do I know? Just by believing the Bible, I guess. It's a wonderful feeling when I have that assurance of His presence. But lately I'm keeping Him at arm's length. I think I'm too mixed up and angry to pray. I know we're some of the lucky ones—I should be grateful that we're provided for. But I'm upset about all the people who aren't.

I didn't think I'd ever miss school, but I do, even kids I'm not really friends with. I miss Andrea most of all. I wish I could hear her voice or just send a text!! It's been a whole week without power and my dad still doesn't want to go and see if her family needs help. I wish she lived closer, 'cos then I know he'd do it. I wish I knew how to convince him that we need to. I'm waiting on God to do that.

PART THREE

SARAH

AGE 16, JANUARY 11
DAY ONE

I thought it was so cool when the power went out. Especially when Mom said I could stay home from school. I figured she really just wanted me to be around to help with Jesse but I didn't care. I'm not crazy about school and a day off is a day off.

Jesse is almost three but we call him 'the baby,' and he cooperates by acting like one. My mother loves it. She always said Richard and I grew up too fast. Anyway, Jesse's not really ours—he's Aunt Susan's, but she was going through a messy divorce and asked my mom to keep him for awhile. The divorce went through, but we've had him for two years now. I feel like he's my baby brother.

So with the power out I thought it was the perfect opportunity to pretend we were in the nineteenth century—you know, like those people on that reality TV show? They had to live without electricity or modern conveniences for one full month and they acted like it was sheer misery. I didn't feel sorry for them because it was, like, a TV show—they were probably getting paid a fortune. They HAD to complain to make it interesting. We, on the other hand, would take it gracefully, as if we were living in the time of *Pride and Prejudice*. No electricity? No problemo.

Only, I was wrong. But I didn't know that yet.

The gas stove worked, so I made us scrambled eggs. There was still running water, so we filled two pitchers and the tub. I dug out all the candles I could find, and I've been lighting them because it's a dark sort of day, what with the snow and all. Mom tried to call Dad to tell him to pick up milk and toddler food on his way home but then we found out the phones are dead; and even our cell phones aren't working.

Weird.

"This must be a huge power outage," I said.

"Get Richard," Mom said. So I woke up my older brother. He's home from college for the winter break. I guess it's good he's here during this outage but usually I'm glad when he's away. See, my dad works overtime a lot so Richard thinks he's gotta be like a father to me. I hate that about him.

"Power's out," Mom told him, when he appeared, still rubbing sleep from his eyes. "I need you to run down to the grocery for me."

Richard grabbed a banana and went out. I was relieved that he had to go and not me because I didn't feel like getting bundled up, first, and second, when there's no power we have to walk ten flights down to the street. We live on the top floor of our building.

LATER

So Richard's back. But he didn't get much from the store. They would only accept cash and Richard had $11. Mom rifled through her things and found $40 and sent him back out. But when he came home the second time the only real food he had was one additional canister of baby formula, a package of hot dogs and a few energy bars. He also got the last half-gallon of milk the store had, and one six-pack of bottled water. It took a long time for him to come back. He said the place was jam-packed and everything was selling out.

I remembered after he left that I had $100 of birthday and Christmas money I'd saved for a shopping spree with Lexie and Andrea, but it was too late to give it to him. I hope the store will have more stuff tomorrow. I'll go and spend my shopping money, and maybe my dad will replace it for me so I can go to the mall after this is over.

Richard disappeared a third time and brought back two cups of hot chocolate and a package of blueberry muffins from the Methodist Church on Main Street. They had a stand out front and were giving them out. But he could only carry two up all those stairs. I hope the elevators will work tomorrow when I go to the street!

With no stores open and nothing working, it actually got boring to be home. I almost wished I was at school. Mom used the oven for a little while to put out heat but my brother says she can't do that. He says we'll all die of carbon monoxide poisoning if she does that for too long. (That was scary.) And when Richard saw we'd washed the dishes, he said it was stupid!

"Fill up any container we have," he said. "The water could stop coming at any time for all we know."

Mom and I looked at each other. "Uh-oh," I said.

"What, has it stopped already?" he asked.

I nodded. He rolled his eyes and walked off, shaking his head. He's so negative he makes me sick. But I wished I'd thought of filling up a lot of little containers.

Now he's wracking his brain, trying to figure out a way to warm up the apartment. He says the problem is that any open flame would build up carbon monoxide just like the gas stove. We have one space heater, but it's electric, so it's useless. We've only lived in this building for nine months and this is the first time we've lost water as well as electricity. It's also the first time we've had no heat. I don't like it.

LATER

I wish Dad were here. He'd know what to do. Richard is playing dad, which is really annoying as usual. He saw me heading to the bathroom and said, "Sarah."

I wondered what pesky thing he was going to say now.

"If it's yellow, let it mellow. If it's brown, flush it down."

When it sunk in, what he'd said, I made a face and turned to go on.

"I mean it, Sarah! All we've got is that water in the tub to make the system flush. Don't waste it! In fact, we should only flush once a night, because we don't know how long this is going to last."

Ugh. There went my *Pride and Prejudice* fantasies.

When I got back Richard said, "Has anyone called Dad? We need to tell him to pick up a kerosene heater. We should really have something like that here. While he's at it, he should get water and more formula."

"The phones aren't working," Mom said, making a face.

"Use your cell phone," he said.

"That's not working either," Mom said. "Unless you want to go out on the balcony and try it there. Maybe we just have bad receptivity today."

We're all wearing sweaters but Richard grabbed a hat and gloves and went out to the balcony. He took all the cell phones and tried them, one at a time. He was out there so long I went out too. Far away, probably ten to fifteen miles in the distance, there was a plume of black smoke rising into the air. It was far from the blocks of rooftops that comprised our little city.

I nudged Richard. "You see that?"

He looked at the smoke. "Yeah. It's a fire."

"So what's happening with the phones?"

"They don't have power," he said. "It's not just coverage. They're dead." We returned inside.

"I know mine should be charged." He looked at me, because I was always losing my charger and had "borrowed" his in the past without asking. Then he got a funny look on his face and plopped down on the sofa.

"At the store I heard people saying their cars weren't working. And the street was weird, quiet like. I couldn't put my finger on it. But there was NO traffic. No buses, no trucks, no cars, nada." He got up and went back out to the balcony. I saw him leaning out to look down the street, first one way, and then the other. He came back in. I was examining my nail polish, trying to decide if I should put on a second coat, waiting for him to make a point.

"I have a terrible suspicion I know what's going on," he said. "I've heard about something that could cause this, a complete black-out, a failure of electronics."

"What?" Mom asked.

"Wait. I'll be right back," he said. "I want to check some things out." He went out and was gone for about an hour. I did my nails and put on makeup because I had nothing better to do. When he came back, he looked different. Really weighed down, or something.

"Did you find anything out?" Mom asked.

He nodded. "Yeah. Nothing's working."

"We already knew that," I said.

"Yeah, well, it's not a regular power failure," he said. "This is something else, probably an electromagnetic pulse."

"A what?" I asked.

"Electromagnetic pulse. A solar flare causes it. We just learned about this at school. It's from the sun. It knocks out everything electronic."

He started explaining what that meant but I got upset and didn't want to hear it. I had been trying to enjoy the outage, even starting this journal by candlelight. I was a modern-day pioneer, or a—an author, like Jane Austen, writing in longhand, lighting candles! I'd already layered up on clothing because the only heat we have is residual from being on the top floor of the building, but it was going away fast. Richard was ruining it! (He thinks he's so smart just because he's in college.)

My mother started crying and I ran to my room so I wouldn't have to hear him talking about it. I flicked on the TV to hear what the news had to say--only the television was dead, which I should have expected. As I sat there in the quiet, I realized that if Richard was right, and there's no transportation, that my dad is stranded at his job. No wonder mom was crying. Stupid Richard!

I couldn't stop thinking about what he'd said. We can't get in touch with Dad? And, how is he going to get home if his car won't start? And if he can't get home, he certainly can't bring us a kerosene heater or any other supplies, like for the baby. I got a sick feeling in my stomach. And then it hit me. Richard was wrong! He had to be! We couldn't survive if there were NO electronics, and our government wouldn't be so stupid to let something like that happen. So I just don't believe what he said. It's too far out. Besides, there's no other choice if I want to be okay and not lose my mind.

RICHARD. IS. WRONG.

LATE EVENING

We're sleeping in the living room. It seems warmer if we're all in one room. Mom says Dad will probably make it home by tomorrow even supposing he had to walk. I didn't say anything but I don't see how that could happen. His company is forty-five minutes from home—by car. Even in good weather it would be a stretch to believe that. I think it would take him days to walk, but I didn't say that to Mom. Besides, I'm still determined not to believe that ALL electronics got fried, as Richard said. I have to believe that dad will get here; I just don't think it will be as soon as Mom thinks.

So with the candles lit and scattered around the two main rooms of the apartment tonight, if it wasn't so cold it would have been cozy.

Richard sealed off the doorway to the kitchen with plastic sheeting and duct tape he found in Dad's tool bin. Then he dragged throw rugs and sleeping bags and blankets onto the floor of the living room. I'm using my sleeping bag on the love seat and Mom has the sofa for her and Jesse.

Richard will find out where the emergency shelter is tomorrow—he says every city has to have emergency shelters, even ours, even though we're small as far as cities go. Anyway, since we don't have a fireplace or anything like that, we may have to go there. I think if things don't get any worse—meaning no colder than today—that we could stay right here until power comes back. I told Richard that and he said, "It isn't coming back, Sarah. Not for a long, long time." I rolled my eyes.

"How do you know?" I asked.

"Because every single electronic part that exists and was affected was completely burned out. They can't *be* fixed. They can only be replaced, but the replacements would have to come from somewhere in the world that wasn't affected. And who knows how long that could take. A month? A year? Five years? You wouldn't believe how many things would need to be replaced just to get one major power source back up and running. The figure is astronomical."

I told him he didn't know everything, and I hated him and he should go back to school.

I have a bad temper.

Then I rolled over and went to sleep. Sometime during the night I woke up, probably because Mom was changing the baby. Something felt wrong. My head. It was cold! I got up, groping around to find the front closet and then to find my favorite knit hat. Mom had one candle lit or it would have been pitch black. With my hat on I felt better but I couldn't sleep. I lay there in the dark, thinking. I planned out all the things I was going to do as soon as our electric is back, like use a hair straightener and take that trip to the mall.

SARAH
JANUARY 12
DAY TWO

My hands were stiff with cold when I woke up. I tried a light switch to see if the power was back, but it wasn't. So I was warming my hands over the stove when Richard came into the kitchen and stood there, hands on his hips. I knew he was going to annoy me but I ignored him, hoping he'd go away. He didn't.

"We don't know how much gas we have left, Sarah. It could stop at any time. Don't waste it."

"My hands are COLD," I said. "I'm not wasting it."

"Save it for cooking for Mom and Jesse," he said.

I wish he'd stayed at college.

"Didn't you say you were going to the store today?" he asked. "What are you waiting for? Everyone else will want to stock up on the same things we want." So I got ready to go, taking my mom's credit card from her purse. Richard, watching me, made a sound in his throat.

"What?"

"Cash only, kid. With no power they won't accept a credit card."

I'd forgotten. After I put on two layers of clothes and my coat and boots, I grabbed my saved money from my jewelry box and headed out of the apartment. The nearest grocery is only a couple of blocks away, so I knew where I was headed. There's also a delicatessen, two fast food places, and one gas and convenience shop within a three block radius of our building. These are the places we go to most. I figured I had a good chance of finding some food in one or other of them.

As soon as I left the apartment, the darkened hallway seemed ominous. I entered the stairs, where it was even darker. Creepy. I stood there for a minute to let my eyes adjust and then, after I'd gone down only one floor, I saw a man at the next landing, just standing there. He didn't look like anyone who lived in the building because I would have recognized him.

He'd heard me coming and stared up at me. I stopped moving. It was as though my blood froze. I turned around and ran back to the apartment. I've never been brave. It's not one of my strong points.

He didn't threaten me or anything. I felt foolish as I ran back. But there was something frightening in the look on his face. I could only describe it in one way: He'd looked at me like I was a piece of meat. A THING. The thought crossed my mind that he was a porn addict or something. Anyway, I didn't recognize him and I knew I couldn't go back alone.

Richard was standing on a step-stool in the kitchen searching the highest, seldom-used cabinets for something when I got back. He looked at me with surprise. Before he could say anything, I blurted out what happened. For once I was glad to have him there because he agreed to go with me to the store. He even surprised me by saying, "It wouldn't have been brave for you to go on; it would've been stupid." That made me feel better, but I know, deep inside, that if bravery had been called for, I would have come up empty. Anyway, we started down but when we reached the place where I'd seen the man, he was gone. I was glad.

Outside, the streets were full of people—unusual for such cold weather. Some looked homeless, just wandering around aimlessly, waiting for someone to tell them where to go or what to do.

Richard saw his friend Chad, who lives in another building down the street. He shook his head at us.

"Can you believe this, man?" he asked. He was carrying a small plastic bag of groceries.

Richard nodded. "I know. We're headed to the grocery."

"Good luck with that," he said, his eyes wide. "There's a long line and—"

Richard grabbed my hand and was turning away. "Thanks," he said, and then, to me, "C'mon. We gotta get there before there's nothing left."

"Cash only!" Chad yelled after us. "Good luck!"

I was so happy I had the $100 dollars. When we turned the corner towards the store, we found a long line of people, stretching all the way up the block. Richard asked what they were in line for and found out they were trying to get into the same store as we were.

We got in line at the end. I could see we were in for misery. Richard considered splitting up while he tried the gas and convenience store, but I didn't want to be alone out there. Meanwhile, the weather felt colder than ever and I wasn't warm when I left the apartment. Even with my hands in my pockets they were feeling numb before we'd moved more than a few feet forward. I thought half the town was in line ahead of us, but as we waited the line behind us kept growing.

We moved intermittently, only inches at a time. My feet started burning. Was I getting frostbite? We heard a skirmish from the front of the line. A fight! The line broke up as everyone tried to see what was going on. I didn't. I didn't want to see. I didn't even want to know, so I just stayed where I was.

And then something went *BANG*!

"Someone's got a gun," Richard said, bobbing his head to get the best view in that direction. At the word *gun* I felt my stomach flip. I was going to panic. I'd had panic attacks before and this one came on with wicked speed. In a blink, I could hardly breathe. I fell forward, trying to get a breath. Richard was not in sight. People were shouting and running and some girl started screaming and I wished I'd stayed home, and I didn't know what to do or where to go. I slumped against the building and fell to the ground, not even feeling the snow or ice. I turned my face against the wall, and I didn't realize it was me screaming until Richard came and put his arm around me.

"Hey, it's okay, no one got hurt. Some idiot just shot his gun into the sky to get everyone's attention."

I was shaking, so Richard grabbed my arm and pulled me up.

"C'mon, I'll take you back," he said, turning me towards the building. I started walking with him, still gasping in air. As we walked I felt the panic subsiding. It was like coming back to earth after being in limbo-land—panic attacks were like that—and I realized we were empty-handed. I stopped.

"We can't go back without something for Jesse and Mom." He looked at me with surprise. I was sort of surprised myself, to be honest. Usually if I have a panic attack the ONLY thing I want to do is get home. I don't feel safe anywhere else. And here, I'd heard an actual gunshot and I was saying we ought to go back towards it.

"You sure you can do this? If you want to go back, I'll get the formula."

I did want to go back. But not alone. What if that creepy guy was on the stairwell again? I hate lonely stairwells! While I was thinking what to do, he stepped back to look up the street.

"Looks like it's all over, so you may as well come with me." I wondered if Richard could tell how afraid I was. I was embarrassed. We fell into step, going cautiously towards the store. The snow on the street was slushy ice from all the foot traffic, and I could now feel the wetness in my pants from when I'd slumped to the ground in my fear. At least there was no line to get in because everyone had dispersed. A man going the other way saw us and stopped. He'd been waiting near us in line, earlier.

"Don't bother," he said, in a flat voice. "There's nothing left. The shelves are empty."

"NOTHING?" I asked. I found that hard to believe.

"The store owners took most of the stuff," he said, "during the night. Everything else's been sold. That fight was because two people wanted the same thing—I think it was baby food."

Richard and I looked at each other.

"What about the convenience store?" Richard asked.

"Same story," he said.

Richard blew out a breath. "What about McDonald's? Is it open?"

He shook his head. "People broke into McDonald's—can you believe it? Just because they were so mad that it wasn't open." He scratched his head. "I never saw people so panicked—you'd think we'd never lost power before."

We thanked him and turned to walk home.

Richard stopped. "I'm gonna go see if there's anything left at McDonald's or any of the other places."

"You mean steal things?" My mouth gaped open.

His eyes were steely. "We need food, Sarah. Get this through your head. No trucks will be in to fill the grocery store shelves. Help is NOT on the way. No reinforcements are coming. We gotta do what we gotta do."

I wasn't ready to believe that. "Maybe we should find the shelter."

He looked around at the people and took my arm, nodding in the direction of a guy who was shuffling along the edges of the sidewalk, studying the ground as though looking for lost coins. "You see that guy?" he asked. "I've seen him, before. He's from that halfway house down the street. If there was a shelter to go to, I think someone would have taken him there."

I didn't want to believe there was no shelter, but I was freezing and didn't want to argue.

"Well, I can't go back alone." My voice was whiny. Pathetic. It's so embarrassing to be this way, but I can't help it.

He hesitated. "Fine. I'll walk you back, but let's hurry. Everything right now is a matter of getting to it first. And give me your cash in case I need it." I handed it over.

"Why do you think nothing's open?" I asked. We had to talk in hurried breaths because we were walking so fast. Everything we passed was closed and dark: The travel agency, the beauty shop, and even the check cashing place. I was feeling sick again, as if the panic was returning and so I slowed down. Hurrying makes it worse.

"Probably because whoever owns them couldn't get here." Then he said, "They couldn't open anyway, with nothing working. They can't heat their stores just like we can't heat our apartment. McDonald's couldn't serve food if it was open, because it has no power either." I hadn't thought of that.

"Don't they have backup generators?"

He shrugged. "They probably do, but they wouldn't last long anyway." We walked quickly and fell silent until we reached the building. Richard turned to go but I said, "What if that guy's in there? You can't go, yet!"

He reluctantly walked me all the way up the ten flights of stairs. For once I was sorry we lived so high up. In good weather I liked to sit on the terrace and enjoy the height, the view of the roof-tops, and the breezes. Now being on the 10th floor seemed the dumbest thing possible.

As we climbed up I said, "Maybe dad will bring some stuff with him when he comes home." My brother gave me a strange look.

"What? What is it?"

"You think he's coming home?"

I gasped. "Of course! Why wouldn't he?"

"Think about it, Sarah. He works forty-five minutes from home by car. That's like 25 miles. It was below freezing last night. Even if dad wanted to walk home, he'd freeze to death trying."

"Don't say that!" I cried. "He'll find a way! He'll stay warm somewhere at night and walk during the day!"

My brother said, "Yeah, wearing his regular coat—It's not made for extreme cold. And he might not have gloves, since the car is usually warm. Or a hat. Just think about it."

"It's been cold all week," I said. "I'll bet he was too wearing a hat and gloves!" But I didn't know for sure. And I hated my brother at that moment for telling me these things.

"Don't say this stuff to Mom," I said.

"You think she hasn't had the same thoughts?"

"Why do you always have to be so negative? Can't you just believe for the best—for once?"

He shrugged. "I guess that's why I'm a realist and you—you're a dreamer."

"You don't have to be a dreamer to believe for the best," I muttered. But maybe he's right about me not being a realist. I can't tell. I do like to daydream about living in some fairyland existence where Prince Charming comes and takes me away on his white horse. What can I say? I was raised on *Cinderella* and "Ever After" and *Pride and Prejudice*.

We passed the Methodist church which was now empty; no one was handing out any food or hot chocolate like they had, yesterday. It was a pretty brick building with stained glass windows. It reminded me of the Catholic church we used to go to, only it was smaller. I used to love studying the pictures within the huge stained glass windows of the Catholic church. And there was artwork on the ceiling—there were arches that ran along the aisles and their sides had been painted old style, like an Italian fresco, with saints and the Apostles. I could stare up at them forever—the service bored me—but Richard was always nudging me in the ribs to pay attention. What had happened to my brother? He no longer seemed to believe in God at all. Maybe it was because we'd stopped attending church as a family before we moved here. I liked not going, since I could sleep in. My parents didn't bug me about it, so I didn't go.

But I believe in God. Still, I hadn't once thought of Him since losing the power. I was guilty of not going to church and guilty for a lot of things. But right then and there I said a prayer that my dad would make it home.

With food for Jesse.

And a kerosene heater.

AFTERNOON

Back in the apartment I got warmed by the stove. Richard had told me not to, but my hands were frozen. My feet were too, and so I heated a pot of water and then dipped in a cloth, and put it on my feet. Mom saw what I was doing and didn't say anything, which was nice because the cloth felt wonderful—for about half a minute. Then it got cold.

Richard came home about an hour later. He had a bag of cold McDonald's apple pies and another of chocolate milk. He said other people were in there with him, jostling each other and grabbing whatever they could find.

"I can't believe this," I said. "It's only been a day without power and everyone's acting crazy!"

Richard plopped down next to me, opening an apple pie. "That's because everyone knows this is bad."

I still didn't want to believe that. "How do you know for sure? What if the power comes back later today or tomorrow?"

He looked at me sideways, chewing. "It won't."

"How do you know for sure?"

"Because it's not just the electric, Sarah. It's everything. ALL electronics. It's not just a power outage. It's a catastrophic thing, like I told you, an electromagnetic pulse. It affected everything that's electronic, and that's why people are freaking out. When you can't turn on the news, or drive anywhere, or heat your house or go to a store to buy more food, people WILL panic."

I took a shaky breath. "How long do you think it will last?" My mother came into the room carrying Jesse. She'd heard my question and looked at my brother, listening.

He was silent a moment, looking down and fiddling with the sturdy paper wrapper of the pie. "A long time."

EVENING

I spent as long as possible putting another coat of polish on my nails by candlelight and trying to hold on to my disbelief of Richard's assessment. If I gave in and accepted that we were in for a long time without power, the thought was too frightening. But I was cold—even my nail polish hardened in record time. It's tough trying not to believe things are bad when you can't get warm in your own home.

Richard came in and said, "Why don't you do something useful instead of wasting time on your nails?"

I stared at him for a second. He is such a pain. "Like what?"

"Like go to the pantry and get out the flour and sugar and other things and bake something. Right now the stove still lights. The oven turns on. Use them!" I looked at Mom. I hoped she would take my side but she was busy with Jesse and acted like she hadn't heard anything.

I looked at my hands. "My nails are wet. And besides, I only know how to bake cookies."

"Even cookies are better than a bag of flour," Richard said. "Use what we have and make something!" I was surprised by his insistence.

"Why don't YOU make something?" He stared at me for a moment.

"Maybe I will. But you're a girl, Sarah. You're supposed to know how to cook."

Typical male attitude!

I do heat water for instant coffee for me and Mom, so it's not like I don't do anything.

Richard started baking some kind of quick bread, but in between tasks he came in and talked about lots of horrible scenarios that are going to happen. He said there'll be a run at the banks and all the supermarkets will be sold out like our little grocery was, and then people will panic and get violent.

"I wish you would just shut up!" I finally yelled at him. "Why are you trying to scare us? You don't KNOW if these things will happen! You don't KNOW that the power won't come back!"

He shook his head at me.

"Time to grow up, little sister," he said. He looked at Mom, who was giving Jesse a bottle. At almost three, my little cousin is too big for a bottle, but he refuses to give it up and Mom refuses to make him. She LOVES having a little one at home again. And Jesse, I have to admit, loves being babied. Anyway, Mom was giving Richard a sad look.

"Mom doesn't want to hear it, either," I said. I almost ran for my iPod, wanting to drown him out with music, only I remembered it's useless.

I lit a candle beside the sofa and stared at the wavering flame. It no longer reminded me of a romanticized past, like in Jane Austen's time. I can't pretend this is fun. Poor little Jesse cries every time he's undressed for a change because of the cold.

I pulled out my cell phone for like the seventh time to see if by some miracle it would work. I'm dying to know how my friends are. If I could just hear ONE person's voice on the other end of a phone I'd feel infinitely better. When it wouldn't work, I flung it down on the couch. Tears filled my eyes.

I hate this! I want to take a shower like I do every night and I can't. I want to get on Facebook and see the statuses of my friends. I want to text Lexie and Andrea, and my cousin in New York. I want to get on YouTube and watch something funny. Instead I can't do anything, and I'm lonely and tired and on top of all that, COLD! This apartment feels like a tomb!

It wouldn't be so bad if I thought it might be over soon, but thanks to Richard I can't even lie to myself that it will be.

And I miss my dad. My mother has never been the talkative type, but she is so quiet it scares me. I know it means she's worrying. And the later it gets, the more we feel his absence.

I'm having second thoughts about those people on that reality TV show. They had every right to complain.

SARAH
JANUARY 13
DAY THREE

This is the third—unbelievable—day without power. We've been hearing about disasters that happen when electronics fail. The Hughes from the next apartment stopped by and filled our ears with this wonderful stuff. (I wanted to leave the room but I felt embarrassed because nobody else seemed to be upset like me.) Mr. Hughes said anyone flying in an airplane would have died because planes fell out of the sky. I remembered that smoke I saw rising in the distance and it horrified me to think a downed plane could have caused it. I ran to the balcony. The smoke was still there, no less than yesterday. Whatever was burning was still burning.

"Yup," said Mr. Hughes, when I got back. "That's a plane."

I didn't want to think about it.

They talked about buses and cars that died while on bridges or in tunnels that went dark. They said trains could be underground or anywhere, in the middle of nowhere when their engines failed. It's really too horrible to think about.

I'm miserable. We all are—because of the temperature as much as anything. Richard and I went down the hall today, asking everyone we know if they could lend us a kerosene heater or something like that. Some people didn't answer our knock. The Schusters have a heater but can't do without it. The Powells are bundled up like we are, but had made a fire in an empty terra cotta planter on their balcony to warm up with.

The Powells are different than anyone else I know. They're members of this little church on the outskirts of town—I know, because they've invited me to their service a few times. I've never gone. Richard calls them 'holy rollers.' I'm not sure what that means, but I will say this: Even though they had no heat in their apartment, just like us, and even though they're facing the same realities we are (no power, no stores, no food) they seemed happy. They invited us out to the balcony to warm up, and Mrs. Powell put a big oatmeal raisin cookie in my hands. The little Powells were toasting marshmallows over the fire and behaving as if it were all a big adventure.

Richard started giving his ultra-negative talk about how horrible things are to Mr. and Mrs. Powell. He figured they couldn't possibly know how bad things really were or they wouldn't be so jolly. But they wouldn't have any of it!

"God brought us to this," Mr. Powell said, "and God will bring us through this."

Richard pointed out the plume of smoke, telling them how a plane had probably fallen from the sky. "Think of how many people died instantly," he said, as if to prove his point that things are awful. (That IS pretty awful.)

But Mr. Powell said, "Everyone has to die sometime, Richard. That's a guarantee. Are you ready for that?"

"What do you mean?" my brother asked.

"Are you ready to face God?" He looked at me, too. I was very interested because I don't think I am ready. I wanted to know what he thought could make me ready.

"Oh, that," Richard said, dismissively. "I'll be curious to ask him why he let this happen."

Mrs. Powell smiled wryly. "I think He'll be the One asking questions of you."

"Like what?" I asked.

"Like have you accepted his Son, Jesus Christ, into your heart?" she turned to me, her eyes shining warmly at me. Richard took my arm.

"Hey, uh, sorry, but we gotta get back to our mom and Jesse."

"We're praying for you," Mr. Powell called, as we left. "We're praying for everyone in this building." I looked back, sorry to be leaving the cheery atmosphere. I was thinking of Lexie, because she was something like the Powells. She talked about God sometimes too. I wondered briefly how Lexie was doing right now and images of other friends crossed my mind. I missed them. It had only been a few days since we lost power, but it felt like a lifetime ago.

Richard didn't come back to our apartment. He wanted to copy the Powells' idea of making a fire on the balcony, so he's out on the street hunting for anything like wood or debris to burn so we can do the same thing.

Everyone's eyes looked different to me. Like shell-shock. (Except for the Powells, that is.) I saw dull, hollow pain. It's hard to explain. Maybe it's hopelessness. And I wonder, do my eyes look that way, too? This has just started and we're already feeling this way? HOW WILL WE SURVIVE THIS WINTER? I try not to have that thought, but it comes at me whenever I find myself rubbing my hands together to make them warm; or when I need to use the restroom and don't want to drop my pants because of the cold.

I wonder if by next week even the Powells will feel this way.

And I keep thinking about Dad. Despite everything, I do think he will make his way home. I know he wouldn't just sit back and wait until the weather warms up. He'll find a way. He has to. Sooner or later. Dads do that, right? As I was thinking this I went into the family room to lay down in my sleeping bag on the love seat. Even though it's still early in the day, I'm bummed out and tired. I heard the door slam open and in a few seconds Richard came crashing into the room.

"FIRE!" He cried. "C'mon, we have to get out, NOW!" He practically shoved me off the sofa, still in my sleeping bag.

"Richard!"

"Fire, Sarah! GET UP!"

One glance at his face told me he wasn't joking. I scrambled out of the sleeping bag, my heart pounding in my throat.

"Where's the fire?" I asked, hurrying behind him as he went to find Mom. "I don't know, it's downstairs, but the smoke's coming up the stairwell and if we don't move now we're gonna get stranded up here!"

Mom was on her feet, having heard all this, and already stuffing baby supplies and other things into a large diaper bag.

"Grab whatever you can!" she said.

"No, Mom, we have to go NOW," Richard said. He grabbed my

blanket off the love seat and disappeared down the hallway. When he came back it was dripping wet, and I realized he'd dunked it in the tub, which still has water. He handed it to me.

"Keep this over your head as you go down."

He grabbed another blanket and went to dip it in the tub like the first one. Since we all sleep fully dressed and in our coats anyway, all we had to do was grab anything else we could reach as we hurried out. Somehow I managed to stuff my journal into my handbag, as well as a protein bar and a pack of gum. I wanted to get some things from my room, but Richard cut me off in the hallway, the other sopping blanket in his arms.

"Forget everything!" he yelled. "Get out, NOW."

"What about you?" I said. "I don't see you leaving." Richard definitely brings out the brat in me.

"I'm getting Mom and Jesse—we'll be right behind you." He pushed me towards the door. "Go on, get out."

But I stopped. Mom was in the kitchen grabbing things from cabinets.

"Move, Sarah!" Richard shouted.

"I don't want to leave without you and Mom!" Actually, I was afraid to. I was afraid I'd start to panic as soon as I closed the door to the apartment. Or else I'd panic on the stairs going down and what if I was all alone? What if that awful man was around? What if I couldn't breathe and fainted? What if the smoke gave me a heart attack? I've always been really good at finding things to worry about.

Mom had Jesse hoisted on one hip and was using her other hand to stuff things into a tote bag. She saw us arguing and suddenly made a beeline towards me. Prying Jesse off of her, she practically threw him at me. He started wailing.

"Take your cousin and go!" she ordered. Richard tried to give her the second blanket.

"We have to leave now, Mom," he said. But she turned and kept filling that tote bag, stuffing any and everything into it she could grab.

"There's no time, Mom!" Richard cried, trying to force her to stop scavenging our shelves. Mom started crying.

"You go!" she cried. "I'll be right there!" Richard glanced at me.

"WHAT are you still doing here? Can't you ever listen?" He yelled.

"You're not my father!"

"Don't be STUPID, Sarah! Get out of here!" He came at me but I stood my ground. I wanted to wait for my mother. Then my mom stopped and looked towards me. Something in her eyes was frightening.

"WHAT IS WRONG WITH YOU? GO NOW, SARAH! NOW!" I can't remember my mom ever screaming at me and the shock hit me with such force that I turned and fled, forgetting my fear of the fire and of being alone in the stairwell.

When I opened the door to the stairs, the darkness and smoke hit me like a wall. I had thought Richard was exaggerating our danger but I saw he had reason to be so concerned. I could hear other people lower down who were coughing and crying and I started to cough too, as soon as I hit the steps.

I pulled the wet blanket over us like a poncho, but I was afraid to cover my eyes completely in case we might encounter actual flames that I'd need to go around. But I was blinking from the stinging smoke by the time I turned the first bend. I still had nine and a half flights to get down and I felt suddenly like Jesse and I were both going to die.

Jesse had actually stopped crying from the shock of the smoke, but after that first turn in the stairwell, perhaps from hearing other people below us, he resumed at full pitch, stopping only to cough and catch what breath he could.

He began kicking at me and trying to squirm out of my arms.

"Stop it!'

He ignored me, wailing even louder.

"Stop it, you're making it worse!"

He fought to get free, and I struggled to keep my grip on him. Toddlers can be amazingly slippery if they have a mind to be.

I changed tactics, trying to reassure him. I crooned, "It's okay, baby boy, we'll be fine." Then I had to cough and his sobs grew louder, accented with terrible sounding coughs. All the while I was descending as fast as I could, counting the steps at each turn so I wouldn't plummet us into a wall in the dark.

One, two, three, four, five, six, seven, eight, nine, TURN. And again and again.

I guess the smoke was getting thicker because Jesse's sobs turned to hoarse screams in my ear. I covered his head completely with the blanket. He was already fighting so much that his indignation at this barely mattered.

Every cell in my body wanted to turn back but I knew they were traitorous cells, that they'd only seal our doom if I listened to them. We'd had it drilled into our head by Dad since we got to the apartment that the only way to survive a fire was to get out—or be rescued from the balcony. But no fire trucks were on their way. Going down was our only option.

Dad had tried to give us basic safety instructions for apartment living when we moved to this building nine months ago. Don't use the elevators if there's a fire. Don't use the elevators if the power goes out. Don't open the door to the apartment without looking through the peek hole to identify the caller....that sort of stuff. But this was never supposed to be a permanent place for us to live. Dad planned on buying a property in the country, which Ohio has plenty of, but it still hadn't happened. They were waiting for that perfect property that had everything they wanted, and so far it hadn't materialized on the market—either that or they couldn't afford it when it did.

When I was as far down as the third floor—at least I was pretty sure it was the third floor, I might have lost count—I started feeling faint. I was light-headed, which of course fueled my panic, which in turn probably made the light-headedness worse.

I was afraid I'd drop Jesse, who was still fighting me something awful. Suddenly I couldn't take it. I was terrified and choking and in a panic and in a rage. I thought I might be dying. I actually stopped moving and re-tightened my arms about his little body and I shook him and then growled into his ear, "STOP MOVING, YOU STUPID BABY OR I'LL KILL YOU!"

I felt terrible as soon as I said it. But amazingly, it worked! Jesse grew quiet and still. I guess he'd never heard me talk to him like that before and it gave him pause. But I'd forgotten which number step we were at, and so I had to grope to find the steel rail (which was hot, to my horror). I grabbed it anyway with one hand and hung on, feeling my way, until it stopped at the next turn in the landing.

It was impossible to see. Maybe that alone was enough to feed my terror. Other people were occasionally stumbling out from the building into the stairwell and their panic also fed mine. I thought my heart would beat out of my body it was hammering so hard. But then there was a crowd to move along with and somehow that helped. I used the body in front of me to keep me on track. Jesse was quiet and the thought crossed my mind that maybe he couldn't breathe beneath the blanket and I was suffocating him, so I pulled it off and spoke to him and he immediately began wailing again. I readjusted him, holding him tightly against me, and would have pulled the blanket further over both our heads, but someone behind me was using it and I couldn't get any more of it.

I heard encouraging shouts from below—we were almost down! People were telling us to hurry, to keep going, and it sped us on. My eyes were stinging and watering even keeping them closed, and as we neared the last set of steps, I remembered Mom and Richard were behind us. What if they didn't make it down? Would I lose my whole family except Jesse? Would I end up having to raise a toddler all by myself?

I must have been crying because I felt tears hitting my mouth. Just thinking of Mom and Richard possibly not making it down filled me with hopelessness. I wanted to collapse and give up. My lungs felt empty, airless, and my legs were seriously weak. Honestly, I don't know how I kept moving. Then suddenly we were through the doorway to the vestibule and then a blast of cold, soothing air hit my face and body and someone grasped my arm, pulling me forward.

"C'mon, honey," a voice said, and then I was outside, and this woman, a black woman named Mrs. Murfrees from the ninth floor, patted my arm, saying, "You made it, honey, you made it."

Her little pat to my arm broke something inside me and I sobbed, a cracked, hoarse sob, probably because of the smoke I'd inhaled on the way down.

"There, there," she said, and without knowing I was going to do it, I flung myself at her and into her arms, still holding Jesse on my hip. I don't know if she was shocked by it, but she put her big arms around me and patted my back, making soft sounds like a mother does.

"My mom and brother are still in there!" I gasped.

Her arms tightened somewhat about me. It felt so good.

"They be out soon, you'll see."

We stood there together watching people as they escaped from the building, most of them stumbling and weakened like me. I felt as though my heart would burst, and Jesse still whimpered in my arms, though he was no longer wailing. I spotted the Powells. They were all

108

together, huddling. I wondered if one of them had gotten hurt. Then, somehow I realized they were praying! They seemed none the worse for wear, and I marveled at their calmness at a time like this. I was glad they were praying. I went over to them, and tugged on Mrs. Powell's arm.

"Could you please pray that my mother and brother will get out safe?"

"Oh, honey, of course! We are already praying that no one will be lost to this fire!" She put her arm around me, pulling me into their little circle. As they prayed, I felt like I was in a new world. Did people really talk to God like this? So familiarly? Like they knew Him? It made me a little nervous because I wasn't sure God would like it. If He didn't like it, would He punish us for doing it?

I dropped the blanket because it was turning to ice. I unzipped my coat and tried to get it around Jesse to keep him as warm as I could. Mrs. Powell must have opened her eyes while her husband continued praying, because suddenly she was wrapping a thick scarf around me and Jesse. For some reason, this brought fresh tears to my already watery, aching eyes. I thanked her silently and she nodded with understanding.

When Mr. Powell said, "Amen!" I thanked them quickly and hurried off to see if Mom and Richard had emerged from the building yet. As I walked, I covered Jesse's head in kisses. I was sorry for my earlier anger. Standing there, bouncing him in my arms, I stood and waited helplessly, watching for mom and Richard to be among the survivors who were stumbling out of the building. I couldn't have kept still even if I hadn't been holding him because my nerves were so taut.

Suddenly there were sharp voices. Someone was saying, "This is your d---- fault!" but I didn't even turn to look to see whose fault it was. My eyes were fixed on the double doors leading to the main entryway and then the stairs. I hardly ever think about how much I love my family but at that moment, standing there, not knowing if they were going to emerge alive, I felt a terrible deep love—even for Richard. I felt something people don't often talk about—that love hurts. But it does. It did while I stood there waiting. Because love is mixed with worry and fear. You can always lose the ones you love.

And then Mom and Richard stumbled out. I ran to them, crying with relief. After a minute of coughing and catching her breath, mom took Jesse from me. He had upped the tempo of his wails the moment he saw her. It was then that I noticed my arm was stinging and my eyes and throat were deeply sore.

LATER

We are now at the library along with most of the displaced residents of our building. We don't know for sure if everyone was home, so we can't tell if anyone was left inside. Anyway, those of us who got out are still in shock. At least, I am.

Richard found out that someone was trying to heat their apartment with a fire in a bucket and it got out of hand.

"Idiots!" he'd spat out. "You can do everything right but all it takes is one idiot and here we are without a home."

There'd been no fire department to the rescue because there was no way to contact a fire department. And even if there was a way to contact them, they wouldn't have a truck that worked. I pictured our building burning inside, like a furnace. Here we were, cold and miserable, and there it was, too hot and out of control to be of any use. I imagined the flames licking up all our possessions. First we'd lost power, the use of any and all appliances. We'd lost transportation. We'd lost my father, for all I knew. Now we'd lost everything else.

———————◆———————

So Richard is still fuming and mom seems numb, falling back into a scary silence. She continues to care for Jesse, but she's doing it robotically, without emotion, and the baby keeps reaching out to touch her face, as though to ask if she's still in there.

I'm sitting here staring at books. We are surrounded by books. Each and every one of them is a reminder of all we've lost, because they are books about the world as it was. The normal world. The one we no longer have access to.

Nevertheless, I am telling myself that I will read each and every one. This is my plan. Since I can no longer create the fantasy that our lives are good, I will read and read and not think about how life has been ruined in a mere, short three days. I will escape from reality, one way or another.

"At least we're all safe and alive," I heard Richard say to Mom.

She'd been staring with a stony-faced silence out the window. She must have looked awful for him to actually point out something positive.

She slowly looked at him. "All? Not all." She turned back, returning to her abyss of dark thoughts.

A man from our building was walking past but he stopped. "You're all safe and alive?"

I nodded.

"Yeah, how long do you think that's gonna last?" he asked. I said nothing. How could he say such a thing? I turned to show Richard my exasperation but he nodded his head.

"He's right."

I started reviewing the morning, how quickly we'd been thrust out of our home. When all the residents of the building—as far as anyone could tell—were outside, a number of people discussed our options, what we should do. That's how we ended up here at the library.

During the walk across town, which we did in a long, slow-moving line, I looked around at the others. Like Mrs. Murfree, I knew some by name and many more by sight, but we'd never gotten to really know our neighbors. Not more than enough to exchange a nod or greeting in passing. I'd seen some of them on the elevator or when I'd stopped to empty our mailbox in the foyer but that was all the contact I'd had. The Powells had been friendlier than most, especially Mrs. Powell, but even them I only knew superficially.

I figured that was about to change.

Anyway, the library was chosen as a place of refuge for two reasons. One, it's a public facility, and two, it's a restored nineteenth century building and someone remembered it has actual working fireplaces. I'd forgotten about them. Guess I don't go to the library enough. I do recall that every Christmas it held a Charles Dickens night, and the fireplace was bright with burning logs. I hoped all the old fireplaces would work.

Many kids were crying and even a few adults by the time we arrived. Lots of us thought we had frostbite in our feet. Mine have stopped burning and tingling, so I think they're okay.

The building has three stories but so far we are all mingling in the biggest first floor room because of that fireplace. Nobody knows anything about an emergency shelter—I can hardly believe it. What kind of government do we have, anyway? Aren't they supposed to be ready for something like this? Isn't every town supposed to have an emergency shelter?

I heard some people saying they would be returning to the apartment building because they still had food there. Mom managed to fill her tote bag before Richard forced her out but it's still a pathetic amount of food, all in all.

When it's safe to go back, I hope Richard will. He can get whatever food survived the flames, if any, and maybe some of our clothing and other stuff.

I honestly don't know how we're supposed to get by. I don't have a single change of clothing. I have a hairbrush in my purse, makeup, my useless cell phone, a container of floss, some change, my bus pass and school ID and one pack of gum. Plus my journal and a few pens. We ate the protein bar on the way over. All in all, NOTHING to help us survive!

I took out the cell phone and opened it up. I don't know why. Richard saw me doing it and said, "Why are you wasting your time? It's dead, Sarah. Even if by some miracle power was restored, you'd need a new cell phone. That one's fried."

I just quietly put it back in my purse, even though Richard shook his head at me like I'm hopeless. I can't bring myself to throw it away. I'm glad I stuffed my journal and pens in my handbag, too, or I couldn't be writing this.

When we arrived here, bedraggled and cold and tired, the apartment Super stood at the door, studying every face and nodding us to pass. I wondered why—and then he stopped a lady, and said, "Not you. You're not from our building."

She just stared at him. She looked like a homeless lady, to be honest. Someone said, "Hey, it IS a public building."

The Super, Mr. Aronoff, said, "Not today."

The lady shuffled off. I felt sorry for her. After that, he stopped a few more people for the same reason. Those of us who were allowed in rushed inside like it was going to be a haven, a refuge. But it was cold and dark when we got here just like everywhere else.

But now there's a big fire in the main fireplace, and someone brought a commercial size box of hotdogs, so we're all getting to eat.

EVENING

So now we've staked our claim, so to speak, as everyone is doing. I found a nice little corner near a window (for light) but not too close (because of the cold). Every time you turn into an aisle between the stacks, you find a family camped out, sitting on a pile of blankets, or just cross-legged, sitting against the books. I wish I had my blanket. Richard kept his and mom's, despite their being wet.

We threw them over the chairs to dry and when they're dry we'll lay them on the floor, but I don't see us getting comfortable here. The chairs were going fast so Richard and I dragged a few to our spot and tried to make a small circle. The walls of books give us a sense of privacy.

Overall today was a disaster upon disaster, but something good happened. (If you can call it good.) Richard disappeared shortly after we settled in our corner. When he showed up again, his pockets and hoodie were full of wrapped snacks. It was a God-send, because I had been sitting there fretting over our lack of food. Sure, Mom had stuffed a lot of cans into her tote bag, but she forgot the can opener. All we'd eaten all day was breakfast and a hot dog.

So Richard found a small kitchen in the basement which must have been for maintenance men or something; by some miracle he was the first one to happen upon it. He found a quart of milk, half-frozen, in the fridge. And there were individually wrapped cheese and crackers and beef sticks. It's almost real food. He emptied everything from his pockets and hoodie and was going back to get more but mom said, "Richard." He looked at her. My mother's eyes are sad.

"Leave some for the others."

"Mom, a lot of these people are saying they have a lot of food back at the building. We don't."

Mom thought for a moment. "Today would have been payday. I'd have gone shopping to restock."

"But it isn't, and we can't go shopping," he said.

"I brought some food," she pointed out, nodding towards the tote bag.

"How long will it last?" he asked, folding his arms across his chest. "IF we can even find a can opener."

"When you go back, look for one," she said. And that seemed to

113

settle it. Mom hadn't said, "IF you go back." She said, "WHEN you go back." So Richard took off.

He came back with his hood and pockets full again, but someone saw him leaving the kitchen so he knows his secret is out.

I feel guilty that he took so much, but I'm also thankful for it. Was it right or wrong for us to grab a lot for ourselves? I don't know what to feel anymore.

And he did find a can opener.

SARAH
JANUARY 14
DAY FOUR

Last night once the fire was going well, it got almost cozy in here. The sheer number of us in the building is adding to the warmth. There's a slight odor of something foul—probably a child's dirty diaper, but I can live with that. What I'm having trouble living with is that I saw HIM here. The guy from the stairwell! I guess he does live in the building.

He still gives me the creeps. He looked at me exactly the same way! He's a bad man, I can tell. I told Richard about him, so my brother is staying close with me. He goes with me as far as the restroom, too. (We're using them for now, but they're going to get gross soon. I don't know what'll happen after that. I don't want to think about it.)

I didn't have a candle or a flashlight so I sat near the fire to write. I had to squeeze past a family with small children, explaining that I only needed a few minutes to write in my journal. As I sat there in the mostly darkened room (except for the blaze from the fireplace and a few flashlights here and there) it seemed to me like the whole world had shut down. Four short days ago everything was normal? It feels like a lifetime ago.

Sometime in the evening, I heard singing. Singing! It was a happy sound. As I listened more closely, I could tell it was a religious song. The chorus said, *He lives, He lives, Hallelujah, Jesus Lives!* It must have been the Powells. It helped me fall asleep. I was sure I wouldn't get a wink of sleep between being uncomfortable and worrying about that man being here. But it was a soothing backdrop and I don't remember lying awake for long.

"Did you hear the singing last night?" I asked Richard today. He nodded. Then shrugged. "People living in dreamland."

———————◆———————

I'm sitting near our little window for light but it's another cloudy day that looks like snow is coming.

Mom and I talked about what would happen if Dad got back to the apartment and no one is there. Richard was quiet while we spoke. He doesn't believe Dad will ever make it back. He says tomorrow he'll go to the building and see if the fire's out. If it is, he'll leave a note on our door, just in case. Then, when someone else said they were going back for supplies, Richard went with him. He gave me his army knife before he left, saying to keep it nearby. I stared at it in my hand and realized it wouldn't help me in a million years. I'd be too scared to use it. I wouldn't even know how to get it open. I'm not very strong. I moved my chair close to Mom and I'm staying right here until he returns.

———————◆———————

Richard's back. Enough smoke had cleared for him to make it up the stairs to our apartment but the whole place still reeks of fire. The good news is that the worst damage seems to have been contained to the third and fourth floors. The guy who started it all lived on the third floor. The rest of the place just has smoke damage.

So Richard was able to grab some of our things as well as leave the note for dad.

He HAS to make it back! But each hour that goes by and he doesn't show up makes me feel that something terrible has happened to him. Mom says the not knowing is making her crazy.

SARAH
JANUARY 15
DAY FIVE

If the apartment had a heat source, we'd be returning today. In the middle of the night I felt someone touch me—it was that creepy guy! He'd only touched my arm, but to wake up and see his face was horrifying. I tried to scream but he quickly moved to cover my mouth. I think he's not right in the head—why else would he have done that in a crowded place? Lucky for me, my brother wasn't sleeping deeply and he pounced on the guy, shouting for help. Other people quickly came around and the man slunk off. Afterwards, some of the men with families went after him and forced him from the library. I am now in dread of his ever coming back.

It's hard to describe how upset I feel—I'm shaking inside even though outwardly you can't tell. I don't feel safe. I can't believe he approached me right near my family. He must be desperate or something. But I want to go home. I'd feel safer there.

LATER

I almost freaked when Richard said he was going out with some of the guys to find food. I begged him not to go, but he said, "It's daytime. You'll be safe. That creep is gone, and people like him count on darkness because they're cowards at heart."

"Where do you think you'll find food, anyway?"

He shrugged, but adjusted his hat and scarf and hurried to join the group that was leaving. He started to give me his knife again but I shuddered and turned away. I asked Mom to make him stay and she said, "I think we're safe; and we need food."

"Why don't you come with me then," Richard said, "if you're worried." He nodded his head towards the group getting ready to go. "There are other young people like you." There were a few girls I recognized, but they were seniors in school and we'd never been friends. I shrank back. Besides, I could not see myself out there in this weather, even with Richard. I felt sure if I went I'd either get frostbite or panicked, or both.

After he'd gone, I suddenly realized I'm in trouble. Real trouble. See, I take a daily anti-depressant. It's supposed to help me so I don't have panic attacks, and I guess it does help a little. But the thing is, I've been taking it for months. And aside from what I've got left in my prescription (which I keep in my handbag), what will I do when it runs out?

Somehow I hadn't thought of this earlier. I asked Mom about it.

She lifted her head and listened to me and then frowned.

"We'll ask Richard to check the pharmacy. Maybe we can get you some. In the meantime," and she paused here, thinking. "Don't take it every day. Start taking one every other day. If we can't get more we'll have to wean you quickly."

Her words filled me with dread. For awhile I sat there crying and worrying. If I'm having panic attacks now, while I have this medicine, what will I be like when I don't have it? I'm scared.

I started browsing the shelves for my first escape book when I found a Bible—it's pristine like nobody ever read it. It's not a Catholic Bible, but I have no idea if that makes a difference. It's an ESV translation, which the notes in the beginning explain as "English Standard Version." I'll give it a try.

AFTERNOON

Richard and the others just got back—with food!!! A lot of it. The nearest Wal-Mart is a mile away, and there were two armed guards in front of it. A group of people were arguing with the guards, trying to reason with them. What good is food on the shelves that's only going to rot? Why shouldn't they be allowed to use it when it could save lives, and so on? They were getting nowhere. Richard and our group pretended to leave but they went around the block and eventually found a way to a back entrance.

I should not be happy that my brother is a thief. But right now that food looks awfully good.

They took a lot from the meat and dairy shelves. Mom is worried that it's all spoiled, but other women here are saying the weather has been cold enough to keep it safe. The hams, for instance, still feel frozen solid. I'm not sure if it's from carting them back in the cold or whether they were frozen yet in the store.

Richard was sporting an extra coat and new heavy-duty boots and thicker gloves. He needed them to make that walk in the freezing cold. And he had four canisters of powdered baby formula, two new bottles and nipples and lots of evaporated milk. It's a generic brand, not what Jesse usually gets, but Mom said anything is better than nothing.

He brought winter little kid clothes for Jesse too, and I can't believe it, but he brought me something that I would have been way too embarrassed to ask for. I hadn't even thought about it since it's not my time of the month, but he brought me pads. And he didn't hang around to wait for me to say anything or to embarrass me, either. He just dropped them on my chair and turned back to giving Mom the other stuff.

I have no idea what I would have done without them when the time came, which is supposed to be in about a week. I have to say, it feels like a miracle. (I know it's stolen, but I think God understands.)

Thirst is a problem. No more water is coming from the sinks or the water fountain. One of the men grabbed a sled and loaded it with gallons and gallons of water, but they have to ration them since there are so many of us. Water is heavy and they had to haul it back that whole mile in the cold, so I understand. But it's no fun being thirsty. I remembered the gum in my handbag and I'm using it in tiny pieces because it helps my mouth feel less dry.

Those girls who went with the men brought back dumb stuff like lacy scarves and hair bands and jewelry. One of them was showing off her stuff to her mother and our eyes met for a moment. I could tell she saw my disapproval, but she just looked angry and then ignored me. But really—here we are practically starving and these girls brought back beauty supplies? I like my makeup as much as any girl, but what they took wasn't stealing out of necessity; it's just plain stealing. And stupid.

Anyway, Richard filled as many plastic bags from the registers as he could carry, and loaded it all on a plastic sled. Other men did that too, using all the sleds the store carried. Right now, a big ham is cooking over the fireplace. Someone thought up an ingenious method – a homemade "spit." It doesn't turn, but by manually turning the meat, it will heat on all sides. Mr. Aronoff directed the handing out of paper plates, plastic utensils, cole slaw and potato salad. It's like a backyard barbecue indoors.

I noticed the Powells sitting off by themselves, not eating. I went over to them.

"Aren't you hungry?"

The family looked up at me. Mr. Powell had a determined look on his face. "We still have some rations from the apartment," he said.

"But there's so much here," I said. "Why not save your stuff?"

Mrs. Powell gave me a slow smile. "We don't feel right eating stolen food." She'd spoken very softly, and there wasn't an ounce of condemnation in what she'd said, but I suddenly felt a stab of guilt. I faltered.

"Oh, honey, you go right ahead and eat that stuff," she said. "We're not saying it's wrong for you to eat it."

"But then why won't you eat it?" I asked.

They hesitated. Mr. Powell said, "We're not starving. If we get to the point of starvation, we'll eat anything that's available. But until that happens, I have to know that I haven't put my hand to anything that isn't mine."

I looked down at my food, wondering if I was a complete sinner for eating. Mrs. Powell spoke up again. "Please, go on and eat," she said. "We firmly believe that what we're doing is what WE need to do. It's not what you should feel bound to. God gives grace."

"As a matter of fact, the only time any sin seems to be okay according to the Bible," Mr. Powell added, "is when a person steals to eat. You see, God understands desperation. We just don't feel desperate, yet. But we're not an example you need to follow."

Richard was motioning to me, so I said a clumsy goodbye and wished them luck.

I wish I could say I lost my appetite for the Wal-Mart food after that but I didn't. I saw a big tray of deli meat near Richard when I went over and was ready to help myself.

"That's why I called you," Richard said. "Don't eat any lunch meats or anything else from the refrigerated department of the store. If it was frozen, it's okay, otherwise steer clear."

"Everyone else is eating it," I said, taking a few pieces from the tray. It looked perfectly good, with salami and turkey and cheese slices. My mouth watered just looking at it. I was about to put the first piece of turkey in my mouth when Richard stopped me, taking my elbow.

"Deli meats carry a high risk of bacteria," he said. "Listeriosis. It's been days without power. Don't eat it."

"It's been freezing cold," I returned. "Wouldn't that keep it safe?"

He grimaced and his mouth formed a determined line. He forced my arm down and shook my fork over my plate until the meat fell off. He looked at me again.

"Don't eat it, Sarah."

Richard is such a pest. "Fine!" I was angry and not sure I believed him, but I didn't eat any. I saw those seniors eating it, though. They ate a lot. I'm going to watch them and when they're just fine, I'll tell Richard he was wrong! I can't wait. He thinks he knows everything.

Elizabeth Wasserman came over to me today with an armful of

drawing books and a package of markers and crayons. She lives in my building and is in eighth grade. She used to ask to sit with me on the bus but I never let her because I wanted to save the spot next to me for my good friends. Now I feel sorry that I never let her. Our eyes met a few times since we got here and I nodded at her. So I wasn't too surprised when she approached me.

We're using these books she found on the shelves to practice drawing. She ripped out blank pages from the back of the books—something that would have horrified me before all this—for drawing paper. She's practicing manga, and I'm doing trees and landscapes. I've never been into the manga thing. Besides, drawing trees is strangely calming. I'm making them all green and full and lush—the exact opposite of the world outside right now. It's only January—what? 15th? I'm already losing track of the days without school or a routine. But anyway, it's a long time 'til spring, that's for sure.

"I need more paper," Elizabeth said. She reached out an arm and grabbed a couple of random books from the shelf beside us.

"These aren't glossy like the pages from the children's section, but I'm too lazy to go over there and get some."

"Want me to get some?"

She looked up. "It's right near the restrooms."

I decided not to get some. Thankfully, the odor from that area hadn't yet reached us in our little alcove. I knew it was just a matter of time, though.

I watched her tear out new blank pages carefully, to make sure they didn't have ragged edges. It reassured me that even if I filled up my journal, I could always find pages like she had, that there'd still be a source of paper to write on. I'm not eloquent or super great with words, but I think I'd feel crazy if I couldn't write down what's going on.

EVENING

Richard fell asleep as soon as he finished eating. He looked so tired. It must have been hard, doing all that walking in the cold and snow and especially coming back hauling a big sled of stuff. What he didn't tell us earlier is that they'd had to fend off people who approached them begging. I could tell it bothered him. He said some of them were older; they could have been friends or neighbors; they looked like good, ordinary people, but they were begging for food.

"Please, I couldn't get to a store when this happened," one woman said. "I have two grandchildren at home." Mr. Aronoff was like a drill sergeant, barking out things like, "Don't stop! Don't talk! Keep moving!" He repeated that every time anyone approached them.

I thought about how hard it must have been to see people so needy and do nothing for them. Richard can be a big pain in the butt. But I have to admit he's been great since this happened. I don't know what we'd have done without him.

It's snowing again. Even with just a sliver of moon I can see flakes falling silently out there. As I sit here watching, I feel the weight of this snow. In the past I loved to watch it fall. It used to be pretty. Not so, now. It is a weight on my heart. It means winter continues, that we will struggle to stay warm, and that we can't return to the apartment.

I hear men talking. One has a radio back at the building and he's planning on getting it tomorrow. The others are going back to Wal-Mart. One man said, "Hey, we should only take what we absolutely need to survive."

Another said, "We weren't the first ones to help ourselves, you saw that. And we won't be the last. If we don't take the stuff, someone else will; and we don't know how long we'll need to survive like this. I say we get as much as we can." A round of approval went up. I glanced at Richard to see if he'd wake up from the noise but he slept on.

Mom is sleeping on the floor with the baby snuggled up against her. It struck me that they were often like that now, entwined like Siamese twins. She has one of the blankets we brought and a few fabric baby books, the soft kind, which Richard found in the children's section, for a pillow. I have Richard's blanket. He says he can sleep without one.

We don't talk about Dad. I catch Mom crying from time to time and I'm pretty sure it's about him.

If I think about him being stranded at work, I'll cry too—so I don't.

I pray God is keeping him alive and will bring him back to us safely.

I don't expect to sleep much tonight—not after last night and that awful man. So far the Powells aren't singing. It would help if they did. I wish I had a flashlight so I could read. We're rationing the use of candles—Mr. Aronoff is afraid of a fire. If Richard goes back to Wal-Mart I'm going to ask him to get a flashlight and batteries.

SARAH
JANUARY 16
DAY SIX

Today Mom asked Richard if he'd go and look for Dad. He said, "Mom, I have NO IDEA where to do that."

"Go to his work," she said. "Maybe he's still there. Lots of people probably got stranded there."

I said, "We need Richard here." She just looked at me, so I added, "What if that guy comes back? That creep? And what if we run out of food? Richard can get more." She said nothing, just fell silent, and soon afterwards I saw she was crying. I went over and put my arms around her. She took a few deep breaths. To Richard she said, "If you go back today, get diapers and wipes, and bring as much formula as you can."

"And water!" I added. I didn't mean to shout but the words came out louder than I meant them to and when I turned around, other people were looking at me. But some of them nodded, because they're thirsty too. In addition to the rationed water, there's a kettle they're using to boil snow, but it takes a long time to boil water for everyone. So far, we've gotten barely enough to quench our thirst. Richard did bring some juice boxes and I've had a few—but they're so sweet they make me even thirstier.

As the men were leaving for the trek to Wal-Mart, someone shouted, "Bring another can opener!" A little girl said to her mother, "There's no 'tricity, mama."

"A different kind of can opener," her mother replied.

A different kind of opener—the words rang in my head for some reason. Because that's what life is, now. A different life. A different kind of living and thinking. I don't care about much of anything right now except whether my dad is alive and what we'll eat or drink. I also think about getting fresh clothes from the apartment--which I won't do without Richard—and taking a bath would be heaven! Everything I used to think or worry about seems meaningless.

———————◆———————

It just occurred to me that a lot of people are missing. "Where is everyone?" I asked Elizabeth, when she came over.

She looked at me with big eyes. "Don't go near the restroom. It's super gross. People are sick. My mom said it could be food poisoning."

Even Richard admitted that listeriosis doesn't show up right away, so if they're sick it must be from something else they ate. Maybe the potato salad. Richard wouldn't let me have any of that either.

EVENING

Now I know we've sunken into chaos! The world, I mean. Richard came back from Wal-Mart with a nicked arm—from a bullet! And Mr. Wendell—a father and family man from our building—might die! He took a shot directly to the chest.

When they went around to the back entrance of Wal-Mart like yesterday, there were other people already there, and they didn't want to let our guys in. They had mostly knives and bats, but one man had a gun. He even boasted that he'd just taken it, along with ammunition, from the store.

The two groups argued and things escalated. Finally that man used his gun and that's when Richard's arm got nicked, and Mr. Wendell got shot.

It horrifies me that Richard could have been the one to take that shot. He thinks the guy was aiming at him but missed. I actually started feeling faint when Mom was applying a bandage to his arm. The thought that we could have lost him! He said, "It's okay, sis, I just got grazed a little. No big deal."

But it is a big deal. Mrs. Wendell is sobbing in the next room. Then I heard shouting. Angry voices. Had Mr. Wendell died? I hoped not.

Elizabeth came by and explained. Mrs. Wendell and her daughter had asked if someone would find a doctor. They wanted to stay with Mr. Wendell while someone else got help. But not one person volunteered. Then, after the shouting, someone did. "Mr. Powell," she said. I nodded. He would do that.

Suddenly Elizabeth started hugging me—I guess her mother isn't very affectionate. I felt awkward, but nobody seemed to pay us any attention, and her body was shaking. I hugged her back.

My mom took the baby and went to a corner of the room. I can't see her from where I am but I know where she is; she's gone there before. I guess it's her way to try and be "alone" in this place. She had tears on her face again and I know she's thinking of Dad and how she

123

could have lost Richard, too.

———————◆———————

On top of everything, we didn't even get any new provisions today. Richard said it was hard enough just carrying back the injured guy. Otherwise they might have tried a few smaller stores they passed. Some of the men are very angry about what happened, and talking revenge. Including Richard. The atmosphere is tense. I hate it. I want to go home, even if it is cold there.

Mr. Aronoff just walked over and told me to put out the candle. He's enforcing a curfew. Who does he think he is? The Gestapo?

I'll just write this one other thing that I almost forgot after what happened at Wal-Mart. A new family came today. Mr. Aronoff let them in because the father has a hand-crank radio. They've been trying since he got here to pick up another signal, but so far there's nothing. All we hear is static. It's sad to hear only static when you know there should be radio stations everywhere. It feels like the country has died.

SARAH
JANUARY 17
DAY SEVEN

Mr. Wendell is still with us.

"They brought a doctor last night, and he got the bullet out," Richard said. But he gave me an ominous look. "He's hanging on, but he's lost a lot of blood. And the doctor won't come back. He was on his way home, walking through town when they found him. He's been walking since it started, holing up wherever he can at night." He gave me a strange look. "He's had to trade drugs for shelter. But he's running out. He wouldn't even leave painkillers or antibiotics for when Wendell wakes up. Said he still has twenty miles to go before he makes it to his house and he needs something to barter with or he'll freeze to death on the way."

I felt hopeful when I heard this. "You see? People can make it home if they try long enough. Maybe Dad is getting close to us, only we don't know it!"

Richard grimaced. "Dad's not exactly a doctor, Sarah. He doesn't have drugs to trade or anything else that I know of."

124

"Still—there are decent people who could have offered him shelter. Ohio is full of nice people!"

"Oh, yeah?" He held up his arm, showing me the bandaged site where the bullet had nicked him. "This nice?" He looked around, taking in the whole area within our sight, and motioned out with his arm. "You see all these people? Not a single one offered to help find a doctor for that lady."

"Mr. Powell went for the doctor," I said.

"Yeah, after Mrs. Wendell threw a hissy fit."

"But he went."

Richard paused, slumping back against the chair, his legs pushing out, as he tried to get more comfortable. "If I wasn't so exhausted I would have. But most of these people could have gone. They didn't come to Wal-Mart; they weren't worn out like we were. It just shows you, people revert to animal instincts when they're threatened. And there's never help when you need it."

I gave him a stony stare. "Sometimes there is help when you need it." He just stared back, shaking his head.

Maybe Richard's right. There is no help. And we need it.

Mom is begging Richard not to go back to the store again. But Richard says he has to. He says it's his duty.

LATER

We now have armed guards at the library. I'm not sure I like it. Two of our men went back to the building and returned with guns. They said if they'd brought them to Wal-Mart maybe Mr. Wendell wouldn't have been shot. They could have defended our group. They'd only left them at the building because of their rush to get out safely during the fire.

So they're our self-appointed policemen.

Every day people try to join us here. I've watched from the window when a group of four young adults tried to come in but weren't allowed. There was shouting and cursing and carrying on but in the end they went away.

I have to sit out of view when I look outside. One day a passing man saw me in the window and then tried to come in. Of course he wasn't allowed to—but I felt responsible for his trying. Guilty, too, that I was in here and he wasn't. This is no paradise, but at least there's a fireplace, and bodies, lots of bodies, to keep us warm. There's a barrel fire at the street corner, and the people who huddle around it keep looking at our building. I think it's only a matter of time until a mob tries to get in and overpowers or outguns our guards.

The thing is, they must think we have it really good in here. Ha! Like them, we are doomed to starvation.

Not yet, though. We still have stuff from when Richard hit the kitchen downstairs, and from Wal-Mart. Mr. Aronoff is encouraging everyone to share what they have, but hoarding is the name of the game. I've seen secret stashes spill out here and there. They are quickly swiped out of sight, hidden again. I don't blame anyone. We're hoarding, too. But not Elizabeth!

She keeps offering me food. I don't know where her family is getting it. It's junk food, but it's calories, right? So I take it. I think Elizabeth is using the food as a way to ensure that I stay her friend. She doesn't need to do that but I'm not complaining because I hate feeling hungry.

Outside, the freezing weather continues.

I think it will be winter forever.

After I blew out the candle I couldn't sleep. So I worked on a verse I'm trying to memorize from the book of Psalms. I like what it says but I'm having trouble believing it.

"*I will never fail you. I will never abandon you.*" I said it over and over.

But I do feel abandoned. Hadn't God failed us?

A prayer came unbidden, and flew from my heart up to heaven.

We're living in the library. I want to go home!

126

PART FOUR

ANDREA

FEBRUARY 25
WEEK SIX

When we first came to the Hendersons' house, I lived in dread of them showing up. Imagine their (and our) dismay were they to appear and find out we'd been eating up their food and using their fuel. Sometimes I still feel guilty about it. But the dread is gone. We have no way to know if they're even alive.

Dad says it could take months for them to find a way back, and we'll repay what we've taken. But that's assuming we'll have access to our bank account at some point—and that somewhere there will actually be groceries for sale.

I heard him complaining to my mother about his retirement account. "What good is it?" he said. "It's useless to us now. We'll never see that money. It may as well not exist."

I hope that's not true. But I don't understand that stuff about money losing its value. I hated economics class. I just hope the United States isn't ruined forever.

Dad looks like a boxer who's losing the fight. Weary. Defeated. I guess it is a fight—with Nature or with God, or whatever caused this power outage. He's now using a hand saw to cut down branches in the backyard here. We've gone through all the wood that was here when we first came. Their yard has more trees than ours, which is a good thing.

He cuts for hours every day, because that wood stove is voracious. But fresh-cut branches don't burn well, so we're going through our linens, using strips of fabric dipped in vegetable oil to get them started. Oh—we're using OUR linens, not our neighbors'. I guess if this interminable winter continues for much longer we'll have to start using theirs, too.

One night dad disappeared and came back with our coffee table—in pieces. (Goodbye, coffee table.) We've also burned a clothes dresser, two wooden chairs, and the work table from our basement. I went home with Dad once when he was searching for something to burn. I wanted to get some clothes and things from my room. To my shock, I could hear him banging and yelling all the way from upstairs. He was in the basement.

At first when I heard him yelling, my heart froze. Did we have an intruder? I ran into the hallway and stood listening, wondering if I'd have to hide. But his yelling didn't change and the banging was steady, like he was working on something. I slowly descended the stairs and as I got closer to the basement door, it started to hit me. Dad was talking to himself. Yelling, actually.

I think he takes out all his anger and frustration on the furniture he's breaking up. I was embarrassed to hear him. He was growling out things, like, "So much for democracy! (bang!) So much for progress! (bang!) For technology! (bang!)" Then some cuss words. Then, more angry rants that I don't even want to write. I slunk back to my room and gathered what I wanted. Then I left while he was still down there.

I have no idea what piece of furniture he was breaking up this time. But it's easier to break up our possessions than it is to cut down frozen branches outdoors. It's unreal. This wicked cold spell won't go away. Mom, thankfully, no longer seems concerned about her furniture.

Yesterday the boys and I helped Dad on an outdoor scavenging mission—taking brush from anywhere we could find it. He led us to the only empty lot in the development—the last piece of property that no one purchased yet. It's on the end of the street, right after Mr. Herman's house. He came out while we were filling the sled and spoke to my father. (UGH. He gives me the creeps for sure.)

I don't know what they said but I saw them looking over at me. It made me feel weird. Mr. Herman's house has changed, too. I think he's a crazy person. He put barbed wire over his fence, which already hid his backyard entirely from view. And the front porch windows were actually boarded up. He told my dad it was just a precaution. A precaution *against what?*

ANDREA
FEBRUARY 26
WEEK SIX—DAY TWO

Some people from the other end of the plat were just here asking what we're doing for water these days. It was like the whole neighborhood came out. I guess people are thoroughly sick of hauling in snow and having to boil it. I don't blame them. Somebody knew we were in the wrong house—I heard my dad telling them we had permission to be here. It's a lie, but I certainly wasn't going to say anything.

Everyone had well water around here like us, wells that work on electricity. Dad said nothing about Jim's manual pump. Ours is still broken. I know my dad is planning on using Jim's well when the snow is gone. Why didn't he tell them about the pump? I'm sure there will be enough water for everyone in the plat. We don't see Jim much. He did have bad frostbite on his feet after walking home when the EMP hit. He hasn't been up and about a whole lot, since.

So it's almost the end of February and winter hasn't shown any signs of letting up. The amount of snow we've had is mind-blowing. Either I can't remember having this much snow in the past or we've just never had so much. Walking anywhere new, where there isn't already a foot trail, is difficult. Even with the hot wood stove here in this house, I still have to change and dress quickly—and we have a ton of clothes and stuff that needs washing. Doing laundry is out of the question because it takes so much water. We stick to spot-cleaning. I wear the same clothes for as long as possible. We may not have much in the way of food but one thing we do have is a lot of clothing.

No one is talking about how we're running low on food. The Henderson's pantry was a God-send, but it can't last forever. We've been here two weeks and we've made a palpable dent in the supplies. I have no idea what we'll be eating in two months. When I think how Mom used to go grocery shopping every week, I can't believe we've even made it this far. Pretty soon we'll have to eat stuff no one likes, such as baked beans and sauerkraut. I miss bread.

EVENING

Dad took the rifle off the mantel tonight and started messing with it. Cleaning it off and loading it and unloading it. I think Mom and I were both gaping at him. Mom asked, "WHAT are you going to do with that?"

He said, "Practice shooting. Tomorrow. I may need to hunt, soon."

We both stared at him. Dad hadn't hunted in my whole life that I knew of.

"Do you really think it will come to that?" Mom asked, wistfully.

He nodded. "Yup. Unless someone drops some stuff out of the sky." He continued examining his gun. I waited, expecting my mother to tell him what a bad idea it was. I've heard her say how she hates guns and dislikes hunters. When she fell silent, it felt eerie. It was like a scary moment in a movie when you know something bad is gonna happen.

"Do you really think you have a chance at catching something?"

"I appreciate that vote of confidence," he snapped.

Uh-oh, I thought. Here it comes. They hadn't been fighting for awhile so I guessed it was time for a big one. I started to leave the room.

"It just so happens," my dad continued, his voice like ice, "that I may need to protect this family."

"From what?" asked my mother. She made it sound like it was a ludicrous idea. I couldn't help it and I stopped to hear his answer. If we needed to be protected from something, I wanted to know about it. I think I was hoping he'd say, "From Mr. Herman." Instead, he shook his head towards the front of the house.

"Our *neighbors*, first of all."

Mom looked over at me. We were both stunned.

"From our neighbors," my mother repeated, as if trying to understand. He gave her a hard stare. "Or people like them. Today they came about water. Next time, who knows what they'll be asking for? Or, IF they'll be ASKING."

My mother looked troubled, but just shook her head. I could tell she didn't agree with my dad's actions, but she said nothing further. I was glad. Neither of us was in the mood to hear him lose his temper.

Every night is the same. We're all exhausted from hauling and boiling water and getting firewood and cooking over the stove and cleanup. So we sit around the room for a little while and then go to sleep. I'm even used to being with the family day in and day out, now. The boys have a pile of board games they rotate, though their favorite is RISK. (I hate that game.) Dad actually plays with them, which is nice.

I think about my friends and I feel as though I'm living in a separate world from them. As if they are all fine, going to school and getting on just like they used to. It feels like we're the only ones—us and our neighbors—who have suffered the loss of everything. Lexie and I used to text constantly, even during class. Now life is like living on the moon. I'm miserable.

ANDREA
WEEK SIX—DAY THREE

Jim stopped over and said someone tried to break into his house last night! He'd tried to shoot the intruder but missed. (I must have slept through it. A gun is loud, right?) It's hard to believe that my neighbor actually shot at someone. Dad got his rifle and they started talking guns and defense and bullets and that sort of stuff.

I saw Quentin sitting attentively and looking for the whole world like he was following the entire conversation. But by following his rapt gaze, I realized it was the gun itself that was really the object of his affection. I said, "Don't ever touch that gun! You could kill someone. Or yourself."

My dad spun his head around at us and said, "Maybe you ought have a lesson on gun safety, Quen."

My mom said, "He's too young for that!"

But dad said, "We'll be living around this firearm for now on, so I think he needs it."

"Me, too?" asked Aiden.

My father nodded.

My mother gave a loud, heavy sigh.

"Kids get hurt by guns if they don't know about gun safety," my dad said.

"Not if it isn't loaded," returned my mother.

"And if it isn't loaded," said my dad, "how am I supposed to defend this family if someone tries to break in here like they did at Jim's?"

I felt a full-fledged fight coming on and I stood up to leave the room, but my dad stopped me. "Stay where you are, Andrea!"

I sat back down. He went over to the gun and said, "You, (pointing at Aiden) "and YOU, (pointing at Quentin) AND you!" (pointing at me.) "Come with me!"

He made us follow him to the sliding doors to the back patio. He opened the door wide, letting in the freezing air from outside.

"It's cold," Aiden whimpered.

"Shut up and pay attention," Dad said. He lifted his gun and pointed it out at the yard. "Cover your ears," he growled.

My mom yelled out, "Don't! Don't do it, Peter!" But it was too late. Dad pulled the trigger. A crack so loud it hurt my whole head rang out, and I cried, "Ahhh!"

Aiden and Quentin, covering their ears, ran to my mother, who put the baby beside her on the sofa and let them scamper onto her lap.

"It was too loud, mommy! It was too loud!"

"I know," she said, and I could see tears in her eyes. I was so mad at my dad I wanted to scream but I was afraid to.

He calmly came back and put the gun back in place and then looked at my brothers.

"That's why you should never touch that gun," he said. "Understand?"

The boys nodded their heads, their eyes wide with fear.

Sometimes my dad is the biggest jerk in history.

"Are you crazy?" my mother said. "You could have damaged their hearing! You could have hurt Lily's ears! It made MY ears hurt, from in here."

He said nothing for a moment, then turned and looked at my mom, still holding the boys against her.

"I don't know," he said, lightly. "Maybe I am crazy." And he walked out of the room.

"He doesn't mean that, Andrea," my mother said. She must have seen my eyes. I was probably staring at my dad with disgust.

Afterwards I was too frazzled to just sit there so I got up and walked around the house. As I looked at this home, which was every bit as classy and attractive as ours, I started feeling like it was really a dressed up graveyard.

Really. Think about it. Just like a cemetery, it's filled with dead things. In the kitchen the counters are dotted with useless appliances. They sit there like ghosts, mocking us. The food processor, expensive Kitchen-Aid mixer, microwave--even the electric kettle--they're all useless. Mrs. Henderson must be a lot like my mom, because they have similar taste in top of the line appliances. Her kitchen has a different color scheme but like ours has granite countertops and a tiled floor. Our kitchen has Italian tile—I don't know what kind of tile this is here, but they're equally stupid now. Because you know what tile is like in a cold house? COLD.

All of these surfaces are stone cold. Sometimes my mom wears two layers of plastic gloves when she's preparing food. The little bit of food that we have to make do with. But all the expensive stainless steel and tile and granite is absolutely useless! We're hungry and thirsty while we drown in affluent junk.

What a joke.

Only I'm not laughing.

EVENING

There's less tension in the house tonight. I think that's because we've accepted the facts. What are the facts? That we're living in 21st century pioneer days. My white collar dad is going to start hunting. Only we're worse off than the pioneers because they knew what they were in for; they knew how to cook without stoves and heat a home without central heat. They knew how to grow food. They knew how to save enough for winter, but we didn't save up any food.

We never dreamed we'd have to.

LEXIE

FEBRUARY 25
WEEK SIX, DAY ONE

The weather is still *freezing* cold. I've never seen our wood pile go down so fast. Yesterday a man showed up at the front door asking if he could buy some wood from us. Dad refused as kindly as he could, but the man got frantic. Said his family had gone through all their propane and had been trying to gather enough wood for a fire, but the snow cover was making it next to impossible. Even what wood he could find was too wet to burn.

"All we've got left for heat are candles," he said, with tears in his eyes.

Dad sold him about half a cord, but told him not to come back. We aren't sure we have enough wood to last the rest of the winter since we've never used it exclusively as a heat source before. So then we spent hours hauling our wood indoors to the basement from the wood shed to keep it safe.

"Isn't it a fire hazard?" I asked, as we carried down the first load.

"It could be," Dad replied, "if there's a spark." He eyed me steadily. I'll put an extra fire extinguisher by the stairs. But if that man comes back, he won't be looking to buy wood next time.

"What do you mean?" I asked him.

"He'll know we don't have enough to sell him any; he'll be ready to help himself."

"He seemed like a nice man," I said, remembering the tears for the sake of his family.

"I'm sure he is, when he's had enough to eat and can keep his family warm. But desperate times can bring out the worst in people. May as well not flaunt that we have something he wants."

"Are we going to bring it all down?" I asked, daunted by the size of the task. I was hauling it down in a heavy-duty canvas log holder, but I could see myself getting weary of this really soon.

"No," he said, taking my latest haul and stacking it neatly against one wall a few feet from the stairs. "We'll leave enough out there to make it look convincing. Either that guy or someone else can take it, and we should still be okay. Let's pray we don't have an extended winter. We still have a propane heater I haven't used and a few canisters of propane. We'll get by."

After all that work, Mom broke open a five-gallon storage bucket full of prepared freeze-dried food as a special treat. Our storage buckets were an investment. Our storage room is lined with them. They stack five high to the ceiling and each one is labeled with its contents. Up to now we'd finished off what had been in our refrigerator and freezers, thanks to having the generator. Then we'd started on the pantry, eating a lot of spaghetti and canned sauce, or rice and beans, with canned stew or chili thrown in now and then for good measure.

So now we were opening a storage bucket. As we dug in to it, I got hit with a reality check. I'd seen the buckets for so long, lined up and stacked neatly, but we never touched them. They were strictly for a long-term emergency. Still, I'd read the content labels Mom put on them, wishing at times that we could use some of them. There were buckets of the essentials, of course; flour, rice, oats, wheat berries, beans, and sugar. But others said things like, "Snacks, Granola Bars, Nuts, and Dried Fruit." Or, "Cocoa, Chocolate Bars, Baking Supplies."

Here we were, finally opening one and it felt surreal.

Most of the buckets were filled by Mom, with me helping. There's a couple full of canned meats like ham, chicken, salmon and tuna. One is nothing but sardines and clams and oysters. We don't usually eat that stuff. I asked my mother why we were storing them and she said a few sardines provide enough protein for one adult for a whole day.

"If things get really bad and you're hungry," she said, "you'll eat it." I guess she's right.

Anyways, the freeze-dried food was from an online survival store. It cost a lot, so I knew this was a treat. Even the twins gathered around with interest when Mom opened the bucket and gave the appropriate "ooohs" and "aaaahs," which made me laugh. They didn't even know what the food was, but they were duly impressed anyways! (It was lasagna, twenty-four servings, according to the label; which will probably be enough for two or three meals, because mom says what the manufacturer calls a serving is usually ridiculously small).

Dad has started accompanying me when I do my barn chores. Milking, feeding the horses, cleaning the stalls, feeding the rabbits and chickens, and so on. It feels really weird having him come along. He stays around watching out like a vigilante, holding his shotgun. When I asked him why, he said the Buchanans had already had to stop people from stealing their animals! I couldn't believe it.

I ask Dad every day if we can get Andrea and her family. He still says no.

LEXIE
FEBRUARY 27
WEEK SIX, DAY TWO

I was looking for my dad and found him in the basement. He had guns and ammo laid out on a table and was emptying out a gun cabinet, doing routine maintenance on his stock.

He looked up and saw me. "Hey, baby. What's up?"

I shrugged. "Not much. Just taking a break from the girls."

He nodded, wiping down a rifle. "Good," he said. "Let's do a review."

I knew immediately what he meant and smiled. I like doing reviews with Dad. Since I was little he and my mom have pounded certain things into my head about the rights of a free people. Gun rights were high on that list.

"Why do we keep firearms?" he asked, just as he'd asked me a thousand times before. I gave the answer I'd memorized but it wasn't coming only from memory. I love these quotes and believe them with all my heart.

"'Because no free man shall ever be debarred the use of arms,' Thomas Jefferson."

"Why else?"

"'A free people ought to be armed,' George Washington. And, 'I prefer dangerous freedom over peaceful slavery,' Thomas Jefferson." Dad's face hadn't changed. He was still intent on cleaning and inspecting his guns but I knew he was enjoying this as much as I was.

"Tell me more," he said.

I closed my eyes to concentrate, to see the beautiful words from the founding fathers that I'd painstakingly memorized as part of my home school curriculum. "'Firearms are a right and a necessity to a free people and the means by which not only political power but public order is maintained.'" He smiled.

"One more."

I took a breath, smiling too. "'To disarm the people is the most effectual way to enslave them,' George Mason, father of the Bill of Rights and the Virginia Declaration of Rights."

"And what do you think about these quotes?" he asked. To answer him (and I guess to show off a little, too) I chose another morsel from my memorized cache as my answer. "'To preserve liberty, it is essential that the whole body of the people always possess arms, and be taught alike, especially when young, how to use them,' Richard Henry Lee." He looked up and nodded approvingly.

"I'm glad you and Mom taught me these quotes, Dad," I said.

"I'm glad you're glad." He winked at me. "But we haven't actually spoken about them in awhile. Our principles may be put to the test if people start getting desperate." Looking at the rifle he was wiping down in his hands, he said, "I'm afraid that with what's happened to our country we'll be finding out firsthand just how necessary it is to have our guns—not only for our freedom but our safety."

I felt a mild stab of fear and looked at my dad's face, startled, because his tone was so solemn. Glancing at the rifle in his hands and at the other firearms spread out on the table, I thought it hard to believe, actually, that we would ever really need them as *defensive* weapons. I'd always enjoyed shooting as a sport and even though I was a staunch believer in gun rights, I had never really thought about *our* weapons as necessary to survival. That had always been true for other people, in other times of history. It was important to maintain that freedom, I thought, but not because I'd ever considered that we would need the guns for our personal safety. That's why it had unnerved me when I had to take Dad's Glock with me after leaving him with Roy on the day of the pulse.

My dad met my eyes and seemed to read the doubts in my mind. In a serious voice he said, quoting, "'*Arms discourage and keep the invader and plunderer in awe, and preserve order in the world as well as property. Horrid mischief would ensue were (the law-abiding) deprived the use of them,' Thomas Paine.*"

137

"I know. But I guess that was *really* true back in Colonial days." I was trying to deny that we could possibly be in any danger now, even with the EMP and the widespread scarcity hitting the country.

My dad stopped what he was doing, and gave me a quizzical look. "Darlin'," he said, "Even *before* the pulse gun owners have been saving their lives and their possessions from thieves and criminals every single day. Gun rights have been just as important now as they ever have been at any time in history."

"How come we never heard about that on the news?" I asked.

"The news media is very selective about what they broadcast. You know that. They don't want the country to know how many lives are saved, how many rapes never happen, or how many would-be thieves are stopped because of legally armed citizens. You have to read the right magazines and unbiased news sources like the Drudge Report to get the news that's suppressed by the mainstream media." He paused, picked up his rifle and continued cleaning it. "Even Drudge doesn't give all the news, such as miraculous healings or other miracles that occur—you have to watch CBN or read the right Christian periodicals for that."

I sighed. "Now we can't watch anything, and I guess we won't be getting any magazines anymore."

He took a breath and shook his head in agreement. "That's right. But don't forget—" and he paused to look at me solemnly again. "'*The Constitution asserts that all power is inherent in the people; that they may exercise it by themselves; that it is their right and duty to be at all times armed.*'"

"Thomas Paine," I said, recognizing the words—or so I thought.

His eyes sparkled at me. "Wrong. Mr. Jefferson, again."

"Darn!" I stayed there awhile longer enjoying being with my dad, and he had me clean one of the rifles to make sure I remembered how to do it. I had to put on plastic gloves first, since the cleaning elements are harsh.

"If we hadn't already got these," Dad said, looking over his cache, "they'd be about impossible to buy now. And that's IF we were near a store that sold them, which we're not."

"Why would they be impossible to buy?" I asked.

"They've sold out by now. People are realizing survival is the name of the game. Those that can take care of themselves may come through okay." He paused. He closed the first gun closet, hesitating over whether to lock it as usual. Safety concerns won out over worries about needing the equipment in a hurry, and he finally locked it up. Then he opened a second smaller cabinet next to the first one. "Those that can't—well, let's just say they're in for more than a rude awakening."

I sat down and crossed my arms and just frowned at him. He'd reminded me of my worries about Andrea and her family.

"Dad, we can't just forget about Andrea." He kept polishing a pistol, but I could tell he'd heard me. Andrea was not my parents' favorite friend of mine, mostly because they weren't satisfied that she or her parents were Christians. The Pattersons didn't attend church regularly, and my dad had met Mr. Patterson and found it difficult to warm up to him. I guess they were afraid that Andrea would be a bad influence on me. But she isn't. I know she hasn't given the claims of Jesus Christ enough thought, but I always figured we'd have time to discuss that. I shouldn't have assumed anything.

He nodded. "When everyone gets here later on, we'll pray about it."

"Good." I didn't tell him I'd forgotten about the study. Before the pulse, we were part of a small group Bible study with about five other families. Tonight two of those families—the Wassermans and the Buchanans—were actually coming to our house to resume our study! The EMP had stopped most of life, but we'd managed to communicate with both families via Dad's ham radio. Dad had taken a course to get his ham license, as had Mr. Wasserman and Mr. Buchanan. They'd all made Faraday cages for their radios and now we were benefiting from all that prep.

If I'd known where to find it and how to use it I could have saved myself that long ride to the Buchanan's that time, to ask for help. And get this—Dad's made contact with people as far as India, because there are so many ham operators in the country. Some radios act as repeaters, sending signals further and further on, sort of like a web. So people in India know about the EMP, and they told him most of Ontario was also affected, but mostly it's just the United States. The good news about that is it encourages us to think it was a solar flare and not a terrorist's weapon that started it all. A terrorist group did claim responsibility but apparently no one is taking them seriously.

Anyways, initially there were a few pockets of America that were unscathed—northern coastal Washington, coastal Maine, and very southern Florida. But the subsequent failures of the infrastructure have now taken down their electricity, too.

When I really think about the scope of the EMP, it seems too unbelievable to comprehend.

But I'm excited we'll be having Bible study here tonight! I can't believe I actually let it slip my mind! We don't go anywhere these days of course, and we see no one, so it feels like a really big treat. Plus, we haven't been to church since the pulse. We could ride our horses to get there, but most people don't have horses; Pastor lives ten miles from church and doesn't own a horse, so there's no point in going. I miss church. I miss all our friends. I miss worship. I love the way it feels when the band gets going and the whole congregation is standing and singing together. We have great worship leaders and talented musicians. I love singing my heart out to the Lord—even though I don't have a great voice, granted.

At least tonight we'll see two families and best of all, I'll get to see Blake. I hope I have time to heat water for a bath so I can wash my hair.

I was lost in thoughts about seeing Blake when Dad suggested we do a little target practice. I really enjoy that but I realized mom would probably need my help upstairs to prepare for the evening. Every day has work above all the stuff we did in the past to keep the homestead going. Getting our cooking water, hauling wood to the stove, and so on. With company coming, I knew there'd be even more chores.

As if she'd read my mind, her voice came from the stairwell at just that moment:

"Lexie—you down there? I need you."

Upstairs, as Mom opened a storage bucket of rice and beans, I had another "unreal" moment, the kind where I grasp the implications of what our lives are now, and what they will be for a long time. They come in waves, these reality hits, striking at times such as when you don't flush the toilet after using it because we only flush them once a night. (To conserve water; we save our water from doing dishes in a five-gallon bucket and haul it into the bathroom and use that to cause a gravity flush. Once a day is usually all we can do. Thankfully we have private septic lines that aren't stopped up like municipal systems might be without electricity.)

Other things jar me into awareness that normal life is gone, too:

Flicking a light switch from habit and remembering it doesn't work; feeling like it's always a little darker in the house than it should be—and we have lots of oil lamps. But the brightness is still subdued compared to the usual white effervescence of electric lights. Or going to heat water for tea and remembering there's no electric kettle—everything takes longer now.

Each day brings fresh waves of what it means to live without electricity, and each new day I have to grasp again the ramifications of what life is, and what it's become. It's sort of scary, sort of depressing.

I'm worried about Andrea and Sarah.

EVENING

When the Buchanans arrived, they gave us a much welcome jar of peaches, canned by Mrs. Buchanan the previous summer. We've got canned goods from farmer's markets and other places where people sold their home-canned items, but Mrs. Buchanan's peaches are the best! Anyways, I saw Blake getting his guitar out, so I went over to him.

"Hey, Blake."

"Lexie." He nodded, glancing at me briefly, reassuringly. He hadn't smiled, but that's Blake. He's tall and slim and unassuming, and quiet more often than not. As usual, he seemed utterly intent on what he was doing, which, in this case was tuning his instrument. He strummed it softly, checking the strings for dissonance. I sometimes felt it was an intrusion into his world, if I spoke to him. But I needed to speak to him.

"Did your mom tell you what I asked about getting to my friend's house?"

He nodded. "She did."

I was breathless. "Well? Do you think you can help me?" I knew it was a long-shot. Not only did the Buchanans need Blake around their own home but, for all his talents and smarts, Blake wasn't an accomplished horseman. He didn't love riding the way I did and he practiced much less often.

He shook his head, and my hopes dropped. "Sorry." He looked up. "I'd do it, if it was up to me. My dad says no. We can't afford to have me going off where I might get hurt when the family's survival depends somewhat on me."

A deep disappointment filled me. "What makes you think you'd get hurt?" I asked. He was just like my dad, worrying!

He actually put his guitar down and gave me his full attention. He had very nice amber-brownish eyes. I felt a pleasant sensation run through me which I hoped did not show on my face.

"People are unpredictable," he said. "It might be okay, or we might run into a nut-case. We might run into someone so desperate that at the sight of our horses, they'd be willing to fight for one." He paused. "I'm not exactly fast on horseback like you."

"You'd be fast enough," I said.

"Maybe. But maybe not in an encounter with a psycho. It's a dangerous world out there."

The others started taking seats in the room so I knew we couldn't talk more right then. But I gave Blake a disappointed look. "I hear your father talking, but I don't hear Blake Buchanan talking."

I hoped I'd given him something to think about.

After that, he played guitar while the rest of us sang. Mrs. Buchanan always brought handouts with hymns for the evening, and we used those. Suddenly, life felt sweet—almost like things were normal again. When the Wassermans arrived and joined us—there are five of them, Mr. and Mrs. W. and three kids—the room even began to feel as warm as it had when central heat still worked.

Mr. Wasserman gave a short talk, reading some Scripture in lieu of a proper Bible study. It was the first time we'd all been together since the pulse, so it made sense that we'd be discussing what happened. He suggested the grid going down might be a judgment of God on our nation. He pointed out that the destruction of Jerusalem was judgment, the destruction of Sodom and Gomorrah; He talked about the millions and millions of aborted children, the gay movement, and how these things are clearly sin according to Scripture and could have brought down judgment.

I felt there was some merit in his argument, but I also had problems with it. Before I thought too much about it, I'd spoken up.

"Our nation was also the fattest on the planet. So we're guilty of gluttony too. Does that mean we're being judged for it? How can you pick out certain sins and decide that God's judgment is on account of them?" I turned red no sooner than I'd spoken. I didn't usually challenge adults other than my parents, and wasn't sure what had come over me to make me do it now. I guess in the back of my mind I was thinking of this gay kid at school. He was a nice, harmless guy, and it made me resent the implication that we were being judged as a country for homosexuality.

"I'm only speculating," Mr. Wasserman admitted. "But Sodom and Gomorrah were definitely judged for sexual sins; and a biblical worldview includes the idea that catastrophic events that affect the health of a whole nation are usually the direct result of divine judgment—either that, or they're the natural results of sin, of straying from God's principles of living, which is an indirect judgment, a self-inflicted judgment. Some ungodly practices carry within themselves the seeds of destruction and hardship."

"What do you mean?" I figured he was talking about alcoholism or drug abuse. But Mr. Wasserman was still on the idea of sins of nations.

"Well, take India," he said. "There are millions of undernourished or even starving people in that country, while at the same time they don't eat beef because they hold cows as sacred. I'm not saying beef is the answer for all food needs, but that's one example of an ungodly practice causing unnecessary suffering. Cattle roam around untouched where hunger is rampant because India is by and large a pagan nation. If you look at history, wherever Christianity has spread, the people prosper. All of Europe and the Americas prospered under Christianity. Heck, the ability to read was only saved from extinction in Western civilization by monks in the Middle Ages. Christianity brings blessings. History proves it."

"I don't think the American Indians would agree with you," Blake interjected, wryly. I was grateful to him for joining me with a challenge of his own.

"It wasn't Christianity that killed or drove out the Indians," Mr. Wasserman replied, nonplussed. "It was, in some cases, diseases that the white man brought—unintentionally. No one said, 'Hey, let's get the Indians sick so they'll die off.' It was an unfortunate thing that happened, but not the fault of anyone's Christian beliefs. And as for war and killing, it happened on both sides, and the government got involved. That isn't Christianity killing anyone, that's government doing it."

I suddenly noticed the rest of the room had fallen silent, listening to our debate. My cheeks flamed afresh. Dad and I often got into debates over issues because we enjoyed it, but I'd taken on Mr. Wasserman and

I felt embarrassed.

My mom spoke up. "Honey," she said, speaking directly to me. "I know you've got friends at school who claim to be homosexual and so it bothers you, the idea that God abhors homosexuality. I just want to say," and she looked around at everyone, "that there is probably NO way for any of us to understand the magnitude of how much our sin— any sin—dishonors and insults an absolutely holy and glorious God. But just because we can't plumb the depths of how great an offense our sin is, doesn't mean it is any less offensive to God Almighty. So whether this catastrophe to our nation is because of any sin in particular is less important than knowing that EVERY sin can be forgiven—and we, who are in Christ, are already forgiven."

I couldn't disagree with my mother on a theological basis, but I felt like she'd just made it harder to focus on the issue at hand—what had caused the EMP.

"What do you think caused the power outage, Blake?" I asked. I knew he'd have a theory; and I knew he wouldn't misunderstand me or think I wanted his theological perspective. Blake was, first and foremost, a young scientist. I always pictured him in the future wearing a lab coat somewhere and doing top secret work for the government. Blake knew more about most things than most people knew about anything. Dad affectionately called him "an encyclopedia of useless information," but most of what he knows isn't useless. At least I don't think so.

I was right about him having a theory. He didn't even have to think about it.

"There was definitely an EMP so the only question is whether it was solar or a terrorist attack. If it was a solar event," he went on, "it was likely due to a buildup of magnetic energy in the sun's atmosphere. This energy builds up, see, and then suddenly gets released all at once. It literally flares out, arcing into space—and towards earth—at a million miles an hour. A solar flare is probably the most powerful explosion in the solar system that we know of," he continued. "It's like a billion nukes going off at once."

Sometimes Blake would launch into explanations that were much more detailed than I needed, but that was Blake. If you asked him a question, he fully expected you to be interested in the entire answer, no matter how long or technical or convoluted it might be. His answer right now was no different, only this time I wasn't bored. I wanted to hear every last detail. I wanted to know what had changed our lives so irreversibly and catastrophically. I do believe that God is fully Sovereign, even over space events, but I was still intrigued by how it had happened. I guess I wasn't the only one who felt that way because we all sat engrossed, willing to hear Blake out, feeling awed and yet horrified by what he was saying.

"If it was terrorists," he went on, "they would have had to set off an explosion really high in the atmosphere, like a mile or two up." He looked around at us as he spoke, coming alive with energy. It made him seem extra good-looking, when he got all enthusiastic and onto what, for him, was a hot topic. I wasn't so engrossed that I couldn't stop to admire his intelligent eyes that were alive with feeling, or his brown wavy hair and the beginnings of a beard, while he spoke.

"You mean a nuclear bomb?" Mom asked, lowering her voice. The twins and the Wasserman children had been absently playing with toys on the floor but suddenly they ceased playing, all except the youngest Wasserman who was only three. They looked up, possibly because of the word "bomb," but I suspected it had more to do with my mother's lowered tone of voice. A lowered tone of voice in an adult is like a siren call to a kid to pay attention. They know they're not supposed to hear whatever's being said, and so of course they want to. Mom noticed their sudden interest.

"Lanie and Laura, could you take your friends and show them the toys from the safe room?" she asked.

"We're playing with those toys right now, Mom," said Laura, holding up an easy-sew card in the shape of an elephant. A thick yellow thread of yarn dangled out of it. Lainie nodded emphatically. "Yeah."

"Okay, but go and check on Justin. Let me know if he's sleeping soundly." Justin was in for the night so I knew it was just an excuse to get them from the room. They seemed to know it too, and shook their heads as one (twins have an annoying way of doing that).

Dad said, "You heard your mother." They frowned, but rose to obey. Three-year old Emma Wasserman, seeing the others leaving, got up on her adorably chunky little legs to hurry after, dragging a big baby doll. When they were gone, Blake continued.

"It would have to be nuclear to cause the EMP. So the detonation would set off this instantaneous flux of gamma rays, see? Followed by an enormous electromagnetic energy field disturbance. The rays have photons which produce high energy free electrons, and these electrons get caught in the earth's atmosphere; and then they in turn cause this high voltage electromagnetic wave, called a pulse, an EMP."

"Why does it take everything out?" Mom asked.

"Because it's a horizon event; in other words, it affects everything within the line of sight of the explosion, all the way to the horizon, including our satellites; but then, see, our own infrastructure would keep it going, so it fries more systems, traveling along wires and conductors, spreading its catastrophic effects as it goes. The magnitude of the energy is too much for almost all circuitry it encounters."

"How far an area might be affected, son?" My dad was probably wondering if the reports he'd heard on his radio were accurate, and wanted to confirm their likelihood of being true.

"They figure one blast could reach about 1,000 miles," Blake said. "If there was more than one—who knows?"

My mom looked at my dad. "So this is a nuclear attack? Shouldn't we all be concerned about fallout, then?" She sounded upset.

Blake saw her reaction and seemed surprised. "No, we're not sure," he added, quickly.

"No," echoed Mrs. Buchanan. "We don't think it was."

"We were just being careful, staying in the safe room," added Mr. Buchanan. "In reality, if it was a nuclear attack and ground zero was close by? Our safe room wouldn't be safe enough. It's not shielded enough, but if it was a high-atmosphere blast, it was good enough."

Blake clarified. "We think it was a solar flare."

There was a moment of silence. Blake seemed like he had more to say, but hesitated.

"Is there more?" I asked, to encourage him.

He looked at me with what I thought was gratitude. I happen to know it's important to Blake to get out all that he thinks is important to a subject.

"If it was a nuke, there would have been significant fallout near the blast, but again, it was so high in the atmosphere that there wouldn't be huge gamma particles—instead, the worst offenders were probably dissipated over a large area, instead of causing a so-called hot spot on the ground." He gave me a significant look, because we all remembered how Dad and I and the school kids and Roy had been outdoors for hours after the pulse. If the blast had been close by, we would have suffered radiation sickness or even death.

"I mean, we still can't be one hundred percent sure," he added, spreading out his hands in a helpless gesture. "Most fallout happens immediately, and we really only know about the type of fallout from bombs that detonate on the ground. A ground detonation causes thousands of tons of earth to pulverize into trillions of particles that are contaminated by the blast; these are what gets carried up into that mushroom cloud and then carried by wind. They also start falling immediately, which is the usual type of fallout."

"So, the closer you are to the detonation site, the worse the fallout, but it follows a plume, so it depends on the wind and where it takes it; the largest particles fall right away, but the smallest particles can travel tens of thousands of miles before falling to the ground, and by the time they do hit the ground, they're already less dangerous due to decay. See, the good news is that the worst radioactive offenders begin to decay immediately; but even the smallest particles, those that are invisible and could be inhaled, also decay. I guess I'm saying that even if it was a nuke from an enemy, there may still be some residual fallout, but it shouldn't be significant."

I remembered what I'd read in the encyclopedia, and nodded. Most people believe you can't survive a nuclear fallout, but the facts say otherwise.

When everyone was silent, he continued. He probably had pages more information in that encyclopedic head of his.

"Unfortunately, radioactive elements are absorbed by everything—earth, air, water, clothing—" he paused. "And snow." He glanced at me. It was snowing the day it happened. He added hurriedly, "But actually no one knows for sure how much fallout would reach the surface of the earth from an atmospheric blast high enough to cause an EMP, since a nuclear blast so high in the atmosphere has never been tested. One thing's for sure, though—if there was a lot of fallout in our area, it would settle like dust. We didn't see any evidence of unusual dust after the pulse."

"Of course, we stayed in the safe room for seventy-two hours," put in Mr. Buchanan, "so if there was any dust and debris from a blast we should've missed the worst of it. But you two would be sick by now, or even dead, if there was significant radiation."

147

"So there could still be fallout," said my mom, trying to clarify what we'd learned.

"Yeah, secondhand fallout, so to speak, in the soil and water and even the air, but again, the longer the time elapses between the radioactivity occurring and subsequent exposure, the less radioactivity there will be. Even if you were, say, close to a ground blast, after two weeks in a shelter you could probably start venturing outdoors. Every day would get safer than the day before."

"I thought radioactive elements lasted forever," I said.

He frowned. "Radioactive decay happens rapidly at first; it does slow down over time, but levels drop quickly. The first forty-eight hours after a blast are the deadliest. And the longer radioactive particles are airborne, the less dangerous they are." I could see he was about to go off on a technical scientific discussion, so I asked quickly, "But if a solar pulse caused this, there wouldn't be that danger of radiation, right?"

He looked at me. I swear I could see the wheels in his head shifting gears.

"Not immediately. Very unlikely."

"So a bomb would mean radiation, but a solar pulse wouldn't," Mom said.

"Well, here's where it gets complicated about radiation," he said, sitting forward in his chair. I felt proud of how knowledgeable he was, and felt myself smiling a little in his direction, despite the grim subject of the discussion.

"Whether or not it was solar or a nuclear weapon," he said, his eyes sweeping the room at us, "whatever was big enough to cause the pulse is big enough to take down operations at most nuclear plants. The problem then is failure of safety systems, such as what happened at Fukushima after the Tsunami. So again, just as the infrastructure carries the pulse further than the initial blast could, the same infrastructure takes it into nuclear power plants and causes them to fail. As far as I know, the government hasn't put protections into place to safeguard our nuclear plants against a pulse of such magnitude."

There was a momentary silence while we all digested these facts. I shifted uncomfortably in my seat. He continued, "But there are back up systems in nuclear power plants that should work, maybe for a week or two. IDEALLY, they'll hang in there long enough to power down the plants so that we don't get Fukushimas happening all over the country."

Mrs. Buchanan said, "Tell them how some things might still work."

"Mom, nearly all solid-state semi-conductors would be destroyed," he said.

"What does that mean?" I asked.

Blake shook his head. "It means TV's, radios, transistors, pacemakers, life-support systems, computers, automobile ignition systems—everything you've already noticed—anything with integrated electronic circuits are wiped out."

There was a collective silence. Of course we already knew these things weren't working, but had we really stopped to consider what it meant for some people? Those in hospitals on life support, for instance? Those in need of limited supplies of medications?

"Yes, but tell them what you told me," Mrs. Buchanan insisted. "That some things could have survived."

"It's not likely," he said, "but fine. Okay, if you had a small system somewhere that wasn't dependent on any long wires; if it was say, underground and protected by enough metal, or concrete, or even dirt, theoretically it could still work."

"Like our ham radio in the Faraday cage," put in my Dad.

Blake nodded. "Exactly."

"You mean, if we had a PC that was protected, there's still a world wide web out there that we could connect to?" Mrs. Wasserman asked. She was younger than my mom and Mrs. Buchanan, a pretty brunette with her hair in a long braid.

"Only if it wasn't a global event, and if your connection isn't dependent on the system that got destroyed."

"If only we'd protected more than our radio," her husband said.

"We all feel that way," put in my mom.

"Don't feel bad," Blake said. "Even the military isn't sure how to protect their systems, or what level of protection would work. It's kinda hard to test things when you need a nuclear blast to set up the test situation."

"But why can't they fix it?" I asked. "Why does everyone assume we're going to be without power for a year or more? Dad said it could be many years before we see it restored."

Blake was nodding. "See, we depend upon large transformers to power the grid across the nation. These are extra high-voltage, multiton units, and probably the first things that got fried. If it was a coordinated attack by an enemy, they almost certainly took out our transformer manufacturer, too. Even IF we had enough residual power to do the manufacturing necessary to make new ones, we only have the capability—at our best—to make about fifty a year. Then there's the problem of how to get them where you need them when they weigh 600 tons or more. Plus, most of the biggest transformers in this country are non-domestic. And it costs tens of millions of dollars for a single unit. Under the circumstances, unless the US has already pre-purchased or pre-ordered these units—AND protected them—they won't be quickly or easily replaced."

"So you think the whole country is in this mess?" I asked. Secretly, I'd held out hope that maybe it was only the tri-state area or the Midwest that had been affected. I refused to believe Dad's source from India. Now I felt that hope vaporizing.

Blake nodded. "Probably 85% of it, maybe more."

Mr. Buchanan slapped his knee and began to rise. "It's getting late, folks. We have more to pray about than ever, now that Blake's explained what we're facing. Why don't we pray and wrap things up for tonight?"

I am usually not too shy to pray in our small group meetings. I know these people well enough to feel safe with them, and I can concentrate on talking to the Lord. I told the group about the Pattersons and my friend Andrea, but I got teary talking about them and didn't want to pray aloud after that. I didn't trust myself to pray without crying and I didn't want to cry in front of Blake. But everyone else did pray for people they knew who may be suffering, either friends or distant family members. So I found my voice and prayed for the Pattersons after all. I got pretty emotional, as I feared, but I felt like everyone was on the same page with me.

Blake met my eyes afterwards, which I could feel were still teary.

"Hey," he said, coming over to me. His parents were saying their goodbyes to my folks, so I figured we had a moment.

"I'll ask my dad again about taking you to your friend's house. We've checked on other people from church, so maybe he'll change his mind."

"Thanks," I said. My voice came out flat. It sounded lame, but I really meant it. Then it hit me, what he'd said.

"You've checked on other people? Like, going to their homes?"

He nodded. "Yeah. The ones who live close by. Your friend's house is far—that's the zinger."

"I guess so."

He eyed me a moment, thinking. "Try not to worry too much. God has always kept a remnant, a people for himself, no matter how much devastation happened around or to them. So far, we're part of that remnant. Maybe the Lord will return soon but if not, we are still HERE. We still worship God."

I smiled. This was the best thing I'd heard all night. "Yeah. My dad has mentioned that, too. Thanks for the reminder."

Then Blake did something he'd never done before. My heart started hammering silly. I say 'silly,' because it was such a small thing and yet it had that effect on me. He took my hand and squeezed it, even lifting it up a bit. For a moment I thought he might kiss it, like a knight of old! But all he did was squeeze it, smile gently, and then turned and left.

"See you next week," he said.

I nodded and stood there like an idiot, my hand tingling. Blake was not a demonstrative guy, so I took this as a great sign, coming from him. Overall, it had been a sobering evening, a depressing discussion. Prayer had helped, but somehow that parting squeeze to my hand helped even more.

———◆———

As I tried to sleep I kept thinking about what Blake said. Maybe there were things that still worked. I thought of people out in this cold, people unprepared for winter without power, and how they needed help. I remembered Jesus's words in Matthew when he was warning his disciples about the destruction of Jerusalem. He said, "Pray that your flight may not be in winter." And, "Alas for women who are pregnant and for those who are nursing infants in those days!" I can't help but feel these words apply to our situation today, even though I know he was talking about what happened to Jerusalem in 70AD.

There are babies in each of our families: Andrea's, mine and Sarah's, because they have her cousin. I pray for them as I pray for other things. But I don't feel hopeful.

LEXIE
FEBRUARY 28
WEEK SIX—DAY THREE

I dreamt of Andrea last night. We were in school at lunch with
Sarah, the way we usually ate together. Also as usual, a few guys had
come and sat down across from us, not because of me or Sarah, but
because of Andrea. Sarah and I were trying to ignore the guys, while
Andrea was being all serious with them, like kissing one of them, and
completely ignoring me and Sarah. She was laughing and flirting.
Finally the guys left and I turned to Andrea.

"You don't care about us," I said. "You just want attention." She
started yelling and yelling, standing up and getting all upset. I can't
remember everything she yelled, or maybe most of it was gibberish, but
she was really mad, only she wasn't mostly mad at me. She was mad at
herself—and I think, her mother. Or maybe it was her father. I'm not
sure.

Anyways, I do remember her saying, "YOU DON'T
UNDERSTAND! I NEED THESE GUYS!"

When I woke up, I thought about the dream and felt sorry for
Andrea. I have to admit that she was a big flirt at school. She really did
seem to *need* the attention of boys, though I don't understand why.
(Exactly what she said to me, in the dream!) I don't know what the
dream meant, but it got me thinking again about how Andrea and her
family are probably in need of help. How could they not be?

Sometimes in the past Mom would announce that we weren't going
to rotate food for awhile. In other words, we'd live like most people,
paycheck to paycheck (though Dad's paychecks were far fewer than
most people's, since he makes his money from farming). She'd time
how long we could go without making a trip to the grocery store, and
the longest we could seem to go was about two weeks. This is not using
anything stored, as if we didn't have it. We'd run out of toilet paper, or
fruit, or aspirin—SOMETHING that we needed to buy from a store. So
I figure most people are like that. They need to go shopping every week
or two. And we've had no way to shop since this started, and if they
didn't store extra food, that means they're way past just running out of
a few things. They're probably desperate.

At breakfast my dad seemed pretty content. Mom had cooked up some home-cured bacon from the root cellar and Dad loves bacon. He could eat it every day, only Mom doesn't want to be bothered cooking it that often—not to mention that now we're being careful with food rations even though we are rich in food compared to most people. So anyways, I figured it was a good time to ask about getting Andrea and her family.

"Dad, have you been thinking about us going to check on the Pattersons?"

"Can I come?" Lainie piped in, at once. The twins were as eager to get out of the house as any of us. None of us were used to being home all day every day.

"I want to go, too!" Laura cried.

"No one's going anywhere," Dad said, making me frown at my plate.

"Just to see if they're okay," I added, weakly.

"I don't think so," he said. When my dad says, "I don't think so," that means it's a NO.

"Why not?" I dropped my fork by my plate. I felt indignant that my dad can be this unfeeling and uncaring. "We're supposed to be Christians, aren't we? Aren't we supposed to care about the rest of the world?" I didn't realize I'd raised my voice until I noticed my little sisters staring at me.

Dad sighed. He pushed his chair out and came over to me. "Come on up here," he said. I came to my feet, but refused to meet his eyes. I was too angry. He put his arms around me and I started crying on his shoulder. I didn't know I was going to cry. It just happened.

"Isn't that nice," said Mrs. Preston, seeing us embrace. She probably wasn't wearing her hearing aid and had no idea what was going on, so to her it was a sweet scene. However, I saw her lean towards my mother and whisper, "What's wrong with Lexie?"

"Honey," my dad said, into my ear. "Jesus didn't heal every sick person when he walked the earth. He didn't feed every hungry person. He is GOD and he didn't fix every problem in the moment. He has a bigger plan that we don't understand and this present moment is just a drop in the bucket of eternity. I don't know all the answers, but I do know God is still on the Throne. And he hasn't called me to take care of every needy person out there. If God brings them our way, I'll know it. Like Mrs. Preston. I do want to help if I can."

I pushed away from him to meet his eyes.

"I've seen people out on the road that look like they need help," I said. "They're going right by our house. Isn't that bringing them our way?"

He looked at me for a moment. "No."

Inside I actually felt relieved. I feel bad now that I probably didn't show my dad that I agreed with him. But I do. I realize that we can't possibly help everyone. It's like in this parable Jesus told about ten virgins—five were wise and five were foolish. The wise had oil in their lamps when the bridegroom called them and proper clothing for the wedding feast and they "entered into the joy of their Lord." The five foolish virgins did not have oil and weren't prepared and they were forbidden entry to the wedding feast. When they realized their lamps had gone out, they asked the five wise ones to give them oil from their lamps. And here's the thing: When asked to share their oil, their provision, the five wise virgins *refused.* Why? They said there wouldn't be enough for their own needs if they gave! Jesus himself told this parable.

Our situation is not exactly the same. I think the parable implies that all the virgins knew the bridegroom would be coming eventually; they chose not to ready themselves. Whereas many people now, I think, had no clue we could end up in such a dire situation as what the pulse has caused. Nevertheless, Scripture is always exhorting people to be prepared to face the worst, because the worst, which is death itself, is also the beginning. The beginning of new life, a new start in heaven— *for those who are prepared.* For those in Christ.

Like it or not, I have to accept that many people are unprepared like the foolish virgins, and that we aren't expected to sacrifice ourselves for their sakes. That doesn't mean we shouldn't be generous and try to help anyone, but we can't put our family's survival at risk to do so.

I sat back down to finish my breakfast, accepting that we wouldn't be going to the Patterson's house today.

"I want a bath," I announced. I said it in a tone of voice that I hoped would tell my parents that I NEEDED it. I wanted to take one yesterday to wash my hair before our company came, but it didn't happen. It takes a lot of work to prepare a bath these days. We only bathe once a week or less due to all the heated water it takes. I'm used to showering daily so I hardly ever feel nice and clean anymore.

LATER

We've all had baths. Every time we manage to bathe, I get hit with another one of those reality checks. Taking a bath in water that's already been used by my parents will never feel normal to me! Mom had Justin in the water, too.

The girls would be bathing after I finished—which meant I had to hurry because even with the kerosene heater Dad put in the room, the water cools off quickly. Anyways, I should have enjoyed getting cleaned up at least, but all I could think about was that I don't know when or if I will ever see another hot shower. Then I remembered we actually have a camp shower! I hope I'll be able to use it in the summer if we have enough water. (I can't wait.) It may not be hot, but I just long to feel it running down my head and body without having to lift a finger.

By the sound of things, the twins had just as much fun as they always did in the tub, even though the water was tepid. Kids don't care about that stuff. I had to stay in there with them on account of the kerosene heater, which is a mild fire hazard. It did make the room nice and toasty. Dad says we have "a good amount" of kerosene, whatever that means.

I guess I do feel more human now that I'm washed up. A lukewarm bath in used water is still better than no bath at all.

EVENING

Mrs. Preston has me worried. Her oxygen containers are about used up. The small ones ran out long ago, but this morning when I checked the one she was using—one of the last ones we've got—the gauge was on empty. Mrs. Preston looked happy as pie so I didn't tell her. I watched her carefully every time I came and went and she seemed fine, maybe a little more sleepy than usual is all. So I'm hoping the oxygen isn't vital. We've already fetched all the tanks that were in her house, as well as everything else she wanted from there.

What else did Mrs. Preston want? More than anything, her soups! We don't eat commercially canned soup because Mom says they're full of toxic ingredients. She says it's silly to eat such poison when it's simple to make your own soup, but Mrs. Preston sure loves her canned soup. She had a ton of canned soup, and I've been giving her a can a day, usually for lunch. She lets anyone else have the leftover, because she can't eat a whole can. To us, that's a treat. Mom won't eat it, but she lets us because no food is to be despised right now.

Anyways, besides her oxygen running out, pretty soon we'll be out of soup. I haven't mentioned that to her, either. Mrs. Preston still doesn't seem to be fully cognizant of what's going on—with the EMP and all. I don't think she gets it. She seems to enjoy being here but hasn't once asked when she'll go back to her own house. And the only time she mentions her son, Tom, is when she tells a story about when he was little. She'll be watching the girls playing and suddenly launch into a story about Tom. Dad said not to ask about him, like where he might be right now, because it would only make her fret. Tom has a job that often took him abroad, so we're hoping that he was on a business trip when this happened. Assuming the EMP wasn't worldwide, he may be better off wherever he is. I hope so.

Anyways, I finally unhooked the oxygen tank. I couldn't see leaving Mrs. Preston chained to that long, unwieldy air hose, or having to keep adjusting the nostril hooks, when she wasn't actually getting any oxygen. I told her she needed a break from it and she just nodded.

But I keep worrying. So I spoke to Mom.

"She'll just have to take it easy, honey, and do the best she can without it," Mom said.

"All she does is sit and read until it's dark right now. How can she take it any easier?"

"No, while you're doing chores in the barn she helps me peel vegetables and she even chops them up sometimes. She also watches Justin."

"Still." I watched my mom for a moment. She was kneading dough, and looked totally comfortable. Sometimes I wondered if my mom even missed electricity.

"Will she die without it?" I asked.

"I don't think so." She didn't look up, and kept on kneading her dough.

So I guess Mrs. Preston will be fine. At least, I hope so.

L. R. BURKARD

SARAH

FEBRUARY 25
WEEK SIX

When I looked at Mom's face this morning she didn't look like my mother. She's aged since this started, I'm sure of it. Either that, or she's ill.

"You need more rest," I said. "Let me take care of Jesse today."

It has surprised me, quite frankly, that my mom hasn't been asking for my help with the baby. And I haven't offered—I've been feeling burdened enough just trying to get us a cup of tea or coffee now and then, so I've only had Jesse when Mom went to use the restroom. Which is gross. Both restrooms here are gross. At first we took turns hauling in snow to make the toilets flush but then we realized we'd need that snow to boil for drinking water. But I'm disgusted with what pigs people are. The grossness is getting unbearable. We've talked about walking back to the apartment just to use our bathroom. We had water in the tub for flushing, and if it's still there we have a chance of having better sanitation than what's here.

The stench is another thing. There was fighting this morning because one family is letting their small children use plastic bags in a corner—but it smells. (I can't believe I'm even writing this in my journal.) And Jesse has maybe two to three weeks of diapers left, thanks to what Richard brought from Wal-Mart. After that we have to start using those cloth diapers. Really we should train Jesse so he won't need them. Most kids are already trained by his age and we'd never have the water needed to wash the cloths.

Speaking of Jesse, Mom is holding onto him like he's her lifeline. If Aunt Susan could see this, at least she'd know that no child was ever more doted on. Poor Jesse wants to run around the library and play; he's a kid. But when she lets him explore, he eventually disappears from sight and that freaks Mom out. I told her I'd follow him around but she would rather keep him right with her. If he was well fed and healthy he'd probably fight her more, but even Jess is subdued these days.

I brought us tea, which we lightened with the very last can of evaporated milk. I thought the milk would last longer. I've been putting the opened cans on the inside of the window ledge to stay cold, but this morning someone had taken the one I put out last night. I didn't mention to Mom that it was our last can. She's been depressed enough.

"Where's Richard?" I asked. Her face, as she answered, was dark.

"Your brother went out with the others."

I knew immediately what she meant. I understood her fear. Going "out with the others" meant he was on a food hunt. Food hunts could turn into food wars. Even abandoned-looking stores might have hidden guards, people who were armed and ready to defend their turf. There was always competition, other hungry people, out and about. Any trip to scavenge could turn violent in a moment.

Meanwhile, each foraging trip brought back less and less. I hadn't been venturing out myself, but Richard brought back reports that horrified me: Whole blocks of stores with their windows smashed in, their contents ravaged, trashed, or stolen.

To my alarm, my mother's face slowly crumpled and she dissolved into tears. "I don't know what I'll do if anything happens to him," she said.

"Don't worry, Mom!" I put down my tea and moved my chair next to hers.

"C'mon, let's pray together for Richard and the others."

She gave me a hopeless look.

"I don't think I can pray." Her voice was hollow. "When did you become so big on praying?" Her eyes searched mine. I felt like she was suddenly present with me in a way she hadn't been for a long time. Maybe not since we'd come to the library.

"I guess since I've been reading this," I said, and I reached down for my ESV Bible. I kept it beneath my chair when I wasn't reading. She looked at it sullenly for a moment, then nodded. But she said nothing, and I felt suddenly embarrassed that I'd suggested praying. Who did I think I was, anyway? That God should listen to me? But that verse I'd memorized came wafting across my brain: *I will never leave you or forsake you.*

I said a hasty prayer, thanking God for staying with us and for protecting Richard and the rest of our group. Afterwards, I realized I'd thanked Him for protecting Richard like it was a done deal. Maybe that

158

verse is really penetrating because I guess I'm starting to believe it. I also prayed that this time the men would not come back empty-handed. I couldn't quite make that a thing to give thanks for—my faith wasn't ready to stretch THAT much. They'd gone out and come back empty-handed too many times for me to *expect* a different outcome.

But I'm still worried about Richard. Maybe that promise in Hebrews is for me but not for Richard. Maybe it's for anyone who reads it and believes it, like salvation, but you can't make it extend to cover anyone else who doesn't choose it for themselves. I just don't know.

LATER

It's hard to believe our luck! (Or wait—maybe it's not luck? Maybe God is hearing our prayers!) Richard's back. All the men came back this time with no one injured. They raided an ACE hardware store on the outskirts of town that, miraculously, hadn't been hugely ransacked. Other people had been there but were evidently only looking for food, because they left really good stuff like shovels and flashlights and batteries and work gloves. There were also knives and fire starters, tarps and heavy-duty garbage bags.

I'm not the kind of girl who usually gets excited about heavy-duty garbage bags. In this case though, they also brought stainless steel trash cans to line with the bags. There is one in each restroom but men are already at work in the library's courtyard putting up a tent they brought back. I think the garbage "toilets" are destined for that tent—our outhouse. Someone (not me, thankfully) has to empty the bags each night. It will mean less of a horrible odor around here, and the problem of no water to flush with won't matter anymore.

I expect a flimsy tent won't be much more than a windbreak in this weather, but anything is better than using the gross restrooms. It's actually revolting how piggish people have been. The girls' room looks like a bunch of animals were let loose. I won't describe it, but suffice it to say it is thoroughly disgusting.

Anyway, since this trip brought such bounty, they're planning a return trip before other people empty out the place like they have the grocery stores. The best part is that there were two vending machines which had been jostled around, but not successfully broken into. Our guys smashed them up and so Richard, being the quick go-getter that he is, has dumped a load of packaged snacks in our circle. Yay!

As for water—the shelves were empty, but the guys found a back room which had a few cases of bottles, as well as a couple of gallon jugs. They'd been hidden from view by other stuff which saved them from previous looters. (I call that an answer to prayer!) Richard, magnificently, not only managed to grab two cases for us, but found a plastic bin and a rope and made a "sled" to haul it all back.

I never thought I'd say this, but I'm proud to have Richard as my big brother. He is actually quite okay.

EVENING

After this morning's victory at ACE Hardware, it seemed twice as wrong when the man who was injured way back at the Wal-Mart skirmish died. I guess it happened about an hour ago. His wife was hysterical for awhile, and so the library is fully awake. Candles and flashlights are sending shadows dancing all over the walls and floor and ceiling. I am watching the leaping shadows. They are haphazard, fast-moving, and somehow strangely in keeping with that woman's wails. Frankly, her cries are awful.

I suppose we should have known this was coming. That man took a shot to the chest and had a collapsed lung and had lost a ton of blood. (Richard said he was a smoker, too, so his remaining lung was compromised. I am amazed he lasted as long as he did.) Still. Before the pulse he was just a husband going to work and providing for his family and then suddenly he was in a gun fight and now he's dead.

I did see the Powells sitting with him a lot. Mr. Powell read to him from his Bible and I know they prayed over him. Mrs. Powell is sitting with the widow now, with one arm around her. I'm so thankful they are here with us—the Powells, I mean. I was having a hard time hearing that wife without wanting to join in with my own sobs. And oh—even the Powells started eating whatever food became available. I'm glad. It would have been ridiculous for them to starve. Everything I'm reading in my ESV Bible tells me God would understand!

But even with Mrs. Powell's arm around her, that lady is still sobbing. I heard a girl say, *Man, somebody shut that b_____ up.* The girl who spoke was hidden by a stack between us so I couldn't see her. A different girl's voice added, *Or throw her outside. That'll knock her cold.* They chuckled. I was stupefied that they would be so hard on her.

I heard the sound of a match being lit and shortly afterwards smelled cigarette smoke—ugh. Someone must have brought cigarettes from that ACE store, because most people have been out of smokes for weeks. We don't smoke, but we know this because the smokers have crawled around the library asking everyone for a cigarette.

When people still had cigarettes, Mr. Aronoff made a rule: No smoking indoors. I shook Richard's shoulder and pointed at the little plumes rising over the stack, coming our way. He shrugged. Obviously he wasn't going to say anything to them. I gave him a pleading look—I detest cigarette smoke. Then Mom coughed, and that did it. Richard stood up and disappeared around the aisle to go speak to them. I don't know what he said, but whatever it was, it worked.

Meanwhile, the sobs of that wife—that widow—are quieting down. But we're all miserable, I think. Human pain is hard to hear, hard to share, hard to endure. I felt tears on my face and realized I was crying. Then Jesse—who'd slept through it all until now—came fully awake. He'd been amazingly immune to the noise earlier, but now he started wailing. Mom did her best to settle him. But in the end I had to open a bottle of water and we made him a bottle with that and powdered formula. That shut him up. I can't help but think that soon we'll have nothing to appease him with, and then what?

I offered to take him so my mom could go back to sleep. When she agreed, I felt more worried—she hardly EVER willingly gives up the baby. But I held out my arms to hold him and wouldn't you know that little brat started wailing and carrying on?

"You keep holding him and now he only wants you!" I cried. "He's spoiled."

My mom sniffed and settled back with him in her arms, her eyes closed. "I don't care. I don't care. I've lost my husband; and my son keeps putting his life in danger." She opened an eye and shot Richard a defiant look. "Jesse's the only guy I've got."

I didn't like to hear my mother say she'd lost my father. Each passing day made it less likely he'd survived, but he could be holed up somewhere just like we are. We don't know for sure that he's lost. But I had no energy to argue the point. Also, it didn't make me feel very important, what she'd said; like daughters don't count? I guess I understand what she means. But the way she clings to Jesse means she doesn't get enough rest. Maybe it was on account of the half-light, the shadows splaying around the walls, but her eyes look sunken. I'm worried.

Richard nudged my arm and I looked at him, wondering what he wanted.

"It's been six weeks," he said. "I wasn't sure we'd make it this long."

"It feels like a year," I mused. He nodded.

"Today was good," I said, referring to the stuff they'd brought from ACE. He said nothing, so I added, "Wasn't it? It was like a miracle!"

He just looked at me for a moment. "The miracle will be if we make it for the next six weeks. After that, with spring, we can move out of here. Find a place to grow some food." He looked around, checking that no one was walking by. Everyone seemed to be getting settled back down. There were less lights bouncing around the walls.

"Look." He stood up and began pulling little packets out of his pants pockets. Seeds! I gasped in admiration at his foresight. He'd taken maybe twenty seed packets from ACE, all vegetables, stuff we could grow and eat—I hoped.

"Wow!" I breathed, giving Richard an admiring smile. "Good thinking!" We were both whispering, keeping our voices low.

He nodded. "I just hope we can make it long enough to use this stuff."

I try not to think about the future these days. Every day is difficult as it is. Every day there's not enough to fill my stomach (except today—we pigged out on the new provisions. My tummy's been aching in protest.) I didn't want to think about how long it would be until the snow would finally be gone. But I did try and envision us planting and growing a garden. We certainly couldn't do it from our apartment. I thought about how we could possibly do it and remembered that Aunt Susan still had her two acre home in Indiana. The divorce left her an emotional wreck—which is why we got Jesse—but she still had a home with land. If only we could get there! They used to have chickens, too, I remembered. Just thinking of a roast chicken made my mouth water, full as I am from today's booty.

If we could get by long enough to make it to Aunt Susan's, we'd have a real chance of surviving. So this is now my single prayer and goal: For me and my family to live long enough to get to Aunt Susan's house in Indiana.

I fantasized about how wonderful it would be until I finally fell asleep.

SARAH
FEBRUARY 26
WEEK SIX, DAY TWO

In all the six weeks we've been here, I've had exactly one bath. I can't begin to express how leathery my skin feels. The library has an old-fashioned bathroom upstairs with an old-style porcelain tub in it, and at first Mr. Aronoff made a schedule so that each family could take turns using it. (He became our leader by default. Everyone knows him since he's the Super and he just sort of took charge.) Anyway, everyone had to haul in their own snow. And that turned out to be the problem. Snow. It soon became evident that there wasn't enough snow for baths, because we needed it for drinking water. It's not like we're in the country where there's plenty of the stuff. Even with all the incredible snow fall we've had, there's still only so much in this municipal area.

I was one of the lucky ones who got a bath. Which is astounding when you think that my last name starts with a W—Weaver. Usually, we Weaver's are picked last for everything, because most people start alphabetically with A. At school, in gym, I was always the last girl to get a turn at the parallel bars or the trampoline. But Mr. Aronoff, inexplicably, started with Z. We have no families beginning with Z, and no Y families, either. So we were FIRST! I was thrilled.

It took interminably long to heat enough snow and bring it upstairs, even using a barrel fire that they started in the courtyard. Then we had to use the same bath water. Without soap, except for some baby wipes Mom donated for the purpose. (If you don't have your own soap, you have to bathe without it.) There were no towels, so we used one of our blankets, sharing that, too. Once we washed up and dried off, I had to hang the blanket near the fire or it would've stayed cold and wet for days. That meant one of us had to guard it because things that are unguarded have a way of disappearing around here.

Mom and the baby bathed first. After that I got to go, and then Richard. Mom and Jesse took a long time. The water was tepid when I got to it, and cold by the time Richard did. I couldn't bring myself to hurry my mother. She always used a hot shower to relax in the past, so it's been a hardship for her not to have that. I think they were in there for like twenty minutes. Mom apologized, saying it felt so good she just couldn't hurry. She looked better after that bath and I'm sorry we haven't been able to keep up having them.

I didn't feel quite clean after using tepid water, and I didn't like sitting in it. But I got to wash my hair. I'd give anything right now to have that opportunity. Did I mention the lice? I always shuddered at the mere thought of having lice. Now we've all got them. It's funny how something like having lice pales in comparison to going hungry.

I took one of those bottles of water Richard brought from the hardware store and forced myself to stay in the smelly restroom long enough to wash myself.

I'd wash my hair too, but water is too precious.

Oh—I've finished *Sense and Sensibility*. It's so strange to think they had no electricity back then but it was no big deal. Because they never had it. You can't miss what you never had.

SARAH
FEBRUARY 27
WEEK SIX—DAY THREE

Richard and I went to the apartment today. I had to cover my mouth and nose with a scarf as we climbed the stairs because of the odor. After six weeks, the place reeks of fire. It will probably never go away.

I was afraid to go up at first. Afraid of what I'd find. Afraid it was still dangerous. Richard reminded me that other people from the library had already returned and brought back some of their stuff. We needed clothing and other things, so I went.

Nothing in our apartment burned—Richard saw that last time, but I can still hardly believe it. We might have gotten away with staying there the whole time! It seems like sheer luck that the fire was contained to a couple of floors. When we reached our floor and then the door to our apartment, I felt so excited to be home. I can't believe how excited. But the door wasn't locked and we found out we'd been robbed! I was disgusted—people are so ruthless.

We didn't have much to begin with, but now the pantry was absolutely empty except for some ketchup packets from a fast-food joint. We took them. My room had been ransacked—I don't know what people were hoping to find. Money? I'm glad I already removed that $100! Not that it did us any good. There's nothing to buy anywhere.

Even though I haven't been sleeping there I felt violated just knowing some stranger went through my things. All the drawers and shelves were disordered. I saw my box of nail polishes and felt a stab of sadness. The girl who cared about nail polish was from a different life.

At least most of our clothing was still there. That was what we came for, so we filled up some bags. I changed in the bathroom, moving in record speed because of the cold—I felt better in different clothes, better than after the bath. Most of the water we'd saved in the tub had drained out. There was about an inch left and it didn't look perfectly clean, and it was frozen. I found an empty travel-size bottle and, using the handle of a toothbrush, I pounded the ice and swept it into the bottle with the bristle. As I worked, I started crying. I don't know why I cried, exactly.

I guess because life has come to this. To taking water from a tub even though it's not clean and feeling like it is a windfall.

The mirror in the bathroom was so cold that frost had made lacy designs on the glass which was actually pretty....I was studying it when Richard called, "What are you doing in there, Sarah? It's getting late."

I took a last look around for anything worth salvaging and found a razor. I picked it up and stood looking at it. I turned to the lacy mirror. Standing there, seeing this shadow of my former self (I hadn't realized how skinny I'd become until I saw myself there. Loose clothing hides a lot.) I pulled off my hat and let it drop to the floor. I suddenly put that razor to my hair and I couldn't stop. I went at it like a madwoman, like the barber of Fleet Street, the one in the Little Shop of Horrors, only I wasn't taking a life. But I felt like I was. It felt like murder.

A girl doesn't lose her hair without a sense of horror.

When Richard saw me—after I left the bathroom—I saw his eyes widen. I'd left my hat in there on account of the lice and I was heading to my bedroom to look for another one. He opened his mouth to say something, but then shut it again. He understood. He's becoming a better and better older brother.

We both walked around a little, silent and full of thoughts, remembering. Most of our cabinets were empty like I said, but there was still some cough syrup and—wonder of wonders—lice treatment shampoo! I think we've had it since I was in third grade and there was an outbreak at school. I laughed a ridiculous laugh. There was no water to use shampoo anyway, but finding it somehow set off something inside me. I was holding the bottle in my hands and suddenly I couldn't stop laughing. I knew, even while I was doing it, that I wasn't really laughing, not with joy, not the way you're supposed to laugh. I couldn't stop. Vaguely, I saw Richard coming towards me with a strange look on his face. I couldn't interpret the look. I didn't recognize it. Even if I had, I was unable to make sense of anything at that time. I was still laughing uncontrollably. He came and took me by the shoulders and still I laughed.

He grabbed the shampoo but I was holding it tightly. He wrested it from me and slammed it down to the floor. When it left my hand, the laughing started to subside. He turned me towards him and then I was crying, crying just as hard and uncontrollably as I'd been laughing. He took me in his arms and I threw my head against him as I cried.

"Shhhhh, it's okay," he said, softly. "It's okay."

The crying came from somewhere deep inside me. I didn't want to be crying on my brother's chest. I didn't want to be crying at all. I couldn't help it. I felt my knees go weak, and I collapsed against Richard.

"Sarah," he said, "Don't do this. I can't carry you back. I can't."

That's when I noticed that Richard had tears on his face. He was crying, too. Richard, crying! I couldn't remember ever seeing Richard cry. It brought me out of myself, out of the misery I'd felt, as something stirred inside me for him.

"I'm sorry," I said, wiping my eyes. "C'mon." I turned to go but hesitated. I bent down and took back the shampoo. Maybe a dry application would help the rest of the family.

They still had hair.

———◆———

As we were leaving I saw that all our windows had ice on the inside like the bathroom mirror, which wasn't too surprising since even the library's windows are often frosty. The lack of light, the emptiness, the mess from the ransackers, and the faint whiff of fire, even up on the tenth floor, was demoralizing. Again I felt weak and unstable. I could hardly move, and I envisioned my spirit leaving me like a column of smoke, disappearing into the atmosphere. Maybe I just wanted it to, but then Richard nudged me and we left. My legs moved, though I swear I felt nothing.

"We need to get back before dark," he said.

"Wait." I ran back down to the bedrooms and grabbed some of the baby's stuff and clothes for my mother. I'm glad whoever got in wasn't interested in that stuff. I brought scissors, and all the towels and washcloths I could find to cut up for future diapers. I bet my mom will tell me to do the same thing for my period. That is, if I get it again. I'm two weeks late and the only explanation is that my body is too malnourished to produce it. I'm not going to worry about it.

It felt like we'd run a marathon by the time we got back to the street. The thought of having to make it all the way to the library seemed too ludicrous to consider. It wasn't freezing cold anymore, but it was cold. I knew I was moving, but I didn't know how. I knew my arms were weighted down with the stuff I'd taken from home, but I felt like I was losing feeling in them too. Richard started talking, and I think it was his talking that got me to keep moving. It saved me.

He talked about when we were young, about the days before we moved to the apartment. Dad had a different job then and he was home more. Those were happier days. I didn't know if we were happier then because dad was home more, or if it was because we were younger and life always seems happier to the young. Or if it was just an illusion. Maybe it was happier just because we had electricity then. I couldn't tell anymore. I couldn't remember.

While he was still talking we reached the library. There was a new guy at the entrance, not the one who was there when we left. When he didn't want to let us back in, I fell to the ground, suddenly feeling my exhaustion. While Richard argued with him, I saw that he was armed. Of course. All our guards kept arms. But this time, we weren't the protected ones, inside. We were outsiders to this guy.

That should have worried me. No, it should have horrified me. Or at least made me faint. But apparently I couldn't feel worried or horrified. I was too exhausted to feel anything.

I'd just shaved my hair and seen my skeletal body and somehow the threat of a gun wasn't having the same effect on me that it normally would have. I don't have much to lose, anymore.

Anyway, Richard's argument wasn't getting through to him. He said he'd already had to drive off a dozen people that day.

"Ask Mr. Aronoff, idiot," Richard spouted. "We're from the tenth floor, apartment 12."

"That's what they all say," he answered, but I could see in his eyes that he was no longer certain about us. He called another sentry who, thankfully, did recognize us. The men had to help me get up.

"This world is full of idiots!" Richard fumed, as we went back in.

I wondered vaguely about those dozen people who hadn't been granted entry. I pictured them as lost, wandering souls, slowly starving. I pictured them as though they were a different class of people than we were, not like us, in much worse shape.

But really, they are no different than us. They are no different than I am. In fact, I am one of them.

———————◆———————

When we got back, there was an unmistakable air of tension. Mom said there'd been a fight. Everyone's getting tense about the food situation.

Ever since that first Wal-Mart raid, the refrigerator that was in the library's kitchen has been out in the courtyard, buried in heaps of snow. The men brought it out there and have used it to keep food that is found—or caught. For instance, some people go out every day to catch squirrels. They're kept in there until there's enough to offer a morsel to everyone.

One night there was a rumor that the squirrel we were eating was actually dog meat. I didn't want to believe it but I'm suspicious. (As though it isn't bad enough to be eating squirrel!) At night we hear dogs howling outside. It's hard to describe what a mournful sound that is. Living high in our building, the only animal sound we used to hear was maybe somebody's pet in a neighboring apartment. But howls? These are different. I actually thought it was wolves, but Richard says it's pets who were abandoned because no one can feed them. Either they were abandoned or lost their owners in a tragedy due to "the event." Normally, I'd want to rescue each and every stray animal I could. But we can't rescue them. We can't even feed ourselves. But here's the thing: Ever since that night of the rumor, I've been listening for the howls and haven't heard any. So I think I've actually eaten dog meat. How disgusting is that?

But our supplies are dwindling. Aside from Richard's stash from the hardware store, we've only been eating once a day. There's got to be about seventy people still here. We had more in the beginning, but some left long ago, and all along our numbers have dwindled because people get fed up with the conditions. They remember long lost relatives or friends and take their chances trying to reach them. If we had someone closer than Aunt Susan, I'd try to go too.

Anyway, apparently the man on duty guarding the refrigerator did not want to let some guy see what was left in it. They had a confrontation and people started to panic and finally someone forced open the door of that fridge. It was empty. He was guarding it just to keep up the pretense that we've actually got some food left. So now it's common knowledge that from this day forward it will be every man for himself. Richard says we'll return to the apartment tomorrow. I thought of all that stuff we'd carried here and the work it took. Now we'd be carting it all back tomorrow? I guess we'd rather die at home than here.

Mom doesn't know about my hair, yet. We live with our hats on.

SARAH
FEBRUARY 27
WEEK SIX—DAY FOUR

I woke up early today so I'm writing while things are still fairly quiet. The library is a stinking mess, and I should be happy at the thought of leaving. But I'm not.

I'm anxious about Mom. She was just starting to seem better. She's as thin as the rest of us, but she borrowed a portable stroller from someone—the light, little kind—and had been walking Jesse around the library. Even that little bit of exercise was good for her, because usually she just sits and broods or sleeps and broods. She'd also started chatting with other mothers and I know that's good for her. Mom always had lots of friends and was active on her social media sites and blogs. So I'm worried that if we return to the apartment, she'll return to her zombie-ness. She'll be alone except for us and we don't seem to be enough to keep her hopes up.

Richard has been quiet lately, often deep in thought. If I ask him what he's thinking about, he just shakes his head. When he wakes up

I'm going to try and convince him to let us stay here a little longer. There's no more food at the apartment than here, but at least we've got a fireplace at the library, and people for mom to talk to. I'd rather die of starvation with everyone else than of starvation plus cold all by ourselves.

LATER

So we agreed to stay another few nights while Richard makes more attempts to find food. Everyone had talked about leaving and it seems like everyone has decided to stay, just like us. It's simply too cold out there. It's almost March. I hope the cold breaks soon.

When Richard and the other men were gone scavenging, there was some excitement out front. I heard raised voices but they were too muffled for me to understand what was going on. I looked at Mom and she shrugged.

Then suddenly people in the first room were getting all upset and I heard new voices trying to get order. Someone was calling for quiet. I got up and walked silently to the doorway where I peeked around the edge of the wall. I was hoping it was government people with news of how they were going to help us. I was wrong. It was two men and two women with some unkempt kids. The men looked macho and had tattoos peeking out on their necks and bushy hair sticking out of thick knit hats, and bushy, straggly beards. Not that the rest of us would win a beauty contest—we were all a scraggly bunch by now. But these guys looked like a motorcycle gang, if you know what I mean.

The women looked somewhat less threatening, but their eyes were veiled—I didn't like the look of any of them, especially because each of the men was holding a rifle and one of the women had a handgun.

"Listen up!" shouted one of the men. "We don't want to hurt anyone—but we will if we have to."

"What do you want?" Mr. Aronoff asked. He had his arms crossed and looked like he was hopping mad. Which was interesting, because earlier we'd thought he was at death's door. Some kind of flu had been going around, leaving lots of people weak and sickly. He was one of them.

"Bring your food out," the man said. "Be cooperative and no one will get hurt."

"Food?" said Mr. Aronoff. "We don't have food! I wish we had food!"

"You're lying," the man said. "If you don't bring it out, we'll find it. Anyone who is found with food will be shot." He looked around the room ominously. "Did you hear that, people?" His voice got louder. "Bring us your food or we WILL shoot you!"

No one moved. He took a deep breath.

You're all crazy," he muttered. Then he nodded at one of the women. She was the only one not holding a weapon. Two children were huddled around her legs. She whispered something to them, and then disengaged her legs from their little grasps.

She was short, with dirty-blonde hair, and looked haggard. Her face was very white—she'd probably lost too much weight, just like the rest of us.

Anyway, she started going through the bags of the nearest family. It was the Jensens from the first floor. Everyone knew the Jensens because they gave the best candy at Halloween. I felt badly for them, and watched with a growing sick feeling in my stomach. Mrs. Jensen was holding her children against her as if they were going to try to take them, too. The woman ignored her and kept going through everything they had.

"Hurry up!" the man with the rifle barked.

She stopped, gave him a look (which I couldn't see, being to her back), and then turned and dumped the contents of Mrs. Jensen's bags, one by one, onto the floor. A pack of chewing gum fell into view, which she grabbed with ferocious energy.

"Is that all?" the man complained, when she held up her prize.

"What have you people been eating?" he asked, looking around the room at everyone. Silence.

"WHAT have you been eating?" he shouted, pointing his gun at Mr. Aronoff. Mrs. Jensen said, "Does it look like we've been eating? We're starving just like you are."

"Then why are you in here?" he asked, his tone full of suspicion.

"Because of the fire," one of the little Jensens said, pointing her little finger towards the fireplace. We were still burning ripped up books and old furniture, and there was a good, though not roaring fire, going at the moment.

The dirty-blonde had stopped to listen and he shoved his head at her. "Keep going! What are you waiting for?"

She went to the next family. I didn't know their name, even though I'd seen their faces many times before we came to the library. Again the contents of their belongings were dumped out. Mostly clothing, makeup, socks, a deck of cards—she took the cards and the makeup.

"Hey, stupid!" the man shouted. "We need FOOD not junk!"

She stood up, her eyes and lips narrowed. "Then why don't you look, Bruce?"

"Don't say my name, you stupid b-----!"

She slumped and walked over to the other woman. "I'm not doing any more."

The second woman apparently accepted that the job now belonged to her. She looked around with distaste. "They don't got nothin' here, Bru--. She stopped short of saying his name.

"Keep looking!" he barked. "They're living on something."

I turned, hoping to slink unnoticed back to our alcove, but almost collided with my mother. She'd come to see what was happening too. The two of us managed to stay quiet and returned to our spot. I was wondering if there was a way to hide the last of the baby's food. I told myself they likely weren't interested in baby food, but it did, after all, have nutrition. Were they so desperate they'd take food from a toddler? Yes, I was sure they would.

I whispered my concern to my mother, whose eyes slowly digested what I'd said. She nodded. Looking towards the other room, she reached beneath her chair and grabbed the last few jars. Slowly she rose and went to the nearest stack. Books had been torn up for fuel, but there were still many left. She opened a big book and hid the jar inside, standing it up on its spine. That seemed too precarious, so we faced a bunch of books out that way, putting a jar here and there, behind the books. I went along the shelf and opened more, facing them out, so the ones hiding the little jars wouldn't be conspicuous.

I saw other people watching us and I prayed they wouldn't turn us in. To my surprise, a few others stood up and bringing out their own hidden—but meager—stashes, did the same as we had, putting random books outfacing along the stacks.

I thought of the granola bars from ACE that we still had. We'd been rationing them. I put them beneath the stack, and prayed they wouldn't search there.

Then we waited.

SARAH
FEBRUARY 28
WEEK SIX—DAY FIVE

By the time the men returned from scavenging, the armed bullies had left. They didn't shoot anyone, even though Elizabeth's mother did have six beef sticks in her purse. She started crying hysterically when the lady dumped her purse out. Bruce was so disgusted that he said, "Just take 'em and leave her."

Those of us who'd hidden our food managed to keep it. I was praying the whole time because what idiot wouldn't think of searching the stacks? There was a tense moment when Bruce, in a fit of disappointment, kicked over a portable shelf unit of DVDs. My heart went into my throat because I thought that was just the start. I thought surely now he and his friends would go around the library dumping over all the shelves and thrashing the place. They'd find our little bit of food. Our lifeline. Our last means of survival.

But they didn't.

"We have armed men who will return any time now," said Mr. Aronoff.

"Oh yeah?" asked Bruce. "Where'd they go?"

Mr. Aronoff still had his arms crossed. "To Look. For. Food." The irony was not lost on Bruce apparently, because shortly after that he rounded up his people and left.

Richard was furious. "That does it," he said. "We're getting out of here."

I had no idea where we would go, but those people had frightened me so much I didn't argue. Thinking back on it, I'm surprised I didn't have a panic attack while they were here. Lesser things had given me panic attacks. Just being alone on the stairs of the building could send me into a panic. And now here we were, with our lives in actual danger—potentially—and I hadn't even panicked. It was especially extraordinary because I'd run out of my antidepressant three weeks ago.

It's funny what a catastrophe will do to you. I'm losing weight and getting thinner by the day, but inside I've somehow gotten stronger. When I was laughing uncontrollably yesterday at the apartment, I thought I was losing my mind. Apparently, I still have it.

PART FIVE

ANDREA

THREE MONTHS

Dad went out to canvass the neighborhood to see if he can trade stuff for food—bartering, he called it. Not that we have much to trade. I saw mom rifling through her jewelry boxes so I know they're hoping her expensive jewelry will put some food on the table. He says he can also offer labor like chopping wood (if they have any) or working for them however they need it once the weather warms up. Though it is now April, the temperature is still cold.

Dad made me accompany him in case there was anything to carry back. We covered almost the whole plat and had come up empty-handed. The only house left was that creepy Mr. Herman's. He must have seen us out there because he came to his door. I stayed at the sidewalk while Dad went to speak to him. I didn't even want to be close to that weirdo. I heard him say, "Let's see what you've got." He seemed to know we were trying to barter. After about ten minutes dad reappeared with a big box in his arms! It was a case of macaroni and cheese, bought with an heirloom gold watch that was my grandmother's. For a pair of ruby earrings, he gave two fat summer sausages, still in their store wrap.

"Highway robbery," my father muttered, as he approached me.

"Just think," Mr. Herman called out, behind him. "It can all be back

174

in the family if you give me your daughter! And no one will be hungry."

He was looking at me, and gave a huge grin. He laughed. I looked away. As we left, I wondered, *Had I heard him correctly?* Was he really offering my father food in exchange for—*me*? That man was horrible!

As my father and I started back towards home, I asked, "What did Mr. Herman mean?"

He shook his head. "Don't worry about it."

Later he told my mother about the incident, but somehow I didn't like the way my father looked at me when he told it. As though he expected me to volunteer to go to Mr. Herman to get the jewelry back, or for more food.

Mom, however, took the loss of her jewelry in stride. "You can't eat it," she said.

So now we have fifteen boxes of mac and cheese and two nice sized summer sausages. I never thought I'd see such things as a feast, but that's what it tasted like. It was heavenly to feel full.

We'll be through this stuff in no time, though. I told my dad we ought to set out for Lexie's house. "Right now, with this food, we'll be able to make the trip. We can boil water and fix this stuff on the way."

He looked at me but said nothing. So I added, "Pretty soon we'll be too weak and malnourished to make the trek."

"I can't take Lily out in this weather, Andrea," Mom said.

"Mom, it's April" I cried.

"And there's still snow out there! And nights are still cold!" she returned. "I don't even think your brothers would be able to walk that far. And how would we survive at night out there?"

"We still have camping gear," I said.

"The camper is useless, and I'm not risking getting us stranded out on the road. That's final," Dad said.

So we're stuck here. Who would have thought there'd still be snow on the ground in April? But honestly, I don't think they want to go. My father would rather we starve than show up at the Martins' doorstep needing help. Maybe it's a macho thing. But he'll sell jewelry to a lowlife. He'll go to that man's door. He'd just better not try to sell me! I AM DETERMINED NOT TO EVER GIVE MYSELF TO THAT MAN. I'D RATHER STARVE.

Oh, yeah. When we were out, we found out the Laycocks have died. The Laycocks were a friendly older couple. Mrs. Laycock always tried to get me talking if I walked by. I think she was lonely. Anyway, they had sold their house and were preparing to move. They'd packed up and of course they didn't have much food around.

But they didn't die of starvation. That's the weird thing about their dying. Their nearest neighbor, the man who found them, told us they had canned pasta and spaghetti and sauce in the pantry. They were found fully clothed and lying in bed together just as if they'd gone to sleep peacefully. So they probably died from hypothermia. In other words, they froze to death, right in their home!

I found this very depressing. Why didn't they at least hold out until their food was all gone? I guess they wanted to die with dignity, in each other's arms—before they had to. I wondered if it gave them a feeling of control. Instead of waiting for the inevitable, they took matters into their own hands. I wondered if one day we would do the same thing. We were certainly getting desperate. The mac and cheese will hold us for now, but yesterday something happened that showed me how desperate we really are.

Aiden had been playing downstairs. When he came up Mom noticed something in his hands.

"Come here," she said. Aiden walked over to my mother.

"Let me see your hands." He held them out to her, obviously wondering what was up.

My mother leaned over and carefully looked at his palms, then took something off that had been sticking to one of them.

"This is a grain of rice!" she exclaimed, to me. "It's rice!"

I rushed over to examine the tiny white speck she'd gotten off his hand and sure enough, it looked like a grain of rice. We found more, all sticking to his palms.

"Where did you get that?" Mom asked Aiden. I saw his eyes widen with fear. My mother hadn't sounded angry exactly, but a child can detect the slightest hint of anger in an adult and react to it. Which is what Aiden did.

He shook his head, his eyes wide. "I don't know."

"Where were you playing?" she asked. Aiden didn't answer, just shook his head like he had no idea.

"Mom, he's scared," I said. "He thinks you're angry." My mother should have realized this. It struck me that she wasn't operating at full tilt. I began to wonder how often she'd been skipping meals in order to feed the rest of us.

She sighed and looked at Aiden, pulling him towards her with one arm while the other held Lily. "I'm not angry, honey," she said, softly. "I just want to know, that's all."

Aiden sniffed, still looking very cautious. "Promise you won't be mad?"

"I promise."

He hesitated, looking awfully upset, and then started crying. "But I broked it," he said, between sobs. "I broked it."

"What did you break?" Mom asked.

"I broked the bag!"

Mom and I looked at each other. Aiden had found a bag of rice somewhere? Mom smiled.

"Where's the bag, sweetheart? It's okay, I'm not mad that you broke it."

"Aiden," I said. "It's rice—we can EAT it!"

This time his little eyes widened with wonder and a dawning realization. "It's FOOD?" he asked, surprised.

"Yes! Show us where you found it," I said, as we all got to our feet.

"It's from the game, the one with holes in it."

"A game?" Now mom and I were baffled.

"Corn hole," said Quentin, who had joined us and was standing in the doorway watching the proceedings. "It fell out of the bag." Quentin was light-years ahead of his brother with verbal skills.

My heart sank. "Corn hole?" I was still in a fog, until Mom said, "Corn hole bean bags made out of rice—not beans. I don't care what it's from, we're going to use that rice."

Mom and I rushed to the basement steps. She still had Lily but it didn't slow her down one bit. On the way, Aiden expanded on his story, gleefully now. He'd been tossing the bags up and down trying to catch them when one fell onto something sharp (which turned out to be an ash poker by the fireplace) and split open, spilling its contents onto the floor. What he didn't mention was that he and Quentin had gone hog-wild playing with the stuff, making a huge mess and scattering the precious grain all over the place.

When we saw the mess my mother said, "Andrea, grab the other three bags and get them upstairs." When I'd found them, she handed me Lily.

"Here. I'll be up in a little bit. Boys, go with your sister."

I turned to see what my mother was doing before we left and I saw her on her knees, collecting that rice. She was picking it out of the rug and putting it into her pocket. One grain at a time, maybe a few at a time. I knew right then and there that we were going to starve to death. It was simply a matter of time.

Now I want to know: How much jewelry is Mr. Herman willing to buy?

ANDREA
THREE MONTHS
DAY TWO

So I was wrong, wondering if we'd end up laying down and accepting the end, dying peacefully perhaps, as the Laycocks had. Since Dad is still refusing to try to get us to the Martins' house, I thought that would soon be our only choice. But Mom took me aside tonight, saying she needed to talk with me.

"Your father says everyone is in the same shape we are, which is slowly starving." I looked sadly at her, nodding.

"So what'll we do? What can anyone do?"

My mom sighed and looked like she was holding back tears. "Honey," she said. "We have one option."

This was news to me. We had an option? I looked at her for a moment and then suddenly it hit me, the option she was talking about.

"You mean, Mr. Herman?" Tears sprang to my eyes. She laid a hand on my arm.

"Before you get all upset, just think about it for a minute. He seems like a decent man." Her voice held no conviction, which didn't surprise me since we both knew that was a bald lie.

"A decent man? Really, Mom? What kind of decent man says he'll feed our family in exchange for sex?"

That got her mad. "Lower your voice! Your brothers will hear!"

"They'll find out anyway," I cried. "They'll find out what's going on if we go there! Don't think they won't!" I was crying, now, but for some reason, this only seemed to harden my mother's heart.

"It's not the end of the world, Andrea," she said, in a strong voice. "Worse things have happened to people." She broke off, while I just shook my head back and forth. I couldn't believe it was really coming to this.

"I didn't think you would do it," I said, wiping tears from my face. "I didn't think you would ever really do that to me."

"If it was just me starving, I wouldn't ask this of you. Think of your brothers! Think of your baby sister! You're being selfish," she said. "I would never consider this if we didn't have to!"

"You DON'T have to!" I cried.

"What else can we do?" she cried. She stared at me with wide, wild eyes. "You think I like this? You think I want to sell my daughter for food?" She started crying too. I ran into her arms and she stroked my hair, but we were both still crying. Suddenly, something felt different. Sure enough, there stood my father in the doorway. He looked hardened.

"It's got to be done," he said. He put an arm on my mother's shoulder, and Mom and I came apart. He looked at me.

"Neither of us wants this, but we don't have a choice. You can save our entire family. All you have to do is be nice to him."

"Oh, I like that!" I cried. My voice was full of derision. "Be nice to him? You mean, sleep with him! Just say it, Dad! Just say it!

"Fine!" he yelled, his temper up. "You can save this family by sleeping with Mr. Herman! Got it? It's a small price to pay for our lives!"

"That's easy for you to say!" I shouted. What I said next was a surprise even to myself. "And what makes you think he'll stop with me? After me, he'll want Mom! What'll you do then, huh?"

I didn't wait for his response. The next thing I knew, I was running. My mother made an effort to try and stop me, reaching for me with both her arms, but I shoved her away. I ran through the living room and to the back door. We lived in our coats most of the time, and I had mine on, so I just stormed out. I had no hat or gloves on however, and it didn't take long for me to slow down outside.

But I fell to the snow on my knees, sobbing. I scrunched down with my face towards the ground, refusing to get up despite the immediate cold wetness seeping into my jeans. After I'd sobbed a few minutes, I sat back, my rear end resting on my heels. I took a deep breath.

Maybe they were right and it wasn't such a big deal. Plenty of girls at school had slept with guys just because they wanted to. No, that wasn't right. Maybe some girls wanted to, but most I knew really didn't. They were just afraid of losing their boyfriend. (I guess that's kind of sad. They don't want to, but they do it. And not to save anyone's life. So now it was my turn?)

My whole family would be warm and fed if I did this. I thought sadly of Nate, my ex. If there was anyone I might have wanted to do it with, it was Nate Jackson. He was tall and smart and I'd been thrilled he'd chosen to go out with me instead of Elise Pickering. Elise is one of the most popular girls at school and it was no secret she had her eyes on Nate. But he'd asked me out, and I found out he was fun and yet serious about school. But we'd only gone out a few times when he tried to—you know. But I said no.

After that it seemed like every time he could get us alone, he would try. Each time, I made it clear I didn't want to.

Pretty soon we weren't dating anymore.

The dumb thing is that most kids at school probably think of me as a 'yes' girl. Elise even made a comment to that effect, that it was the only reason a guy like Nate would go out with me.

I guess I've brought that on myself, because I'm a flirt. I like guys to like me, see—but I'm not a 'yes' girl. I've always said no. I've always felt there was something to say no for. Something better in my future. I hoped so, at least.

Now I was face to face with the fact that I'd said no for nothing. Nothing but Mr. Herman. Fresh tears came to my eyes. My knees were freezing, so I got to my feet, but I still wasn't ready to go back in the house. I couldn't shake a feeling of doom. Maybe I'm a drama queen. But there's something about knowing your parents are willing to give up your dignity—your innocence—to feed themselves, that makes you feel like the world is ending. Then I remembered.

It already had.

At least, our world had. The world where we were well-to-do and had everything we wanted to eat, and more.

I slowly started back, thinking of stories I'd read of parents in China who sold their daughters to brothels in order to eat. Or in India, parents who killed baby girls because they couldn't feed them. But it never felt real, those stories. It was as though, despite reading them, I could still hang on to unbelief. That sort of stuff couldn't really be happening, right? Or, if it was happening, it would never touch me. Not here in America. Now I realized grimly that all those accounts were true. Girls were sold into slavery or into prostitution or worse, killed—and all because people wanted to eat.

When I got back inside I could feel my parents' eyes upon me, but I didn't look at them. Even Aiden and Quentin came scampering up to me, eyes full of curiosity.

"Where'd you go, An'?"

"Nowhere," I mumbled.

Baby Lily started crying and my mother bounced her on her shoulder, to no avail. She looked at my father.

"She's hungry."

My father looked at me. As though it were my problem. My fault. I tried to stare him down. I thought he should feel ashamed for what he was asking me to do—sacrifice myself literally, for their sake. But in the end, I was the one who looked away. I'd seen something in his face that really unsettled me. *He felt righteous about the whole thing!*

I left the room and wandered through the cold rooms of the house. Even here at the Hendersons we'd resorted to burning furniture and so everything looked oddly empty, like a house that no one lived in. Stacks of belongings that used to be on the furniture were piled against the walls, including empty ornamental vases (the dried flower arrangements were burned long ago). Also, throw rugs were missing, since they'd all been dragged into the living room to make the floor softer for the boys' sleeping bags.

I wandered upstairs to the bedrooms—relics of days gone by. If things would just warm up, we could return to our own house. I could sleep in my own room. Read, write, do anything I wanted to without having to live in the presence of the whole family day in and day out. I longed for that day. It seemed as if the enemy right now was the cold, not the EMP, not the powerlessness, not the lack of food. Not even Mr. Herman. Just the unending, relentless cold.

Suddenly I found myself falling to my knees again, as I had done outside, only this was different. I knew I would have to give in and let my family move to Mr. Herman's house. At least he was willing to let us all move there, not just me. I definitely didn't want to be alone with him in that house. At least I'd have Mom and the boys and Lily around, too.

But the thing which propelled me to the floor to my knees, wasn't just bleak despair, as I'd felt outside. It was like there was something whispering inside me, telling me that if God was in heaven, then I needed His help. I wanted His help. I knelt there, wondering if I had the right to pray. I hadn't been to church in ages, and I seldom even thought about God. (Unlike Lexie, who seemed to have a lot of faith.)

It was worth a try.

"God, I'm sorry for all I've done wrong." I had to stop for a moment. I thought about all I'd done wrong. It was a lot. WAY too much for God to forgive, I was sure. I thought all the way back to first grade when I had cheated on a test for the first time. I thought of how mean I was sometimes to my little brothers. I thought of guys like Nate—boys I had allowed to touch me in ways I was sorry for. Then I remembered how I'd selfishly pigged out on that box of chocolate chip cookies only weeks ago. My whole family was hungry and I'd eaten the entire box. Had it been weeks ago? That I'd eaten so much? It felt like a year. Anyway, I had no one else to pray to—who is in heaven besides God, right? So I added, "Please, if you can forgive me, please save me from Mr. Herman! And save my family!"

I was deeply certain I didn't deserve to be saved. How could God possibly forgive my deepest darkest blackness?

Then, somehow I remembered something Lexie said once. That we can only be saved when we *know* we don't deserve it. God didn't suffer the pain of the cross for people who are good, people who deserve heaven—he suffered and died in our place precisely because we AREN'T good and *only* deserve death and suffering. If we could be good apart from Him, why would he have become a man to die in such a horrible fashion? Suddenly the idea of why Jesus came and suffered made sense to me. As I knelt there on my bedroom floor, I don't know why, but everything changed. My fear of Mr. Herman melted away. My disgust with my father, my grief at his coldness, ebbed off me like a receding wave. My fear of God himself dissipated like smoke. I sat up, gasping with surprise and amazement.

Every single thing that had happened in my life was every single thing I needed to get me to this place.

I COULD be saved! Lexie was right! Being a selfish, rotten person wasn't my downfall—it was exactly what qualified me for God's plan of salvation.

I cried after that, still on the floor, but my tears felt utterly different than the ones I'd shed earlier. This was a cleansing cry. And I knew, I just knew, that I was not alone in that room. I had the weirdest feeling that God the Son was with me—Jesus Christ! How could I know that? I don't know how, but I did. I was not alone. I AM not alone.

Mom called from downstairs. She usually calls me to help with Lily, so I dried off my eyes and went down.

My parents were both watching me furtively, waiting for my next burst of temper, I guess. I felt their eyes, the silent wondering if I was going to explode again.

I didn't.

———————◆———————

Without that infusion of food from Mr. Herman, this is what we had left in the pantry: A bottle of mustard, some packets of soy sauce and duck sauce, vinegar, baking soda and baking powder, a few cans of sliced mushrooms, tea, coffee, a box of onion soup mix, and chicken bouillon.

Yesterday I prayed that God will save me from Mr. Herman. My spirits are still up since I prayed, but when I look at the pantry I can't help but wonder what will happen when we get through the mac and cheese. Even if mom sells more jewelry, that won't last forever. Maybe she'll buy us another week or a few more weeks of food. But then…???

Then I'd find out if God could answer prayer.

LEXIE

THREE MONTHS

Mr. Buchanan was by yesterday and said they'd lost a few more chickens to thieves. They had to put the chicken coop right up against the house.

"How do you know it wasn't a critter that got your chickens?" my dad asked.

"You know how a coop is a mess after a predator gets in? They kill more than they'll eat and they terrorize the whole roost. You know how loud chickens get when they're riled up and scared. Well, we didn't hear anything. No, this was a human being. Someone who went in nice and calm and didn't stir up the hens but helped himself to a few. So we've got three less layers, now." Before he left, he added, "Don't let the same thing happen to you."

So dad has moved the coop and put up new chicken-wire fencing and it's right up against the house so we should hear if anyone tries to get our hens. Mom says we can't replenish our stock until the weather is warm because there's no electricity to warm an incubator, so we've got to protect what we have. I like it when we let a hen or two go broody, though, even though there are fewer eggs for awhile. (A broody hen won't lay while she's sitting on a clutch of eggs.) But I love it when the chicks hatch. They're the cutest things.

Anyways, we haven't seen anyone on our property. I'm gladder than ever that we're far back from the road—almost a quarter mile, in all. There's a big meadow after the first stand of trees, giving us an excellent view of anyone coming towards the house from the road.

The Buchanans, however, have had three incidents now when they had to fend off intruders. We think it's because their house can be seen from the road. Not only are we far back, but the drive curves significantly, so we're hidden entirely from view of anyone passing. Anyways, when my dad was in the barn with me for my chores, I told him we HAVE to go and see how Andrea and her family are making out.

"It's unconscionable, dad," I said, hoping to sound compelling. "To have everything we need and not do anything to help people we know." His head went to one side while he gazed at me.

"Lexie, every single day that goes by makes it more and more dangerous to be out and about."

"Why?"

"Because people are desperate. Desperate people do crazy things. Violent things."

I finished shoveling fresh hay in the stall for Rhema and stood facing my dad in the semi-darkness of the barn.

"Then why didn't we go at first, like I wanted to?" I asked, feeling my temper rising.

He frowned. "I'm sorry, honey. There was NO good time. There was no good time. It's always been risky and it's a risk I don't want to take." He said it twice as if to reassure himself—or maybe me, I wasn't sure.

"There is no good time for many things," I said. "Unless we make the time for them. But if you won't help me, one day I'm just going to saddle up Rhema and go for myself."

He stared at me.

"That would be foolish. Please say you don't mean that."

"I do mean it." I hated to say that to my father who has always been fair and loving to me, but I was really mad.

"Lexie, I'm surprised at you," he said. I felt badly, but held my ground. Would I really take off by myself? I wasn't so sure.

"How on earth would that help your friend?" he said. "If you took off on your own and showed up at their door? You'd be one more mouth to feed, that's all."

I suspected my father was only saying this to dissuade me from the idea of taking off on my own. I knew the thought frightened him. Heck, it frightened me. But I only said, "I have to know, Dad! I have to know how they are. I am sure Andrea needs us!"

"How can you be sure?" he asked, incredulously. "You can't be sure of that! I think you're lonely and you want a friend around." He turned away, moving over towards his horse's stall.

I hesitated. I did want a friend around. But was that all? I thought of all the times I'd had thoughts of Andrea and her family, unbidden, just floating into my mind. Like when I prayed. And the thoughts were always the same: That she needed help. That her family needed help. I wasn't TRYING to create a crisis. I just felt sure, somewhere deep in my being that she and her family were in one, a crisis. And that we, considering all we knew and had, could help.

"I'm sure because I feel it every time I pray!" I declared.

My father said nothing for a moment, and stood, stroking Promised Land's handsome head and mane. He took a deep breath and turned towards me. Slowly he came over.

"You can't think only of yourself and your friend. What would happen to your mother and sisters and little brother if anything happened to me? Or God forbid, to both of us?"

"What's going to happen?" I cried. "You act like the whole country has gone crazy! So the Buchanans lost a few chickens! Big deal! I'm talking about saving a whole family!"

"I have to think of my family first," said Dad. "Your friend lives a good distance away. If anyone forced us to give up the horses we'd be opening ourselves up to exposure and hunger and Lord knows what else." I stared at my dad, feeling like I didn't know him. Where was the warm-hearted man I'd grown up with? The man who let me keep Millicent, my pig, until she died a natural death because I'd grown fond of her and couldn't bear to have her butchered?

"But dad, it feels so important to me when I'm praying. Haven't you always told me that when you can't shake off thoughts or themes during prayer it could well be God speaking to your heart?"

He gave me a cynical look. He sighed. "Lexie, if God wants us to get the Pattersons, he'll have to tell me about it, too."

I was silent for a minute while I finished up my chores. "So you think I can't hear from God?" I asked, finally. "That I'm just imagining him speaking to my heart?" I was insulted but also, unaccountably, hurt. My father didn't trust my perceptions.

"Honey, I'm not saying that. I'm just saying that nowhere in Scripture do I see an injunctive to listen to my daughter when it comes to making decisions that affect the whole family." He waited until I met his eyes. "I'm not saying you're not listening or hearing correctly. I'm just saying I need to hear it, too."

"Have you asked God about it?"

"I have," he said, pulling the stall door shut and closing the latch.

"But I will again, if that's what you want."

"That's definitely what I want."

"Okay." His eyes met mine, steadily. "You have my word. I'm not guaranteeing we'll do anything, Lexie. I'm not guaranteeing it. But I'll go before the Lord and see what happens."

"Thanks, Dad."

His eyes, which I could see in the lantern light, were somber. I had a battery-operated lantern for the barn which was less of a fire hazard than the oil lamps we used in the house. I grabbed it from its hook so it would light our way back. On moonlit nights the snowy landscape shone almost like daylight, but I liked having the lamp just the same.

As we walked in silence back to the house, I took a moment to give a word of thanks to someone else.

God, I love you!

Dad said, "I do have one condition."

"What?"

"If I pray and I DON'T hear God telling me to get the Pattersons, then you have to drop the subject for now on. Don't bring it up again." His eyes were dead serious. "Deal?"

I took a breath. I'd just been thanking God because I trusted my father to keep his word and pray. And I trusted that God would speak to his heart, just as He'd spoken to mine.

"Deal," I said.

Before bed I asked God to speak to my father's heart loud and clear. I need him to have peace about going for Andrea and her family. There's a segment of preppers who are alarmists, always thinking the worst, always shouting how the end will be anarchy and chaos and each man for himself. I think my dad must have heard too many of their dire predictions and it went to his head.

I hope he comes to his senses.

**LEXIE
THREE MONTHS
DAY TWO**

I'm so excited! Dad told me this morning at breakfast that he'll speak to the Buchanans about getting the Pattersons! It seems too good to be true! I think I just stared at him with my mouth open for a minute.

Then I got up and went around to him at the end of the table and gave him a hug. I had tears in my eyes, I was so relieved.

As I was returning to my seat Mrs. Preston said, "I'll take one of those!" So I stopped and gave her a hug, too. She's always been way big on hugs. I don't mind when we're at home or her house but I never liked to see her open arms at church, in public. I don't know why, it embarrasses me. Anyways, I wasn't embarrassed now so I gave her a good one.

I noticed she wasn't looking her best. I think it's because she's out of oxygen. My parents are both denying there's a problem. I don't understand them.

But I'm too happy to worry over that right now. I can't believe it. We're going to get the Pattersons!

"So when can we leave?" I asked, taking a bite of my cinnamon-oatmeal pancakes.

"Now, slow down," Dad said. "I have to see if the Buchanans will help. I'm not going out there just the two of us. There's safety in numbers. Besides, how could we help that whole family if they need it, if there's just the two of us? If the Buchanans will come, that'll give us enough riders to take back every one of the Pattersons. If they won't go, neither will we."

That stemmed my excitement. As if I needed more to depress me, he added, "And if we do go for your friends, they won't be able to take any belongings with them to speak of. They're lucky each of us can fit an extra body on our horses, so don't even think we're gonna get their gear—or go back for it. Not a chance."

"Okay." There was nothing else to say. I just hoped the Pattersons would be okay with that.

"You know," my dad said, looking at my mother as though they'd discussed what he was about to say. "They may not even need or want our help. Not every man will get up and go into another man's house just like that."

"A starving man will," I said, with assurance. Dad just gave me a look. I could see he wasn't convinced, still, that Andrea's family might be starving. As long as he's willing to go, I don't care. But inside, every thought of Andrea fills me with a sad, empty feeling. So now I've got to pray that Mr. Buchanan will lend us the help of his family. Going on horseback makes it a little tricky—you can only expect a horse to cover so many miles a day. But if we leave early and bring plenty of hay for them, we might be able to coax them back the same day. They'll be carrying more bodies on the return trip—it'll be hard on them. But horses are powerful animals. And they'll just have to do it!

My only other worry was Blake. He probably hadn't ridden for hours and hours, ever. And this wasn't going to be a joyride.

EVENING

I can't sleep. I'm too excited about the prospect of finally seeing Andrea and being able to help her family. Also, now that Dad has agreed to go, I'm getting worried. What if the Buchanans won't help? What if Dad's right and there's danger out there? What if one of us gets hurt or loses a horse? What if the Pattersons aren't even home? Or what if they've starved to death already? Or frozen to death? What if? What if? What if!

I can't stand it!

LEXIE
THREE MONTHS
DAY THREE

My heart is leaping for joy.

Dad and I saw the Buchanans this morning to discuss getting the Pattersons, and they've agreed to help! My conviction about Andrea's family being in dire straits seemed to matter more to Mr. and Mrs. Buchanan than to my own parents—but I guess it doesn't matter as long as we'll be going.

At first Mr. Buchanan wanted Blake to stay with the little ones from both our families, but Blake spoke up and said he wanted to go; let my mother watch the kids. So that's what will happen.

I can't wait for tomorrow! I'm helping Mom prepare supplies for our saddlebags and I'm getting so excited I can't stand it! She's laughing at me for being giddy.

I think my parents still don't get how important this is.

SARAH

THREE MONTHS

I've accepted that my dad is not coming back. Honestly, that seems like a small thing next to the fact that we're slowly starving. I'm not even really mourning for him. I feel guilty about that. How could I not mourn for my own father? But maybe he's doing better than we are. Maybe he found a place to hunker down for the winter and is now on his way back. But even the idea that he's doing better than we are doesn't give me any comfort.

I guess I'm angry. I didn't know I could feel this angry. I'm angry that he didn't find a way to get back to us; angry that we weren't more prepared for something like this; angry that we're hungry and thirsty!

I'm crying as I write. Maybe I am mourning for my dad. I guess deep down inside I know he probably isn't doing better than us. In fact, I don't think he's still alive at all. He'd have come back if he was alive.

Richard has moved us out of the library. We've taken the few meager bits of sustenance we had, a bottle of water (I'll explain about that in a minute), some books to rip up for tinder, and the rest of our stuff, and returned to the apartment. There was no longer a reason to stay—no food, no water, and a few of our own men were getting to be bullies. They started doing shifts, taking turns supposedly to keep watch, but they were more like Nazis, not letting us move around freely or even talk after "curfew."

We're out of baby food and canned milk. Jesse doesn't even cry anymore. For awhile I thought his cries would drive me crazy. Our empty, colorless lives were difficult—but a baby crying because it's hungry is unbearable. Children don't understand why you can't feed them. Their crying is a form of human torture.

My mother looks like walking death. She is wasting away, and there isn't a single thing I can do about it. She still clings to baby Jesse like he's all she's got.

I'm writing this with the feeling that it may be my last entry. Richard took out a deep stock pot and made a fire in it for warmth, but the smoke is noxious and it won't last very long. Our apartment doesn't even feel like home to me. Besides the robbery, there is smog and dirt on all the windows, and I have no clue where it came from. The fire? I don't see how. Anyway, the effect of the gloom is that it seems like a tomb in here.

EVENING

We've moved again. Richard had been exploring the garage level of the building and found a door leading to a set of steps going even further underground than the garage. So now we're in a boiler room, though of course the boiler is long dead and cold. But being underground, the room is actually warmer than our apartment. Even the library wasn't this warm unless you were nearer the fireplace than our little spot.

When he came and told us he'd found this place, my mother registered what he'd said but there wasn't the faintest spark of hope in her eyes. Still, I mustered what little energy I could and helped her get to her feet. Once she got moving, she seemed better. I'd been in my room and found a few pieces of candy in the closet—they were in the pocket of an old pair of jeans. We each took and sucked on one slowly, almost with reverence. When my mother's piece was too small for Jesse to choke on, she gave it to him, putting it on his outstretched tongue gingerly.

"Want more," he said, as soon as he'd finished it.

My mom shook her head. I still had a sliver in my mouth, so I gave it to him. "Want more," he said in a moment, holding out his once chubby fist. Poor baby! We spent the whole walk down the ten flights and the extra two, trying to quiet his cries. The candy had given him enough energy to complain, and that was probably all. I wished I hadn't found it. Every day I keep thinking that unless someone comes to our rescue we can't survive much longer.

SARAH
THREE MONTHS, DAY TWO

I had an unusual encounter back at the library. I haven't written about it before now because I needed to think it out. There was this man—wait, let me explain what was going on.

There were less of us by now. Lots of families had gone with all their stuff because we'd run out of everything. Even before that, people were starting to get sick and some families left to escape the illness. I don't even know what it was. Flu? Pneumonia? All I know is I heard a whole lot of coughing and moaning.

Anyway, all we had left was that big old fireplace, still being fed with books. The ashes were spilling out all over the floor, but whoever had been cleaning them either got sick or had left because no one was doing it anymore. The fire was getting weaker by the day. Then, the temperature climbed from the single digits to just below freezing, and then, gloriously, it was in the forties! We still needed the fire, but the warmer weather felt heavenly.

Until we realized there was no more water. No more snow meant that even our ridiculously small rations of drinking water disappeared. A few blackened puddles here and there were all we could find, and even boiling didn't seem to make that clean. We knew there were streams outside of town and small branches of the Miami river, but they were FAR. Starvation had been looming on the horizon for weeks, but now we were facing the fact that we were going to die from dehydration instead. I think dehydration is worse.

The only reason we'd stayed as long as we had at the library was because there wasn't any food or water back at the apartment either. But one day Mom said we might as well die at home rather than the library. We were planning on leaving the next morning. That's when I had this "encounter," as I call it now.

Richard had risen early and gone out scavenging as he often did. Many days he came back empty handed but not always. (Once he came back with a big bar of chocolate. I found out you can't eat chocolate with a dry throat. I actually thought it was choking me. I finally let a small piece melt on my tongue—which took a really long time— because I was desperate for the calories. But I don't think I'll ever look at chocolate the same.)

Anyway, every time Richard went out, Mom hated it. She was sure she'd never see him alive again. I don't know if she was afraid that he'd get killed on the street or if she thought she would die before he got back.

So there we were, me and Mom and Jesse. They were still asleep and I had woken up but I had no energy to do anything. We were listless and without hope. All along, I had managed to hang onto a small thread of hope. Maybe it was from my Bible reading. I'm not sure. But now I felt hopeless. I didn't even have the desire to read anymore. In a library!

Someone tapped me on the shoulder. When I looked there was this man, tall, thin but not haggard like the rest of us. He had a peaceful look on his face. It startled me so much, and afterwards I realized it was because I hadn't seen such a look on anyone in a long time. There was no anguish, no pain in his expression. Still, I was suspicious because I didn't recognize him.

"Would you like to give your mother and brother a drink?" he asked.

I blinked, figuring I was dreaming. When he didn't disappear, I think I just stared at him. I couldn't believe what he was asking. I glanced at my mother. She was sleeping with Jesse on her chest. Jesse's eyes were open but he just watched us, quietly. He'd been getting more and more listless and lethargic by the day, even by the hour. Mom and I refused to say it aloud but we knew he was dying.

"I can't," I finally said, with indignation in my voice. Who was this idiot who thought I was withholding life-giving water from my family? How on earth was I supposed to give anyone a drink when I had nothing?

"There's no water," I said, annoyed.

"Follow me," he said, quietly. "There's water."

I wondered vaguely if he was just trying to lure me from safety, but something in his expression of assurance made me follow him. He gave me no feeling of personal threat but it bothered me that I didn't recognize him. If he was from our building, or if he'd been in the library all along, I certainly didn't remember him.

Anyway, he led me to the door which led to the basement and that's where I stopped. There was no way I wanted to follow this stranger to a lower level, alone. He looked at me, and I swear he could read my thoughts.

"It's okay," he said. He turned and looked back into the other rooms. As if he'd called her to come, I saw Elizabeth slowly making her way towards us. She was suffering from hunger and thirst as much as the rest of us, and looked almost drunken as she walked. I was glad to see her. Without a word, she came and joined us and we proceeded

193

down the stairs. I took her hand and she managed a little smile.

"What are we doing?" she asked.

"Getting water, I think," I said. Her eyes widened and she looked at the man as if for the first time, taking notice of this person who was apparently going to save our lives.

"Is that your dad?" she asked.

I shook my head. "No." I shrugged, letting her know I had no clue who he was.

When we got downstairs he led us right past the kitchen and into a little room that held what I guessed was a water heater. There was condensation on the outside of it and I stared at those drops as though they were pennies from heaven. I had a temptation to put my mouth right on the outside of the thing and lick them up. The only thing that stopped me from doing that was his presence.

"In here," he said. I noticed then that he was holding a bowl and a wrench. He used the wrench to turn a screw, then another, and then he placed the bowl beneath a pipe. In a few seconds, water began running into the bowl. When it was more than half full, he turned the screws again and stopped the flow. He gave me the bowl. My eyes were twice their normal size, I'm sure. There was a question in his eyes, and I wondered for a second what it meant. Elizabeth, despite the wonder of what was happening, was leaning against the wall, her eyes closed. She was on the point of exhaustion. And it hit me: The question was whether I would drink first or offer it to my friend. I nudged her and said, softly, "Elizabeth."

She opened her eyes and saw the bowl I was holding out to her. She just stared at it for a moment, blinking. I put it to her lips and she started to drink. She suddenly came to life and took the bowl in both her hands.

"Easy!" I cried. "Don't spill it."

She slowed down a little but was still taking big gulps. She seemed then to suddenly remember that I was thirsty too, and gave me the bowl. I took a long, cooling drink. The water was absolutely the best water I'd ever had in my life. It felt like the sky had opened, as though the sun had been gone for a long while but now was shining again. I'd almost finished the rest when I realized the man must be thirsty too. I stopped, looked at him uncertainly, and then offered the rest to him.

He accepted the bowl and took a good sip, then handed it back to

Elizabeth. She finished it quickly. He gave me the wrench saying, "Try it."

I did what I'd seen him do, loosening the screws to a valve, telling Elizabeth to have the bowl ready. We filled it again, not all the way so it wouldn't spill. Then I remembered seeing empty plastic water bottles strewn around, even downstairs where we were.

"Let's fill the water bottles!" I cried. "Everyone needs this water!"

The man said, "There's water in the pipes, too. It was frozen until now but it's all been melting and you can access it." He went on to explain that many pipes had burst in the cold spell but these old pipes in the library hadn't. Someone had taken the precaution of wrapping them in insulation a long time ago. There was a light in his eyes as he spoke—as if he'd been there, as if he knew exactly when it had happened. I had a fleeting thought that maybe he'd done it himself.

I looked at him with profound gratitude. Our lives were saved. At least for the time being.

I asked, (I don't know what made me do it, I think I must have felt instinctively that he was an angel or something), "Why did God let this happen?" I was referring to the EMP, the loss of lives, the devastation, and sorrow.

He looked at me with without the slightest hint of surprise at my question. He said, "Because of His great love."

I thought he'd told me why God gave us this water. That wasn't my question.

All I could think about was all we'd lost, our old life, my dad, our apartment. The answer could not be because of God's great love!

"So many people have died! No one can get anywhere to help other people. Think of those who couldn't get to a hospital. Or family members—like my dad—who never came back home!"

His eyes took on a faraway look. "The secret things belong to God. The question," he added, "is this: When the Son of Man returns, will he find faith on the earth?" I was so surprised by that response that I said nothing. I think I just gaped at him stupidly. I didn't understand what he was talking about, or what it had to do with all the suffering I'd seen, or all the suffering I knew was still ahead.

He waited as if he knew I hadn't done questioning. And I hadn't. "What about all the people who died because they couldn't get medicine? Or those who may have starved? They all died before their time!" He had taken the wrench back and was tightening the screw just enough to keep water from running out and being lost. He grimaced slightly with the effort, then ran his hand along the insulated pipe as if to admire the workmanship.

I could picture him being a craftsman of sorts, a careful, methodical artist. *A carpenter?* The thought hit me like a brick. Was I talking to *Jesus Christ?* As soon as the thought came I brushed it aside. Was I losing my mind?

He turned to leave, placing the wrench gently beside the pipe on the floor. He looked at me. I've never seen eyes like his. Penetrating. Calm. Unlike everyone else's eyes, not discouraged. Peaceful.

"Do you think perhaps they were worse people than you?" He paused. "No. Unless you repent," he said, not unkindly, "you will all likewise perish."

I recognized those words.....from somewhere. Elizabeth was standing back waiting for me. We'd filled a bunch of bottles with water and placed them in a row. They stood waiting to be brought to others. She seemed oblivious to our conversation, as if it was above her head.

"They died for no reason," I said, hanging onto my indignation. "Why did they have to die before their time?" I felt certain that I could ask this, as if I knew, deep down inside, who I was talking to, as impossible or crazy as it seemed.

"C'mon," Elizabeth said, touching my arm.

"Before their time?" Those were the last words I heard him speak. He gave me a look I can't describe. He wasn't ridiculing my question, but somehow answering it. *No one dies before their time.* That was his answer! I could believe it or reject it, but that was all the answer I was going to get. I started gathering bottles to bring upstairs. With my arms full I turned around to thank him. No one was there. He'd vanished!

"Where'd he go?" I asked.

Elizabeth shrugged. She behaved as though the whole encounter was uninteresting—except for the water. But not me. I've been mulling his words around my head ever since. I don't question my sanity regarding him, either. There was something in the way he spoke! Every word is burned in my heart. I turn them over and examine them, again and again. I know there's stuff I need to understand, such as, how does repenting change my destiny? He said, "Unless you repent, you will all likewise perish." Likewise perish. What does that mean?

I found the reference in the Bible. Jesus was talking to his disciples who had asked if the eighteen people who died when the tower of Siloam fell on them were worse sinners than everyone else. The idea was, "Did they die because of their sin?"

Jesus said, "No; but unless you repent you will all likewise perish."

It obviously didn't mean that a tower of Siloam was going to fall on them too. But the eighteen died suddenly, without warning. Maybe that means they weren't ready. They hadn't thought about their future or their destiny. So if I repent, it means I'm thinking about my future. I'm thinking about how I'll face God someday.

I'm not as smart as Richard, but even I can get the idea that when we see death around us it is to remind us of our own mortality. Our own future. And to repent (according to the dictionary, which I found in the reference section) means "to feel remorse, contrition, or self-reproach for what one has done or failed to do; be contrite." It also means, "To make a change for the better as a result of remorse or contrition for one's sins."

I would go to confession if I could get to church. But I can't. So I've confessed my sins to God as best I can, and I will try to have faith. It seems weird that I am ready to believe in God now when the world has turned upside down and I'm possibly dying, when I didn't really care about God when things were so much better.

I wish I'd known then, how good things were.

Anyway, that was my encounter. I'm keeping it to myself, because everyone would say I'm crazy if I told them I'd seen and spoken to Jesus. But it must have been him—didn't he call himself the *Living Water?* Hadn't he claimed that if you drink HIS water you would never thirst again? Obviously he wasn't talking about normal human thirst. He was talking about something deeper, something foundational and more important than a temporary answer to a dry mouth. I've been thinking about this since it happened, and my conclusion is that he meant eternal thirst. (Doesn't everyone have that? The feeling that there's more to this life than just this life? I can't be the only one who feels this way!)

Anyway, I guess he could have been an angel, but I still think it was Jesus. As INSANE as that sounds, I really do. I know for sure he was no mortal man.

The water lasted for eight days—eight glorious days when we

didn't have to feel the shadow of death hovering quite so closely over our heads. We stayed at the library because of it, and even Richard's scavenging seemed to prosper suddenly.

Mr. Aronoff nearly died from that illness going around but he got up when he saw us giving out water that first day. He demanded to know where we'd got it. I told him. He acted as though he was angry someone had shown mere girls a water source, something so important, but hadn't thought to show him first.

It reminded me of something I'd just read in my Bible. After Jesus rose from the dead he appeared first to a *woman.* Not only that, but he gave her the express mission of telling the Apostles of his resurrection. This was in a time when women were looked down upon! It made me feel more certain the man I saw and spoke to was Jesus!

Anyway, Mr. Aronoff took over rationing out the water. Being in charge seemed to energize him in fact, and he became his old diabolical self. No one knew how much the pipes held, and so he insisted upon us using as little as possible. No washing. Drinking only.

No one else could remember seeing the man Elizabeth and I described. (I'm glad Elizabeth saw him, too!) Just in case, I went searching the whole library for him but he was nowhere to be found. I wasn't surprised.

Anyway, so now we're here in the sublevel garage where there's lots of water in these pipes (unlike our apartment, where they *had* frozen and burst). But I'm not sleeping down here. It's too yucky.

SARAH
THREE MONTHS, DAY THREE

Today I discovered another reason besides the water and the higher temperature that Richard brought us down to this dismal basement. Unknown to us, he'd been saving mouse traps he picked up on his foraging expeditions. Almost every store he'd gone into searching for food had mouse traps. People had emptied the shelves of anything edible but they'd always left the traps. He says there are more mice (and probably rats, too) down here than elsewhere in the building.

So get this—he fills them with ketchup (he has a lot of little packages of ketchup that were still in the apartment) and he's skinning the dead mice! The first time he brought us cooked mouse meat I thought I would vomit. I mean, if there'd been any food in my stomach, I would have. Richard got way annoyed with me for not eating, but it was all I could do to stop the dry heaves.

Mom ate, and fed baby Jesse—just little teensy bites. Jesse's stomach has been empty for so long she was afraid he'd be unable to digest a lot of food. Not that there was a lot. I think Richard cooked up five mice and it was still a meager amount of meat.

When it was almost all gone, I suddenly felt a stab of hunger. I haven't eaten in so long I almost forgot what hunger feels like. I'm beyond hunger. Richard held out the last bit of meat to me.

"Take it, Sarah. You haven't had anything."

It didn't look like a mouse. It looked like a bit of cooked meat. I ate it.

When this is over—if I'm still alive—I'm going to rip these pages from my journal. I will tell no one I ate mice to survive. I will forget, myself, that I did this. The only thing worse I can think of would be to eat dog, and I think that already happened.

Soon it will be warm enough for us to try and make the journey to Indiana. I've seen people on horseback from the balcony, and I've seen two horse-drawn wagons. I'm hoping my $100 will get us a spot on one of those wagons for part of the trip. Perhaps that's why I didn't get to spend it on anything else—God knew we'd need it now.

LEXIE

THREE MONTHS
DAY FOUR

We're going for Andrea and her family! I got up at the crack of dawn so I could take care of the animals and my other chores before the Buchanans got here. My stomach is churning with anticipation, but I'm also a little afraid. What if my dad's been right all along and this is a dangerous trip? What if the Pattersons are fine and we're doing this for nothing?

All I can do is trust that my impressions during prayer are from the Lord.

———————◆———————

Now that we're back home I can tell what happened.

Blake and his family got here yesterday just after dawn. I was still out by the rabbits, throwing some straw beneath the cages so their droppings will turn to mulch when things warm up. I didn't hear him coming up behind me so when he touched my shoulder, I jumped.

"Sorry," he said. He wore a stern expression but his eyes were soft. Blake rarely smiles, so this wasn't unusual.

"No problem. I'm glad it's you!" Something about him seemed friendlier than usual. "Thanks for coming and helping," I said.

"Sure, I know Andrea and you are good friends." He gave me a sideways look. "I've wondered about that, actually. You two are so different."

I nodded. "I know. We are very different." I figured he was referring to the fact that Andrea dresses fashionably and wears make up while I'm more the country girl type. Heck, I AM a country girl and it shows. I don't wear makeup and I don't like fancy clothes; that's just me.

"Both our families have twins. We saw each other at this meeting for twins and their families, and that's how we started talking. Sharing

200

twin stories. We just became friends after that." He nodded. I felt like he wanted to say something else. I looked expectantly at him.

"So you feel like the Holy Spirit wants us to do this? To go for her family?"

His question surprised me. I loved that he asked me directly. It was to the point and without a hint of mockery. There are moments when you speak to another person and get a glimpse of where they're at, spiritually. This was one of those moments. Blake understood, which meant he had to have had his own moments with God when he felt the leading of the Holy Spirit. I suddenly felt closer to Blake than I ever had.

"Yeah, definitely. Every time I pray."

He nodded. "Then this is the right thing for us to do. I mean, you can't trust someone else's perceptions of what God is telling *you* to do, but if it lines up with Scripture and doesn't raise any alarms, then it's worth considering. At first my parents weren't any keener on doing this than your dad, you know."

I nodded. I could understand that. I was asking them to leave their homestead for a whole day or more.

"But they went before the Lord on this one. Just because you've been so sure the Holy Spirit is speaking to you." He paused. "Just for the record, I'm glad they agreed."

"Me, too!"

Afterwards we fell silent and I became very aware it was just the two of us there alone. He touched my arm, and held it.

"Keep your horse near mine on the ride," he said. "I'll try to keep an eye out for you."

I was thrilled by this show of concern but I had to hide a smile. Considering my horsemanship was far superior to Blake's, I had already decided to keep an eye on him! Still, my heart rose at his words. He cared.

"Thank you."

His eyes held mine and I wondered briefly if he was going to kiss me. It was way too early in the morning to think of kissing anyone, but if he'd tried, I would have let him. He didn't. I was relieved, although a part of me would love to kiss Blake Buchanan. Just not at 6 o'clock in the morning. Even without the kiss, I felt as though something new was now between us. He'd come out to talk to me alone. He'd told me to stick close to him during the ride. I felt certain my secret crush for Blake was no longer one-sided.

He kept a hand on my elbow as we walked back to the house. Even through my coat I was uber-aware of his hand on my arm. It felt nice.

Inside, my mother was still making breakfast. Dad had wanted to leave as early as possible but you can't rush my mother. She'd already made coffee and fried up bacon and was using a griddle on top of the wood stove to make her famous pancakes.

"Hot oatmeal would have been faster," Dad said. "Even scrambled eggs."

"I'm not sending you out there on a long ride without a good, full breakfast," she'd said. Personally, I was glad. Our packs included snacks like nuts and trail mix and granola bars, but a full stomach went a long way on horseback in the cold.

There was a lot of talk about possible threats to our safety and how best to avoid them. Dad and Mr. Buchanan stood bent over a topographical map for ages, discussing routes and alternate routes. The two trains of thought went like this: We could either stay off-road as much as possible to avoid being seen, which would mean slow-going on the part of the horses; or, we could take the roads and make better time, but be more visible. In the end, my dad and Mr. Buchanan agreed to use the roads. Even rutted with pot-holes and muddy from this long, cold winter, they're still faster than crossing unfamiliar ground and rougher terrain. Any of our horses could go down in a single unexpected gulley or ditch—it was too great a risk.

After breakfast, we did a last-minute check of supplies and stowed our packs. Everyone but me checked their guns. I don't have my own yet, and after that day on the road having to carry one, I think I'm glad I don't. I've had enough training to handle one properly, but I'm not sure I could ever use a firearm against another human being. But as I watched Blake check his magazine, handling his 9mm confidently, I sort of envied him.

When we gathered in a circle for prayer before leaving, I felt hopeful and confident. Last night's misgivings had vanished.

We started out in a walk and slowly picked up the pace, encouraging the horses to a trot, and then a canter. It was impossible not to make noise, what with all the hooves hitting the ground, but Dad turned us off the road to cross an open field, bringing us close to the tree line so we wouldn't be so obvious. After that, we came out onto what used to be a highway—only it's now quiet and lonely, dotted with dead cars here and there, like every other road. When he stopped to stare down at a pile of mud, we all pulled up into a little circle.

"What is it?" Mr. Buchanan asked. We were all wondering.

"It's tire tracks," my dad said. "Will you look at that? There's some kind of vehicle that still works!" Sure enough, we looked down and now saw an unmistakable line of fresh tracks made by tires.

"Maybe we should try our cars," Mr. Buchanan said, scratching his head in thought.

Blake spoke up. "No. This had to be an older model car. Without the electronic components of modern cars, it wouldn't have been fried by the EMP. You'd need an old car for it to work, now."

"How about that," my dad mused. "Seems I should have hung on to that '57 Chevy after all."

"Everybody should have hung on to a '57 Chevy," said Mr. Buchanan, wryly.

"Okay, let's get moving," my dad said.

We rode, mostly in silence, for the next half hour. I stayed close to Blake, falling behind him purposefully so I could keep an eye on his seat and how he was doing. We hit a badly potted stretch of road and the others fell into line. We were on the wrong side of the road, and Blake fell into some furious maneuvering to get his horse across without hitting a hole; His position on the saddle looked precarious to me and I spurred Rhema with a shout to get beside him. Falling into line on the other side, Blake looked a little pale, but otherwise fine.

"Go ahead of me," he said, nodding. "I can't watch you if you're behind me."

I raised my eyebrows in surprise but did as he said, suppressing the urge to laugh. How could I tell Blake I was the one who needed to keep an eye on him? I didn't. I enjoyed his concern and didn't want to ruin it.

There was lots of time to think while we rode. Despite the signs of spring coming on, the fresh-tipped grasses peeking out and even a few early irises here and there, the world seemed quiet and lonely.

As we got closer to Andrea's neighborhood, more and more cars sat dead in the road. We saw signs of looting. Broken windows, shards of glass glimmering in sunlight as we approached. Other times glass wasn't so obvious, but Dad or Mr. Buchanan, being in front, would shout a warning and the rest would carefully lead their horse away from the area.

We wound around roadblocks, falling into a line whenever we needed to. I had the sense, suddenly, of living in a post-apocalyptic world. I had to remind myself that dead cars did not equal dead people. Just because vehicles didn't work didn't mean society was wiped out. But it felt that way. Dad stopped suddenly at a PT Cruiser on the side of the road. There were people inside!

"I think they're asleep," he said, loud enough for us all to hear. A window was broken on the passenger side, and he circled around. Then, suddenly he spurred his horse away, shaking his head. He motioned with one arm for us to follow and we fell back into place.

I looked at Blake, wondering.

"There must be a foul odor."

For a few seconds those words rang a blank inside my head and then suddenly they fell into context. Those people weren't sleeping! I had a big lump in my throat after that.

Maybe that was why I wasn't paying attention a little while later when suddenly Rhema skidded off the side of the road, taking me down the slope of a gulley. Lots of Ohio roads have deep gullies on the sides to hold water, because our soil is heavy clay and doesn't absorb it quickly. The gullies catch the runoff. Now, one of them almost caught me.

Blake had hollered at the last minute for me to watch out, but it was too late. I was sure my horse was going to fall completely, perhaps on top of me. I tensed for the impact, but she never went down. Rhema is such a good horse! She gave a protesting whinny and stumbled a little but kept me seated.

"What happened?" My father had swung around and come over.

"I don't know. I guess I let her wander too far over."

"Pay attention to what you're doing, Lex," he said. "I'm glad you aren't hurt. You're lucky. Is she okay?" he added.

I nodded, patting her mane. "She's fine."

After that scare I paid more attention. And I felt humbled. Maybe Blake did need to watch out for me! But it took my mind off the ghost cars. And then Dad had a close call with Spirit when we hit a patch of mud that was hiding a big pot-hole. We had to wait for Spirit to regain his confidence. He'd come to a stop, snorting and whinnying. Dad coaxed him to move along. In the end, I had to dangle a carrot a few feet ahead of him to get him out of that ditch. Spirit can be cantankerous. It was a good thing my mother had thought to pack snacks for the horses!

"I'm glad you aren't hurt, old boy," my dad said to him afterwards, stroking his head. To us, he added, "About three more miles to the plat."

We were keeping to a steady, slow, trot, passing newer developments now. One man was out on his lawn as we passed, holding a big sign. It read, CASH FOR FOOD. I considered riding over and giving him the lunch Mom had packed which was tucked in a saddle bag. But Dad just kept going and I knew he'd get angry if I detoured. I think we all felt badly for that man.

I noticed smoke rising from the chimneys of older homes, which heartened me. They had a means of heat, a way to cook food. Strangely, the affluent huge houses looked empty and desolate. Like Andrea's house, they were impressive and sturdy but probably lacked alternate heating methods like a simple woodstove. I shook my head at the irony--the wealthier people could be worse off now than their humbler neighbors who had long heated with propane or wood. *The first shall be last....*

I don't know if it was because the sky had been growing overcast, or due to the large silent houses we passed, but a growing sense of desolation began overtaking me. Were these huge homes really empty and desolate? Or was I just imagining it? I couldn't tell. I saw images in my head—people who died in those big houses, unable to stay warm or because they'd run out of food. It was morbid and I knew it but I couldn't stop. It made me more and more anxious to reach Andrea's—I was worried about what we were going to find.

When we turned into the plat, I gave Rhema a little spur with my heels. She'd been so well behaved and I could tell she wasn't too winded. It was far past noon, but we'd all made it safely and in one piece.

We dismounted in the backyard. Blake and his mom took the job of seeing to the animals. We'd let them drink from ponds on the way, so water wasn't an immediate concern. I hurried to the door and knocked as loudly as I could. My dad came up behind me. I knocked again, searching for a doorbell, but found none.

"I'll go around to the front," Dad said.

I kept knocking, and then cupped my hands to peer inside. It was dark and empty-looking. I felt a sense of despair. Had we come all this way for nothing? And what had happened to Andrea and her family? I'd probably never know. I ran off the steps and started rounding the house, but stopped to rap on a basement window. I knelt down to peer inside, but like the upstairs, it was dark and empty.

I met my dad on the front stone steps. "There's no answer," he said, his hands in his pockets. I rang the doorbell. Dad put his hand gently upon mine.

"Honey, doorbells likely don't work."

"Oh, yeah." *One dumbbell (me) hitting a dead doorbell.* I rapped on the door instead, taking off my gloves to hit it hard with my knuckles. Again, my dad's hand covered mine, softly.

"They're not here, honey."

I looked up at him. "We need to get inside. See if they're in there."

He sighed. "If they're inside and can't answer the door, there's no point in going in. It would be too late for us to do anything to help."

I forced back tears. To say I was disappointed would be a huge understatement. Blake joined us and saw my expression.

"How about we check with the neighbors? Maybe someone knows something." I thought that was a good idea. My dad slowly nodded.

"May as well ask."

Mr. Buchanan and Blake went to the nearest house on the right, which was a few hundred feet down the street. Dad and I took the house on the left.

I saw some smoke coming from a chimney and pointed it out to my father. "Look! There's definitely someone home, here!"

He nodded. When we reached the front door, I rang the bell, already forgetting what my dad said, that they didn't work any longer. He gave me a gentle look and knocked loudly. We waited. I was beginning to think no one would answer when the door flew open and Andrea stood there, her arms opened wide to embrace me. She looked thin and strangely different, but wore a huge grin.

"You came!" she cried, tears popping into her eyes. "I prayed you would come!"

"You prayed?" I asked. Andrea was not one known for praying. I looked at her with appreciation. "Good for you! Every time I prayed, I felt we had to come."

"Really?" She stared at me, her mouth falling open.

"Really. My dad didn't want to, but we had to."

Dad hollered for the Buchanans and soon we were all inside. I noticed a rifle against the wall right near the front door and wondered if Mr. Patterson had thought we were intruders.

He was already talking to my dad and Mr. Buchanan, his face grim, but he was nodding. Andrea and I had stopped to examine one another, suddenly feeling shy. The difference in her was that she wore no makeup and had lost weight. But she shrieked with excitement and grabbed me into a bear hug. We hugged and laughed and were embarrassed that we hugged, and then she took my hand to lead me further inside.

"I'm so glad you're okay," I said. Andrea gave a humorless laugh.

"We're not okay. I'm so glad you came! Like I said, I prayed you would!"

"Andrea, that is so cool!" I exclaimed to her back, as I followed her through the house. She turned and smiled sheepishly. "Yeah, I guess so."

As we moved on, I looked around at the home. It was rich looking and stately but strangely bare. "So, are you living with your neighbors?"

She explained the situation to me, the absence of the neighbors, the woodstove. I felt sad about her neighbors, but it made sense for them to use the house.

"How's the baby?" I asked.

"Fine. Here she is," she said, motioning me into the open living room area. As I said hello to her mom and brothers, stopping to give Lily my attention, Andrea greeted my dad and Mr. Buchanan who had come in after us with her father.

"Thank you for coming," Mrs. Patterson said, over and over, to each of us. All the family was bundled up, the boys looking up at me from the floor fully dressed in coats.

"We're trying to conserve wood," Mr. Patterson said, sounding apologetic. I think he was attempting to explain why the room was cold. We could understand that. If Dad hadn't been piling up wood for years, we'd have been outside every day chopping to have had enough for this winter.

"Well, that's why we're here," my dad said. He explained we'd come to offer shelter and food. Sanctuary. He told how I insisted on coming, insisted God wanted us to. My cheeks flushed with heat. Blake touched my arm.

"Wanna help me carry in the stuff from the saddlebags?" Mrs. Buchanan had already started bringing in the sacks, but there was more to get. We had lunch in there, sandwiches, thermoses of soup and snacks. We were all hungry after the ride.

Gratefully, I nodded. I saw Andrea looking interestedly at us. She and Blake knew each other by sight but that was all. Usually if there was a guy around, it was Andrea talking to him, not me. I felt proud. Silly, perhaps, but I couldn't help it. Blake *is* cute.

We went out to get our gear. Andrea hurried to join us, so I introduced her to Blake as though they didn't already know each other's name—to give them a proper introduction. For the first time in my life, it seemed like Andrea got shy. Later she told me she didn't know how to act with a church-going guy. She knew Blake and I went to the same church, and found that knowledge slightly intimidating. I laughed at that. But I was glad. I'd much rather Andrea feel shy around Blake than bold, which she is around most guys at school.

Mrs. Buchanan handed us things to carry in and we unpacked lunch in the dining room. The look on the faces of the boys about broke my heart. They looked like they hadn't seen food in a long, long time. Andrea and her parents tried to be nonchalant about it, but I could see they were excited about the food too. Besides the trail snacks, we had simple sandwiches on homemade bread and thermoses of soup and coffee—except for my thermos which had hot cocoa. I gave most of my food away, feeling like Santa Claus. Actually, we all gave most of our food to them.

Afterwards my dad hurried us to get moving. He figured we wouldn't be back before nightfall but he wanted to get us there as quickly as possible. The Pattersons could take very little. Mrs. Patterson had a hard time letting go of baby gear. Finally, with everyone on horseback, our saddlebags bulging with the loads, we set off. I was ecstatic. Everything had gone perfectly—we were saving the Pattersons! Maybe I was a little too proud of myself, proud of the fact that I'd heard from the Lord and followed His leading. Maybe I shouldn't have been preparing a little victory speech to vindicate myself to my dad after all his needless worries. Or maybe it was just inevitable, what happened.

We were halfway back to the farm. Blake had one of Andrea's brothers on his horse, and my dad had the other. Mr. Buchanan had her father and Mrs. Buchanan, her mother. Baby Lily was wrapped up inside Mrs. Patterson's coat with an extra blanket around them. I, of course, had Andrea. (Dad had suggested Blake take Andrea, which about set my blood boiling. I had no idea I would feel jealous so easily! Anyways, I cleared my throat, saying I wanted to take my best friend. I tried not to meet Blake's eyes. I didn't want him to know I was jealous. Thankfully, my dad agreed with my suggestion.)

With all the extra weight, we were moving slowly. You can only push a horse so much. Dad had considered letting the horses rest overnight but there was no shelter for them, and we hadn't brought enough food anyway.

We were passing a street of stately homes, large edifices that shouted *wealth*, trotting lightly, when we all heard it: A single, sudden *crack*! It was so loud it felt like an explosion had gone off. I couldn't tell which direction it came from, or where it had gone.

The horses startled, rocking us precariously for a few seconds though I don't think any of them actually bucked. I heard Blake saying, "Whoaaaaaa!"

Promised Land came to a complete stop. Blake and I drew up beside his mother, while I sent a questioning look at my dad. *Was this an attack?*

A voice rang out: "Give us a horse and we won't shoot again!" I didn't see the speaker but I could now tell the voice had come from a huge home to our right. It WAS an attack!

My dad had instructed us to gallop away from danger if it was at all possible. He said the likelihood of someone hitting a moving target was low.

"RUN!" He cried, now. We shouted and spurred our horses to get moving. More shots rang out. *Somebody was actually shooting at us!* I broke into a cold sweat and started praying beneath my breath. I heard a shriek, and my heart went into my throat. It felt like I'd swallowed it. Had Mrs. Buchanan been shot? Or Mrs. Patterson?

We kept moving, the horses struggling to gallop beneath their loads. The shots grew fainter. We covered about half a mile. Andrea was huddled in front of me as if trying to make herself smaller. My heart pounded loudly in my ears. I hoped everything was okay but I heard shouts from another rider. It was Blake. A stab of fear cut through me.

When I slowed Rhema and turned her around, Blake had gone up to his dad's horse, which had stopped. Blake moved aside. We saw instantly that Mr. Patterson, still seated in front of Mr. Buchanan, was unconscious. His head, bleeding heavily, hung down, and he wasn't holding on anymore. Only Mr. Buchanan's arms were keeping him up there, and I could see it must have been difficult to guide the reins while supporting the man.

Mrs. Patterson cried, "No! Is he all right? Is my husband all right?"

My dad went over and dismounted, giving his reins to Blake while he examined Mr. Patterson. Mr. Buchanan was already shaking his head in the negative. After checking for a pulse, the look on his face told me—It told all of us—that something awful had happened.

I didn't think he could have died. People can't just die instantly like that. Or so I thought. But Blake dismounted, handed me the reins to both the horses, and helped my dad lift the limp body and put him face down across the horse's back. My dad unbuttoned his coat and removed his scarf. He wrapped it around the dead man's head, I guess to stop the runoff of blood. The twins looked frightened and confused.

"Is my daddy hurt?" one of them asked. I think it was Aiden.

Mrs. Patterson had stared in shock while they moved her husband. She started sobbing. "Oh, no, no, no, Oh, God, no! Help me down," she said, and started writhing from her seat.

Mrs. Buchanan said, "I'm sorry, there's no time. We need to get home, first." Her voice left no room for objections. I knew she was soft-hearted; being firm at this moment must have cost her some difficulty, but she knew we needed to be safe. She spurred her horse to start off and we followed. Andrea was crying. I couldn't hear it but I could feel her body shaking between my arms, stretched around her to hold the reins.

"I'm so sorry," I muttered, miserably. "I'm so sorry." Inside, I knew it was my fault. I was the one who insisted on making this ride. I thought the Pattersons would be safer at our house.

So much for being safer.

L. R. BURKARD

LATER

I had a hollow, dull ache in the pit of my stomach for the rest of the ride home. It made my sore rear end seem like nothing, my aching leg muscles a trifle. Everything felt unreal—or is it surreal? A part of me was unable to grasp that Andrea's father lay across Mr. Buchanan's horse, dead. Another part of me was sickeningly aware. I was scared the rest of the way, constantly looking around for other people who might be a threat. We stopped occasionally—briefly—so my dad could consult the topographical map. He kept us away from houses as much as possible. It made the ride even longer.

It grew colder after sunset. We moved slowly in the dark, a silent, somber train, and I was numb in my hands and feet by the time we got back. To our joy, my mother had a waiting pot of stew, and cornbread, and most of us ate as though we were famished. The Pattersons were unable to consume much—either from grief, or because they'd eaten a huge lunch. Their stomachs weren't used to large amounts.

The atmosphere should have been joyful after a rescue, but was instead grave. Mrs. Patterson stopped crying. But she looked like she was in a trance. Going through motions with no feelings evident. Mom and Mrs. Buchanan helped her wash off her husband's bloody head and prepare him for burial. I don't know what they did exactly, as we were shooed from the room. Mrs. Preston was silent, her sympathy showing in her eyes which followed Mrs. Patterson sadly. I think she identified with her, being a widow herself.

Andrea and I went upstairs, sitting far from the little ones (despite heavy protests and efforts to join us). We hugged and cried. This time there was no embarrassment. I was sorry, I said, for coming for them. If we hadn't come, her father would still be alive. But Andrea shook her head.

"It's not your fault. If anything, it's mine."

"Yours? How?"

"My dad was getting ready to ...." Here, she pursed her lips in an effort not to cry. "To..to sell me to a man at the end of our street!" She kept her voice low on account of the children. "I would rather die than go there, so you see I needed you to come."

"Your dad wanted to...to SELL you?" I whispered fiercely, hardly able to believe what I'd heard.

She looked away, her face wet with tears. She proceeded to tell me about the creepy guy at the end of the street and how he had food—for a price. She told me that just last night her father had told her privately they were out of time, the family was starving. She needed to understand there was no choice in the matter; she would have to do whatever it took for the preservation of her family.

"He didn't say, I'm going to sell you, but that's what he meant." She looked up at me to see if I understood. "Thank you, Lexie, for coming. You saved me from that! What happened to my dad wasn't your fault. I think I *wished* him dead!" She burst into sobs. Aiden came over sleepily and climbed into her lap. She cuddled him.

I put my hand on her arm. "Andrea, your wishing him dead didn't make it happen."

She looked at me, blinking back tears. "How do you know? How do you know it wasn't bad karma or something?"

I thought frantically for what to say. See, there's no karma in the world—or anything, for that matter—that is more powerful than the sovereignty of Almighty God. But how could I explain that to her in a way she'd understand?

"Since your dad died, then you need to understand it was his time to die."

She looked at me hopefully.

"How do you know that? How can you be sure?"

I swallowed. I'd been feeling guilty myself because of her father's death. I realized at that moment it was not for me to feel guilty. GOD had allowed it to happen. We'll never know why, but he had. Unless I was the one who pulled the trigger of the gun that shot him, there was no responsibility for me to bear.

"Because the Bible says even a sparrow doesn't fall to the ground without the Father's will. We may never understand why, but it was his time."

Andrea mulled that over for a minute. "How do you know the Bible is true?"

I hesitated. This was a legitimate question and worthy of discussion. "There are lots of reasons why I personally believe it's true," I said, "but if you want to know why many of the greatest minds in history have accepted it as truth, then you should study books on it. It's wise to question anything you believe. But Scripture has an amazing history—it really is a miraculous book."

Andrea just looked at me questioningly, so I added, "The Bible is the only book in the world that has given predictions of future events—hundreds of years before they happened—which were fulfilled exactly. I mean, prophesies with explicit details. It's a human impossibility to make such predictions that come true!" She nodded thoughtfully, so I went on. "Most of the predictions about Jesus were made 700 years before he was born, like his name, birthplace, triumphal entry, the way he would die, even his burial—they were all foretold with precise detail. And Jesus fulfilled over 300 prophecies! The odds of that happening are so astronomical they're not even considered odds. "

"I didn't know that," she said. My mind was still spinning, thinking of stuff I'd learned long ago, reasons for believing that were now just a part of me, no longer something I had to weigh or consider: I said, "Archaeology supports the Bible, and there's no other book from any religion that can offer you reasons for our existence, reasons for what is wrong with the world, and what will happen to us after we die. There's no other book like it," I repeated, "because it's the Word of God. If you did believe that God wrote a book, wouldn't you want to read it?"

She nodded.

I had a thought. Why not give Andrea a copy of the Bible? We always kept extras on hand just for the purpose of giving them away. "I'll be right back," I said. But I picked up my Bible, bound in dusty pink leather and full of notes I'd scribbled during Bible study time or devotions. I handed it to her. "We have extra Bibles so I'll get you one you can keep, but you can take a look at mine until I get back." I handed it to her so that it was open at the book of Matthew, a good place for a newbie to start, I thought.

I went to my dad's study and found a brand new copy of the Bible. It wasn't as pretty as mine, didn't have the dusty pink leather, but it would do. Then I went and sat in front of the bookshelves in my room. I had a few I thought might help Andrea. *Mere Christianity*, by C.S.Lewis, *The Case for Christ: A Journalist's Personal Investigation of the Evidence for Jesus*, by Lee Strobel, and *The Sovereignty of God*, by Arthur W. Pink. Of all three, I liked *Mere Christianity* best, so I'd suggest she start with that one.

When I gave them to Andrea, I said, "Take your time reading these. And feel free to ask questions. Between my dad and our Bible study group, I'm sure we'll have someone who can answer them, or a book that can."

"Are you still having Bible study with other people?" she asked, surprised.

I nodded. "Yeah, Just those of us who have transportation. Horses."

"Wow, it's like life is normal here," she said, darkly.

I chuckled. "You might not think so once you start helping with chores. We have a ton of work to do every day."

Andrea nodded, undaunted. She took each book in her free hand and looked it over briefly. Aiden slept soundly. She still looked crestfallen, which was certainly understandable. I tried to think of something helpful to say but came up blank.

"I guess my dad's in a better place," she said, finally. Her tone was closer to a question than a statement, but I couldn't confirm that hope. I didn't reply. I didn't want to say how his spirit could be facing an eternity apart from God and heaven—that would be like pouring vinegar in a wound. I wasn't sure of Mr. Patterson's beliefs and whether he'd ever opened his heart to the Lord, so I said nothing.

"C'mon," I said, "Let's find Blake and get something to eat and then get some sleep."

"Wow, we can get something to *eat*!" I stood up smiling, and helped her carry Aiden back to the sleeping bag he was using for now.

This was what I'd had in mind when I asked my dad to get her and her family. Feeding them. Keeping them warm.

It was past midnight and we were all exhausted, but no one questioned me when I got our biggest and heaviest cast iron skillet and made popcorn over the woodstove. I used a whole cup of popcorn. One cup of kernels makes a huge bucket of popcorn, and if I'd put any thought into it I would have chosen a stock pot to hold it all. But Blake and Andrea held bowls to the sides of the skillet and chuckled as they caught the kernels as they popped out once the pan had filled to its limit. Some spilled out on the floor but my mother didn't even scold me. We seasoned it with garlic salt and butter. Even Mrs. Patterson, looking sadly distraught, ate a bowlful. Andrea couldn't get enough butter on hers.

"I thought butter didn't exist anymore," she said. We laughed, including Blake.

"As long as cows or goats exist, we'll have butter," Dad said.

She shrugged, and then chuckled. "I guess."

The Buchanans were staying the night after all that riding. Our safe room became their guest room. Upstairs, the little ones slept while Andrea and I continued talking. We talked a long time, making up for the twelve weeks we'd been out of contact, and sharing stories of how we'd lived since the grid went down. It's wonderful having Andrea here. (If only her dad hadn't had to die for it to happen. *Sigh*.)

Before we fell asleep she said, "Remember what you said about Sarah?"

Earlier, we'd discussed Sarah and wondered how she and her family were doing. I had rashly stated maybe we could help them too.

"Well," said Andrea. "I think you'd better see what your dad thinks before you go planning any more rescues."

"I know," I said. "I will."

I started praying for Sarah but fell asleep before I'd gotten too far. I didn't even update my journal with all this until today. Anyway, when I mentioned Sarah to my dad this morning, he shook his head firmly. I know that look. I wasn't surprised, especially considering Mr. Patterson's fate.

"No way, honey. We put all our lives in danger yesterday. You realize it could have been you or me or one of the Buchanans? It could have been a few of us or all of us. We can't take that risk again."

"Dad, what are we supposed to do, just hole up at home for the rest of our lives?" I hated the thought.

He paused. He'd been stacking wood in the holder next to the stove. "Sooner or later there will be restoration. The government even now is working to get back up and running, believe me. We have military bases around the globe that weren't affected. That means that even while we speak, there are forces that have power. They can bring the needed equipment to start the rebuilding. It may take years, I don't know, but it won't take your whole lifetime." He pulled off his heavy-duty work gloves and tousled my hair. He used to do that a lot when I was little, and I still liked it.

"Okay, Dad."

I'm still worried about Sarah, though. So is Andrea.

———————◆———————

The Buchanans planned on leaving after breakfast but they sat around sipping coffee and talking with my folks a little longer. Andrea, Blake and I listened in. Mr. Buchanan said sobering things, such as while the country is "down," he wouldn't be surprised if an enemy took the opportunity to come in and try to take over. Most people, such as in big cities (if they survived this far) would be at the mercy of an invader he said, because they aren't armed. A large number of Americans are outlawed against that privilege. Liberal politicians, my dad said, always attack the citizens' right to keep arms—and helplessness was the result.

"Liberals say it's safer if you outlaw guns, which is absurd, because when you do that then ONLY criminals have them. Criminals don't care if it's against the law to own a gun—they get them underground. Only law-abiding, good citizens lack a gun when they might need it due to these stupid laws. *A free people is an armed people."* The others nodded in agreement.

I enjoyed how Dad got passionate when he got on this topic. He'd always told me guns are the great equalizers—especially for women. A woman with a gun can defend herself from even the strongest attacker. That's why he had me learning gun safety since I was about seven years old.

The talk moved on to things at hand, such as burying Mr. Patterson. The Buchanans needed to get back to their own home but agreed to let Blake stay on to help with the digging. Before they'd gone, my dad had disappeared for awhile. He came in now carrying two bags, which he gave Mr. Buchanan.

"This'll keep until you get home and cook it or dry it or whatever you're gonna do."

"What is it?" Blake asked.

Mrs. Buchanan answered smiling, "It's meat."

"Pet food," quipped Mr. Buchanan.

Meat? Pet food? It was *rabbit!*

His wife elbowed him in the ribs affectionately. "Don't say that! They're not pets."

When Mr. Buchanan was in a good mood, he was a big joker.

Dad had butchered a kit of rabbits. I found out later it was part of the bargain he'd made, sort of a payment for helping us get the Pattersons. He did that for my sake. You can see why I love my dad.

The men got started outside digging the grave. Andrea and I took the baby upstairs to the bedroom. My little sisters were already there, and then Andrea's brothers came up and all of us had fun talking to the baby. We were delighted each time she made the smallest sound in reply. Justin is a cute toddler, but Lily is an infant—they're like two different animals!

I was glad Aiden and Quentin could be distracted from their grief, even if just for a few minutes.

Watching the kids, I got thoughtful. I always assumed I'd get married after college and have a family. I'd have a baby just like Lily. I thought of Blake—would I someday have a baby with Blake? There was no going to college for now, but Blake was still Blake. Available. My eyes wandered to Andrea and I felt a sudden stab of worry. Andrea flirted with any guy around. So far, I hadn't seen her flirting with Blake. I hoped it stayed that way. I hoped she would continue to feel shy around him. What if he decided to like Andrea more than me? She's prettier, for sure.

Suddenly it occurred to me that Mr. Patterson had lost his life only yesterday and here I was, worrying over who was prettier, me or Andrea.

I'm a stupid, selfish jerk sometimes.

———————◆———————

Mrs. Patterson picked out the spot on our property to bury her husband. In summer, it's a hilltop shady oasis, with a majestic oak standing tall and erect like a sentinel. I like to ride Rhema up there, then dismount and relax with my back against the tree, daydreaming while I look out at the countryside. When the fields are covered in soy it looks like an endless, undulating sea of green—only the occasional car crossing your line of vision far away reminds you there are roads crisscrossing the countryside. When the corn is tall, you can't see them at all. Those are summer visions.

Last summer feels like a world away.

Right now the ground up there, just like everywhere, is cold and hard. It took Blake and my dad two hours to dig about four feet down, which Dad says is deep enough to keep animals from digging up the body.

Will I still sit up by that tree in nice weather? *I doubt it.*

With the grave dug, Blake and my dad carried Mr. Patterson out to the cart and the rest of us walked together behind the lumbering cart up the hill. Mr. Patterson was wrapped in sheets and then a blanket. The men lowered him gently into the ground. All the Pattersons were crying.

I cried, too. I felt miserable and couldn't wait for it to be over. Dad read Scripture; I remember one in particular: "The dust returns to the ground it came from, and the spirit returns to God who gave it." That's from Ecclesiastes 12:7.

We each took a turn shoveling dirt over the grave. I had just finished my turn when my dad said, "Everyone, quiet, please."

We stood listening. I heard nothing. Looking around at the countryside, it looked bare and sad. Winter's mark was still everywhere, from the hard soil to the empty, brown fields surrounding our property.

"Look!" Dad was pointing down towards the road frontage of the farm. Since the trees were still bare there was little cover despite the thick stand of trees and brush that in summer and fall acts like a privacy fence between us and the road. We saw a group of people turning into our property. Most were entering right through the brushy area, with a few on the actual driveway. At the same time, a few emerged from the brush, already coming out to the grassy pasture between it and the house.

"What on earth...?" said my mother.

"C'mon," said Dad. He waved us to follow him. "Lex, load everyone onto the cart. I don't want anyone outside until I know who these people are and what they want."

"What about my husband?" said Mrs. Patterson, through a tear-streaked face. She pointed at the grave, still open.

"I don't like it any more than you do, but we have to see to our safety before anything else," said Dad. "I promise you, as soon as I know it's safe, Blake and I will come back and secure the grave. Most animals don't go roaming until nightfall, if that helps any."

She sniffed. "I'll stay and finish," she said, in a low voice.

My mom and dad exchanged glances. "I'm sorry, I can't let you do that," Dad said.

"What?" She seemed shocked. My mother took her arm, motioning at me to come and get Lily, whom she held in the crook of her other arm. I got the baby but Andrea took her from me. I think she feels

218

proud of how well she handles her baby sister. Anyways, we hurried to climb into the cart. Mom somehow got Mrs. Patterson to come along. Dad barely waited for us to get settled on the straw before snapping the reins. We took off with a jolt. As we went downhill we lost sight of the approaching group.

I felt no sense of danger. My father was being his usual overly cautious self, I was sure.

"Who do you think they are?" I asked Blake, who had settled between me and Andrea. He took a breath, thinking.

"Marauders."

"Really?"

He shook his head. "Remember how we lost chickens to thieves? Our root cellar was raided, too. These might be the people responsible. They go around looking for anything they can use—or eat, actually, and they're not looking to buy the stuff."

I felt my first sense of alarm. "But it's broad daylight," I said. "Wouldn't they wait for nightfall?"

"Why wait, when they've got that many people on their side?" he asked.

When we reached the house, Dad was issuing orders before we got inside. To my mother: "Hon, unlock the gun cabinets and bring up our stuff. Blake, go with my wife. Wait—take a radio and try to reach your folks. If they're not past five miles out we may be able to reach them. We're gonna need all the help we can get." Our walkie-talkies had a five mile range, and I prayed his parents were within it.

He turned to me. "Lex, show Andrea and the kids to the safe room and how to lock themselves in."

This scared me. If Dad wanted them in the safe room then he must really think there might be danger. Violence. The idea of an armed gang descending on our property suddenly sent my heart thudding.

Dad was looking through his binoculars as I ushered everyone out of the room towards the basement. I heard him say, "It's *Roy!* Roy is leading this gang! And they're armed."

Hearing his name depressed my spirits further. That man was trouble. He'd locked my father in his basement where he could have frozen to death during that sub-zero cold spell. Who knew what else he was capable of?

I led Andrea, her mother, and the kids to the safe room. Mrs.

Patterson looked around curiously. I could see she was new to the concept of such a room. The children seemed oddly happy to be getting enclosed. Lainie was already explaining to Aiden and Quentin how there were lots of games and toys in the room. I guess I expected them to protest at being shut up down there, but fear had taken hold of everyone. I showed them how to lock the room, giving quick instructions to stay quiet if they heard noise but couldn't identify the source. They were not to open the door for anyone except one of us.

Andrea grasped my hand before I left. "I'll be praying," she said, with wide eyes.

"Thanks. I will, too!"

Once the door was locked behind me, I turned and saw Blake taking three rifles from my mom, who'd taken them from the vault. He came and handed me one, our eyes meeting. He looked calm. Serious, but calm. I was glad. Around his neck was a messenger bag, which I guessed carried extra loaded mags for the guns.

"Did you reach your folks?"

He grimaced. "I'm not sure. Reception wasn't good. But if they were able to hear me they'll be back, I'm sure."

Upstairs, my dad was still at the window, binoculars in hand. It's a quarter mile from the brush to the house, and the gang was getting close.

"It's Roy, alright," he said, his voice grim. "And they've got guns as well as bats and crowbars." He looked frankly at me and Blake. "This is not a friendly visit."

"Who's Roy?" asked Blake.

I reminded him who the bus driver was, and how he'd imprisoned my father the day we lost power.

We joined my dad at the window, careful to stay behind the drapes. My mother joined us.

"What if I take a storage bucket or two and put them out there? Maybe they'll just take the stuff and leave."

My dad was quiet a moment. "I wish I knew that would work. But I'm not sure. If one of us goes out there, who's to say whether they'll shoot on sight?" He sighed. "We can't take that risk."

"Lex, you and Blake take the windows in our bedroom. Keep an eye out for anyone trying to round the house. Your mom and I will take the front windows here."

"What if someone tries to go around the other side?" I asked. We had a wide property, and it was going to be near impossible to keep all the perimeters safe without more people to help us.

"We'll do the best we can," Dad said. "Maybe they'll run if we give them trouble."

We were turning to head for our posts when Dad said, "Wait. Let's pray." We formed a little circle holding hands, while he said a quick prayer for safety, for blessing, and for no loss of life if possible.

As Blake and I hurried down the hall to the master bedroom, he said, "We have an advantage. We're on a hill and they still have ground to cross. They're in the open." There were tree breaks on either side of the property, potential hiding places, but right now the gang seemed contained right in front of us. They were getting larger as they neared, and we opened our windows enough to get the barrels of our guns outside, pointing towards them. Far behind them was the brown, bare break of trees. They stood out quite obviously, which made me wonder if they were really intent on mischief. Maybe they were seeking help of some kind. Maybe they just wanted to talk.

"I can see Roy," I said. "I think. If it's him he's lost a lot of weight."

"It's probably him. Most people have lost weight."

We watched them coming on. They stopped and seemed to be discussing something among themselves. My father ran into the room.

"I'm going to take the first shot, aiming to miss. I just want to scare them off. Don't start shooting unless they return fire."

"Dad, what if they just want to talk?" I looked out at them. "They're not even trying to hide."

"You don't approach people with crowbars and guns when you just want to talk," he said. He paused. "They're probably assuming we're liberals—unarmed sitting ducks."

Blake snickered.

"They're not here to talk, Lex." His face was dark with concern. "Let's pray we can scare them off."

After he left, we waited uneasily, waiting to hear that first shot. My dad's words echoed in my brain, but I had a feeling of unreality. *This couldn't really be happening! We couldn't really be defending ourselves from lawless attackers! This was still America, wasn't it?*

"I don't like this," I said. My insides were churning, reminding me of the moment I saw Mr. Patterson slumped over on Mr. Buchanan's horse.

"There's nothing to like," said Blake. He'd checked and double checked his rifle and now got settled as well as he could, kneeling on the floor. I quickly rose and tossed him a pillow. I was using one beneath my knees because otherwise I was too low to aim well.

I hoped my hands wouldn't shake too much to shoot. I looked over at Blake, marveling at how calm he seemed. Then I saw he was shaking slightly too. Our eyes met.

"We can do this," he said.

"We have to." I nodded.

It helped me to know he was scared too. Before I'd merely been glad Blake had stayed behind. Now, I was deeply grateful. The mob coming across the lawn far outnumbered us.

I had a thought, and gasped. "We forgot Mrs. Preston! I didn't take her to the safe room!"

Blake looked over, but shook his head. "You can't go, now. If we hold the fort she'll be fine. If you leave and they get in, we're all in trouble."

I prayed silently that Mrs. Preston was asleep and would stay out of sight until this was over. She often slept through "hell and high water," as my grandmother used to say, right in the center of things in her favorite chair in the living room. I hoped that would be true today. The high water was perhaps a euphemism. The "hell" seemed to have come.

Crack! My dad had made his shot.

We came to attention at our posts. How could I have looked away? This was important! To my surprise, the gang stopped in their tracks. Some of them lifted their guns. They were going to return fire! But one man quickly turned and faced the group, his hands in the air. I don't know what he said, but they started turning back. Had that one shot scared them off like we hoped?

For a minute it seemed it had. But two men began running towards the right side of the property, still in the direction of the house.

"That's us," Blake said, taking aim.

"But they didn't shoot back," I said. "Dad said to shoot if they returned fire."

"He also put us in charge of maintaining the border," Blake said, sounding very militaristic to me. But he was right.

Then came Blake's ear splitting shot. I jumped, blinked, and then focused to take one of my own. I aimed in the direction the men were running, slightly ahead of them actually, knowing I'd miss if I tried to shoot directly at a moving target at that distance.

More shots sounded. Two of the intruders had stopped to shoot, but the majority of the gang had turned and was running back the way they came. The two Blake and I had aimed for also turned and headed for the line of retreating figures.

Three more shots sounded. One of the men returning fire fell to the ground. His buddy took off after the others.

I ignored the fallen man, watching the beautiful sight of their retreat. I saw Roy taking a beating with the butt of another man's gun. He'd probably assured his buddies we would be easy targets. They hadn't expected a fight!

Sitting back, relief slowly washed over me. In fact, I felt giddy. Then faint. Was I going to faint? I took a few deep breaths. How could I be such a sissy? And especially in front of Blake!

"Are you okay?" When I looked up he was coming towards me. He held out a hand to help me up and then, to my great surprise, smiled and took me in a big bear hug. I love Blake's smiles, which are rare, but to be followed by a hug was downright awesome.

"Praise God," he said, into my ear. All my faintness vanished and I took in his scent—which happened to be the smell of gun at the moment. I reveled in the feel of him holding me. It was heavenly.

Then we came apart. Just *before* Dad entered the room.

I was definitely feeling weak. It isn't every day a girl takes part in a gunfight! It was going to take awhile to really feel safe again.

"We scared them off," Blake said.

Dad nodded, but looked unhappy. "They'll be back."

My heart constricted. "How do you know?"

"Because Roy knows we've got food, here. I never told him any details, but I'm sure he put two and two together. Plus, we're a small farm. All farmers are better off than most at a time like this. They've probably already hit a farm or two—maybe more. I don't think they'll let us go so easily. And next time it'll be harder to run them off. They'll be more prepared, knowing we're armed."

I swallowed.

He looked at Blake. "I hope we can depend upon you, young man, to help us out a little longer?"

"Sure," said Blake. "I'll contact my folks."

"You can use the ham radio?" I asked, surprised. It looked like a nasty thing to me, full of switches and knobs and all kinds of mysterious interfaces. I'd never wanted to take the time to learn how to use it until the EMP, and since then there hadn't been time for me to learn.

Blake looked surprised by my question. "Of course," he said. "How do you think my parents learned?" He gave a wry expression, making me shake my head and smile as he walked off with my dad. That was Blake.

My father reappeared in the doorway as I was putting the pillows back on the bed.

"Lex, take the front window in the dining room. We'll take turns keeping watch. You first."

I sighed. "Can I get something to eat, first? I feel a little faint."

He looked at me. He realized how difficult this had been for his teenage daughter. His eyes softened.

"I'll take the first watch." He came towards me and gave me a hug. "I'm proud of you, you know. You and Blake did a great job."

"I'm scared about next time."

"I know. I guess we should have shot to kill from the outset. That's what safety experts tell you to do."

"Then why didn't we?"

Dad hesitated. "Because I believe in mercy. Think of how God had mercy on us, saving us despite our sin."

"So if they come back....?" I asked.

"We have no choice. We shoot to kill."

"You think there's a chance they won't come back?"

"No, unfortunately, I think they will."

The Buchanans are wonderful people. They could have insisted they needed Blake at their own farm. They're just as vulnerable to attack as we are. But they let him stay. We've been taking shifts, keeping watch. Even Mrs. Patterson and Andrea take a turn, which helps a lot. It's been three days since that mob came.

I hope they never return.

Today I've brought my journal during my watch. Dad thinks they'd never make the mistake of coming during daylight again, but since it's still light outside, I can write. Keeping watch is boring.

"Lexie, can you help me do my puzzle?" It was Laura. "No one will help me."

"Did you ask Mrs. Preston?" Mrs. Preston was a reliable standby for helping with the simple games and puzzles the children favored.

"Mrs. Preston's asleep," she said, her voice flat with disappointment.

"Well, wake her up. Just give her a little nudge." Mrs. Preston slept more and more these days. Her oxygen tanks had run out. She could sleep through any amount of noise. But if you touched her it almost always woke her up.

"I tried," she said, turning her head sideways, and with a shrug.

"How'd you try?" I asked. "You know you have to touch her."

"I did." She shrugged again. "I pulled on her arms and I even got on her lap and tried to open one of her eyes."

I held back a laugh. "You tried to open her eye?"

"Yup. I pulled her eyelid up, but it didn't work."

My amusement vanished. "What do you mean, it didn't work?"

"I couldn't find her eye. It was all white. I wanted her to look at me." She sighed. "Will you help me or not?"

I rose and rushed into the living room to Mrs. Preston who was in her favorite chair. Her mouth was hanging open. She didn't usually sleep like that. I tried waking her, calling her name, tugging her arm, touching her face. She felt cold. I even did what Laura had done, trying to open an eye, but it *was* all white. Her pupils must have been way high in her head.

I started shouting for my mom, who was in the kitchen. She and Mrs. Patterson rushed in. Dad ran in and went for his rifle but I said, "No, it's Mrs. Preston! I think she's dead!" I was crying now.

Everyone began gathering in the room. Blake entered, rifle in hand. I shook my head and then motioned towards our grandmotherly neighbor.

Silence fell. Someone took in a shaky breath. It was Mrs. Patterson. She'd only met Mrs. Preston since coming here but another death must have been too close to home for her. She quickly left the room, her

hand over her mouth. Andrea's troubled eyes met mine. She started
ushering the children out of the room while my mother and father
continued to examine Mrs. Preston. My sisters left reluctantly, both in
tears. We seemed to have a lot of those around these days—tears.
Including my own.

"She's still alive," my mother said, finally. "But I don't think she'll
be with us by tomorrow."

Four of us carried her into my bedroom, at my request. I'd returned
to using it since the weather had warmed, but Mrs. Preston was still
using our futon and didn't have a room of her own. I wanted her to be
comfortable and have a place of privacy, of quiet. She'd always
enjoyed the liveliness of our household but somehow I felt it was more
fitting she be moved away from the hustle and bustle. She did not come
to or respond to us. Mom had said she wouldn't be with us by
tomorrow. I felt like she was already gone.

We lingered there, talking in low voices as if it was sacrilegious to
speak around the dying. Mom left to check on dinner, and Dad went to
feed the animals and milk the cow. Andrea came back. We sat on the
edge of the bed and I told her what a good neighbor and friend Mrs.
Preston was. I told her how she always had chocolate for me, and of the
many hours we'd spent at her house just because we could.

My dad poked his head in the door. "Any change?"

I shook my head. In a sharp voice he said, "Lex, aren't you
supposed to be on watch?"

I'd completely forgotten. I hurried from the room, my heart
pounding. Downstairs, I took a quick survey of the front, not expecting
to see anything. Wait—was that movement? Dusk had fallen, and at
first I thought my eyes were playing tricks on me. It looked like a big
dark cloud was on the property coming towards the house. As I
watched in horror, portions of the black cloud began moving out to the
sides, going towards the outer perimeter of the property. The gang was
back! Some were only yards from the house! I stood up so fast I
knocked over a chair and then ran around yelling, "They're back!
They're back!" Everyone scrambled to get their guns. I heard a shot.

They're shooting already! Then I heard the pounding of feet,
getting louder. Someone banged at the front door, right near my post.

To say I was frightened would be a gross understatement. I was
terrified.

SARAH

We are back upstairs in our apartment collecting whatever useful gear we can find to make the trip to Aunt Susan's house in Indiana. But we are a skeleton crew in the most literal sense. Skeletons of our former selves.

Jesse—wait, I'm crying. I can't write.

LATER

Jesse is gone!

We buried him in the cemetery of the Catholic church (although technically we're not members of the parish). Richard dug the grave and I read a Scripture. I chose Psalm 23, because it seemed the right thing to do. My mother was all cried out and just stood woodenly, not making a sound. Richard was still shoveling dirt back over Jesse's little wrapped up body when a priest showed up. We didn't even think to look for one or to ask permission to dig. I guess we figured they'd abandoned the place, because the church was locked.

Anyway, he was thin like us. Maybe not quite like us, but his robes were hanging about him loosely, suggesting he'd lost a lot of weight.

I wondered if he would tell us not to bury Jess there. If he would make us take him somewhere else. But when he saw the grave, how little it was, he just stared down at it, at Richard shoveling dirt, and his shoulders began to shake. I realized with a jolt, he was crying! He put his hand upon my mother's arm—and that did it. She sank to her knees in grief. I fell down beside her, both of us crying silently, tearlessly.

We don't cry tears. I think we have no water in our bodies for them.

Jesse had been listless for the past week and so unresponsive that I'd already come to terms with the fact we were losing him. I felt almost glad he wouldn't be hungry anymore, wouldn't be suffering the way we were still suffering.

The priest asked if we were Catholic. When my mom said yes, he disappeared for a few minutes and came back and then administered Extreme Unction over the grave, over Jesse. While Richard closed the grave with earth, the priest, Father Benedict he said, insisted we follow him back to the rectory. It was attached to the church and so we went. Richard would follow when he'd finished. I honestly don't know how he had the energy to do that work.

We followed Father Benedict to the kitchen, a large room meant to accommodate more than one priest. He had us sit at the table. He motioned to a man who turned and got busy doing something, his back to us. When he came and set bread and water in front of us, we stared at it in shock. *Bread and water!* It was like a feast. We hadn't had a clean glass of water that we hadn't had to collect from a pipe in so long it felt heady, like having champagne at a wedding. Then we stared at the food while the man, unbelievably, refilled our glasses.

I looked at the priest. He nodded. We fell eagerly at the bread, but my mother said, "Wait." She carefully cut the loaf into three pieces—one for Richard. As she cut it, the man brought a little dish with seasoned oil in it. We dipped our bread into the oil before eating it. I don't think it was olive oil. It should have tasted plain, maybe even nasty. But it wasn't. It was good.

He asked if we were members of the parish and my mother hesitated. We hadn't actually bothered to register with the church when we moved into the apartment. She tried to explain. She didn't volunteer that we weren't good Catholics, didn't go to church as a rule. I had made Communion and Confirmation at our old parish, and that was the end of church-going. I considered telling him about my encounter with Jesus at the library. I thought better of it.

This was yesterday. My stomach ached after eating. I wasn't used to stuffing my face, even with bread. Right now I'd love to have another piece of it.

Richard has his seeds, I have the $100 of mall money I never spent, and we are going to make a new life in Indiana. If we get there. He's managed to find us a tent and some camping gear, a few knives, and matches for a fire. That's it.

I haven't said so to Richard, but I sense my mother will not make it to Indiana. If not for that bread from the priest, I don't think she would have made it out of town. I guess we'll see.

The thought of continuing on, just the two of us, Richard and me—is so surprising. I've always been the weak one in the family, the one who panics, fears, loses it. I shouldn't have made it this far. I shouldn't be alive when Jesse isn't. I shouldn't be able to go on if my mother is not. Maybe I'm kidding myself and I won't make it out of town either.

I hope for Richard's sake that I'm wrong.

LEXIE

The pounding on the door changed into hard whacks. Someone was hitting it with a solid object, something heavy, trying to bang it down! My mother rushed into the room, rifle in hand.

"Lex, open the window, for crying out loud! You need to take a shot if you get it!"

"Mom, they're right out there! Someone's at the door!" They pounded again, and she went over to the door, slowly, aiming her rifle right at the middle of it. *Pound.* Something cracked the wood, right in the middle. And then my mother, my gentle, loving mother, shot right near the spot where it had cracked, aiming just a little higher up. We heard a thump. Then the sound of someone running off.

I peeked out from the side of the window. I couldn't see the door but I did see part of a body.

"You hit one of them," I said. The body moved. The man, holding one arm against his middle, and bent over in half, appeared, leaning heavily on the rails of the porch. He was trying to walk away.

"He's leaving," I said.

To my surprise my mother unlocked the door and then, even as he turned in horror, shot the man again, this time in the head. He fell instantly.

Outside, we couldn't really see anyone distinctly but we heard movement, like people running off. My mother rushed down the steps and took a few shots towards the sounds. The black cloud had dispersed, meaning they could now be anywhere on the property. I hoped they would go for the animals and forget about us in the house. If they kept trying to gain entry, it seemed inevitable they'd succeed. My mother came back to the front door and stopped, staring at the crowbar still stuck in the wood. She handed me her rifle and tried tugging it out, grasping and pulling, but to little effect.

"Help me, Lex," she gasped.

Together we were able to pry it loose and we took it inside, and then locked the bolt on the door behind us. I wondered where Blake was. I saw no sign of Andrea or the kids, either, so I prayed they'd gone to the safe room.

My heart was thudding painfully in my chest, and I was blinking back tears. *What a watchman I was! Practically useless!*

My mother touched my arm. "Hey, it's okay. We'll get through this. Trust in the Lord."

I nodded. She told me to get down on the floor, my back against the wall beneath the window. I was to look outside from time to time, but most of all, stay alert for intruders who might get in the house. If anyone crossed the threshold into the room, I was to shoot to kill. (She also reminded me to "holler like a stuck pig," in that event. Another of her southernisms. I knew this meant she was as tense as I was.) She ran off to check another area of the house.

I stared at the open doorway, praying no one would appear in it. If they did, I'd have to shoot. I heard more shots, but couldn't tell which direction they came from. I had no idea if it was enemy fire or our own. Suddenly, my ears perked up. *Someone was running towards the room.* My heart flew to my throat as I raised my rifle. *Stay cool*, I told myself. *You can't afford to muck this up.*

My mom poked her head in.

"Lex they're all in the back. C'mon!"

I ran behind her, glad not to be alone when and if I had to face the enemy.

I saw Dad and Blake kneeling at windows facing the back. I fell to my knees at a window that looked out at the left side of the property. This side had the fewest windows and needed a sentry. I could just see the black outline which was a side of the chicken coop.

"We can't let them get any animals," Dad said. "If they get a single chicken, they'll be back for more. We need to make them wipe our farm off their radar."

I wondered how he proposed to do that, but said nothing.

"Keep your eyes on the barn and the coop," he said.

Neither task was easy, particularly watching the coop. The moon wasn't full and, although I could see the outline of the hen house if I squinted, I wasn't sure I'd see if anyone tried to enter it. I hoped the chickens would put up a noisy fuss if they got disturbed. The barn, fortunately, had a solar light over the door which didn't give a bright blaze, but was something. My fear was they'd somehow find a ladder and climb into the barn by some other way. However, they couldn't exactly take the cow or a horse out of a window. If they were going for the big stuff, they'd have to use the door.

"So you don't think I need to stay in front?" I asked, thinking of the easy approach to the house the gang would have now, with no one around to spot them.

"They're after the animals and looking for a root cellar," Dad said. "They're not typical burglars trying to get at valuables."

"They want meat," Blake added, darkly. I remembered the Buchanans had already lost a bunch of hens to thieves.

"What about the guy who tried to break down the front door?" I asked, "Mom had to stop him." I couldn't bring myself to say she'd had to shoot him.

"He was a fool. Only a fool would do that, knowing we're armed," Dad said.

"I've put out all the lamps," Mom whispered. "They can't see us, but we can see them if we let our eyes adjust." I stared at seeming blackness, seeing nothing. I could see the treeline where the sky made a slightly lighter backdrop, but on the ground I couldn't make out much of anything. Would my eyes really be able to adjust? Then suddenly I saw movement. Someone was approaching the chickens.

"Dad, the coop!"

Everyone shifted into a shooting position. Mom got up.

"I'm going upstairs," she said. "I think I'll have a better shot from the kids' room."

"We've got to take a shot from here," Dad said. "We can't wait. The lock on that coop isn't strong."

"Take it," she said. "But I'm still going up."

"I've got a shot!" Blake hissed.

"Take it, son," my dad said.

Crack!

We saw dark figures scattering like balls on a pool table. Suddenly we were all shooting as the moving apparitions came into and out of range. Ghostly figures came stalking beneath my window but I spotted them and sent down warning shots. Further away, I saw three go down. My heart was pounding wildly, throbbing through my veins in a way that was almost painful. I knew I wasn't holding the rifle as steadily as I should be. Every creeping figure outdoors filled me with dread, so I banged away, but it was like operating on pure adrenaline. I emptied a magazine and reloaded as quickly as I could. I always found reloading a chore.

Mom came back and knelt beside my father, sticking her rifle through the opening of the window. Blake appeared at my side.

Suddenly I heard from outside a deep guttural man's voice. "Aim for the windows!"

Blake and I started blasting in the direction of the voice, probably not something my father would have thought sound defensive practice but it must have worked because we neither felt or heard any return fire. It was to our advantage that the majority of their weapons were not guns. I heard my mother make an odd exclamation in her throat and my heart froze. Had she been hit?

"Mom?" I called. I couldn't hide the fear from my voice.

"I'm fine," she said. But I felt as though it had been a close call and suddenly my blood was boiling. I don't get angry often but when I do, I'm formidable. (I like to think so, anyways.) They'd tried to hurt my mother! That, and the encounter at the front door suddenly loomed in my mind as unacceptable dangers.

It was like something inside me snapped into place, and all my training came into play. My nerves steadied, and I took aim. I was a good shot. Years of target practice were behind me. I no longer saw innocent people out there, people who were hungry. I saw attackers, invaders. I saw threats. I zeroed in on a dark figure making his way, zigzag, in the direction of the front. I took a shot.

He fell.

For a few seconds my newfound coolness left me and I broke out into a cold sweat.

"Great shot," said Blake. I looked over and actually saw a smile glint out in the dark. That helped me pull it together. I returned to the battle, started shooting at one intruder, then another, sometimes missing, but seeing others fall. Some fell because of Mom and Dad or Blake; and then, in a wave of sheer ecstasy, I saw a black cloud of maybe seven men turn and run.

"They're running away!" Mom cried, happily. She'd managed a whispered shout but I think she would have sounded it from the rooftop if it had been safe to do so.

"Keep at them!" Dad barked. "They need to know not to come back."

We raced to the front of the house, leaving only Dad at the back. I saw a few dark figures and shot in their direction, but I have no idea if I hit anyone. Blake joined me at my window.

More dark figures came shooting out from the sides of the house and we sprang into action. They were quickly fanning out as they ran, but Blake concentrated on the left and I took the right. We hadn't even had to speak about it, it just happened, each of us taking a different side to focus on. Later I thought of that as a good sign. It meant we had a natural knack for working well together.

A volley of return fire sounded, close.

"Get down, Lex!" Blake had never called me Lex before; only Lexie. I ducked down, but with a glow in my heart.

"You be careful, too," I cried. Another volley of shots rang out and hit the house. We fell to the floor.

"Someone out there's got an AK," Blake said. "Guess he was a latecomer to the party." The next volley came from closer range and bullets flew into the room, hitting the walls behind us. The glass of our dining room hutch shattered, sending a wave of shards cascading to the floor. I found that incredibly upsetting. My mom crawled over to our window, and she whispered, "Give me space."

I moved aside. My mom had a look I'd never seen on her face before.

"I've got babies in this house!" she growled, peeking over the sill with her rifle at the ready. "I'm so mad I could spit nails!" Then suddenly she fell silent, motioning to us to be quiet too. Moving her rifle to point sharply to the right, she aimed. She moved it even further, almost pointing the gun back inside the house, it was that far over.

Crack! Then, a thud. It was right outside the window. I felt weak with fear, realizing how close the guy had gotten.

"We need to get that gun," Mom said.

Blake said, "Not yet! There could be more—"

"Hey!" Someone was yelling to us from outdoors. At that moment my father edged into the room. "Hey, don't shoot!" the voice called again.

He came and peered carefully out. "I can't see anything," he said, his voice low.

"It's me, Roy!" came the voice. "I didn't know they wanted to hurt anything," he said. My father practically snorted.

"Look! I'm unarmed," Roy called. And then we saw him. He was coming towards the house, his arms up in the air. The clouds seemed to move aside and let a stream of moonlight through. It was the first good moonlight we'd had all night, but I could see Roy pretty well now. I didn't see anyone else.

My dad put his face to the window. "You brought them here, Roy!"

Roy stopped moving for a moment, uncertainty on his face.

"I didn't know they would hurt anything," he said.

"You're lying!" my father returned.

"He thinks we're dumber than a stack of bricks," my mother murmured. I would have snickered at this southernism if I wasn't too busy being creeped out by Roy.

"No, really," Roy said. He started walking towards us again. "I didn't know, honest! They woulda killed me if I didn't tell them somewhere to find food."

My dad had his rifle pointed out. He lowered and raised the lever, causing an unmistakable click as it snapped into place. Roy stopped.

"Turn around and don't look back," Dad ordered.

"C'mon, I'm just a bus driver," he began, his legs moving again.

Crack! The shot whizzed past him and Roy stopped, seemingly surprised.

"C'mon, man, I'm just looking for some food. I'm starving, man, really."

Dad readied the gun again, the clacking sound winging out into the night so Roy had to have heard it. "Turn around and keep going," my dad said.

Roy shook his head, and kept shaking it. "There's nowhere to go, man," he said despairingly, drawing out the syllable. "Just give me something, anything, to keep me alive, huh? That's all I'm askin'."

My mother said, "Should I get him something?"

Amazingly, I, too, felt sorry for Roy.

"Absolutely not!" My father's tone surprised me. He was seldom harsh, but he sounded that way now. And then, without warning a second man was at our window, and he swung something hard and black towards us. We flew out of range, all of us falling on one another, and then he was climbing in and I saw him holding that big black thing, I guess it was a crowbar, over my dad's head. There was just enough light from the night sky to see that awful silhouette in the dark, and then I screamed. Someone else screamed, too, I think it was my mother.

Crack! The man fell! He fell right onto Dad, who pushed him away quickly. My mother had a flashlight out now and I'd hardly grasped what happened, didn't even have time to wonder who had made the shot, but saw my father get back and rush towards the window. Someone else was climbing in! It was Roy!

"Watch out, Mr. Martin! *Move!*" came a scream from behind us, from across the room. I thought for a confused moment that it was Andrea's voice, but it couldn't be Andrea. She was with the kids, and besides, she'd only just started taking gun safety lessons with Dad. She'd had maybe two or three lessons, and had only taken a couple of shots in her whole life.

Again, the same voice screamed: "Move, Mr. Martin! *Move out of the way!*"

My dad, startled, did. The second he moved, there was a shot.

Crack! Roy froze, staring in at nothing, as if seeing nothing that is; then he fell backwards. He'd gotten one leg straddled across the window sill, but it slithered off as he fell. The shot, we saw later, had landed directly in the heart. I turned to see who our sharp shooter was.

To my shock, it *was* Andrea.

SARAH

So we're stuck in the apartment for at least another night. Mom is sick.

I am praying she doesn't die like Jesse.

The apartment is a moldy, disgusting mess from the pipes that burst. There is nothing here for us.

When Richard first starting catching mi—*rodents*, is what I'll call them—I thought things could not get worse. Then I got used to eating again. It was protein, right? I thought everything would be okay. We would survive.

Then Jesse died.

And now Mom's sick.

If she gets worse—or *dies!*—I don't know how I'll take it.

LATER

Mom's hot with fever! Richard is going to walk to the nearest hospital to see if there's any medicine. Our cupboards were emptied by the looters so we have nothing, not even aspirin.

I guess I fell asleep waiting for Richard to return because I just woke up from a dream.

In it there was a really skinny man, skinny like us. He came slowly towards me and suddenly I thought I recognized my father! I ran towards him. As I got closer, I saw it wasn't my father. I didn't know who it was. But he kept coming closer and then I saw. It was him! Jesus! The guy who showed me where to get water at the library!

He took my right hand. I didn't see him speak, but I heard words. At first I didn't understand them but after I woke up, I thought I did. I'm pretty sure the words were, "There is no suffering on earth that can compare."

That was the whole dream. I feel disappointed. Compare to what? Compare to what? I still wonder.

Lying here awake, something about that dream is niggling at my brain. Like I'd heard that line before, somewhere. I don't know where.

I can't quite recall it.

Richard is back. The hospital was deserted, completely looted and messed up; and he found no medicine anywhere. He went to get some water from the sub-basement.

———————◆———————

Now he's back from the basement. The water is running out! Great! Another source, gone. So much for staying here. If Mom isn't better soon, we'll all die together.

———————◆———————

Somewhere in the middle of the night it started raining. We ran outside onto the balcony with every bowl, cup and pot we had to capture it. The downpour got heavy, drenching us in seconds. Richard and I danced in it, knowing it was life-giving water. Maybe we danced because it was a sign of spring. Maybe it was because somehow we are managing to survive—barely, by a hair, by some provision that appears just before we truly perish.

Looking back, it seems there have always been small provisions just in time to keep us alive. Except for the baby. But Jesse's in a better place, at least. As for us, we need these little miracles to live.

I have to believe they will keep coming.

SARAH
ONE WEEK LATER

It's just me and Richard, now. I can't talk about what happened with Mom.

I'm putting this journal away, hopefully to pick it up again in Indiana.

LATER

I have to write. As we were leaving town we passed a Protestant Church. I think it was called Redeemer Fellowship. Anyway, there was a sign out front, the kind that can be changed to say different things each week. What it said will be forever burned in my mind. It read, *"There is no suffering that can compare to the glory that is to be revealed."*

It could not be a coincidence that the sign finished the sentence in my dream! When I saw the sign I got so excited, I told Richard about the dream.

"What does that mean?" I asked. "The glory that is to be revealed?"

He shrugged. "I don't know." We walked on. After a minute or two, he said. "I guess it means heaven." Another silence passed. He added, "If you believe in that stuff."

I thought about the dream and then I thought about that sign.

I do believe in that stuff.

LEXIE

We didn't want to bury them on the property. Roy's remains, and those of the other members of his gang. They don't belong here.

Blake and my dad loaded them in the cart and drove until they reached a ditch on the side of the road. It was deeper than most, and had a lot of spring growth.

May they rest in peace. (They won't. God is a God of justice.)

Life has changed forever. You would have thought it was the EMP that would make me say this—that life has changed. After all, we live without technology, without appliances, without running water and hot showers. But I feel like Roy and his gang changed us even more.

Take Andrea, for instance. Who would have thought she'd leave the safe room—where she and the others were truly safe—and take a rifle from the vault (which should have been locked, but wasn't!) and come up to throw her hand in with ours? She said it would have been harder for her to continue to hear fighting and not know who was winning, or who was getting hurt, than it was to stay there and just be safe. And her dead-on shots that night? She says it was beginner's luck! I don't think so.

(Sometimes I wonder if our getting the Pattersons was really to save them, or if their coming was just so that Andrea would be here to save my dad! Maybe it was for both reasons.)

But no one feels carefree when we're outside. It's like the world isn't safe anymore. How long will we live in the shadow of that night? I don't know.

There was another shadow that haunted me too. The feeling that we didn't have the right to kill anyone. Blake has no misgivings about that. He says self-defense is a constitutional right; that the intruders would have killed us without a qualm; and that we did the right thing. I actually don't question whether it was the *right* thing to do, defending ourselves the way we did. I just can't bring myself to feel good about it.

I should mention Mrs. Preston regained consciousness the day after all that commotion and noise and violence. She hadn't a clue about any of it and we left it that way. She was cheerful even though she couldn't even sit up. Her voice was weak. She said to me, "Don't forget to take a piece of chocolate from the tray." I realized she thought she was in her own house. I didn't say otherwise. The last thing she told me was she'd been dreaming of heaven, had seen Jesus. He was smiling at her, a really big smile.

I like to think she is standing beneath that smile, today.

I miss her more than I knew I would. I've adopted Butler as my own cat (the girls claimed Moppet). I wanted Butler because he's the 'miracle cat,' the one who scratched Justin and didn't leave a mark.

Andrea and I are homeschooling. Mom and Dad are our advisors, our guidance counselors. They basically laid out a course of study that utilizes the books we have, and we have designated hours to read and study each day. I think I'm learning more now than I ever did in class.

Blake comes by often. He's mapped out an off-road trail, not too differently than the way I rode to his place when I wanted help finding Dad. He's gotten to be an accomplished rider now that he makes the trip so often. We worried about him at first, going out alone on horseback (while there could be more Roy and his gang types about) but he's always arrived safely and gotten home as well.

In some ways we're one big family now. No one has said anything about the Pattersons returning to their own home. Andrea and her mother wish they could have brought more stuff with them, but there's no question of them going back. They have nothing to survive on there. (Mrs. Patterson doesn't even do gardening! She's been learning with us.)

I don't relish having two little brothers all the time. Aiden and Quentin fight among themselves, and they fight like cats and dogs with my sisters. When I start to get really annoyed I just remember that if not for us they could have died, and then I can handle it.

We've seen signs of civilization reviving. Some people came by on foot selling candles—they were candle-makers before the grid went down, specializing in soy, scented candles. Now they make "long lasting" and "emergency candles." We didn't need candles, but dad spoke with them a long time and says it's good to see people trying to make an honest living.

We've had five instances where looters came around after Roy's gang. Two times people succeeded in stealing animals—six chickens and two rabbits in all. So Dad found someone who breeds dogs. We now have a German Shepherd and a Great Dane (named Mozart and Bach) and we've had no disappearances since. Whenever the dogs bark it still puts me on edge, though. Andrea and I usually hold hands and pray until Dad sounds the all clear.

Now and then I think about the old days and wonder if they'll ever come back. I still have my iPad underneath my bed. I miss *so* many people. But I try not to think about them because there's no mail and no way to get in touch with anyone unless they're neighbors. We did find out that five families who live within a mile of us are still in their homes, eking by. Andrea and I were talking about school the other day and Sarah came up. We have no idea how she's doing. I pray for her and her family.

In the old, old days when our country was poorer it used to be everyone knew how to do food storage in case of hard times. Then it got to seem like only paranoid people did. But Dad says before the EMP there was a growing population of people just like us, normal folks who saved for a rainy day or emergency. In other words, there are pockets of preppers all over the country who prepared the way we have. He believes God raised up a remnant to survive and worship him. There will be other survivors too, of course, but definitely a community of faith.

It's good to know this. It's good to know we're not the only ones who got through this past winter. Someday, maybe soon, life will get back to the way it used to be.

There's only one thing I don't want to return to the way it was. My relationship with Blake. Blake sits next to me every week at Bible study, we ride together, and we hold hands a lot. He's become a good listener, because I talk a lot while we do stuff around the farm. Somehow he finds time to come over and hang out with me while I do chores. Last week, he'd been helping me catch chickens that were slated for butchering and I'd fallen down after losing my grip on a hen. I laughed as he grasped my hand and pulled me to my feet. Right there outside the coop in broad daylight, when he pulled me to my feet, he kept on pulling until I was up close to him. Our eyes met. I knew he was waiting to see if I would pull away. When I didn't, he kissed me.

They say a first kiss should be special? It was! *Sweet,* is how I'd describe it.

I wouldn't want to kiss anyone else, but I loved kissing Blake. Someday, I want to be Mrs. Blake Buchanan. I can't wait!

For Reflection

"When life did not make sense to Habakkuk, when all he saw on the horizon was appalling and dreadful suffering for himself and God's people, he responded this way: "Yet I will rejoice in the LORD; I will take joy in the God of my salvation." He turned his attention away from suffering and fixed it upon the more vital issue of salvation.

In your own times of severe distress, which are you more aware of—your suffering or your salvation? What the Puritan Thomas Watson recognized will always be true for us: "Your sufferings are not so great as your sins: Put these two in the balance, and see which weighs heaviest." We can rejoice in our salvation even amid great affliction when we recognize how much worse we deserve because of our sins.

From, *Living the Cross Centered Life*, C.J. Mahaney

RESILIENCE, Book Two in the *PULSE EFFEX SERIES*, picks up the thrill-ride where ***PULSE*** left off!

"BAR OF EXCELLENCE RAISED TO NEW HEIGHTS!"
L.R. Burkard is back with the next tale in her dystopian series, and the bar of excellence is raised to new heights with this top quality literary offering!

DEENA PETERSON, Blogger, Book Reviewer

In this action-packed sequel to *PULSE*, author L.R. Burkard takes readers on a spine-tingling journey into a landscape where teens shoulder rifles instead of school books and where survival might mean becoming your own worst enemy.

DOWNLOAD FREE CHAPTERS OF *RESILIENCE*:

http://www.LinoreBurkard.com/READER_EXCERPT_RESILIENCE.pdf

(Enter the address into the browser for best results)

RESILIENCE is available in print, kindle, and ePUB. Audio coming!

DEFIANCE, Book Three in the *PULSE EFFEX SERIES,* continues the heart-pounding suspense!

"ACTION, ADVENTURE AND SUSPENSE"
Will captivate readers!
> **MARK GOODWIN**, Author of *The Days of Noah Series*

"AMAZING STORYTELLING!"
In *Defiance,* the riveting story continues with even greater urgency."
> **ANGELA WALSH**, Publisher and Editor, Christian Library Journal

In this third installment of the PULSE EFFEX SERIES, survival means resistance must give way to defiance.
But can ordinary teens and their families withstand powerful forces and keep hope alive?

DOWNLOAD FREE CHAPTERS OF *DEFIANCE*:

http://www.LinoreBurkard.com/Excerpt_DEFIANCE.pdf

(Enter the address into the browser for best results)

DEFIANCE is available in print, kindle, and ePub. Audio coming!

Afterword

If you start surfing the web for information regarding a possible EMP, you will find lots of great information. You will also find lots of *mis*information. For the purpose of this story, and because my research supported the idea, I have vehicles dying at the moment of the pulse. After I finished the book I saw research suggesting that many vehicles would not die from an EMP, but only from a HEMP. (That is, a high-altitude nuclear electromagnetic pulse, such as would occur if we were attacked by an enemy.)

I faced a choice: Either I could change the story, leaving more vehicles working, or turn the pulse into a HEMP event. I chose to leave it ambiguous—though leaning in the direction of a solar pulse.

For a more thorough overview of common EMP myths, check out http://www.futurescience.com/emp/EMP-myths.html

Regardless of the transportation issue, on a personal note, I do recommend that everyone, no matter where you live, keep a pantry stocked for an emergency. Whether or not an EMP occurs, the fact is that other things happen: jobs are lost, the economy suffers downturns, hurricanes and other storms occur, all of which can be more bearable to live through if you have basic food and water supplies on hand. Whatever your budget, you can buy one extra can of a nutrient-dense food each time you shop, and store it. Do the same with water. After a year or so, begin to use your stored food, *making sure to replenish whatever you consume.*

And there's one other thing you can do, something which can only benefit everyone: Pray for our country and our planet!

Wishing you safety and peace,

Linore

PS: Take advantage of my reader bonus, below! It's a small thank you for reading my book.

READER BONUS: *As my thank you, please accept a free PDF: Andrea's Epilogue-- her thoughts about life since coming to live with the Martins but before the* sequel, *RESILIENCE, opens. (This book began with Andrea so it's only fair she gets a chance to close it.) Simply join the mailing list by visiting my website at* http://www.LRBurkard.com

You'll also get a link for a second free PDF: "Where Do I Start? Fool-Proof Preparedness for Beginners."
Go HERE:
http://www.LRBurkard.com

BEFORE YOU GO:
CAN YOU REVIEW THIS STORY?

Readers rely on reviews to know whether to purchase a book or not. If you enjoyed this story, please write a few lines telling why others might like it (without giving away the entire plot) on places such as Amazon or GoodReads, or BarnesandNoble.com. It will be much appreciated!

WANT MORE BY THIS AUTHOR?

Read L.R.Burkard's Regency romances written as Linore Rose Burkard. Go to Amazon.com or http://www.LinoreBurkard.com.

Other Titles

Before the Season Ends – The first installment of the Regency Series sparkles with heartwarming and humorous romance in the vein of Georgette Heyer.

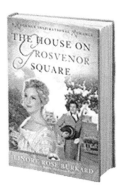

The House in Grosvenor Square – Mystery, perils and adventure—as well as romance—beset Miss Ariana Forsythe, our lovable heroine from ***Before the Season Ends***.

The Country House Courtship – The third volume in the Regency Series finds Beatrice Forsythe, younger sister of Ariana, ready for a romance of her own. Two eligible men, one country estate, and one feisty heroine make for a country house romance like no other!

Made in the USA
Monee, IL
17 January 2021